CHANCE
to BREAK

CHANCE to BREAK

a novel

OWEN PRELL

NORTHLOOP
BOOKS

North Loop Books
2301 Lucien Way #415
Maitland, FL 32751
407.339.4217
www.northloopbooks.com

NORTHLOOP
BOOKS

Printed in the United States of America

ISBN-13: 978-1-54561-926-1

For my parents

to Linda —
wishing you happiness,
on and off the court!

Owen

What saves a man is to take a step. Then another step.
It is always the same step, but you have to take it.

Antoine de Saint-Exupéry

The mark of great sportsmen is not how good
they are at their best, but how good they are at
their worst.

Martina Navratilova

Monday

(Love-all)

1

I came to tennis in an unremarkable manner. My mother, who first played the game in the postwar Surrey of her childhood, simply packed me into our Ford Country Squire station wagon at age seven with a small-gripped Jack Kramer Autograph and drove me down to the Veteran Avenue courts for a lesson with Win Brenneker, the resident pro. There had been no discussion among my parents and me beforehand about learning the sport. And probably very little afterward. "How was it?" they each must have asked me. "Did you have fun?" Whether I nodded or just shrugged my shoulders – I can't be certain all these years later – my mother penciled in another lesson for the following week on the oversized calendar of family activities she maintained on the fridge, and that was that.

Looking back, what seems extraordinary is the extent to which my life has been affected by my taking up tennis. I am tempted to add: for better or worse. But that's only because of my recent catastrophic downfall. I don't wish to sound melodramatic but there's really no other description that does it justice. Before that, any casual observer would have viewed the role of tennis in my life as positive. I mean, people don't usually consider regular participation in a recreational sport to be some kind of a scourge. Tennis is supposed to be a game you can play for life. Not one that will ruin your life. But I now realize a plausible argument can be made along those lines. Sadly, I myself seem incapable of reaching that judgment. Like Heisenberg's uncertain atom, I am much too close to my own momentum to separate coincidence from causation. If that sounds like a cop out, so be it. To be clear: I make no bones about taking responsibility for my predicament. *Mea culpa, mea culpa, mea maxima culpa.* I've never understood the impulse to blame fate or others for one's situation. I'm just not quite ready to name tennis as a co-conspirator.

Win – short for Erwin, although no one called him by his given name – was at least six foot two in his canvas Jack Purcells and had huge, deeply tanned forearms covered in blond hair. The way he brandished his own Kramer Autograph and the sun caught his Marvel Comics jaw and aquamarine eyes, he looked like he belonged on the beaches of Hermosa or Redondo or Malibu with one of the massive Hobie Alter surfboards of the era. I was so in awe of Win that it took me several years to realize I had actual talent – I have always been agile, with excellent hand-eye coordination – and consequently I could relax and feel at home on the court with the other boys who progressed to Win's intermediate and advanced groups.

By this time I lobbied my parents for and eventually received a Dunlop Maxply Fort, still wooden of course, but more stylish than the hard-edged Wilson racquets. 'Rocket' Rod Laver played with the Dunlop and was the reigning world number one, having achieved the incredible feat of two Grand Slams, once as an amateur and once as a professional. I actually served as ball boy in a match Laver played against his fellow Aussie and longtime rival, Ken Rosewall, at the Pacific Southwest Championships held on the hard courts of the L.A. Tennis Club in Hollywood. It remains one of the thrills of my life, and though I wish I could say I have been judicious about trotting this anecdote out in conversation after a friendly hit or at a party when the subject of tennis comes up, the truth is I recount it shamelessly, like an aging D-list actress might claim a one-night-stand with Warren Beatty.

My involvement with tennis is actually a tale of two worlds, the concrete courts of California, where callow confidence is tolerated, even encouraged, and the damp, uneven grass courts of England, rife with effusive apologies ("Sorry, so sorry, terribly sorry!") for all manner of things – a missed forehand, the weather, a broken drinking fountain – that barely masks the bitterness boiling within. The New World experience – Southern California in my early youth and Northern California in college and beyond – was one of seemingly limitless abundance and eye-squinting glare: gallon containers of fresh squeezed orange juice, eight lane freeways coursing with chrome-laden, V8-powered cars, platinum blondes in bikinis and their bronze-muscled boyfriends, endless days of sunshine (often smog-tinged), the scent of eucalyptus trees, as non-native as most of the people, and just the faintest unease that calamity lurks, be it drought or earthquake or wildfire. The Old World experience – my high school years in Oxford – was one of being an interloper in the crumbling corridors of tradition and majesty: ancient stone cathedrals of learning and power, out-dated class divisions based on the happenstance of birth and fusty nuances of speech (accent *and* vocabulary), somber college dons getting about on rickety Raleigh bicycles or maybe a rusty Morris Minor, over-sweetened fizzy bar juices with little discernable juice and no ice, the smell of diesel fumes from double-decker buses, and the ever-present reminder that the better days of empire reside in history and not reality.

Playing an actual tennis match against a worthy opponent, however, or even just rallying without score keeping, is a kind of sanctuary. Once the game is commenced, locale or nationality or relative wealth or sophistication becomes utterly meaningless. The only thing is the ball – consistently fuzzy and optic yellow the world round – meeting racquet strings and shooting back across the net to bounce between the lines. You can lose yourself for an hour or more in the pure, metronomic repetition of groundstrokes – topspin, flat and slice; cross-court, down the line and inside out – punctuated with the occasional put-away volley or overhead. And if the game is a sanctuary then the court itself is a temple, the recti-linear dimensions – always measured in feet – representing a sort of Euclidean perfection to suitably challenge the stride and reach of two (or four) players. Hermes, that most Olympian of gods, would surely have been a tennis player. The patron of sports and athletes, he was quick and cunning, and moved freely between the worlds of the mortal and the divine. He patrolled the boundaries, as a tennis player roams the baseline, but was known as a trick-ster, the type to throw in an unexpected drop shot or underhand serve. Jung considered Hermes a guide to the underworld and the messenger between our conscious and unconscious minds. I never perceived tennis to have a dark side, but maybe I have been fooling myself.

I am standing on the corner of Market and Eighth Streets in San Francisco. Diana Shohara, my divorce lawyer, stands next to me and touches my arm sympathetically. Her shoulder-length hair is lassoed in a practical gray elastic band. With her sober charcoal suit and thoughtful, epicanthal eyes, the moment assumes an air of solemnity that strikes me as both appropriate and absurd.

"You sure?" she says. "You've been through a lot."

I have declined her offer of a cab ride back up Market Street.

"No, I'd prefer to walk. I could use some fresh air."

The sun is breaking through the fog layer and it feels warm on my face, ought to feel good in fact, if I didn't have such a pervading sense of nausea and emptiness.

"Oh Trevor, I'm so sorry. I feel like I've let you down."

"What are you talking about? You were terrific. I've let *you* down. Putting you through that whole ordeal and then settling out like that."

"Don't worry about it. I have a feeling Judge Towling was going to grant legal custody anyway, so you didn't really give up anything. You still have visitation. And you probably won a ton of goodwill from your wife."

I can tell Diana instantly regrets her choice of words. That *wife* hangs in the air like the anachronism it surely has become. But we both pretend it doesn't matter and I give her a quick hug as we say our goodbyes and watch her disappear down the broken escalator into the Muni station, taking the steps confidently in her heels.

My mind goes blank for a moment and then reverts to its first moment of consciousness this morning, when I traversed that nebulous journey from sleep to waking. As if willing myself back in time, alone in bed but irrationally hopeful as to the day's outcome in court, I reregister the two thoughts that actually vied for my attention: It is the summer solstice and I won't be able to play tennis today. Given the laundry list of burdens my devil mind could have fastened onto, either through justifiable worry or simple masochism, these issues seem utterly inconsequential. Even setting aside the strong possibility (now reality) of losing legal custody of the girls, not to mention my marriage itself, my psychological quiver held plenty of poison-tipped arrows. That the lease term of the South of Market loft I occupy expires in ten days and can't be extended, this being the loft that my now-bankrupt real estate company once used as a sales model for the building and rented to me after my separation from Annie in its capacity as debtor-in-possession. That my company's destiny in bankruptcy court is liquidation not reorganization, despite the fact that our underlying assets are solid and we never over-leveraged ourselves like the others who triggered the subprime mortgage fiasco. And moreover: that I no longer hold a meaningful stake in any assets, real or personal, except a motorcycle (used, Italian) in the basement garage of the aforementioned loft. But I suppose my mind had already baked all that nasty stuff into the overcooked pie shell of my existential reality. So there it was and here it is: the longest day of the year, the opening day of Wimbledon as it happens, and no possibility of playing tennis to mark the occasion.

As if to suspend disbelief, I reconsider the possibility of squeezing in a quick hit at the club, even just forty-five minutes on the ball machine. But I know it is impossible. I have a meeting in an hour with Fred, my erstwhile business partner, along with the loan officer and the outside counsel for First Regency Bank, the lender for our larger real estate loans in default. A revised asset allocation plan is on the agenda and it will not be a short discussion. Even if by some miracle it doesn't drag on all afternoon, I promised Fred that the two of us would sit down immediately afterward and iron out the logistics of our LLC's liquidation. Staring ruefully down the empty Muni escalator, I realize it *will* be the year's longest day, both figuratively and literally.

Prior to walking into court this morning, Diana cautioned me to defer to her, that Judge Judy Towling already had all the information she needed to make her ruling and that my and Annie's presence with counsel was just a formality. That all made perfect sense, until I saw Annie in the hallway with her lawyer, Calvin Wanamaker. She looked, in a word, marvelous. She has always been a handsome woman, with her practical Midwestern cheekbones, wavy ash blonde hair and athletic frame. Even when she was carrying those extra pounds for a year or so after the birth of the girls, men would notice her. But seeing her this morning, she positively glowed. And it didn't take a genius to figure out why. I'd seen that particular glow once before, early in our relationship. It was the unmistakable glow of a woman in love.

I managed to fake a facsimile of composure as each lawyer and client duo waited for the clerk to open the courtroom door, even jokingly referring to Cal Wanamaker as 'the loyal opposition' for Diana's benefit (he has been, according to Diana, nothing but courteous and professional throughout the proceedings). And even in the courtroom, rising and sitting in ritual obeisance upon Judge Towling's arrival, I deported myself responsibly. It was only after Diana responded to her that we were ready to proceed with her findings that I found myself inexplicably standing up to address the court. And then all hell broke loose.

Subsequent events are still something of a blur but I do recall that I somehow prevailed on Annie to meet with me in private, over the vehement objection of her counsel and the strenuous disapproval of mine. My purpose was instinctual and unpremeditated: so that I could look her in her eye and try to understand one last time why she was divorcing me and seeking sole custody of the two girls we'd raised together the last fourteen years. For the umpteenth time I apologized for having jeopardized our financial security by pledging our assets (which Annie and I had long ago placed in a family trust, to safeguard the girls should we both perish) to First Regency Bank to renew the company's line of credit. I've been over this in my mind endlessly and I never get any clearer answer than this: I never expected the financial markets to collapse the way they did and, given I had signatory power for the trust, I didn't want to worry Annie. But it was wrong, as I've told her before, and I said so again this morning.

A part of me might wish to cut myself some slack for the unforeseen series of events that occurred in the run-up to the global economic meltdown of 2008. No less than Alan Greenspan, the ex-Federal Reserve Chairman whose own decades-long legacy of non-inflationary expansion stood in utter ruins, has admitted, with the dispassionate precision that only an economist can muster, that this was a "once in a century collapse." The only problem is, it was smack in the middle of *my* century. Or more to the point, mine and Annie's.

What I also recall, with something approaching clarity, is that Annie finally departed from script. Yes, I should have told her about the asset pledge, she agreed, but the divorce was about more than that. It was, as she put it, that I "disappeared from our marriage." Not overtly, she continued, but in little increments. She then trotted out a list of particulars demonstrating my having gone walkabout – the long hours spent at the office, out riding my motorcycle, playing tennis (yes, there's that dagger now, Hermes) – all of which left Annie feeling sad and lonely. So when I neglected to inform her about the collateral it was the last straw.

"No, that's not true," she'd corrected herself. "Your affair was."

I was shocked, beyond incredulity. "My *what*? I never had an affair."

She looked clinical, almost disinterested, like a schoolteacher sending a chronically errant child to the principal's office. "Emotional affair, then. I presume she was a player at your club, with all the tennis references. Siobhan, was it?"

My mind was suddenly flooded and I could feel my face flushing. I fought the impulse to correct her ignorance of Gaelic; she'd pronounced the name "*See*-o-ban" instead of "*Shiv-awn*." But that would give it away, wouldn't it?

"Annie, I swear to you, I don't know what you've imagined but I never…"

"Please, Trevor. Spare me. I read the text messages."

Indignation replaced defensiveness. "You did *what*?"

"If you're going to tell a woman other than your wife how hot she looks, you probably shouldn't leave your phone on the kitchen table when she texts back."

"So you…?" My voice trailed off, as the futility of my protestations began to dawn on me.

"Yes, I looked. Wouldn't you? Call me crazy, but I thought marriage meant there were no secrets of that sort to hide."

"Annie, you have to believe me, she meant nothing." The cliché-awfulness of that phrase was immediately apparent to me so

I stopped myself from going on. Wait a second, a corner of my brain wanted to argue: aren't clichés trite because they're true? But Annie's war-weary smile served to muffle me.

"Trevor, listen to me. Very carefully. It doesn't *matter* to me if you consummated an affair. I assumed you did but that wasn't the issue. What I came to realize is that I couldn't rely on you anymore. Not for your affections and certainly not for our financial well-being. You deceived me and you betrayed my trust. At some point I realized I needed to move on."

I took it in in stunned silence. All these months I'd been convinced I needed to atone for the surreptitious asset pledge. And now that the greater truth of my malfeasance was revealed, what else could I do but capitulate and give her the settlement she'd been asking for? She'd already assured me that custody was just a technicality. That I was still going to be Sky and Abby's father and participate fully in their lives. I knew all that already. But what I didn't know was how in love she was with another man. So much so that she finally could summon the generosity to give me the closure I'd been lacking. And in the process provoke new regret on my part that surpasses by magnitudes what I felt before. Everything she said and did told me clearly: my wife has finally written me off as a husband and it is too late to win her back. It will now and always be too late.

"Fuck!"

I say it reflexively, in a harsh whisper that attracts no interest from anyone on the sidewalk around me and does nothing to alter my regret. I tilt my head back then stare at the chipped and faded Muni station logo. Christ – me, of all people! How could I not have known better? After what happened to us in Oxford. Did I learn nothing at all?

Without any pause my high school years in England, complete in their miserable verisimilitude, come flooding from the recesses of my brain's neurons into my consciousness. It was such a painful time in my family's history that I have come to refer to it as the 'Oxford Wilderness Period' in the perhaps vague hope that euphemism will dull the ache. The stated reason for the move was so my father could be a visiting faculty member at the Oxford Centre

8

for Management Studies (or OCMS), the precursor to the present-day Saïd Business School. But that was a lie. What my parents never admitted to my sister and me, and what Meg and I didn't learn until after our return to the States, was that my father was in fact unemployed and enduring a midlife crisis of epic proportions. Six months prior he had resigned his tenured professorship at UCLA's graduate school of management in order to found a technical publishing company with a colleague, and had rashly personally guaranteed a bank loan. This was 1975, in the wake of the Arab Oil Embargo and in the midst of the worst economic recession in America since the Great Depression, a period of high inflation, ignominious capitulation in South Vietnam, unremitting Cold War tension, and overall malaise. When the fledgling company suffered a seemingly insurmountable setback, my father panicked. Bill Davis, member of the Greatest Generation, who'd braved Omaha Beach and the Bulge, who'd deftly navigated the choppy waters of career, marriage and fatherhood with seeming aplomb while his post-Eisenhower contemporaries were going all Rabbit Angstrom or worse: he not only flinched, but flat-out panicked. Worried that they would lose everything, he convinced my mother to sell our home on Hilgard Avenue at a fire sale price, convert the dollars to pounds sheltered in a Channel Islands bank, and essentially flee. Maybe he viewed it as a strategic retreat, like the British Expeditionary Force evacuating from the beaches of Dunkirk, but it was actually a self-imposed exile, with the rest of us along for the ride.

There were no real obstacles once the decision had been made, apart from the underlying shame and deceit upon which it was based that corroded it from within. My mother's British citizenship meant the three of us with U.S. passports could obtain residency visas from the Consul General in Los Angeles. I imagine the Home Office was both pleased and befuddled by our emigration, as Britain's own recession was, if anything, worse than the one Americans were enduring. This was an England mired in massive labor unrest despite a Labour government in power, an England not far removed from the devastating economic toll of rebuilding after the war, an England of racial division and post-colonial self-doubt, well before the reinvigorating effects of the Channel Tunnel, the fall of the Iron Curtain, and the cod liver oil austerity of Margaret Thatcher. What we saw upon arrival in London, our jet-lagged eyes bleary but incredulous, was studded leather-clad skinheads roaming the King's Road and transit workers picketing tube and railway stations. It was a far cry from Rule Britannia.

Once situated in a rented Jericho neighborhood row house, we attempted to recreate some semblance of family normalcy. Each day my mother packed my increasingly confused and rebellious sister and me off to our respective Oxford public schools (public in the British sense, as in the cold showers, rigid discipline and inedible dining hall meals of Orwell, Waugh and Greene). Meanwhile my father dressed and departed with leather briefcase in hand for Templeton College, where he would – unbeknownst to us – audit a few classes and read in the library. He had somehow wangled those privileges from an old Wharton classmate who was on good terms with a Fellow at the OCMS, but that was the extent of his integration into Oxford academic life. He was home in time to join us for afternoon tea and we were none the wiser. My sister would spend her free time hanging out with a group of misfit American and European girls who listened to ABBA, experimented with cigarettes and boys, and drank lager and lime at a pub on Cornmarket Street that served underage teenagers. For my sins, I found refuge on the dozens of grass courts that dotted Oxfordshire rather then risk more extra-curricular bullying at the hands of several thuggish upperclassmen, whose ringleader had inexplicably targeted me with his taunts and intimidations. Nothing seemed to deter this lout, certainly not my wholehearted agreement that Americans were "poofs and wankers, the lot of us." He had the unhinged, malevolent look of someone whose home life was so miserable that being sent away to borstal – the Brit version of juvy – would have been an improvement. He outweighed me by at least three stone, from appearances all muscle, and his mates referred to him simply as Stomper. I presumed this was a nickname, but given the steel-toed Doc Martens he wore, as menacing a pair of civilian boots as seemed possible, all scuffed up and black, I wasn't interested in finding out firsthand how he'd earned it. So I saw to it that, apart from my actual classes, I spent zero time loitering on campus and instead hurried along in open view and on perpetual high alert for my tormentors. Maybe tennis served as an escape, not as the intrinsically joyful pursuit it had been years before, but it was survival just the same.

While he was alive my father – who in most respects was a decent and honorable man – never spoke candidly to me about our move to England. I believe he'd somehow convinced himself that it had, in retrospect, all happened for the best. Indeed, upon our return to the States he rebounded to resume teaching at UCLA for the remainder of his career, although in an untenured position, and his long and seemingly contented marriage to my mother must also be counted as one of his great blessings. As bleak as my own situation is, and I acknowledge it is far worse than my father's was in every aspect, I try to take some comfort from his successful recovery from our Oxford Wilderness Period. F. Scott Fitzgerald famously said there are no second acts in American lives, but surely that booze-fueled self-fulfilling prophecy has been proved wrong time and again. Isn't the redemption myth as honored in our culture as baseball and apple pie? True, Annie has divorced me and taken up with one Jeffrey Schreiber, aka the Man with no (Evident) Flaws. True, my real estate development company has fully succumbed to the subprime mortgage debacle of two years ago. True, Skylar and Abigail view me with contempt and pity, respectively, and I can only imagine that Jeffrey Schreiber provides, in contrast, a shining example of male virtue, with his thriving medical products business (focusing on wheelchair-bound children no less!), his eco-friendly Prius and his humble, earnest manner. True, my parents were inconveniently killed almost a year ago, taken out in their Acura on Ventura Boulevard in broad daylight by a drunk and stoned nineteen-year-old named Gasparo Echevaria Nuñez running a red light in his uncle's Buick at eighty miles an hour. I say inconveniently because, as tragic as their demise was in any regard, the timing meant I could reinvest my half of their estate in my teetering company, in effect doubling-down at the roulette wheel in Vegas. My bad, as the kids say today. And all true, all maddeningly, depressingly true. Yet – and this is the critical point I must make – I have won tennis matches that seemed as hopeless.

One singles match my sophomore year at Cal, during our improbable run towards the 1980 NCAA title, stands out in my mind. I was down a set and five games to love, and forty-fifteen to Stanford's Paul Hearn (who once reached the round of sixteen at the U.S. Open), and the humid Georgia heat was beyond sweltering. Even Coach McKittridge, who shouted all the right encouragement ("One game at a time, Trevor! Just get the break!"), later confided that he'd given up on me. And somehow I found a way to fight back. "How did you do it?" my exultant teammates wanted to know, as they embraced me after the match. At that moment, I was too exhausted to introspect and too naïve to improvise. Even now, I can't really understand it. Was it single-minded determination? Better execution? A change of attitude? Sheer luck? A monumental choke on my opponent's part? I don't know. What seems most palpable to me and what I sometimes relive, as a sort of sense memory of vindication, is the scent of the star jasmine in full bloom that ringed the Bulldog Athletics Complex courts, an utterly intoxicating aroma. It's a pity the climate in San Francisco, where I've lived the past two decades, is too cold for the species to reliably flower. But to be fair, the Bay Area has other attributes that aren't available in Athens, Georgia. I don't wish to sound ungrateful or downcast. I really don't.

I realize I've been standing above the Muni escalator for some time, and Diana Shohara might actually be back at her desk by now. Most men would find Diana attractive, me included. According to my friend Dore Berringer – he and Diana are both partners at Asbury & Hollington LLP – she is available and, so he swears, possibly interested, but dating your divorce lawyer seems about as icky and misbegotten a notion as dating your therapist. Besides, all I can think about is Annie. I cannot fathom not being married to her. No longer sharing the first words of the day, the first coffee. No longer making love to her, the way our bodies used to fuse in sympathetic harmony. And now that pleasure, denied to me, is apparently reserved for Jeffrey Schreiber, aka The Man with no (Evident) Flaws.

I briefly revisit the murder fantasy I concocted for Jeffrey Schreiber, complete with pistol shots from my father's old Army .45 ("It's nothing personal, Jeffrey," I tell him before firing) and disposal of the body in the bear-infested Desolation Wilderness of the High Sierra. But this mental indulgence, formerly suffused with righteous retribution, has somehow lost its luster and now seems gratuitous. I mean, really – what's the point? My friends haven't said it to me in so many words, but their encouragement of late has been a sort of, "Come on Trevor, buck up – it's time to accept it and move on." I'm sure they are right. And I simply cannot.

Suddenly I feel famished, desperately so. My watch reads eleven-fifteen and I realize I haven't eaten anything. I normally eat three meals a day, including a decent breakfast – oatmeal and fruit, or some eggs and toast – so my blood sugar is flatlining. I scan the surroundings and spot one of those faux bohemian coffee shops that trade in downscale chic. Beggars can't be choosers, so I make a beeline for the New Vienna Café.

The place affects a grungy vibe but seems clean enough, with an enormous old-fashioned brass espresso machine that emits gurgling noises and blasts of steam like something from Willy Wonka's chocolate factory. The woman behind the counter is twenty-something, with pale skin and black hair, several piercings and tattoos, and a surfeit of cleavage.

"What can I get you?" she asks.

"A double cappuccino, please." I scan the offerings in the glass case, which are numerous. "And a pastry, I think. What's fresh?"

"The cinnamon apple crumb cake came in this morning. It's yummy."

"Done. A piece of that as well."

She makes the cappuccino first, taking real pride in her work: carefully measuring and tamping the ground coffee beans, steaming the milk fully, and then completing the process by drawing a leaf with a swizzle stick in the foamy crema. She smiles conspiratorially as she cuts a large hunk of coffee cake, then dishes it up.

"That's five twenty-five, please," she says, after ringing up the order.

I hand her my Visa card and watch as she swipes it in the register's reader, trying to keep my eyes from staring at her chest. With such lovely breasts, I think, why muck it up with the tattoos and body piercings? Then her expression changes, as if reading my mind. Nothing negative, really, just puzzlement. She hands the card back to me.

"It says it was rejected. Do you want me to try another?"

Now it's my turn to be puzzled, although my confusion lasts less than a second and is replaced with a sickening comprehension. Followed closely on its heels by an embarrassment of a peculiar and completely unfamiliar type. I have never had a credit card rejected before. I feel naked and ridiculous, like everyone in San Francisco can see I'm a failure. Not just a failure, but also a fraud. Even this woman, who under ordinary circumstances I would have no need to impress, must be wondering: Who is this loser?

I reach for my wallet, reinsert the useless credit card and rapidly consider my options. I have a First Regency debit card, but I know there is nothing left in my checking account, which is why I've been using the Chase Visa card for my meal purchases. Like a driver crossing the Mojave Desert on a dwindling tank of gasoline, however, I've been in a state of blithe denial about my circumstances. On some level I knew that the payment on the most recent Visa statement was overdue, but it still feels something of a surprise that the steadily purring engine that was my financial liquidity has suddenly quit without so much as a cough or splutter and, to belabor the automotive metaphor, I now find myself rolling to a stop on the side of the road.

"Um, I've got three bucks in cash. I guess I'll just have the coffee."

I hand over the singles and shrug apologetically. I would prefer to run from the place but that would only confirm my loser status. Besides, I really need the coffee. She takes the money and smiles, pushing the plate with the coffee cake towards me.

"My treat."

I look at her and feel ashamed for my negative thoughts about her piercings and tattoos. This is a genuinely kind-hearted soul.

"Thank you. Are you sure?"

"Absolutely."

"That's really nice of you. Thanks again." She smiles again, in a way that makes me think that I have made her day, instead of the other way around.

I take my coffee and cake to a table as far away as possible and sit down. I pretend to occupy myself with a leftover business section of the *Chronicle* but the do-gooding barista won't be deterred: she beams at me, oblivious that she is rubbing salt in the wound, effectively killing me with kindness. I force a smile and salute her with my fork and then tuck into my meal. The hot cappuccino with its smooth caffeine jolt, along with the sugar rush of the coffee cake, work their magic and I feel momentarily better. But after I take a few more bites and sips, the cold prickliness of reality reasserts itself. I am broke and soon to be homeless, with no rational plan to address either. And unlike Blanche DuBois, I have no desire to depend on the kindness of strangers.

2

Market Street is the true heart of San Francisco, even though Tony Bennett doesn't mention it in his signature song. I stand again at Market and Eighth Street and look in either direction: southwest towards the Castro and Diamond Heights, then northeast to the Ferry Building and the Bay beyond. I've passed this intersection hundreds of times but standing here now it feels alien to me. Heartless even, as if its very existence bodes me ill.

My phone rings. It's Lindsay Furstad, Annie's younger sister. I hesitate and almost decline the call, but I've always adored Lindsay so I press 'Accept' and start walking down Market towards Seventh.

"Hey there."

"Hi Trevor. How are you?"

"Annie told you already, right?"

"Yeah, but I don't want to talk about it."

"That makes two of us."

I pass a homeless guy holding a cardboard panhandling sign. The sign reads: 'Will beg for money.' We lock eyes and I imagine all he sees is a middle-aged white dude in a serious suit with an iPhone, not the colossal fuckup who actually stands before him, so I give him my best 'mind your own damned business' expression and keep walking.

"Listen, Trev, I know you know this goes without saying it but I'll say it anyway. I love you and you'll always be my favorite brother-in-law, okay?"

"I'm your only brother-in-law." She remains silent so I fully take in what she said. "I love you too, Lin."

"It totally sucks," she says.

"No argument here." I fleetingly consider asking her to loan me some money but immediately dismiss the notion. At least for now. "How's Liz?"

"Pretty down on the whole marriage thing. She's convinced the judge won't have the balls to overturn what she insists on calling 'the will of the people.'"

"Oh, he will. He'll do the right thing, just you wait and see."

"You really think? He's got to know they'll be gunning for him."

Liz is Lindsay's fiancée. They were all set to be married after the California Supreme Court declared the state's restrictions on same-sex marriage unconstitutional two summers ago, but the reception space they coveted was booked until mid-November so the wedding didn't take place until just after the California electorate barely adopted Proposition 8, which amended the State Constitution to prohibit same-sex marriage. The approximately 18,000 gay marriages that had been performed before Election Day remained legally valid, but Lindsay and Liz's marriage was nullified. Talk about a pair of pissed off lipstick lesbians. Their only hope now, short of moving to Massachusetts or Connecticut, is the federal lawsuit challenging the constitutionality of Proposition 8, whose closing arguments District Judge Vaughan Walker heard two weeks ago. Complicating the matter, in true San Francisco fashion, Judge Walker is both an establishment Republican (appointed to the bench by none other than the first President Bush) and, I have been reliably informed by friends who belong to the Bohemian Club, a closeted homosexual. Conventional wisdom says that Walker will overturn the discriminatory ballot initiative, but Liz has become embittered by the whole process and isn't prepared to get her hopes up.

"What's he got to lose?" I say. "He's got lifetime tenure and every one of his fellow gay men will have his back."

"So to speak."

I laugh out loud. "Nice."

"I hope you're right," she says, not sounding at all convinced.

"It's going to happen sooner or later. Why should straight people be given a monopoly on the misery of marriage?"

"It's good you aren't bitter," she says.

"Give Liz a hug for me, all right?"

"Will do. And you take care of yourself, okay?"

"Okay." I pause a split-second, then venture: "Hey Liz?" But it's too late; she's already rung off.

"Chickenshit," I say to myself and I fight back the urge to throw the phone through a storefront window. I've never considered myself either a victim or a wide-eyed optimist, preferring to take the long view that small but incremental improvement is about all that mankind can hope for, but our civilization's recent lurches from one colossal miscue to another, whether in matters of economics or human rights, has been exacting a toll on me and my loved ones and I am starting to take it personally. Lindsay Furstad is one of the sweetest, most generous persons there is, and, though I'm sure many of the people who voted to deny her and her equally wonderful fiancée their impending nuptials did so with no individual animus, I'm equally convinced more than a few acted out of fear and ignorance. Just as many who helped perpetrate the sub-prime mortgage implosion were motivated, in their financial decisions, by greed and envy. Let he who is without sin cast the first stone, the Gospel of John says, though as I walk along Market Street my thoughts don't linger on rectifying injustice. There's a more immediate concern: my total lack of funds. How does that quote go, how the prospect of being hanged concentrates the mind wonderfully? Well, I'd use a different adverb, but I'm feeling more than a little focused.

I lift my phone and speed-dial my sister, Meg. She answers her cell phone on the first ring.

"Can you call me back in five minutes?"

"Um, sure."

"Okay, call me then."

I hang up and fume as I keep walking. What, the laundry needs folding before she can talk? The brownies aren't out of the oven yet? She's in the middle of posting another thrilling entry on her mommy blog? I would never denigrate the hard work Meg does as a housewife, holding down the fort for her husband Manny and their two children, Max and Zoe, but she must know what I've been contending with.

To distract myself I open the Wimbledon app on my phone and check to see if there have been any more upsets, near or actual. But order seems to have been restored at the All England Club, after the nasty scare the tournament endured earlier.

This morning, getting dressed for court, I flipped on the television and was pleasantly reminded that another fortnight of Wimbledon coverage had commenced. The grass courts are never as pristine and green as on opening day, and Hannah Storm, anchoring the joint NBC-ESPN broadcast, looked resplendent. Her face soon betrayed concern, however, as she reported that a major upset was brewing and to none other than Roger Federer, the reigning Wimbledon men's singles champion and the consensus pick among tennis cognoscenti as the greatest player of all time. I stared at the screen, transfixed with disbelief, as Hannah's colleague, Patrick McEnroe, delivered the shocking news: Federer was down two sets to one and was only a game away from losing the fourth set – and the match – to a Colombian player named Alejandro Falla. I had never heard of Falla but this guy was obviously playing the match of his life, on Centre Court no less. Improbably, he took the first two sets from Roger 7-5, 6-4, and even though he lost the third, 4-6, he was now serving at 5-4 in the fourth, up a break and one hold away from surely the greatest upset in tennis history. As Brad Gilbert then chimed in to remind us, Federer had only recently (in the French Open) had his streak of 23 straight Grand Slam semifinal appearances broken, a record of DiMaggio-like proportions. And that happened in the quarter-finals and to a powerful Swede, Robin Soderling, the very man who'd upset Rafael Nadal the previous year after the Spaniard had gone undefeated at Stade Roland Garros the prior four years. This was the *first round* of Wimbledon, and Falla, unseeded in the tournament, was barely in the top 100 in the world. His lifetime earnings were probably less than Roger Federer makes in a typical month.

I figured I had about fifteen minutes before I needed to walk to the City Hall courthouse, so I watched the drama unfold. Alejandro Falla, wearing basically a t-shirt and gym shorts, and sporting a two or three-day growth of beard, walked out to serve for the match. Jeez, I thought – he could at least have shaved for the occasion. Roger, in contrast, looked refined in his whites, his shorts cut Bermuda-length and his shirt crisply collared and bearing a custom gold 'RF' logo. His face couldn't mask the truth however. He was deeply concerned that he would lose.

Was it for Roger, I now mull, a 'wonderful concentration of the mind'? Perhaps so. I myself have felt the looming sting of defeat in match situations, the narrowing of the space-time cone of possible good outcomes, though of course for much lower stakes. There is another flipside, though, to being on the brink, one that I would do well to consider in my present circumstances. When you've got little left to lose you gain a certain sense of freedom, a feeling that you can just go for it.

It may seem the height of arrogance to compare myself to the great Federer, although we do share some similarities in style of play. I too use a one-handed backhand, I like to attack the net, and I often have trouble with two-handed lefty opponents (Falla falls in that category). There, however, I must humbly bow and cede the stage to my superiors. I am a strong club player, with a 5.0 USTA rating, but the pros are above 6.0 and I would lose to guys who wouldn't get a game off Federer or even Falla. And yet… when I take my racquet back for a topspin backhand, step in and really connect for a winner, my follow-through fully extended and the ball literally jumping off the court, I feel worthy. Worthy of what, I'm not exactly sure. Maybe of being part of a tradition, of caring about the game. This may seem quaint or even misguided, especially given my current circumstances. But there will be Wimbledon and tennis long after I am gone, so why shouldn't this matter? I just hope my legacy is something other than: He played tennis pretty well, but screwed up the rest of his life.

Federer, being the great champion he is, did wonderfully concentrate his mind. His opponent, no doubt feeling the pressure of serving for the match, soon found himself down fifteen-forty. For Federer, it provided a crucial chance to break, even the fourth set and, most likely, go on to win the match. All Falla needed, however, was a couple of solid first serves to get to deuce. Instead, he netted the first serve and spun the second into Federer's justly feared forehand. Like a prizefighter sensing an adversary is vulnerable, Roger stepped into the forehand and crushed a topspin return down the line. Game, Federer.

As happy as I was for Roger – and I'm a big Federer fan – I actually felt sorry for Falla. He still led two sets to one and the fourth set had yet to be decided, but everyone watching understood his moment had passed. And he had nowhere to hide, no one else to blame. In the final reckoning, he let it slip away. In a way, it might have been easier if he'd just shown up for the match and performed as expected, putting up a respectable fight and going down three sets to none. Maybe even winning a set in a close tie-breaker to demonstrate his mettle. But after tantalizing the crowd – and himself – with the prospect of the greatest upset of all time, this was much harder to accept.

I try calling Meg again.

"Hi stranger," she answers. "Wow, right on time. You must really want something."

"Do I have to want something to call?"

"Of course not," she says. "But you usually do."

"How are Manny and the rug rats?" Meg and her husband, Manny Ramos, have a son, Max, and a daughter, Zoe, aged 10 and 8, respectively. I used to get the girls together with them fairly regularly when we visited my folks in L.A., but not since the car accident. For the record, Manny's parents emigrated from Spain, not Mexico – Meg is touchy on the subject.

"Manny is working too hard but he promised we could go to Disney World next month. I was booking the flight when you first called."

"But you live twenty-five minutes from Disneyland."

"Exactly. What kind of vacation would that be? So… what *do* you want, Trev?"

"Annie got legal custody of the girls. I just came from the courtroom."

"Jesus, Trev, I'm so sorry. I knew it must be soon that the judge was supposed to… oh God, how are you doing?"

"I'm okay, I guess. It's not like it was unexpected. No, that's not true. I mean the okay part. I'm a mess, if you really want to know. But I'll survive. It's what we Davises do, isn't it?"

"Tell that to Mom and Dad."

Meg took our parents' deaths especially hard, being the youngest and never really outgrowing her childhood dependence on them for emotional and, occasionally, financial support. Manny manages a small chain of supermarkets in Downey, a suburb southeast of Los Angeles, and while he does okay, Meg never had a desire to work professionally after becoming a mother and they have struggled to make ends meet. My mother named Meg after Margaret Bourke-White, the photo-journalist, a woman my mom evidently admired for her feminist independence, but Meg has never exhibited the slightest interest in photography, journalistic or otherwise. Her singular passion, apart from managing the busy lives of Max and Zoe, is blogging about it. But who wants to read someone's mommy blog, other than other mothers seeking validation for their own choices and lifestyle? Maybe June Cleever has really come a long way, baby, but can't she just co-parent with Ward in self-satisfied enlightenment without sharing every mother-loving detail?

I pause at the light at Seventh Street and take a deep breath. For of course I *do* need to ask her for something.

"I was thinking about that bequest Mom's Aunt Philippa made to her. I really think we should try to get that resolved. What if I talk to the solicitor again?"

"It didn't sound like he was going to be persuaded."

There's a sudden coldness to her tone, which I naturally chalk up to the investment she made in one of my real estate funds with her half of our parent's estate. Jesus, I think – does she still blame me for that? She understood the risks.

"Maybe we just have to try harder. I have a little time. How about you spot me some travel expenses and I fly over there? He'd have nowhere to hide if I confront him in person."

My mother's Aunt Philippa, her own mother's only surviving sibling, died just a month before my mother and just a week shy of her 100th birthday. If she'd made it to the centenary mark she would have a received a congratulatory telegram from the Queen, something she was looking forward to. But no matter: she lived a long, full life even though she never married or had children. In her young adulthood, she'd volunteered as a spotter for the RAF during the war and received an OBE from King George VI. Later, she became an accountant and lived in Newport Pagnell, about an hour north of London via the M1 motorway, working her entire career for Tickford, an automotive coachbuilding and engineering firm most famous for its association with Aston Martin and Lagonda. By the time of her retirement from Tickford she'd socked away a sizable nest egg, of which she willed seventy-five thousand pounds to her niece, Victoria Moore Davis. Unfortunately, she'd named as the estate's executor a particularly recalcitrant solicitor, one Rupert M. T. Salmons, Esquire, who has yet to release any funds to my mother's estate in almost a year and shows no signs of doing so anytime soon.

"You want me to front you the travel expenses?"

"Well, it seems only fair, Meg. When I dislodge the inheritance, you'll be getting a sixty grand windfall." It's probably more like fifty-seven thousand at the current exchange rate but it's simpler to round up.

"*If* you dislodge it. That other solicitor already sent him letters and got nowhere."

I say nothing and let the silence accumulate. "How much do you need?" she asks. I can hear the suspicion in her voice and I do a quick mental calculation.

"I think six thousand ought to be enough."

"Six thousand?! Are you kidding? Do you have any idea what five days for four in Orlando costs, all in?"

"Meg, you gotta spend money to get money." I almost point out that my building deals averaged a thirty percent return on investment, and this would be more like a thousand percent return, but given our history I don't.

"You think my kids are going to care about that when their holiday is cancelled?"

"Seriously, Meg, you don't have an extra six thousand in the bank?" As soon as I say this, with the inevitable edge in my voice,

I know any chance I've had of convincing her is lost. Game, set and match.

"No, see Trevor, we're what you call the lower-middle class. If at the end of the month I cover the mortgage, manage to save a little for college tuition and have enough leftover for dinner at the Olive Garden, I consider that a success. Especially the way my last investment went. Anyway, hey, I should probably dash, so let me know how it goes, okay? I'm really sorry about the custody thing but I'm sure you're going to work it all out."

"Bye sis." I hang up and mentally kick myself. I really think I have a shot with this asshole British solicitor, who's otherwise just going to eat up my great-aunt's estate in legal fees.

I pass a white BMW touring motorcycle parked on Market and sigh. I've been resisting making this call but I have no choice, so I look up a phone number in my contacts directory and dial it. A pleasant female voice answers, "Malloy Motors, how may I direct your call?"

"Is Gary there?"

"He's with a customer right now. Who can I tell him is calling?"

"Please tell him it's Trevor Davis and it's urgent."

"Um, okay, just a second."

I keep walking – I'm now midway to Sixth Street – and I listen to dead air in my left ear for the better part of a minute. Finally, Gary Malloy gets on the line.

"Jay-sus, Trevor, what's so fucking urgent? You didn't crash the Griso, did you?"

Gary speaks with the particular nasal twang of a Northern Irishman. He's Catholic and has given me no end of grief about my being half-English. The only thing that makes me even tolerable in his eyes is a shared love of motorcycles, especially Italian ones, although he is more partial to Ducatis than Guzzis.

"Nah, it's fine, totally brilliant. You going to be in your shop for a while?"

"Uh, yeah. Why?"

"Tell you when I see you."

I hang up and check e-mail. A newsletter from my tennis club with upcoming events, some merchant solicitations, and a message from Fred telling me that we're meeting at 1 pm in a third floor conference room at First Regency Bank, but whose real purpose is to make sure I'll be there. I tap out a quick reply — *See you then* – and press send. It's too noisy on Market Street to hear the *whoosh!* but checking the Sent Messages box confirms it went out.

I reach Sixth Street just as the light turns green and cross. My phone vibrates in receipt of a text message but I'm still sufficiently spooked by the UPS truck that almost ran me over this morning on my way to City Hall that I wait until reaching the sidewalk to look. I'm hoping it's from JP, probably my best friend if I had to choose one, who is flying to a job in Africa via Germany, but it's Dore (short for Theodore and pronounced like the wooden rowboat). *Diana just told me. Fuck. You okay?*

I text back: *Mustn't grumble.* I cross Market and start walking down Sixth. Dore texts back: *Don't pull that stoic British shit. Lunch?*

Keep calm and carry on. I crane my neck and spot the 'For Sale' sign. The listing must be almost a year old. No surprise, really, in this market. No bank lending officer would go anywhere near this kind of thing. I once convinced Fred to do a walk-through of the building with me several years ago. The bones were actually pretty good, typical post-1906 mid-rise construction – brick façade over steel girders – and the price was bargain basement even then, less than sixty dollars per square foot, but Fred couldn't get out of the building fast enough. "Kevin on steroids," he said. This was an inside joke of ours about spec construction, a reference to the movie *Field of Dreams.* The Kevin Costner character builds a baseball diamond in the middle of his Iowa cornfield because a voice tells him, "Build it and he will come."

The light at Mission turns red so I cross Sixth and keep walking. The partial haze has fully burned off – it never quite amounted to fog – and the north side of Mission is bathed in sunlight. Even though I prefer using the outdoor courts at the club, I never play without a tennis cap so the unaccustomed sun feels good on my face.

Haha! Seriously, lunch?

Pressed today, but thanks. For everything.

I know Dore beats himself up about his role as real estate lawyer in the collapse of my company, maybe even how that contributed to the demise of my marriage, but in my mind he is in no way responsible as I've tried to reassure him. No one forced me to secure the bank loans the way I did and, at the time, it seemed beyond risk. Dore has counseled filing for personal bankruptcy several times, in concert with Diana, but I told him what I tell her, that's the coward's way out. I know this infuriates him – "Why do you think Congress *enacted* the Bankruptcy Code anyway?" – but I'm damned if I'm going to ruin my credit rating for seven years just to make the lawyers feel better. What would I be protecting anyway? Annie was going to get my half of the home equity and our share of the LLC's remaining value. The rest is just crumbs.

I feel more energetic, the caffeine and sugar now fully in my blood stream, and I increase my pace. The old Chronicle building looms ahead on the right. It still houses the newspaper staff but the majority of its space is sublet to a tech incubator called 'The Hub,' its floors teeming with über-cool twenty-somethings all toting Mac laptops and cross-marketing their start-up models. I make a mental note to chide Fred for not buying the building on Sixth when we could, then I realize how preposterous that is on any number of levels.

Anytime, Dore texts. I figure that concludes the conversation – that's the weird thing about text or email messages, you are never sure – and put the phone away. I would like to hear from JP (short for Jean-Paul; his father, Pascal Martin, emigrated from Lyon in the fifties) but he's probably somewhere over the Red Sea and besides, I know my news will upset him. A lot. JP has been seeing a graphic designer named Deirdre for over a year and lately it's been getting serious. Our mutual friends are divided over whether JP will remain a bachelor forever, with each passing year producing more affirmative votes. What I do know, however, is that JP is a closet romantic and would like to settle down with the right woman and start a family. So how to explain that he dates and beds a seemingly endless supply of attractive young women? Well, for one, despite his being my age, JP can easily pass for forty, with the kind of George Clooney-esque looks that would be annoying on anyone less intelligent and interesting. So the obvious answer is: because he can. But more to the point, JP was briefly and disastrously married in his late twenties and I know that wretched episode is still seared on his emotional retina so as to nearly blind him to the benefits of marriage. My news will in no way encourage him to propose to Deirdre the graphic artist. But is that really a bad thing? Ah, well, this is certainly the wrong day for me to answer *that* question.

I catch a glimpse of my walking profile in the plate glass window of a storefront and, despite the distortion, it more or less corresponds with how it has looked for the past three decades. Which seems both normal and odd, since I know I don't really look like I did when I was twenty. My hair has gone grey and thinned, my face is lined, and my chest is less muscular. After a long tennis match, I certainly don't *feel* the same as I used to. But otherwise, in my head, I seem very much that younger version of myself – with similar desires, hopes and fears. Up until the last year or so I felt I had more wisdom and less insecurity than my younger self, but recent events have taken a certain toll on that viewpoint. Maybe that's why my march through middle age – I will turn forty-nine in a couple of months – has taken on the feeling of a headlong plunge.

I remember a particularly candid conversation I had with my father a few years ago in Los Angeles. I took him to see the updated *Casino Royale* in Beverly Hills – Bond films were always a shared passion – and afterwards the locale must have jogged something because he regaled me with stories of his youth, having hot chocolate at Brown's on Highland as a kid, how his father picked him up from Union Station after the war and immediately took him to the Pacific Dining Car for a huge New York strip steak. He told me that even though he was in his eighties, he felt in many ways the same boy who went to Los Angeles High School; the memories were crystal clear, not just factually but emotionally, like the anxiety of asking Pamela Beresford out on a date and the elation of her saying yes. The only thing that was different was his event horizon: he had a sense of the looming day of reckoning, of the accelerating finiteness of life. I took in his words and understood them intellectually but not on any deeper level. Lately, however, they have resonance. My approaching half-century mark, though arbitrary, has imbued in me an unwelcome sobriety. How does the scripture go? 'The time has come to set aside childish things.' Well, in my earlier forties I could pretend, at least to myself, to have purchase on a kind of youthfulness, to imagine a life full of possibilities still ahead of me. That notion now seems untenable, as dated as a thrift store suit with wide lapels. My mother used certain expressions that stuck out in Southern California for their Englishness, one of my favorites being: mutton dressed up as lamb. Well for me, approaching fifty with no assets, no means of support and no spouse feels like mutton dressed up as lamb – and headed for the slaughter.

I check my watch – almost noon – and take advantage of the lack of pedestrians on Mission to quicken my stride. The area is almost immediately better: new modern office towers, busy stores, nice cafés. It's almost like I've crossed over the border from Juárez into El Paso. The City of San Francisco's master plan after the 1970s was to focus development South of Market, which occurred in fits and starts in the 80s but really took hold, in my mind, with the construction of a new Museum of Modern Art in 1995 on Third Street just across from the Yerba Buena-Moscone Convention Center complex. While some consider the design already passé – the museum selected a little-known Swiss architect named Mario Botta – the more practical achievement was to provide a reason for the City's artistic and social elite to venture below Market Street. The museum has been spectacularly successful, with a huge increase in its endowment going hand-in-hand with many well-curated exhibitions.

I consider walking up Third but instead continue down Mission one more block; either route gets me home in the same time. I glance in the lobby of a boutique hotel on the right and observe the busy reception area. This is one of about a dozen such hotels owned by Chris Weymouth. Chris and I collaborated on one small development project and almost went into business together full-time. I wonder, not for the first time, whether my fortunes might have been different if I'd managed to put my personal discomfort at working with Chris aside and done the deal.

Chris Weymouth and I had hit it off immediately. The same age, height and build, we shared all the same intellectual and cultural touchstones of an upper-middle-class American with a progressive capitalistic bent. I remember the trouble started, however, after we each invited our respective significant others to join us for a dinner some eight years ago. A seemingly enjoyable event, complete with delicious food and wine at one of the trendy restaurants then springing up South of Market, I happily deconstructed the evening at home with Annie afterwards.

"Isn't Chris great?" I asked.

"Seems nice," she responded tepidly.

"You don't seem very enthusiastic. What's the matter? He's doing incredibly well and I think he's only going to do better."

"Why does he bother pretending she's his girlfriend? He's obviously gay."

I looked at her, stunned. "What are you talking about?"

"Come on, Trevor. He's completely gay! I mean, of course, there's nothing wrong with that. But why does he have to hide it? He even has a crush on you."

"That's ridiculous! Can't two men like each other without there having to be a sexual undertone? He's simply metrosexual. You should hear the way he talks about women. Didn't you see the way he was touching Yasuko? Trust me, he's straight."

"Whatever," she shrugged, unconvinced.

True or not, I don't know why it bothered me so much, but I couldn't help but examine Chris's behavior more closely when I was around him, which was quite often as we considered a closer business relationship. His smiles in my direction that I had previously taken to be just appreciation now assumed a bigger significance. He would comment to other business associates what a clever observation I had made, or how valuable I was to the hotel project we were discussing. Meanwhile other evidence mounted at an alarming rate: the feminine tics and mannerisms, almost out of a homosexual cliché guidebook; the lack of any interest in sports; the obsession with fine wine and opera (don't straight men like Puccini as well?!); the deference to me in social situations, as if I were the alpha male. I tried to ignore all these signs, even as

I rationalized the inconsequentiality of his sexual preference. We were contemplating a business partnership, not a domestic one. But what I was truly dreading finally came to fruition.

We were doing a walk-through of his latest hotel and Chris wanted me to see one of the regular rooms. It was large and well-appointed, modern without being obtrusive, typical of his aesthetic talent and attention to detail. I told him so and thanked him for showing it to me.

"Any time. I mean it. *Any* time." His eyes held mine several beats too long, his mouth forming a deferential soft smile that I could only imagine he'd learned from Yasuko and her Japanese neo-geisha tradition. I couldn't wait to get outside and get away from him.

Jesus, I thought, storming away – a fucking pass? Must he be so fucking oblivious? Doesn't he realize I'm straight? Happily married (which I was back then, more or less)? Now he's gone and ruined everything. I knew my gaydar must be rusty but his straidar – or whatever the hell it's called – must be nonexistent.

I briefly considered sitting him down and confronting the situation. Look Chris, I would say. I really like you and I very much want to do this deal together. Unless I've got things wrong, it seems you might like me in a way I can't reciprocate. Can we shelve that and just get on with the business at hand? Who knows, maybe that would have worked. But I was too chicken to try. Why, I wonder now? Was it just that I assumed it was doomed to failure, that he would be so embarrassed by his miscalculation that he would break off our working relationship? Or could it be that I was, on some distressing level, confused by my own attraction to him (for genuine but non-sexual reasons) and felt somehow to blame for leading him on?

In any event, I took the coward's way out: neither confronting him nor going through with the deal. I used Fred as the excuse, saying my CFO couldn't make the numbers pencil out, but I believe Chris suspected the real reason. It was a classic lose-lose situation: what could have been a mutually beneficial and successful business arrangement foundered on the shoals of misunderstanding and fear.

Annie sympathized with me and we joked about it afterwards in the ways socially enlightened heterosexuals do, ways that would otherwise verge on the politically incorrect if it weren't for our clear and unmitigated tolerance and liberalism. After all, Annie's sister was a lesbian for God's sake! Of the seven deadly sins, I have no doubt mine is pride. Too late, I realized to my surprise and chagrin, it is a lot easier for me to be friends with and even love an attractive, bright lesbian than a good-looking, intelligent gay man.

I am now home, if I can dare to use that term for a residence I must soon vacate. I enter the building lobby and quickly make my way to the corridor upstairs. Once I spot the loft's front door I yank my tie off; inside, I slam the door shut behind me and tear off my suit jacket as if it were lined with anthrax powder. I kick my shoes off, unhitch and toss the belt and unzip my trousers so they fall below my waist just as I start upstairs, my stride to the first step ripping the lightweight worsted wool. I pause to survey the damage – the whole front inseam is torn from the zipper down to the seat – but I shrug and keep going. I don't plan on wearing this suit anytime soon. On the upstairs landing I pause to observe the loft, forcing myself to pretend I'm a stranger viewing it for the first time. Any reasonably enlightened visitor, I'm convinced, would praise its addition to the City's housing inventory, with the acid-washed concrete floors (concealing radiant heat), 18 foot ceiling, and beechwood and glass kitchen. It was not cheap to design and construct but then quality rarely is. Why cut corners and build a piece of crap?

"Fuck it," I say out loud. I grab hold of my shirt on either side of the now-opened collar and pull hard. But the fabric proves surprisingly strong and nothing happens. Christ almighty – you pay for quality, you get quality! Renewing my effort, the second button finally pops, then the cloth gives way in a cotton-cleaving crescendo. This seems to momentarily quench my rending-of-garments thirst, so I sit on the edge of the bed and calmly remove what remains of the tattered shirt and trousers and pull on a t-shirt and a pair of Levis.

Back downstairs I glance at the TV screen, momentarily consider checking in on Wimbledon, even for one minute, but decide against it. Instead, I search for and locate a file box, rummage inside and find the small document I want, and stuff it in the front pocket of my jeans. Now with purpose, I grab phone, keys and wallet, all of which I place into the pockets of my black leather jacket. Then I zip on boots and dash out the door.

The loft unit has one deeded garage space, but it is an unusually long one so it fits both the Maserati and the Guzzi with room to spare. I glance briefly at the Quattroporte, literally *four doors*, but focus my attention on the Guzzi. If the large sedan weren't leased I might have more present-day appreciation for its sinuous Pininfarina lines.

I always had a grudging admiration for Moto Guzzi motorcycles, with their distinctive V-twin motors and shaft drive, but nothing that kept me from riding a succession of Hondas and BMWs. Until one day I spotted a Griso. It was such a handsome bike, so raw in its masculinity and yet refined in its Italian aesthetics, that I knew I would have one. This was three years ago when the fortunes of my real estate company were very different, so the $15,000 splurge was almost a rounding error on the balance sheet, especially as I netted close to $7,000 upon selling my BMW R1150.

I straddle the Griso, insert the key and switch on the ignition. The tachometer needle swings all the way up and back – I've never found out why, maybe some kind of self-diagnostic procedure – and I confirm the gearbox is in neutral, engage the clutch and press the starter. The 1200cc engine comes to life, the distinctive rasp of the four exhaust valves amplified by the custom Lavizzari pipes and the concrete confines of the garage. I twist the throttle open a couple of times, leaning each time against the bike's pronounced lurch to the right from crankshaft torque, and let the engine warm up. The rumble between my legs reminds me yet again of the one time Annie consented to ride on the Griso, when she first felt the vibration and teased about why guys and their biker gals like to ride Harleys. Just sit back and enjoy yourself I joked back, and she dutifully complied. Her thighs gripped the brown leather saddle with her arms wrapped tightly around my black leather jacket and her feet perched on the passenger pegs while encased in long zippered boots, the ones we bought together in Pisa on our honeymoon. All that cowhide and throbbing pistons: it was like foreplay in a bad porn movie but it actually had the desired effect. The girls were both asleep when we got home and as soon as I paid the sitter (we didn't really need one at their age but Annie insisted because we were going to dinner on the motorbike), Annie smiled a devilish, come hither smile, her hair still delightfully askew from the wind and helmet. We rushed to our bedroom and made raunchy, passionate love.

I shake my head to snap out of the reverie, strap on my helmet and carefully ease the bike past the Quattroporte. Once through the garage door I quickly accelerate in first gear, the outsized exhaust note reverberating down Minna Street. A flick of the handlebars and I'm onto Third Street, back on the throttle and up into second, then third gear, almost 50 mph on this crowded midday thoroughfare, then a fast downshift to sweep onto Harrison, a much wider, one-way avenue. The light is just changing to green up ahead at Fourth and there is no traffic whatsoever in the center lane so I punch it, still in second gear, the engine's massive torque feeding in just near the point where the front wheel will break free from the pavement, then shift to third near the redline, then fourth, past 80 mph now, which is totally irresponsible – the posted speed limit is 35 – but I'm both completely alert, in control of the machine, and feeling utterly reckless. At this rate I can make it through the green light at Fifth Street for sure but then I'll need to haul on the brakes since the lights are timed for the posted speed. Or I can just let her rip.

It isn't so much a conscious thought or even a repressed desire as a… what? A realization, I suppose. That if I keep pouring on the throttle and accelerating I will crash into something so hard that I will almost certainly perish. But what if I don't, and just horribly maim myself? That would certainly be a fate worse than death, to use the hackneyed expression.

And so, for whatever reason – primitive self-preservation I suppose – my right wrist slides forward and my fingers grasp the front brake in unison with my right toes pushing down on the rear, not exactly a panic stop but given the bike's ABS system it might as well be. I decelerate so quickly that I forget to engage the clutch and, as I come to a complete stop, the Griso's engine stalls with a heavy forward lurch. The sudden silence seems both shocking and sobering, like a nighttime power outage that reminds you how tenuous modern civilization really is, and did you really forget to store some candles, just in case? My heart is pounding and the helmet's visor starts to fog from my heavy exhalations and for the second time today – the first being the UPS truck near-miss – I feel that enervating, tingling sensation of excess adrenalin coursing through my body with no place to escape. And I realize, with absolutely no sense of irony, that I'm still in the middle of Harrison and if I don't move right away some other truck will rear-end me and finish the job I almost set out to do.

I re-start the Griso, stomp on the shifter repeatedly to get to first gear, and ease the clutch out. My hands twitch nervously and I flip my helmet visor up, taking a couple of deep breaths to try to calm myself. Jeez, I try to console myself with false amusement, that was some double cappuccino that girl prepared! But it is a feeble and unsuccessful effort. For the dark clouds in my head quickly reform, centering mostly on Annie and her cursed boyfriend, Jeffrey Schreiber, aka The Man with no (Evident) Flaws. I brood on her – and his – happiness. I consider adding the word 'presumed' before happiness, but this I know would be a false qualifier, wholly without basis and inserted only to throw myself a minuscule psychic bone. I saw full well from Annie's body language in court how happy she is, or more correctly, has become. And it eats at me like the hydrochloric acid I remember from 9th grade science lab, all fuming and corrosive. The acid *itself*, I know, is not dangerous, no more than a 110 horsepower motorcycle, but in the right circumstances it can be as deadly as detonating dynamite.

I feel chastened by my near-misadventure and proceed along Harrison in second gear. The truth is, I have absolutely no death wish, although I have certainly perceived in myself a new acceptance of my mortality since the death of my parents and my breakup with Annie. It's not that I *want* to die, it's that I would feel more or less at peace if my ticket got punched at the half-century mark. To be clear, I haven't fulfilled all my aspirations by any stretch, and I truly hope to be taken quietly in my sleep in my late nineties after playing a spirited game of tennis the day before, but if I were told tomorrow that I had some finite time to live, six months for instance, I don't believe I'd feel the sense of tragedy that I would had my life only spanned a quarter-century. Except, it would be lovely to see the girls to adulthood, with thriving careers and maybe husbands and families of their own.

Now on Mission, the Griso rumbles past Sixteenth Street. I pull over and park in one of the diagonal motorcycle spaces in front of Malloy Motors. Flanking me are a dozen other bikes, some with dealer plates belonging to the shop and others of visiting customers. There are a handful of Ducatis, several Triumphs, a stunning yellow Aprilia, and a handsome, white Moto Guzzi V7 Classic.

Gary Malloy stands just outside the doorway, puffing on an Embassy Mild with its distinctive blue metallic band and chatting with a man in racing leathers. I blip the throttle before shutting it off and Gary looks over. I roll the Griso onto its kickstand and dismount.

The man in leathers takes a closer look at my bike and then furrows his brow.

"Is that a Special Edition?"

I nod, yes.

"I thought they were only available in Europe."

"They are," Gary chimes in with a smirk.

Mr. Racing Leathers ruminates on this a moment, starts to form another question then reconsiders. He shrugs and heads inside the shop.

"You still riding that Italian piece of shite?" Gary asks.

"Is your mother still fucking Ian Paisley?"

Gary cocks his head appreciatively. "Afternoon, Trevor."

"Afternoon, Gary. How's business?"

Gary snorts and takes a final drag on his cigarette before dropping it to the sidewalk and stomping it out with the toe of his sneaker. Before buying the motorcycle shop, Gary had a short but reasonably successful career racing on the European Grand Prix circuit. After a nasty spill at Silverstone – he keeps the scarred helmet behind the counter of his shop to dramatize the need for buying quality safety equipment – he decided it was time to visit a cousin who'd already emigrated from Belfast to San Francisco. Gary's goal: to seek his own version of the American Dream.

"Everyone's a fucking tire-kicker. That bastard shows up on a Monster he bought used off fucking Craigslist and he's bent my ear the last half-hour about the new Streetfighter. Good job you rolled up – he was just working up the fucking nerve to ask for a test ride but there's no chance in fucking hell he'd purchase a new bike."

Gary is rail-thin and good-looking in a dark-haired David Bowie sort of way, although several inches shorter than my six foot one.

"Sounds like he might be interested in my Griso."

Gary looks thoughtful a moment, then suddenly dismissive. "I'm telling you, man. A fucking tire-kicker. I guarantee that suit he's wearing has never been within fifty fucking miles of a race course."

"Gary, I need a favor."

"Sorry, don't believe in them."

"Seriously…" I begin but he cuts me off.

"I am fucking serious." He registers my mild annoyance and spreads his palms, granting me permission to continue.

"When do you figure Guzzi will start exporting SEs here?"

"The coming model year, but they probably won't ship the first bikes until March. Fucking Italians. Brilliant engineers. And crap businessmen."

Gary rode for the Ducati factory team, so he knows from whence he speaks.

"So you think my bike might still fetch a good price?"

"Ah, so that's it." Gary smiles in self-satisfaction, his mind already calculating his sales commission. "Sure, I could consign it for you, just say the fucking word. For *that*"– he points to my Griso with admiration – "I'd find a fucking buyer."

"What do you figure, asking price?"

Gary ponders a moment, his appraising eye taking in the Griso's distinctive Tenni green paint job.

"Should go fourteen, I reckon."

"Those pipes cost me a thousand Euros extra." The stock factory exhaust was the only thing I didn't like about the Griso, an absurdly oversized canister that resembled a bulging codpiece on an Elizabethan madrigal singer. The aftermarket Lavizzari dual chrome pipes look much classier and sound better as well.

"I know, I fucking installed them. Maybe ask fifteen."

"That's great. But here's the catch. I'm having a little cash flow situation. I can't wait for a consignment sale."

"You want me to advance you the fucking money? What do I look like, the fucking Bank of Malloy?"

"Gary, you might consider broadening your cursing vocabulary. There are other words than 'fuck.'"

He glares at me with the cold fury of a genuine Irish Republican nursing generations of hatred over his motherland's occupation.

"Fuck you, you fucking English fuck." With that he turns and walks inside.

Jesus, I think. Why do I keep insulting the people I need to give me money? I'm normally very good at raising funds from prospective investors so I am both distressed at my currently disastrous people skills and genuinely concerned that I don't have the cash to eat another meal. I take a deep breath, reassess, and walk inside Gary's dealership.

Gary is standing near the office in back, looking over some paperwork. But he also sees me approach past the rows of new Triumphs and Ducatis and doesn't turn away. I take that as a good sign.

"Gary, jeez, I am so sorry. That totally came out wrong – I was just trying to lighten the mood in an awkward moment." Gary just listens.

"I absolutely hate playing the sympathy card but here's the thing. My business is in liquidation, I'm getting divorced, my apartment lease is up, my credit card just got rejected and I literally, *literally*, don't have two nickels to rub together."

I fish in my pocket and pull out the Griso's pink slip.

"Okay, we agree the Griso is worth at least fifteen grand. It pains me to sell it – you of all people know what that bike means to me – but I have no choice. I'll sign this pink slip and you pay me what you want. I just need some cash today."

Gary stares at me a moment, as if assessing the legitimacy of my sob story. I believe I detect a note of tenderness in his eyes, or is it pity? He walks over to the other side of the office and returns with a checkbook. He scribbles on a Wells Fargo Bank check, rips it out and hands it to me. I glance down and see it is in the amount of five thousand dollars and payable to Cash.

"Gary, are you kidding me? You just said it was worth three times this amount."

"Take it to the branch up the block. I'll phone the manager right now and tell her to expect you."

I put the check down and shake my head. "I can't take this. I thought we were friends, Gary. This is how you treat your friends?"

He looks at me and that cold Northern Irish fury returns to his eyes.

"Friends? How are we friends? Because we shoot the shit about motorbikes? Have you ever had me over to dinner in your nice San Francisco home? Stood me for a pint at a bar?" He grabs the check and waves it at me. "This is business. I'm doing you a fucking favor but you don't need to say 'thank you very much,' you can just sign the fucking pink slip and take my money and be gone."

With that he puts down the check and walks away.

I slump against the desk, my heart racing, and consider my options. The proverbial bird in the hand versus trying to find another buyer – some stranger – who might pay me more. In cash, today. I look around to see if that guy in the racing suit is still in the showroom but he's nowhere to be seen. Jesus. Gary is robbing me blind but what can I do? He knows damn well how desperate I am because I told him so. And like he said, it's just business.

I dearly want to walk out. I can actually feel my amygdala flooding and demanding my body to tear up Gary's check and storm out. If indignation were blood-soluble it would be pulsing through my veins. But somehow, something else fights its way through to my frontal cortex. It's an expression as old as the Old Testament: pride goeth before a fall.

I calm myself enough to think, force myself to. Is that all it is now? False pride? The knowledge that someone has bested me, someone I thought might treat me better? Or that I've done this to myself, allowed my situation to get so vulnerable that I have no alternative but to take a sucker's deal?

And having asked the question, I immediately know the answer.

3

The F line streetcar drops me on Market Street at Battery and I quickly cross the wide thoroughfare against the light, clutching my right hand to my jacket pocket to feel the reassuring thickness of a number ten envelope filled with $4900 in $100 dollar bills. From the bulge in my right front jeans pocket I know the $98.50 in smaller bills and change remains there as well. The vintage wooden streetcar continues down Market towards the Ferry Building, its steel wheels *humming* against the rails, and I try to ignore the incongruity of the scene: me in my motorcycle gear, carrying all that remains of my net worth, amongst the high-rise buildings in the modern part of the city that I have worked in and developed for over two decades but that now seem as foreign as the 1920s era Milanese streetcar in which I just rode.

I meet Fred Kashani in the lobby of the First Regency Bank building. Fred is my longtime business partner and usually nothing ruffles his feathers, yet he seems a bit anxious, probably because I texted him from the bus to tell him not to meet in the conference room upstairs, and my attire must add to his concern. I'm sure he was expecting business clothes. He is dressed in a two-button navy suit with an open-necked white shirt, as natty as ever.

But Fred won't let much get in the way of his typically fine manners and he offers his hand to shake. "Hello, Trevor."

"Good to see you, Fred."

"Everything okay?" he asks hopefully.

"Well, you know. These are challenging times."

He attempts a smile, then nods his head with understanding. "Indeed."

"Listen, I know we're supposed to meet with the bankers upstairs…"

"In..." Fred interrupts, checking his watch, "five minutes."

"Okay, so I'll make it quick. Let's find a place to talk."

I start walking towards the private banking section of the bank's retail offices and Fred has no choice but to follow. I open a glass door, enter, and spot one of the young women who handle deposits and other services for the bank's VIP customers.

"Hi Jolene."

"Hello Mr. Davis," she says brightly.

"Jolene, do you have a place where Fred and I can talk privately for a few minutes?"

Fred looks at his watch again with concern. "Trevor, I don't know if..."

"Any place will do," I say, more to reassure her than to placate Fred.

"Um, sure," she says unsteadily, then continues, "I think the small conference room over there is free." She points down the corridor.

"Great, thanks!" I say with outsized buoyancy, as I guide Fred's arm gently but firmly in that direction.

The small conference room has a corporate aroma of leather chairs, legal pads and thermos-jugged coffee. Fred closes the door behind us and takes a seat at the round, four-person table. He seems reconciled to the fact that our bank meeting will not go off as expected, although he must wonder how much deviation there will be.

Fred's real name is Farid but he only uses that within his Iranian-American community. After our relationship solidified I began using it as well and he didn't seem to mind, but it ultimately became more confusing for others because his business cards are printed as 'Fred Kashani' and he introduces himself that way to every non-Persian. Fred is of medium height, in his early forties, and good-looking in an Omar Sharif meets Tom Hanks sort of way. We've been business partners for fifteen years and I count Fred as one of my true friends, as honest and considerate as they come. Fred came to the U.S. in the upper-middle-class exodus after the fall of the Shah and ended up attending Cal for both under-graduate studies and business school. After the invasion of Iraq in 2003 I got a window into Fred's teenage years, when he was a recent immigrant with rudimentary English trying desperately to fit in, despite rampant anti-Iranian hostility in the wake of the hostage crisis. By the time of George W. Bush's military adventure in the Persian Gulf, Fred was a middle-aged American citizen, confident in his fluency, an upstanding member of the Bay Area business community. Yet I clearly remember the pain on his face as he relived the fear and shame of being stereotyped as one of those 'Arab towel heads' by ignorant bigots.

One of my pleasures has been getting to know Iranian culture through Fred, and I find it very appealing, a unique combination of Old World courtliness, French sophistication (the women with their dress in particular), American entrepreneurism and Jewish intelligentsia. Fred and his lovely wife, Niloufar, have invited me into their home for family events – they have a delightfully precocious five year-old son named Moraad – where Niloufar serves delicious Persian specialties that always include the crusty rice dish, *tah-deeg*. I forever ingratiated myself to her by praising her *tah-deeg* and asking for seconds when she first served it to me. Although now I wonder if, after the news I will deliver to Fred, she will be disposed to ever cook for me again.

"I just passed that mid-rise on Sixth. It's still for sale." I say this in an offhand manner, more to ease into what I need to tell Fred than to suggest a business opportunity. He just pulls his facial muscles into a momentary smile, betraying nothing in the way of interest or impatience.

"Fred, I know we don't have much time so I'll cut right to it. I'm not going to be able to join the meeting upstairs."

Fred takes a moment to absorb my news, which at this point is probably not wholly unexpected.

"Might I ask why?" he asks. I sigh and lay my palms on the table.

"Of course you can, and I'll tell you whatever you want. But the short answer is, I need to leave on a trip. Right away."

"Is this related to your court hearing this morning? How did that go, by the way?"

"Well, it's finally decided, which I suppose is some sort of relief. Annie will get custody of the girls. And, as you know, I won't be keeping any of the house, or my share of the business."

"I'm so sorry, Trevor. I really am."

"Thanks Fred. I appreciate it."

When I invited Fred to buy into Davis Holdings, LLC, we agreed that he would receive, after a three year vesting schedule, one-third of the company, with me and Annie retaining the other two-thirds. So even though he is a substantial owner and the day-to-day managing partner, his fate has been inextricably linked to my personal and financial downfall. I feel terrible about that, but at the same time realize that the collapse of the subprime market was the true culprit in deep-sixing our business, and there was nothing I could have done about that to shield Fred from our current circumstances. Luckily, he'd been prudent and socked away most of his partnership proceeds for more than a decade prior to the downturn. It was not the outcome he'd hoped for, but Fred has done very well.

"So, anyway," I continue. "I won't be able to meet with the bank guys. Or with you after. I'm not sure how long I'm going to be out of town but I likely won't be able to clean out the loft unit either."

"I see." For the first time, Fred is visibly annoyed. Not only am I bailing on crucial business meetings, with all the messy financial and legal details to be hammered out, but I'm leaving him in charge of my personal belongings, knowing that the bank as principal lender may demand we re-let the loft immediately. For all he knows there is soiled laundry strewn all over the place and dirty dishes piled up in the sink.

"What if your consent is required on a particular provision?" he asks.

"I trust you, Fred. I'll sign whatever you agree to."

My cell phone rings and I dig it out to ID the caller. It's an unfamiliar number with a San Mateo Peninsula area code. I consider ignoring it but I could actually use the interruption.

"Excuse me, Fred." I step to the side of the conference room and accept the call.

"Trevor Davis."

"Mr. Davis?" It's a woman's voice, with a pointed tone, almost strident. "This is Sandra Morgan at the Portola Equestrian Academy. I have Skylar in the office with me."

"Is she okay?" I ask.

"She's fine. But I'm afraid you're going to have to pick her up. She's been expelled for rules infractions."

Skylar and Abigail were starting out the summer break at separate camps, according to their abiding passions: English riding for Sky and ballet dancing for Abby. Annie is supposed to collect them at the end of the week after returning from a hiking trip to Yosemite. It went unsaid but her presumed hiking companion is Jeffrey Schreiber, aka the Man with no (Evident) Flaws.

"What infraction?" I ask.

"Infractions, plural," Sandra Morgan says. "The rules are quite clear. The first violation of a safety or ethics rule earns a warning and the second an expulsion. It's all spelled out in the camper agreement which parents sign."

"I'm sure it is, but what did she... what are you claiming she did?"

"Skylar was outside after lights out last night. Today she was riding without a helmet. What time can we expect you this afternoon?"

"I'm afraid that's impossible. I'm leaving town on business. Did you try reaching her mother?"

"Yes, but there was no answer on the numbers we have listed. I'm sorry to inconvenience you, Mr. Davis, but you'll need to collect your daughter. For the safety of our campers we can't permit these kinds of violations."

"You can't give her a warning?"

"That's what the first violation is. And her attitude continues to be ... uncooperative at best."

"Could I speak with her please?"

"Certainly, just a second."

I shrug my shoulders apologetically at Fred, who has been checking his smartphone and looking antsy.

"Hi Dad," Skylar says.

"Hi sweetheart," I say. "Listen, honey, can you please do me a favor? Can you apologize to Ms. Morgan and tell her you won't violate any more of the camp rules? I know how much you want to do this camp."

"I told her I was sorry, I just forgot to put on my helmet. But it's like Nazi Germany or something around here. I mean, Jesus, what's the big deal about lights out? I wasn't even tired."

"Sky, please listen. I need to leave town on business, it's kind of an emergency, so there's no way I can collect you from camp. Can you please make nice with the staff? Whatever it takes, okay? I really appreciate it."

"Yeah, whatever."

I hear some muffled voices talking on the other end. Thank God, I think – she's smoothing things over. Then, from a distance but clear: "This is total bullshit!"

"Mr. Davis?" Sandra Morgan is back on the phone. "Skylar will be waiting in the office for you to collect her. Thank you."

"Wait," I say. "Can't we figure out a…?"

"Good day." And she hangs up.

I look over at Fred whose face manages to convey both sympathy for my plight and anxiety about the meeting.

"I'm sorry, Trevor, I really should go."

I walk towards him, still in a daze from the phone call. I agreed via email with Annie yesterday that I'd be on call this week for the girls, given her Yosemite trip. But even with the Griso money there's no way I can afford to linger in San Francisco all week, so I mentally scramble to come up with a way to park Sky someplace so I can deal with my great-aunt's inheritance.

"I understand Fred, no problem."

So typical – he's apologizing to me. Fred holds out his hand so I clasp it in a firm handshake. He bows his head slightly as I release his hand.

"Do you need anything?" he asks. "Some spending money?"

"No, I have that covered. Thanks. Just do me one favor."

"Anything."

"Kiss your wife tonight and tell her how much you love her."
Fred nods solemnly.

"Don't take any crap from these guys, okay?"

Fred laughs. "They have already realized you can't get blood from a stone." Fred turns serious again. "Take good care, Trevor."

"Thank you," I say. "*Merci.*" I pronounce it the Farsi way, stressing the first consonant.

"*Khahesh Mikonam.*" And with that he walks out of the conference room towards the elevator bank.

"Go Bears," I say, even though Fred can no longer hear me. I feel a rising anger towards him as he disappears from sight, which puzzles me until I realize why: I was hoping he'd have been upset – even angry – at my leaving him in the lurch. True, he's always been exceedingly polite and conflict-averse, but his behavior in the face of my news was like a duck contending with a sudden summer shower. Unexpected perhaps, but nothing that can't be shrugged off. Has he become inured to my failings? Annie exhibited a similar war-weariness this morning. God, I'd so much rather they berate me for my betrayals than purse their lips in resignation. Fred used to look up to me with a respect that could border on hero worship. And what remains now? Mildly irritated acquiescence?

I glance at my watch and immediately try to push these thoughts away. I need to focus on the task at hand. So I hastily depart the conference room and go in search of Jolene, the deposits officer. I find her alone at her desk, still eager to treat me as the valued bank customer I was – she surely knows otherwise, doesn't she? – so I pull out the envelope full of cash and ask about a more practical way to travel with this much money. I've been thinking about the problem of going overseas without a valid credit or debit card. Cash may be king, but legitimate folks don't use stacks of hundreds to buy airline tickets. And even though I've never been mugged or pickpocketed in San Francisco, why tempt fate now? My luck hasn't been stellar lately. And I have no margin for error.

Jolene seems completely unfazed by the cash – she must be used to dealing with much larger amounts – and she brightly suggests a new product called a Cash Passport. She explains that it functions like a credit card but is a hybrid of a debit card and a traveler's check that employs a small chip to maintain the card's balance and that can be recharged at any participating bank worldwide. I say a silent oath to myself to use that recharge function

46

soon, as five grand doesn't go very far on a trip to London, and I instruct Jolene to deposit my cash onto the card. She tells me that there's normally a thirty-five dollar fee for the card but she'll waive it, given I'm a longtime preferred banking customer. What's this, another random act of kindness? Or the next float in the Trevor Davis summer solstice pity parade? But I'm no stranger to this office so I thank Jolene and justify her munificence, however small (yet significant in my dire straights), as my due for all the pain the bank's commercial loan department has caused me.

I walk out onto Market and immediately cross the street, then regret my decision as I'm now out of the sunshine beneath one of the several skyscrapers along this stretch of Market across from Sansome and I feel every cold draft of wind. Seeking warmth I turn left on Second Street, past the recently closed (but not yet re-leased) Rand McNally store and I consider for a microsecond that in times past I would have ducked in to browse the shelves filled with guidebooks and maps and travel memoirs before an impending trip. A victim of 2008 or the demise of physical books? No matter, really, since I wouldn't be buying any units of inventory, even if they were still stocked and displayed.

I quicken my stride. There is direct sun on me but I still don't feel warm and now my feet are uncomfortable, unaccustomed as they are to walking so far in riding boots. I dodge through the heavy pedestrian lunch traffic, mostly twenty-somethings it seems, full of purpose. I am intent on one thing: making it past Mission to Minna and the loft. But now I am stuck behind a young couple pushing a doublewide stroller, one of those supremely cool and expensive models of a brand with at least one umlaut over an extra, unnecessary vowel. The stroller, I can see, holds a bright-eyed toddler to starboard and another to port. As I swing past them I glance back to take in the parents: he no more than thirty, clutching a latté and sporting a scruff of beard, much like Alejandro Falla earlier (memo to *prior* investor self: short Gillette stock), she of similar age, blonde and thin-lipped and advanced yoga fit, glancing down at the kids with a combination of tenderness and concern and – could it be? – smugness. They could all be versions of me and Annie and the girls from a decade ago, minus the self-satisfaction of course, on their way to the playground at Yerba Buena Gardens, an urban oasis of sand pit, spongy rubber mats, climbing structure and tube slide incongruously perched atop Moscone Center, which hosts important conventions ranging from the political (e.g. the doomed Mondale-Ferraro Democratic ticket of 1984) to the corporate (Steve Jobs annually presides over the Apple Worldwide Developers Conference in his iconic black mock turtleneck and jeans).

It's been years since Sky and Abby played at Yerba Buena Gardens but it seems like yesterday, a time of such innocence and family contentment that I recoil from the memory. There is a lull in the car traffic on Second so I dart across to the west side and almost duck into the small alley named after Ambrose Bierce, until I remember that it does not give onto Mission but only turns right onto another alley named Annie, two obvious strikes against it. So I am now forced to walk down Second towards Mission in plain view of the couple with the tandem stroller on the opposite side of the street should I so choose to look, which I shouldn't but do anyway. How can I judge their happiness? For all I know they are miserable – we all know how outward appearances can be deceiving – and besides, what does that matter to my situation? No, I won't begrudge them their paradise, if that's in fact where they reside. I have my own marching orders and it doesn't do to compare.

By now I'm well past them, and thankfully with the light so I can cross Mission in stride, with Minna now fully in sight. I turn right, just steps from the loft and I'm about to reach for my keys when I'm startled by the sound of screeching tires and wailing, tuned exhaust note, so I look up to see… what appears to be *my* Maserati peeling out of the building's underground garage. What the …? As the Quattroporte flashes past, the driver a couple of feet away, I catch a glimpse of him behind the tinted windows and see not a drugged-out teenager intent on a quick score but a man in his thirties, astute and professional, wearing leather gloves and staring calmly ahead. A look, in sum, consistent with a bank repossessor, not a car thief.

"Motherfucker!"

I'm not prone to swearing out loud in public. Really, I'm not. But… I mean, under the circumstances, can you blame me?

4

I glance at my watch as I pull onto the Fourth Street on-ramp for the 101 South: 2.55 p.m. Christ, all the time wasted – just gone – on top of the money blown on this god-forsaken Hyundai. Okay, take a deep breath because… I need to let it go. It's a choice right now; dwell on the negative or find something positive. You got your serve broken but there's a chance to break right back. It's not irreparable. I've got a 'Cash Passport' now and while the balance of $4,900 has already been dinged – *completely unnecessarily*, my mind cries out – I do have wheels, an actual, functioning automobile, like any other self-respecting Californian. I can still collect Sky and, who knows, maybe the freeway traffic will be kind. So… Just. Let. It. Go. But my mind doesn't want to cooperate. And so it rewinds the tape of the last few hours and presses the 'play' button. Maybe we'll learn something useful by doing so, it seems to want to argue. That's how we can do better next time. I doubt it, I want to say back. In that direction lies madness.

What I get is a montage of all moments with a common denominator: money. Handing over my remaining dollar bills for a latté. Holding the Wells Fargo check for the devalued Guzzi. Having to rent a claptrap subcompact when I could have moved the Maserati from the garage this morning, instead of leaving it in the assigned parking space any trained bank repo man would know to try first.

For most of my life money has been a largely abstract concept, a bunch of numbers in a bank account that I rarely experienced on a tangible level. I trusted that some fiscal safety net was there and, until my Chase card was rejected at the coffee shop, it always was. Maybe the account balance had fewer digits in my twenties, but there was never a doubt that I'd have a roof over my head and a meal to eat. Once I was gainfully employed, payroll checks were automatically deposited, mortgage payments were automatically deducted, and ATMs dispensed cash like the computer-driven machines they are: clinically and without question. In their later years my parents' assets became less and less relevant to me. I always assumed I would someday inherit something from them – they'd reestablished their own solvency in the wake of the Oxford Wilderness Period and eventually owned their Encino home free and clear – but I neither counted on it nor needed to. That is, until I did. And that money is long gone, having fed the collective maw of estate taxes, loan refinance calls and alimony payment offsets. So now I'm living off the discounted residue of an impulse motorcycle purchase.

I reach for my phone and risk taking my eye off the traffic to check for emails. Scanning quickly I find nothing worth reading except one from JP. Finally!

Hey buddy. Just landed Frankfurt. 'Don't mention the war!' Rwanda project will be balls to the wall, 24/7. How goes on your end? Dare I ask? Let's grab a beer when I get back. JP.

I'd like to respond but that would be dangerous while driving. No, come on, that's not true: I *could* dictate using voice recognition. The truth is, I'm just not ready to share. Which is odd since I share pretty much everything with JP. Is it because I'm still unsure of my game plan? Or that he's heading into the Heart of Darkness and won't be able to help? So I check my watch and wonder if I packed enough. Or left the loft in reasonable enough shape for Fred. Thank God that Rosa, the cleaning lady, is coming tomorrow. Did I remember to leave her a tip? Yeah, I must have; I can picture myself inserting a twenty in an envelope and writing her name before I dashed for the door. Good. She always does a nice job.

So… what *did* I manage to stuff into my (large) Wilson tennis bag? Pair of khakis. Tennis shoes. Toilet kit. Socks. Underwear. The old rule of thumb used to be, just remember the passport and credit card, since you could always buy whatever you needed. Things are different now. So I'm glad I thought to toss in a paperback copy of *The Sun Also Rises* – I've been meaning to re-read it for months – and a handful of Twinings English Breakfast teabags.

There's something about those glossy red crenelated wrappers that is oddly soothing.

The speed of the traffic flow increases as we approach the 280 turnoff and I realize: I'm really doing this. Then I have a pang of doubt as I remember Abby, at her ballet camp. What if she gets injured or sick before Annie can collect her on Saturday? The likelihood is low but I've always thought of myself as a responsible parent, notwithstanding recent evidence to the contrary.

Should I call the camp and inform them? But, of what? My departure on an unexpected business trip? They have their camp protocol, calling each parent and then the listed emergency contact, which in our case is Annie's sister, Lindsay. Besides, nothing is going to happen. Unlike Sky, Abby would never get sent home for a rules infraction. The girls may have been born together but they are as genetically dissimilar as any pair of ordinary sisters. Which, in nature and nurture terms meant distinct personalities and appearances. Annie and I decided early on to refer to them as 'the girls' and not 'the twins' for that very reason. Sky is muscular, brown-haired and fiercely independent. Abby is slender, blonde and sweet to the point of shyness. Anyway, Abby couldn't be at a better place right now than her dance camp in Pacifica. The truth is, I want to reach out to her more for me than for her.

So instead I drive and congratulate myself on including that extra twenty for Rosa. I might need the extra cash but no more than that hardworking Mexican single mother of three. Oh yes, it feels good to be generous but this wasn't just charity, rather a personal vote of confidence for my changing fortunes. Like going for a really big first serve when I know I've got my (usually reliable) second. Hear that, money gods? You assholes? I'm feeling confident! Shit, did I just jinx it by saying that? Nah – superstition is for losers. I used to play a guy who avoided stepping on the lines between points. It didn't help him beat me.

And what about removing the two bottles of wine from the closet and leaving them with a note for Fred? One was a Gevrey-Chambertin, Clos Prieur, from 2002. A stellar vintage of my favorite wine, the quintessence of pinot noir. The other was a Brunello di Montalcino, Poggio Antico, from 2004. The Italian first cousin of the Burgundy, if such a thing exists. Was it pride, to make me feel better about leaving him to contend with the loft and the LLC? They were in fact the last two bottles in my possession. I had several cases more at the house that I left behind when I departed, so I suppose those belong to Annie now. In a way, that wine represents all that was good in our marriage, apart from the girls: meals cooked in our open kitchen shared with family and friends, lingering at the reclaimed walnut dining table over conversation, laughter and dessert. Jeez, this really is not helping at all.

Okay then. Let's focus on the task at hand. I'm driving south on 280 now, approaching the Sand Hill Road exit. So, you masochistic moron, did that accomplish anything? What's the takeaway? Next time you default on the lease payment of your luxury sports sedan, don't park in your usual space? Or is it something more fundamental – more universal – about debt or risk or marriage or life. Think, damn you! There has to be something there, some nugget of gold, to justify all this panning through tons of sludge.

I scan the Hyundai's plastic interior and try to find something nice to say about the vehicle. It's almost new. It runs. Come on, the choice was a no-brainer, wasn't it? Given my vow, as soon as Jolene handed me the Cash Passport, to avoid all but the most necessary expenses in order to preserve what that miserly Ulsterman had paid for my Griso. So every decision becomes rudimentary, like triage in a MASH unit: select the cheapest option to get me where I need to go. Budget and Hertz each have a location equidistant from my loft, according to the iPhone? Easy, choose Budget. Budget has a compact at a sixty-nine dollar daily rate or a subcompact at fifty-nine? Simple, choose the subcompact. Return the car to SFO and incur a twenty-dollar drop off fee or to the Financial District and figure out a BART ride to the airport? That was more difficult, involving some unknowns, so I figured better the devil you know and opted for the drop off fee. Of course, there are always complications.

The sole employee manning the Budget rental counter on Howard Street printed the receipt. Perry, as his orange nametag identified him, had been exceedingly courteous in the face of my clearly agitated state. He was African-American, about my height and age, with salt-and-pepper dreadlocks.

"It ain't no Cadillac," he joked, when I asked what that meant exactly, a *subcompact*. I took back my license and charge card and rapidly scanned the receipt.

"Hey, you said it was only fifty-nine bucks plus the drop off fee."

"It is, before taxes."

The receipt listed a bevy of state and local taxes, including a special San Francisco tourism fee and an airport concession fee separate from the drop off fee.

"Are you kidding me? What's with the tourist fee? I'm a local."

Perry shrugged and laughed. "Don't make no difference to them. I figured you didn't want the collision damage waiver so I took that off."

"You figured right." I forced myself to smile. This guy was just doing his job. "These are challenging times, Perry."

"Don't I know it," he said.

The starboard tires chirp against a stretch of raised lane markers that deviate from true, so I jerk the steering wheel to the left. I'm doing about sixty-five and the rental car wallows disturbingly, only regaining its equilibrium after some awkward oscillations. So this is what fifty-nine bucks a day gets you, plus taxes and junk fees. A Hyundai Accent. I'm not sure what the name 'Accent' is supposed to connote, other than an accent on small. Small interior and small engine – all for the small wallet. Compared to the Quattroporte, the Accent is… well, it's ridiculous to compare the two cars, truly a matter of apples and oranges. Or more appropriately, apples and kumquats. Henry Ford sold millions of the Model T well into the late twenties because they were basic transportation for people whose only frame of reference was the horse and buggy. But if you had more than five hundred bucks to spend, there were dozens of alternatives, with names mostly forgotten today and a few (like Oldsmobile and Chevrolet) that are still relevant. To its credit – and I'm trying very hard to be charitable – the Hyundai has all the modern safety features we've come to rely on, such as disc brakes, seat belts and air bags. But in the automotive scheme of things, the Accent is basic transportation. It would have been nice to part with the Maserati on my own terms. I grip the plastic steering wheel and readjust myself in the uncomfortable cloth seat and try to forget the leather grandeur that was the Quattroporte. But what's the use of grumbling? So I say it again: basic transportation, that's all I need.

That's all my father required in high school with the Ford Model A his buddy Pete Swigard drove. I remember him telling me that once he and Pete had girlfriends they were set, as happy as lords. My dad would transfer from the passenger to the rumble seat in back with his date and Pete would park in a secluded spot near Griffith Observatory, allowing the two couples to neck and slake their thirst for swing music with the radio blaring until they could fully quench it on the weekends, dancing with hundreds of fellow swing-crazed Angelinos way past midnight at huge ballrooms like the Aragon and Palladium to the big bands of Tommy Dorsey and Artie Shaw.

I've been thinking about my parents a fair bit lately, not so much in the mourning sense – they've been dead just over a year and I believe I'm past most of the shock and grief – but to remind myself who they were and what their legacy means. It sounds like a cliché but I'm sort of glad they didn't live to see the demise of my marriage and career. And though their dying in a senseless car accident was tragic, the fact that they lived long and eventful lives and didn't suffer the lingering decline of the aged and infirm must in some sense count as a positive. My mother in particular, the ever-whimsical Victoria, would have appreciated the irony of two octogenarians getting wiped out on a clear, sunny day in the San Fernando Valley after having survived Hitler's Blitz of London and the D-Day invasion, respectively. In fact, my parents had been home less than one week after attending ceremonies in Normandy to commemorate the 65th anniversary of D-Day. Given how profound an effect World War Two had on both their lives, and especially my father's, their perishing on the heels of that trip to France seems some kind of cosmic bookend, the meaning of which I'm still trying to figure out.

William Davis (his friends and family all called him Bill) was a nineteen year-old 2nd Lieutenant on June 6, 1944, with no prior combat experience and, as he once told me, both the supreme confidence that he would survive and the abject fear that he might panic or otherwise screw up. If he was to be believed, and I have no reason to doubt his version of events, he acquitted himself with honor intact. However, I also believe that he saw things that day and in the weeks and months to come, horrible and life-changing things, such that he literally came home a changed man. Or, more accurately, *as* a man, since he was certainly little more than a boy before. My father had his ups and downs (including the aforementioned Oxford Wilderness Period) during what must be counted a largely successful life: solid if not spectacular career; long marriage to a loyal, loving (if complicated) woman; and the legacy of two children, four grandchildren and many friends. But for him everything came back to that solitary stretch of sand known as Omaha Beach. Try as I might, I'll never fully comprehend what he endured or how he transcended that completely understandable fear. I do know that I've never faced anything comparable in my life and never expect to. And furthermore, though it embarrasses me to admit it, I'll always be envious of him for his moment of challenge and triumph. I remember Annie once expressing relief that we had girls, not boys, since she'd avoid having to deal with toy guns and watching war movies on TV or, God forbid, seeing them embroiled in the real thing. What's with the male fascination with fighting and weaponry, she asked? Don't they realize how terrible warfare is? I can't remember my answer but I think I know. It's not that we males are inherently violent or even that we enjoy pretending to inflict grievous harm on another. It's that, hard wired over millennia, we have the understanding we might be called to combat. And deep down we wonder how we'll fare. At least I do.

5

I walk towards the Hyundai, now loaded to the gunwales with riding gear, and open the driver's side door. Skylar stares at the car and then looks at me with a mixture of incredulity and disgust.

"What's this?" she says.

"Rental car."

"Where's your car?"

"The lease ended. This is just temporary."

I toss it off casually, as if it's all part of some master plan. She looks at me dubiously and, with exaggerated reluctance, opens the passenger door and gets in. She slouches in her seat as I maneuver the miniature sedan around the circular dirt and gravel driveway, kicking up clouds of chalky dust in our wake. Strands of black horsehair cling to the thighs of Sky's tan cotton jodhpurs and the Accent's rental car aroma mingles with a horsey-sweaty scent and the fresh lavender smell of Sky's hair.

"Where's my phone?" she says.

"I don't know. Where'd you have it last?"

The answer comes to her and her face darkens into an angry scowl.

"Shit, they wouldn't let me keep it. Mom took it."

"Okay, that's where it is then."

"You mean you didn't get it from her?"

I give her a look like, 'are you kidding?' and remind her to buckle her seatbelt.

She reaches towards the car radio and punches the power on, unleashing Mick Jagger and Keith Richards in full wail. I'd had it tuned to a classic rock station approaching Crystal Springs Reservoir to distract me. She immediately turns it off and scrunches her face disapprovingly.

"Don't you listen to anything from, like, this century?"

"The Stones are still going strong. They've stood the test of time."

She rolls her eyes, a seemingly reflexive response to any opinion I might offer. She makes no motion to fasten her seatbelt.

"Sky, please." I indicate my own seatbelt and she rolls her eyes anew.

"I will. When we're past the driveway." She scans the car's interior with disapproval. "This is a piece of shit."

I resist the urge to agree with her – what would that accomplish? – and we drive in silence until Portola Valley Road, where I slow to a stop. She lets out a melodramatic sigh and buckles her shoulder belt.

"Happy now?"

I give her a perfunctory smile and accelerate east towards 280. And consider her question. I'm certainly not happy, not in the conventional sense, given my psychic burdens: the grief over my failed marriage, the worry about my bleak financial situation, the inconvenience of retrieving my eldest daughter from her equestrian camp when I need to fly to London. As is my nature, though, I look for tendrils of hope in this miasma of misfortune. Sky didn't, in fact, get injured – she was just kicked out for riding without a helmet. And here she sits, in all her teenage, pouty confusion, maybe willing herself to trust that I am still her loving, steadfast father, despite ample evidence to the contrary. We may be driving back to San Francisco in a piece of crap Korean subcompact but the grass-covered hills of Portola Valley, remarkably still green on the summer solstice, beckon us onward. If you look closely enough, and set an intention, aren't there always reasons to be happy?

Once back on 280 heading north, I update Sky on our situation in the spirit of the 'no bullshit' policy I initiated with the girls after the separation. How her mother and I have resolved the legal custody issue; and how Annie is now unreachable, having left town with Jeffrey Schreiber, aka the Man with no (Evident) Flaws, to go hiking in Yosemite. How Abby is still ensconced in her ballet camp and presumably will remain so for the rest of the week, barring expulsion for wearing an inappropriate tutu. (Sky, of course, takes umbrage at my attempt at humor at her expense.

But a) I feel entitled, b) she knows I only tease affectionately, and c) I believe I detect some appreciation on her part that I'm able to put it in perspective, i.e. that I'm not angry about her foolish behavior, which has squandered a top-notch – or so we were told – hunter-jumper camp experience and the thousand plus dollars it cost.) I remind Sky about my mother's Aunt Philippa and the modest but still significant sum that Aunt Meg and I were due to inherit before this obstinate English solicitor, one Rupert M. T. Salmons, made it his personal crusade to uphold the letter but not the spirit of British estate law, thereby rendering null and void the express intent of his deceased client. And I recount, with as much candor as I can muster, how my long-suffering credit card was rejected this morning in the New Vienna Café and why, apart from the measly five thousand dollars I managed to get for my prized Moto Guzzi, I am penniless. Not just illiquid – I actually spend about a mile of freeway time explaining the meaning of this term – but flat broke. And how I believe a face-to-face with Rupert Salmons Esq. is my only hope for replenishing my financial coffers sufficiently to start over. At this point we are approaching Daly City, beyond the bucolic rolling countryside west of Stanford University and in the higher density suburban sprawl, the car dealers and shopping malls of Serramonte, and the industrial parks and mid-rise office buildings of South San Francisco.

"So, what are you saying, exactly?" she says.

"That I need to fly to England tonight and I don't know who you can stay with. Do you have any ideas? You getting kicked out of your camp wasn't part of my plan."

"Oh, so I suppose it's all my fault?"

"No. I mean, not the part about why I need to go. That's my doing. I'm just laying the situation out here."

She takes it in, reflects on it a few seconds.

"You can just leave me at Mom's house. I'm old enough."

"Sorry, not an option. I'm sure you'd be fine but I don't plan to be arrested for child endangerment."

"I wouldn't tell anyone. I don't even need to leave the house. I can live off cereal and frozen pizza and shit."

"Yeah, well – forget it. It's not going to happen."

"So then what?"

"How about I ask Aunt Lin and Aunt Liz if you can stay with them?"

"No way. I'm not spending a week in that lesbian freak show."

"Sky! What are you talking about? I thought you adored them?"

"I do, sort of. No, I do, they're great. But every time I stay there it creeps me out. I mean, it's not like they're recruiting me for their team or anything. They even ask me if I have any boyfriends and shit. I mean, as if! But there's this gay vibe like, 'I'd be okay if you were a sister too,' so I really, really don't want to hang there, alright?"

"I listen to some of your friends at school and I have to say, it's like homophobia is the new racism."

"Dad, I am fucking not homophobic!"

"Good. Then do me this favor, okay? Because as much as I'd like to spend some extra quality time with you, I need to make this trip."

Sky broods a moment then suddenly brightens.

"I have the perfect solution," she says.

"Yeah?" I say skeptically."What's that?"

"I fly to London with you. We can have the quality father-daughter time that I know you so deeply cherish and you can get your money."

"What? No way. I'm not, I mean – I can't look after you while…"

"You wouldn't have to babysit me, Dad. I'm fourteen, I can look after myself. And it's not like I haven't been to Europe before. We were there just a couple of years ago so I know my way around."

"Sky, this is out of the question. Your mom is expecting to collect you at the end of the week. I can't just leave the country with you. Apart from everything else, it's a complete violation of the custody agreement. I could probably go to jail."

"I won't tell anyone," she says.

I laugh, more of snort actually. "You won't need to. We can't exactly hide the fact. There are airline records, immigration documents, all sorts of things. Besides, even assuming that all could be worked out, there's an even bigger problem."

"What's that?" she asks.

I sigh. "I can't afford it. As it is, I barely have enough money to fly myself there and spend a week or two sorting this thing out. I have no idea what the airfare will cost but with no advance purchase I'm pretty sure it's hefty. I can't stretch the budget to pay for another ticket."

She chews on that. Good, I think – we've put this one to bed. Which still leaves where she's going to stay, but I figure even if Lin and Liz are out of the picture there has to be a friend of hers who's in town, some parental favor I can call in.

"I've got it," she says. "I'll just withdraw some money from my bank account."

"Sorry," I say. "That money is for your college education."

"No it's not. I have a separate college fund, remember?"

And I remember that she's correct. One smart thing Annie and I did early on was invest funds in one of those 529 plans for each of the girls, money that could appreciate through their school years and be accessible for higher education. The share price took a hit after the stock market tumble but with any luck by the time the girls turn eighteen there should be enough to at least get them through four years of undergraduate study at a public school.

"Sky, I really don't feel comfortable having you withdraw money from your bank account to fly to London with me. I'm sure your mother would not approve."

"Dad, you owe me." Skylar says it like a bridge player laying down a winning trump card. I immediately know where she is going with this and I dread it.

"Sweetie, let's not rehash about…"

"You said 'no bullshit' Dad so come on, what's it going to be? You cost me Moondancer and you know it. So you owe me big time."

Moondancer was Skylar's horse, an Arabian jumper that was stabled in Golden Gate Park before we sold him last year. To say she loved Moondancer would be an understatement. Annie and I tried our best to shield the girls from the economic realities of our divorce but some adjustments had to be made. For Sky, that meant Moondancer had to go. The stable and vet fees alone were costing a fortune. And so her riding instructor put us in touch with another horse-crazy girl's parents who were only too happy to pay $35,000 for a well-trained, pedigree six-year old show jumper. In most respects, Abby and Sky still live a very privileged existence, continuing to attend a top private school (thanks largely to Annie taking a job last year as the school's director of admissions). But Sky has not gotten over the loss of her beloved horse, something she holds me personally accountable for.

"Sky, we've been over this. I'm sorry we had to sell Moondancer but we've all made sacrifices. Look at me, I just sold my motorcycle today. And look what we're driving."

"You don't need to remind me," she says. "Total piece of shit."

"Honey, I know you blame me but it's not healthy to go on doing that. Believe me. Don't you think I blame myself? I live with regret every day. Every single day. I can't change the past but I can try to fix what's happened, make our lives better. And I could sure use your help."

"Don't play the victim. It's not attractive."

"Goddammit, Sky, don't you..." I start to splutter, my face flushing, my grip on the steering wheel tightening, before I somehow manage to regain control and shut my mouth. I take a deep breath and start again.

"I do ask you to speak to me with respect. I'm not playing the victim. I'm asking for your assistance. There's a big difference. I can't force you to stay with your aunts, or anyone else for that matter, but I wish you'd reconsider."

Sky broods so I focus on driving. The Accent's motor buzzes as it struggles to maintain seventy on the uphill portions of the freeway with the two of us aboard and all of the riding gear and luggage in back.

"Dad, I hear what you're saying."

I heave a quiet sigh of relief. "That's great, darling. Thanks."

"Which is why I'm going to help you get what you want and I want."

I glance at her, not sure where she's going with this. "What do you mean?"

"Well, you want to get the inheritance and I want Moondancer back. I figure if we work together, we'll accomplish both goals. Okay?"

"Right…"

"So," she continues, "I'll use my money to come with you to London so I can help you buy him back. This way everybody wins."

"Sky, we've been over this. I just can't…"

"Dad," she interrupts, "just think about it, okay? I could be a big help. I'm smart and resourceful and… I'm motivated."

"I hear that." And, in the recesses of my mind, the way crazy notions sometimes do, this one gains an initial purchase and starts to accrue some semblance of plausibility. Nothing like true rationality, but somewhere further along the continuum from totally absurd towards marginally conceivable. So I try to think it through, holding the idea up to the light of reason to see whether it makes any sense at all.

It's true that Sky and I haven't spent much quality time together the past year and that our relationship has been rancorous and dysfunctional. Whereas Abby has felt sorry for me and views me in a certain pathetic light, Sky has focused her anger and bitterness chiefly in my direction. I'm convinced that only part of this is the result of family events, and mostly stems from the normal hormone-soaked confusions of being a teenager. But in the perfect storm that my life has assumed lately, Sky has laid her angst on my doorstep with all the irrational, emotive fury that a fourteen-year-old child of divorce can muster. Throw in the entitlement factor seemingly endemic to upper-middle-class American life, and it's been a recipe for acrimony bordering on hatred.

No, I think, regaining some perspective – it's been a nightmare dealing with Sky so how's that going to be any different going to London with her? Jesus, I can't believe I'm even entertaining the notion. There are a dozen reasons why it's a terrible idea, each one compelling. And yet – could it possibly work? It would only be for a week anyway, actually less than a week. There's that horse stable in Hyde Park where Sky rode when she was eight. She could ride there. It could fill in for the camp she was supposed to be doing. I'd tell Annie it was the best I could do under the circumstances.

After all, Sky was kicked out of Portola – Sandra Morgan would verify that – so I had to improvise on the spot. And once I get the funds from the inheritance I'll reimburse Sky for the travel. No harm, no foul.

I stop myself again. Am I insane? Annie will crucify me. And Sky has been so irrational lately, so mean-spirited, she'll make my life even for several days a living hell. But still… why not give her a chance to prove herself? I've been saying lately, even when it's been especially rough, you can never give up on your kids. Or yourself. So why not give her a chance to demonstrate that she's worthy of my trust? And as for Annie, what can she do? Divorce me? Take everything I own? She's already done all of that, and more.

"Look, Sky – even assuming for a second that we were to go through with this, I'd need your absolute pledge that you'd cooperate in every way possible. No misbehaving, no acting out. This trip is life or death for me, financially, and I can't have you messing it up. I'm going to have to be at the top of my game to bring this off and if you start to go off the reservation that's not going to be possible. Understood?"

"Absolutely," she says. She pauses then we each look at each other. "So we're really going to do this?"

"Yes. No. Maybe. I don't know. I mean, I don't see how. For starters, we don't even have your passport. Hasn't it expired?"

"It's at home!" she says. "I know exactly where it is."

"And then," I continue, "there could be visa issues. I seem to recall something about kids needing to travel with both parents otherwise they have to carry some notarized affidavit from the other parent to prove they're not being kidnapped."

"Give me a break," she says. "It's not like I'm a little kid. I can speak for myself."

"That's what I'm worried about."

She shoots me a dirty look.

"Anyway, I just don't want to run into trouble at Heathrow. The English can be sticklers for rules." Christ, don't I know it. God damned Lawn Tennis Association.

Sky remains silent so I concentrate on the task at hand. Like a tennis player in a tight match – or any sport for that matter – the key is to not get ahead of yourself, just focus on one point at a time. This shot, this moment. Win the rally then move on to the next one. Before you know it, there's a game in the bag, and then a set. That's got to be my approach now. Who knows if Sky can really find her passport? Or if it's still valid. I can't sweat those details yet.

I follow the signs for the Golden Gate Bridge until the freeway ends and turns into 19th Avenue, approaching the southwest part of the City, near the Zoo and the sand dunes that line the Great Highway along the Pacific. If I'd been driving back downtown I would have taken 280 East, towards the Bay Bridge, but there's no reason to return to the loft now. So I follow an older, more familiar route. I'd say a route home, although that's not correct. It's the route to Skylar's home, and Annie and Abigail's. But no longer mine. Still, it is a familiar route, one I can navigate on autopilot as I've done countless times, driving the four of us back from the airport or from road trips to L.A., a book on tape playing on the car stereo or maybe my best of Eighties songs mix. So many trips, so many experiences, stretching back to the car seat days. Nothing anyone might point to as extraordinary but all tiles in the mosaic of a family that, when viewed from enough distance, tell the story as well as Sargent or Seurat. Sometimes you have to look away from a picture, if the beauty seems too real. And just stare ahead.

When we pull up in front of the house on Washington Street it looks the same. Same Spanish tile roof and smooth beige stucco exterior with red brick trim. Only the garden appears a little scruffier. I guess Annie has cut back on the landscape service. It isn't the priciest house on the block, nor the most modest, but it fits right in – a well-crafted Edwardian-era home in Presidio Heights. This isn't an over-the-top neighborhood like Pacific Heights, or stuffy like St. Francis Wood, or even hip like Noe Valley, but classy. Broad, clean streets and generous property setbacks. Close to the nice shops and restaurants on Sacramento Street and a quick Muni express bus commute to the Financial District. And since the Army departed the Presidio, even more desirable. There was no question I would move out after Annie and I separated; the only issue was the amount the house would be valued and whether she'd be able to buy out my interest. As Diana Shohara expected, Annie's lawyer made a forceful, cogent argument that my undisclosed collateral pledge to the bank had fraudulently jeopardized Annie's stake in the house. And so, as part of the divorce settlement, I signed a quit-claim deed granting her full title. The mortgage won't be a picnic for her to manage on her own, but we'd paid it down considerably before things went south. With her new job at The Francisco School, she can just about cover it.

I help Sky unload her saddle and tack and lug it to the garage.

"Why don't you put this stuff away while I go find my passport?" she says brightly. I nod in dumb agreement, feeling a bit overwhelmed to be back on this familiar, hallowed ground but without Annie present. It's an unsettling feeling, not exactly strange, just awkward, like returning to a school campus after graduation. So I watch Sky let herself into the house with the hide-a-key, disable the alarm, and dash upstairs. I open the garage, pleased to see that the same combination code (Annie's birth year) still works, and put away the horse gear. I close the garage door just as Sky comes running up, waving a passport above her head in her right hand.

"See, I told you I knew where it was! And I found my passbook too!" She produces a Bank of America passbook with the left hand and holds them out for my inspection.

I examine the passport first. The girls aren't able to get U.K. passports – I only got mine several years ago due to a change in British law making adult children of female citizens eligible – but a valid American passport will be sufficient to get a tourist visa at Heathrow. Assuming I can finesse the custody issue, that is. To my surprise, Sky's passport doesn't expire until next April. I'd figured that its five-year validity would have ended already. Next, I look at the bank passbook. This was always something Annie maintained with the girls, trustee accounts for deposits of extra allowance or birthday gifts of cash, started when they were in kindergarten to nurture the value of saving. I don't expect there is much in the account, maybe $750 or so, so I'm doubly surprised to see the balance is almost two thousand dollars. A pang of guilt washes over me. It would be like smashing a kid's piggy bank to clean out Sky's account. Christ, I think. Annie is going to be livid.

"Sweetie, it's incredibly generous of you to offer to do this, but I can't let you. Come on, I'll call Aunt Lindsay and see if you can stay there. I'm sure we can arrange some riding lessons at Golden Gate and I'll give you some money for movies and meals out. Kind of like your own private vacation."

She looks crestfallen, not angry or belligerent like in the car, but sad and disappointed.

"I thought we agreed," she finally says.

"No, we didn't agree to anything. I said I'd think about it. And I have. It's just not practical."

She takes that in for a moment. Then she fixes me with an expression that looks older and wiser than her years. One I've seen before and marvel at – because it makes her look so much like her mother.

"I understand, Dad. I don't blame you. I know I've been a shit to you lately and you don't trust me. I wouldn't trust me either. I'm sorry if I've let you down. It was stupid and careless of me to ride without my helmet. But just so you know, I really meant what I said, about making this a win for both of us. You can call Aunt Lin. I'll stay there."

I listen to her, watch her tell me this – exactly what I've wanted her to say – and detect not a hint of manipulation or insincerity, just wholesome contrition. Which of course breaks my heart. For she's absolutely right: I haven't trusted her and, among all the reasons why taking her with me to London makes no sense, this is the one I've been stuck on. I've imagined standing near the curb at Piccadilly Circus, a frenzy of cars and buses in the roadway, with Sky having a nuclear meltdown for some nonsensical reason and jeopardizing my whole trip. And in this instant I feel I've betrayed her with my mistrust.

I smile a sad weary smile and reach out to embrace her. These moments have been too few between us lately, nonexistent really, and, perhaps feeling something reciprocal on her part, she hugs me back. When we let go, she reaches quietly for her passport and passbook. And then the strangest thing happens. I keep holding onto them. And words come out of my mouth that seem possessed of their own volition, certainly none that I am intentionally uttering.

"If you want to come with me, I'd be happy to have you."

Sky looks at me closely, as if gauging my seriousness. Her eyes betray a hint of elation – or is it victory? – and then she smiles.

"Do you mean it?"

"Well, I guess I do. God help me, I do. Are you in?"

"Hell yes. Let's do this!"

And with that, the wheels are set in motion. The only remaining thought I have, which lingers like a drunken party guest at midnight, is: am I truly my own worst enemy? No, that's a rhetorical question. Or… is it?

Tuesday

(Love-15)

6

I wake from one of those sleeps where you're not sure if you've really slept at all. *There's* a paradox if you want to think about it, but I don't. I just want to stretch my legs, drink some water and get the taste of Bordeaux *vin ordinaire* out of my mouth.

The airplane cabin is still dark but the light peeking around the drawn shades indicates daytime. I glance at my watch: forty minutes after midnight. I take it off and reset it eight hours forward to GMT. Okay, 8:40 a.m. London time, although figure an hour earlier in our actual geographic time zone. Where does that put us, over Iceland? Or maybe approaching Scotland. Sky reclines next to me, her eyes closed. Good, she's sleeping, no small feat in these economy class seats. She'll need to be well rested for later. And I'll need her at her best.

Christ, we really made it, didn't we? At least… this far. The jumble of events leading up to us actually boarding the Virgin flight replays in my head and I shudder involuntarily, then shake my head in disbelief.

When Sky and I entered the Laurel Village branch of Bank of America, our task seemed straightforward: withdraw the balance in Sky's account – $1,946.73 according to the teller we first approached – and drive to SFO. But things rapidly became more complicated. Half an hour later we were still there, Sky and I now sitting at the desk of the branch manager, Roberta Maggiore, while Ms. Maggiore stood at the opposite end of the bank conferring by telephone with a superior at B of A headquarters. The atmosphere in the bank had been relaxed when we entered, more like a Starbucks than a financial institution, but it now was tense. As I sat next to Sky I was acutely aware of the video cameras attached to the walls. They must be recording us, I realized. There will be hard evidence. Even the older security guard, formerly bored and slouching at the bank's entrance, now stood alert and focused on Skylar a few paces away, as if he considered her a credible threat to draw a gun. My goal still remained: to help Sky get her money. But I was actively formulating a fallback plan that wouldn't jeopardize my departure for London, with or without my daughter. And one that didn't involve getting arrested on felony charges of bank fraud or kidnapping a minor.

I realized back at the house that Sky had become highly motivated by the prospect of repurchasing Moondancer, for she showered and repacked for our anticipated flight in record time. But until the bank teller – and then the manager – politely inquired about the reason for the withdrawal, I had no idea just *how* motivated. It's as if my eldest daughter, previously listless and cynical, had found a purpose in life and she'd suddenly begun pursuing it with the zealotry of a medieval crusader. Sky lashed out at the bank manager (apparently a recent transfer to the branch, so she'd never met Sky before) with such a profanity-laced tirade that it would have mortified me had not the embarrassment been overshadowed by more practical concerns. It was all I could do to calm my daughter down and remind her (in a hasty sidebar outside the earshot of the reeling manager) that if she didn't get a grip on her emotions she could pretty much kiss our trip – and Moondancer – goodbye. I disliked invoking her beloved horse in this manner, for the unwitting equine has become some sort of perverted Holy Grail for Skylar, making it – for better or worse – the carrot *and* the stick. Exacerbating the situation, Sky is tall and well developed for her age, and I believe Ms. Maggiore actually felt intimidated physically. The petite bank manager looked barely over five feet tall in her red canvas espadrilles.

Sitting at that desk with the manager still on the phone, I didn't give us a one in five chance of getting out of there with Sky's money. And that's after I'd enlisted Dore's help as a banking law expert in an impromptu conference call. Okay, this might have been overkill, but I couldn't think of anything else, and the poor bastard no doubt still felt sorry for my rough outing in divorce court earlier so he picked right up. Rather than calm the waters, though, this escalated the stakes to a wacky degree. For once Dore sized up Ms. Maggiore's unreasonable intransigence – she was invoking a one day technical hold on an insignificant account closure by a customer offering a valid passport as proof of identity – he became so outraged (feigned or genuine) that he threatened to pull all of Asbury & Hollington's business with B of A. Which, I was surprised to discover, he could credibly threaten because he's the chair of the firm's finance committee. Who could have predicted that? I mean, seriously, you couldn't script this kind of thing if you tried. What I was hoping is that, at that very moment, Ms. Maggiore was discussing with her colleague at headquarters the merits of jeopardizing a major international law firm client for the sake of an extra day's float on a teenager's paltry savings account. But what I also knew is that Roberta Maggiore was by then emotionally invested in the outcome. And as history often shows, that can be problematic. Roberta Maggiore had been rudely insulted by a teenage girl and had lost face at the hands of the girl's father and his high-priced corporate lawyer. And when people feel humiliated they often make decisions irrationally and poorly. In this rapidly escalating poker match, what truly worried me was having Ms. Maggiore call our bluff and investigate why, after years of regular deposits to her modest trust account, a certain Skylar Davis had presented herself with a parent in the middle of a weekday requesting an immediate and total withdrawal of her account when that particular parent wasn't even on the account's signature card. And when that parent had, that very morning (unbeknownst to said bank manager), been adjudicated to no longer have legal custody of his daughter. Either way one looked at it, it seemed there was a great deal for everyone to lose and very little to gain. But Sky seemed oblivious to all of this; she just looked like she wanted to run the hapless bank manager through with a broadsword if she could get her hands on one.

Ms. Maggiore, who seemed to have been doing most of the listening in her phone conversation, said a final few words and then hung up. She looked briefly in our direction, averting her gaze when her eyes met mine, then she walked over to the teller and conferred with her.

"Remember," I said to Sky, "whatever they decide just say thank you and we'll be on our way."

"Bullshit, it's my fucking money. They can't keep it if I want to withdraw it. Your lawyer friend said so."

"Sky, I'm totally on your side here." I tried to banish the worry from my eyes and to project a soothing calmness for Sky's benefit. Then I saw the bank manager striding towards us. "Let's be chill, okay?" This unintentionally cracked Sky up.

"'Let's be *chill*?' Where'd you get that, the old farts dictionary of homie slang?"

"Damn straight. That's what I'm saying. Just be chill."

"Mr. Davis," Ms. Maggiore said, "could I have a word with you please?"

"Of course." I stood and followed her as she walked several steps away. She then stopped, put her arms nervously at her side and addressed me.

"I've discussed the matter with our main office. While this is highly irregular and, I've been assured, it's within my power as branch manager to impose a precautionary hold on the account closure per the terms of the deposit agreement, as a courtesy for a longtime customer we're going to permit an immediate with-drawal. I've instructed one of our tellers to prepare a cashier's check in your daughter's name for the full amount of the balance."

This was unexpected news, a combination of both good and bad that I hastily tried to process. We'd get the money – that was good – but as a cashier's check? Would that work? By then I didn't trust this diminutive bank manager so maybe this was just another way for the bank to delay payment.

"We very much appreciate it," I said. "But since you're granting the withdrawal, cash would be preferable. Like I said, Skylar found a better investment opportunity at my bank. We'll be making a deposit there right away."

Ms. Maggiore did some mental processing of her own, so I quickly added: "I again apologize for my daughter's language. She had a rough day at camp but that's really no excuse."

"No, it's not," Ms. Maggiore said. "I'm sure your bank will have no problem with a Bank of America cashier's check. Good day." And with that she turned and walked away.

I considered pursuing her but this clearly seemed the best result I could expect. It reflected pettiness on her part because she could just as well have given us cash, but I figured, as long as we were able to convert the deposit to my Cash Passport and pay for a flight to London, we'd be fine. I could have gotten snarky with the bank manager – the "longtime customer" they were concerned about obviously wasn't Sky – but as the saying goes, don't let the good become the enemy of the perfect. A cashier's check was good enough.

I walked back to Sky. "Good news, you're getting your money."

"Damn right I am." She seemed completely oblivious to the legal bullet I'd dodged. Not to mention the high level law firm and banking machinations that had ensued. If there weren't real people and their livelihoods in the balance it would have been comical.

"Hey," I said, "how about a little gratitude?"

"Thanks, Dad."

I smiled and did my best imitation of a gangsta rapper, shoulders hunched, arms forward and hands pointed downward like guns. "That's what I'm talking about," I said. Sky rolled her eyes and the security guard did a double-take. And we got the heck out of the bank as soon as the teller handed Sky her check.

In contrast, adding the money to my Cash Passport at First Regency Bank turned out to be a snap. Then we were finally on our way to the airport. But I'd underestimated the cost of the airline tickets.

Arriving at the SFO international terminal after four, we first tried British Airways. They had a flight to London boarding within minutes but the agent said it was already full. The second flight was departing in less than three hours, but the main cabin was sold out. I inquired about seats in business class but they cost over four thousand dollars each. Impossible. So we tried Virgin Atlantic next.

Virgin's flight was almost full but they had two seats available in economy. The problem was the fare: with surcharges and taxes, flying one-way would cost each of us one thousand seven hundred and sixty-three dollars. And double that for round-trip. I started to hand over the Cash Passport for two one-way fares then hesitated. Sky would need a round-trip ticket, but that might max out the card. I did a quick mental calculation. With Sky's B of A money, I had $6,846.73, less $112.28 for the car rental. Damn, I wasn't used to debit cards, where charges are incurred immediately. Sky was right – the Hyundai *was* a piece of shit. I recriminated again about the Quattroporte getting repossessed. In my next life, I thought, I'll start a rental car business. Once the purchase price is amortized, it's all gravy. Plus, you can sell the used cars when you update the fleet and make even more. Nice business model.

So we were down to $6,734 and change. I struggled to do the math in my head as the Virgin ticket agent and Sky waited.

"Sir," the woman said, "if we're going to get you on this flight I really need to ticket you." I was vaguely disappointed that she had an American accent. The British Airways agent had been English.

"Let's make mine one-way and my daughter's round-trip." I handed her the Cash Passport. That would still leave almost $1,500 on the card. Not very much, especially in an expensive city like London, but we'd have to make it work. I just needed to meet with the solicitor, Rupert Salmons, and convince him to release those funds. One shot at a time, I told myself, just construct the point.

"Dad!" Sky said. I looked at her and we exchanged a silent acknowledgement about what this meant. She'd be flying home without me.

More to placate Skylar, I said to the Virgin agent: "Any way we can fly standby?"

"That won't change the outbound ticket price. And the return could go higher."

"We can make mine one-way too," Sky said.

"No way," I said. "Hers is round trip."

The Virgin agent was now regarding us appraisingly and I realized this, too, could go sideways. In the heightened tension of post-9/11 air travel, airlines have a lot of discretion about who they let on their planes. Sky and I certainly didn't fit the profile for terrorists, but tell that to a ticket agent steeped in institutional paranoia.

"Are you sure?" the agent said to me. I fixed Sky with a look – 'please let this go' – then gave the agent my most reassuring smile.

"We're sure."

The available seats were not together and I initially considered that a boon, figuring it would give each of some needed space. We'd already spent more time together in stressful circumstances than was customary or advisable and we hadn't yet arrived in London. But the ticket agent took it upon herself to rearrange some seat assignments and I wasn't going to risk setting Sky off by refusing the agent's generosity. Now, seeing Sky asleep next to me, I'm glad. She looks more like the little girl she was than the young woman she has become. She and Abby do share some traits, including one in common with their mother: they sleep completely immobile and silent. It truly can be disconcerting, but maybe that's because most people I've known intimately are restless sleepers, snoring or tossing and turning or at least moving their lips occasionally. But not Annie and the girls. They might as well be corpses. Which is why it takes me by surprise when Sky suddenly opens her eyes and says: "Where are we?"

I check my watch. "I'm not sure. Near Ireland maybe. You can sleep some more if you like."

Sky stretches her arms, sits up, then reaches for my watch.

"When did you get this?"

"Don't you remember? It was Grandpa's."

I unfasten the Longines and hand it to her. She examines it – a relatively simple, elegant timepiece fashioned from stainless steel and gold with a brown leather strap – and hands it back. I refasten it on my left wrist.

"I miss Grandma and Grandpa," she says.

"I miss them too."

"Do you have anything else of theirs?" I shake my head, no.

"You and your sister each got some of Grandma's jewelry. Auntie Meg and Zoe too. Max has Grandpa's war medals."

Sky nods, as if taking this all in for the first time. I know it isn't, but maybe she's not yet fully awake.

My father didn't own this watch very long, in fact barely a week before he died, but it has assumed outsized sentimental value for me because of the circumstances of its acquisition. For it was given to him during his trip to Normandy at a ceremony for the 65th anniversary of D-Day by the mayor of Vierville-sur-Mer. I don't need to take the watch off to recite the inscription engraved on the back:

To
William G. Davis
U.S. Army
From the grateful
citizens of France
June 6, 2009

My mother told me that when the mayor presented the watch to my father, and similar timepieces to a handful of other elderly American veterans, there wasn't a dry eye in the house, the house being a local village restaurant. It was especially poignant for my mother given her own connection to France and the war. Yes, I tell myself, it's fortunate they got to make that trip before they perished. We all have to go sometime, don't we?

I unfasten my seat belt and bench press myself out of my seat. "You want anything?" I ask Sky.

"You going to the bathroom?" she asks.

"Uh huh."

"Spend a penny for me."

I smile, pleased she's in good humor and dusting off this family Britishism.

"Will do."

My knees require the entire journey along the cabin aisle to go from painful to a dull ache. Once in the lavatory I give myself a close inspection in the mirror. So this is what almost fifty looks like? The circles under my eyes I can mostly blame on the overnight flight – it's called a 'red-eye' for a reason – but otherwise I can't avoid ownership of the gray hair and lines. And yes, that angry red splotch below my right temple. The mirror truly doesn't lie. How much, I wonder, is repairable? I don't mean artificially – I'm not so vain as to contemplate surgery – but by a change in lifestyle. If there is a strong mind-body connection, and I don't understand why there wouldn't be, surely my haggard appearance would benefit from some inner harmony. Well, that's what I'm on this trip for, isn't it? Try to get myself a little financial breathing room, a chance for a fresh start. At what, I'm not sure. The Bay Area job opportunities I've been responding to the past six months, many requiring vastly less experience than I possess, have come up a big fat zero. A headhunter I met with put it most succinctly, in the peculiar jargon that certain professions seem to adopt: I don't have enough runway. Meaning, she explained, most companies don't want to hire someone whose career longevity is only a decade or so. I remember smiling and suggesting that what she was really trying to say is that I'm too fucking old. She laughed, but didn't disagree.

The irony, of course, is that before it came crashing down I was pursuing the American Dream, what every U.S. President and every member of Congress, Democrat or Republican, trots out in every reelection speech as the national imperative and entrepreneurial ideal: starting a business and building it up to be successful, with a payroll and an employee pension plan and, oh yes, plenty of tax revenues for Uncle Sam. But what the Great Recession (as the pundits are now referring to it) demonstrated is that there are no government bailouts for small businesses. The huge Wall Street investment banks were literally "too big to fail," and other corporate giants like General Motors and AIG also got rescued, but the little fish who were supposed to be the engines of capitalism got left by the wayside.

As the traditional land of opportunity becomes less hospitable to me, in more ways than one, it isn't lost on me that my British passport gives me the right to live and work in Merry Olde. Well, the entire European Community too, but let's focus on the UK for purposes of this discussion. I've never seriously considered availing myself of this benefit before – and why would I after the negative experience of the Oxford Wilderness Period? – but now that I actually think about it, it's probably no different there. Ever since Maggie Thatcher's tenure as Prime Minister, hasn't Britain been in the throes of some bizarre infatuation with all things

American, from Rambo to Reaganomics? Even Tony Blair, on the surface both intelligent and not a Tory, mangled the meaning of the so-called Special Relationship and infamously became 'Bush's poodle' in flouting international law (and parting company with NATO allies like France) by invading Iraq. So, I must ask myself, would setting up shop in England, derisively referred to as a "nation of shopkeepers" by Napoleon Bonaparte, offer any benefit? Or would it now have all the cold-hearted capitalism of the States along with the nasty leftovers of British pedantry and snobbishness? I suppose I shall find out soon.

Sky and I spend the remainder of the flight in silence, she attempting to doze and me letting my mind wander. On long final approach into Heathrow, our seat backs in their upright position and our tray tables stowed, Sky stares out the cabin window over the starboard wing. Since we broke through the clouds it's been a continuous landscape of gently undulating hills, a classic vision of bucolic Albion.

"I always forget how green it is," I say.

She ignores my comment, perhaps rightly consigning it to the bin marked 'useless nostalgia' and asks, all business: "So what's the plan?"

"Clear immigration. The watchword there, 'father-daughter vacation.' Clear customs. The watchword there, 'nothing to declare.' Find douchebag solicitor and clear inheritance. The watchword there, 'will not be denied.'"

She looks satisfied, then momentarily not. "You forgot something."

"What's that?" I say.

"Repurchase Moondancer. The watchword there, 'never should have been sold.'"

I open my mouth to respond, as automatic a mechanism for me as breathing, then stop myself. Whatever I say, I realize, will only complicate things for the worse. So instead I put my hand on Sky's wrist and squeeze it. I hope this and my affirming smile communicate enough vague solidarity to avoid further elaboration.

"Let's talk specifics," she says. "When are you meeting with the guy?"

"Well, that has to be worked out."

She looks puzzled. "You mean you don't have something arranged already?"

"This all happened pretty fast. But don't worry. His office is in London and I'm not going to be deterred. Remember the watchword."

"Dad, seriously. What if he's on vacation or something? How are you going to do this if he's not available?"

"Sweetie, there are no guarantees in life. But you've got to have a little faith. Your old man is on the job."

The 747 flares over the runway and settles on its undercarriage with a solid *thump* combined with the *screech* of static tires meeting moving pavement. The reverse thrust and deceleration hold our immediate attention, and then a Virgin flight attendant with a Scottish accent gets on the PA system to welcome us to London, more Emily Mortimer in *Dear Frankie* than Maggie Smith in *Prime of Miss Jean Brodie*, although I'd want to hear her say "girls" to be sure. We are now taxiing to the terminal and passengers are fidgeting with personal items, including Sky, who can't seem to find something in the seat pocket in front of her until she does, the ear buds for her iPod mini. Everyone seems to be in high anticipation mode, can't get to the gate soon enough, so looking forward to arrival. Except, it seems, for me. I am wondering if I've made a fatal miscalculation. If my recently irresponsible and naïve teenage daughter isn't, with her newfound purpose and maturity, absolutely correct. What if I'm not able to arrange a meeting with the solicitor? What do I do then?

7

Since our Piccadilly Line train resumed travelling underground, beyond the surface stations that made it seem like a fish out of water, Skylar has been looking at me expectantly. We are decelerating again for the next tube station, and as soon as I see the lettered tiles – Gloucester Road – I nod to her and stand up. This is as far as we dare go into central London and risk paying too much for lodging. I recall that budget hotels line the Cromwell Road, but we're still close enough to South Kensington to feel we're actually in the West End and not the humdrum outskirts like Hammersmith or Chiswick.

With my tennis bag on my back I help Sky with her suitcase and we make our way onto the escalator and up to street level. She's holding up okay, really not all that bad given the circumstances, so the imperative now is to find a decent, inexpensive place to stay and, if possible, keep her awake until evening. I know from experience the only way to conquer jet lag is to tough it out the day of arrival. Just like pushing through a tough set when you feel tired and your opponent is moving you around: no pain, no gain.

In retrospect I realize I needn't have worried about entering the country with Sky. The immigration officer at Heathrow couldn't have been less interested in her status, and he stamped our passports (I used my American one to be safe) with standard six-month tourist visas and handed them back to me without a word. The only surprise was running into Bennett Dixon at the baggage carousel as we collected my oversized tennis bag.

"Hey Trevor!" he'd yelled at me. "You playing in the seniors at Wimbledon?"

It took me a second to recover from the shock of being recognized and register who was calling me by name. Bennett belongs to my tennis club and is a solid player but he's not someone I typ-ically hit with, except doubles if he needs a fourth. I like Bennett – he's got good tennis etiquette and has fun on the court, two big virtues in my book – and normally I'd be happy to engage him in conversation. But he was traveling with his wife and I was worried that she might know Annie and would report seeing me in London with Sky. Not that I'm keeping this trip from Annie. I'm planning on contacting her later, on the assumption she's still beyond cell phone range in Yosemite, but I didn't want to be preempted.

"I *was* playing," I joked back, "but McEnroe took my spot. You going?"

"We are. Centre Court seats right through next week."

"Fantastic," I said.

"You?" he said.

"Nah. I'm here with my daughter on a little family business."

I introduced Sky to Bennett and his wife, Naomi – I'd met her once or twice before – and Bennett and I made small talk about the long flight and the tennis, what a close a shave it was for Federer, then I inched towards the customs exit. I was pretty sure Bennett knew about my divorce and my company's collapse, as things like that tend to get around a club locker room, but he'd never said anything. Not that it would concern him. Bennett owns a very successful wine importing business, exclusively French and Italian producers. He comes to London every June, before heading to the Continent and visiting some of his suppliers and spending August at his vacation house in Provence. What a great job to have, assuming you like good wine and European travel. I have often shopped at Bennett's store on Fillmore Street and I have only the highest regard for his taste. Sure, one can spend fifty bucks most places and get a delicious wine, but the trick is buying something tasty for twenty or twenty-five. If he weren't such a nice guy, I'd be envious of the bastard. At least I can take him in straight sets.

"Nice running into you," Bennett said. "Next time, I need to pick your brain about real estate." He looked annoyingly preppy with his wavy brown hair, chinos and Lacoste polo shirt.

"Okay, next time!" I said, mustering more conviction than I felt. Just what I needed, giving some free advice to Mr. Moneybags on renegotiating a lease or hiring a contractor. I suppose it's no different being a doctor or a lawyer – you're constantly getting hit up for advice. It's just easier to swallow when there's paying work coming in the door.

"Now what?" Sky says. We're standing on the Cromwell Road, a busy thoroughfare with a near-constant stream of buses and taxis, cars and motorcycles. I look around and try to size up a suitable candidate. I rule out the high-rise hotel on the opposite side of the street – it looks too modern and therefore expensive – and I scan the offerings on our side. They look more upscale than I remember, either boutique hotels or cozy Bed and Breakfasts trading on the solid sandstone charm of the Victorian architecture.

"Let's walk a bit," I say. Which earns an immediate eye roll from Sky. Oh Lord, I think, she's already wilting. This might take some doing to stick to my guns, budget-wise. I've already decided that since lodging will be our biggest expense and the most fungible – any room with two beds will do – I'm going to have to be strict about economizing. We start walking, or rather I do and Sky grudgingly follows, dragging her roller suitcase behind her. I notice a poster advertising an all-Beethoven program by the Royal Philharmonic Orchestra at Albert Hall. To lighten the mood I point it out to Sky.

"Your mother would love that, wouldn't she?" Annie is a big classical music fan, a regular season subscriber to the San Francisco Symphony since I've known her.

"Dad, you really need to move on."

"What's that supposed to mean?"

"I think you know. I mean, she's moved on, hasn't she?"

I stare at her, my mouth agape at the thoughtlessness of her remark.

"Look," she continues, "I know how you feel about her and all, but… I mean, she's my mom so I'm not going to diss her, okay?"

"Who's asking you to diss her, for Chrissakes? I just said she would like the concert. What's wrong with that?"

"Okay, right Dad. I get it. I guess we're bailing on the whole 'no bullshit' thing, but no problem."

"You want no bullshit? Fine, I'll give you no bullshit."

I'm about to continue, really lay it out there for her, but I stop. It's not that I can't, I mean it's nothing I haven't said to the girls already, how sorry I am for what's happened, how I still love their mother, but I just don't have the energy or heart to go there right now. And, like Sky said, she doesn't want me to disparage Annie in her presence. I wasn't planning to, not directly, but whatever I say is going to have an undercurrent of blame. So I'd rather not.

"Okay," she says. "I'm waiting."

"I think we should find a place to stay." I say it like that's my meaningful 'no bullshit' statement, stressing each word equally, not as if I want to segue to another topic, but she's having none of it. She puts her hands on her hips, tilts her head sideways and gives me an eye roll worthy of Sarah Burnhardt.

"Jesus, you are such a fucking pussy."

I am mostly inured to her potty mouth but this kind of language in a personal insult shocks me. Somehow I curb the reflex to go parental and chastise her. That, I know, will get us nowhere. So I just start walking. She has to follow and sure enough, after several seconds, she does.

I'm furious at Sky but this is sadly an all-too familiar sentiment lately, so I'm well-practiced in making the emotional leap towards sympathy and, inexorably, self-blame. And because that's never a happy destination for me, I force myself to mentally shift gears. To something practical, like how I'm going to approach Rupert Salmons. I already have his office address and telephone number, but this is going to take a more clever strategy than just phoning him up and requesting a meeting. The solicitor that Meg and I hired made enough of a nuisance of himself that Salmons will know who I am and will likely want to avoid me. Jeez, I lament for the umpteenth time, why can't he just do right by Aunt Philippa? She clearly intended to make my mother the beneficiary of her bequest.

Salmons's stated reason was as lawyeristic as they come, and therefore maddeningly irrefutable. Especially as Salmons is the executor of the will and accordingly serves as its sole interpreter unless we challenge him in court. Which would be expensive, uncertain, and has the punitive twist in England of incurring opposing counsel's costs if we lost. As our solicitor explained, Salmons is relying on a form over substance argument, invoking the precise language of Aunt Philippa's bequest, which reads: "to my lawful niece, Victoria Moore Davis." Because, technically speaking, my mother was neither Philippa Moore's niece nor named Victoria Moore, even though she long ago assumed those roles in the eyes of everyone who mattered, including the British government. How does the Shakespeare quote go? "The first thing we do, let's kill all the lawyers."

Growing up, my mother was as English to me as she was to anyone else, with her Received Pronunciation accent and her British mannerisms and sensibility. It was only when I was ten and I overheard a conversation my parents were having that I learned she'd been born in France. I was as shocked as if I'd discovered she was a paroled bank robber, so they sat me and Meg down and she explained the whole story, or as much as she knew. She'd been born Victoire Durant in 1933 to a bourgeois Catholic father and a bohemian Jewish mother in the city of Poitiers. They either never were married or got divorced soon after my mother was born. In early 1940 before France fell to the Germans, the mother – my real grandmother! – convinced herself that her daughter would be safer in England, so she arranged for the then-six-year-old girl to be evacuated into the care of a foster agency in London. The assumption was that she intended to follow her daughter when she could, but she never did. Young Victoire was almost immediately placed with a childless couple, Richard and Evelyn Moore, who called her Victoria and raised her as their own in the town of Shepperton, or more accurately Evelyn did, as Richard spent the next five years in North Africa and Italy driving a 10-ton Mack truck furnished by American Lend-Lease in an RAF ground support unit. At some point after the war it became clear Victoria's mother would not be reclaiming her daughter, and they eventually obtained a British passport in her name, presumably based on her school records and their foster placement papers. Victoria was by now English for all intents and purposes, without a shred of a French accent, but Richard and Evelyn Moore never formalized the adoption. Perhaps they (wrongly) assumed the foster agency had done so. Complicating matters, as the solicitor that Meg and I hired discovered, the foster agency's offices in Marylebone had been bombed by a V-2 rocket in early 1945 and their records destroyed. It's only conjecture on my part, but I imagine Richard and Evelyn didn't wish to risk upsetting Victoria by inquiring about her mother, who for all they knew had been shipped off to Auschwitz under the deportation laws of Vichy France. I knew my grandparents well enough before they died to understand they were classic stiff upper lip types, not the sort to indulge in exploring one's feelings or enjoy seeing that in others. And while they certainly wanted to do the right thing – my grandfather in particular had an unparalleled sense of duty and fair play – Victoria was their only child and they also must not have wanted to risk her birth mother reasserting custody if by some miracle she were still alive. So they left things as they were, which was perfectly fine for all concerned and would never have caused anyone an iota of trouble until Aunt Philippa's bequest. And, more particularly, me, with my pressing need to receive the half of it I now consider mine, legally and morally.

"How much further?" Sky asks. She's still several paces behind me so I stop and wait for her. Looking around, I see the first promising prospect for lodging, the Viceroy Guesthouse tucked between two larger establishments a few doors up the Cromwell Road.

"Let's try that," I say. Something about it, the modest hand-lettered sign, the frilly linen window treatments, speaks to it being affordable.

"Whatever," she says. When we get to the entrance steps I reach to help Sky with her suitcase, but she rebuffs me.

"I got it," she says, annoyed. I raise my hands in mock surrender, jog up the steps and reach for the door. At least she deigns to let me hold it open for her.

Inside, we are immediately assaulted by a garam masala kitchen smell, not unpleasant but far from subtle. The walls consist of a scratched and stained eggshell wainscot, which extends vertically several feet before giving way to flocked muslin wallpaper. The floor is covered with a worn paisley-patterned carpet, leading towards a reception area whose most prominent feature is a large, apparently wooden, elephant covered in paper money, an assortment of currencies including British pounds, U.S. dollars, Euros and, by the look of it, Indian rupees.

"No fucking way," Sky says, and she turns on her heels and starts walking back towards the entrance.

"Wait a second." She spins towards me and unleashes a furious glare not dissimilar to the one I received yesterday from Gary Malloy, although it feels like earlier today in my body's discombobulated circadian clock.

"I know you're worried about money but this is ridiculous!"

"Let's just ask how much it is. Even if we don't stay, we need a point of reference for the next place."

"Dad, I'm tired! Can't we just go back to the Stanhope Hotel? It looked fine."

"What it looked is expensive. Come on, you know we're on a tight budget."

Sky pauses enough before responding so that we both become aware of a faint tinkling and rustling noise. It slowly gets more noticeable and we both turn and observe a woman approaching. She appears Indian, maybe fifty, and is clothed in a red and ivory sari. Dangling from her wrists, earlobes and neck are countless gold bracelets, bangles and other ornaments. The effect, as she moves, is to sound like a human wind chime.

"Good afternoon," the woman says formally with a British Indian accent.

"Good afternoon," I say. "My name is Trevor Davis and this is my daughter, Skylar. We just arrived in London and we were wondering if you have a room available. Two beds, bathroom en suite if possible."

The woman beams, as if she's unfamiliar with guests introducing themselves in this manner. I can't help myself; back in England I revert to an overt politeness to mask my Americanness, no doubt a defensive holdover from youth.

"Very pleased to meet you both. I am Mrs. Chatterjee. Yes, indeed, we do have such rooms available. And all of our rooms have bathrooms, actually." She adds this last part with more pride than affront.

"Wonderful. Could I ask the rate?"

"Certainly." Mrs. Chatterjee consults a log on the desk in front of her. "A room with two singles is one hundred sixty-five pounds a night." She softens her mouth into a smile that is more sexy than matronly and I realize I've sold Mrs. Chatterjee short.

I turn to Sky and I'm about to ask her if that sounds okay, but my daughter's expression and body language say: don't bother. She appears no less uncomfortable as any moderately spoiled, post-progressive white American teenager with jet lag would, when confronted with The Viceroy Guesthouse as the choice for London accommodations.

"We should go, Dad." She says it with a measure of restraint and I'm relieved, given what could have come out of her mouth. Roberta Maggiore didn't get off this light.

"I understand." I turn back to address Mrs. Chatterjee. "Thank you so much. We'd like to consider it, so I'm going to make some inquiries to determine if this is the best location for us. We're here in London on some important family business." I emphasize the word "important" with the most serious facial expression I can muster and Mrs. Chatterjee nods sympathetically, as if in total understanding.

"Well, jolly fine and good then," she says. "We hope to see you again soon." Amused, I nod farewell and follow Sky, who has miraculously been revitalized and is already out the door and halfway down the steps to the Cromwell Road.

When I reach her she's standing with her arms crossed.

"Which way?" she says. I nod the direction we were heading before and she pulls out the handle on her suitcase and starts walking.

"What a freak show," she continues. "'Well, jolly fine and good then.' She belongs in *A Passage to* frigging *India*. Thank God we're not staying there."

"Have you read it?"

"Read what?"

"*A Passage to India*?"

She looks at me as if I'm a moron. "Like, it's a movie? You know, with the guy who played Obi-Wan in *Star Wars*? Mom made me watch it for a paper I had in social studies on colonial history. Totally boring, like some British version of *To Kill a Mockingbird* but without Scout and Jem and Boo Radley."

This seems a puzzling non sequitur but then I grasp the connection Sky is making between the plotlines of the two stories.

"That's really insightful, Sky. I never thought of that before."

"Gee, thanks, Dad. Now can we find a place to stay?"

"Sure. But let me ask you something first."

She looks at me sharply, brimming with irritation.

"Yes?"

"What's your biggest fear?"

"Dad, seriously. I'm tired and, in case you haven't noticed, more than a little cranky. Can we *please* just find a hotel?"

"Your biggest fear."

"You mean, other than standing on a dirty London street, exhausted, wondering if I'll ever get to lie down?"

"Other than that."

"Why are you asking me this stupid question?!"

"I want to know."

I don't know if I'm probing to bond with Sky or to discover what's at the root of all her hostility, but I don't want to let it go. Just as Sky doesn't want to go there. I see her gauge my resolve and wrestle with whether to answer. Or maybe she genuinely doesn't have one.

"No."

"No what?"

"I'm not going to fucking tell you."

"That's ridiculous." I'm annoyed and my own jet lag isn't helping. "What, you don't trust me? Or you just don't want to give me the satisfaction."

"Whatever."

I've seen this expression on Sky's face before. Pure stubbornness. Or, as a John Wayne cowboy character in a fifties Western would call it, cussedness.

"If you tell me we can stay at that nice hotel we just passed."

I can see the temptation materialize and linger on her face, then just as quickly get banished.

"No."

I'm incredulous. "You mean you won't tell me? Even to stay in the place you want?" But she just stares me down, her eyes resolute and murderous.

"I mean it Sky. If you won't tell me, we're going right back to the Viceroy Guesthouse and checking in there."

"Fuck you. Mom's right. You are a selfish fucking bastard."

I literally, I mean *literally*, see multicolored stars in front of my eyes, I'm so livid. It's all I can do to restrain myself from hauling off and slugging Sky. Could Annie really have…? Or is this just an angry, vengeful teenager talking? I force myself to take a deep breath and my vision clears just enough to see a thin, cruel smile forming at the edges of my daughter's mouth.

8

The two young women sitting near me in the Internet café on Earls Court Road alternate between checking their Facebook accounts and chatting in what sounds like Danish or Swedish. Thankfully the café is air-conditioned, as it's unusually warm for London. And more good news, I feel like I'm actually getting somewhere. Which is a far cry from just twenty minutes ago, when I was sitting on a sofa in the television lounge of the Viceroy Guesthouse and feeling completely useless. You know that feeling, when you're convinced you're a worthless good-for-nothing, basically a pimple on the face of humanity? Of course you do.

Sky was upstairs in our room, pouting or maybe even tearing the place apart, for all I knew. Honestly, I didn't really care as long as she wasn't sleeping. At four o'clock in the afternoon it was still too early to succumb to the jet lag. Don't get me wrong, I was certainly tired, in that uniquely disoriented way, but I forced my eyes to remain open by drinking some strong black tea – I congratulated myself for bringing the Twinings – and watching coverage of Wimbledon on BBC Two. Although the tennis wasn't cooperating: the match was a boring, lopsided affair between Andy Murray and an unseeded Czech. The BBC could have switched to a more interesting match, but no chance of that, with the Scotsman being Britain's best hope to win a major since Fred Perry in 1936.

The lounge was an anachronism, with the threadbare chintz sofa, flocked wallpaper and small screen cathode ray tube television. At least it's color, I consoled myself with something approaching humor. I knew I was risking a major rift with Sky by following through on my threat and returning to Mrs. Chatterjee's guesthouse, but with the exchange rate at about $1.50, anything close to the two hundred and fifty pounds per night cost of the kind of place she wanted to stay at would put the CashPort's burn rate, in the argot of Silicon Valley, at less than four days, even with a bare bones meal budget. As it was, I had to drag out Moondancer and flog the poor beast once more for Sky to agree to re-enter the Viceroy, and when I left her in the room she was not a happy camper. As much as I hate being the bad guy, someone's got to be responsible. And I know from decades of running a business that there are always unexpected expenses. But even factoring in ten percent for cost overruns, our burn rate now is no better than five days. Just enough to get Sky back on a plane home at week's end. And then what about me? It's not worth dwelling on. I simply must free up some cash.

This jolt of reality and the crushing ennui of the tennis match forced me up off the sofa. I hit the power switch on the TV – there was no remote – and dashed for the stairs. Time to get in the game, so to speak. Much as I would have liked to rest and recuperate, the draining hourglass that is my financial liquidity wouldn't permit it. I knocked on our room door as a courtesy, in case Sky was undressing, then opened it and entered. But it was empty.

"Sky?" I called out. "You in the bathroom?" A quick look revealed she wasn't there either. I was momentarily concerned, in the way that is ingrained in any parent, then I reminded myself she's fourteen. Maybe she just needed to take a walk and blow off some steam. I know she has some cash on her, about twenty quid or so, so maybe she went for a snack. She knows where we're staying – although I'm sure she'd rather forget – so it's not like she can get lost. She speaks the language and she's city-savvy. I even reminded her earlier to look right at intersections, and the Greater London Authority, in its protective benevolence, actually paints "Look Right" on the pavement at most street corners as a caution to Americans and Europeans. Because I already know about cars driving on the left, what I wish is for them to also paint something useful for me. Some message that I'm on the right track: "Keep at it" or "Don't Despair," like those electronic freeway signs in *L.A. Story* that communicate with Steve Martin's character. But this is London. The best I'm going to get is "Mind the Gap."

Now that I'm at the café, should I still worry? I checked with Mrs. Chatterjee in the lobby but she hadn't seen Sky go out. Well, if I'm going to do some Internet research, I thought, I might as well take the tennis bag. Perhaps I can talk my way onto a nearby court for a hit after some time at the computer screen. After all, I haven't exercised in two days and I'm going to need to be at my best when (not if – must stay positive!) I meet with Rupert Salmons. Okay, perhaps this is a rationalization, but as Jeff Goldblum's character says in *The Big Chill*, it's impossible to get through the day without two or three juicy rationalizations. And if so, I'm already behind.

So let's take inventory: I've made a good start in only fifteen minutes and my £1 bought me a whole hour. With that and the two sausage rolls at £1.35 each – breakfast on the Virgin flight only went so far – I feel pretty good about my economizing. Except I also had to spend £25 for a new SIM card for my phone, after discovering my mobile service was dead. All I can figure is Ma Bell knows I've defaulted on my credit card bill and froze my account. Technology, it giveth and it taketh away.

Still, it's truly amazing what you can learn on the Internet. One wonders how we ever managed without it. But I suppose people have been saying that sort of thing forever, whether about the invention of the automobile or the printing press. I still believe humanity advances with slow incremental improvements, partially offset by occasional setbacks, but I will acknowledge that once in a while there's a bigger leap forward. Maybe the Internet is such a leap, although my list of civilization's great achievements would focus on simpler things, more tangible and immediate. Such as a bottle of chilled, crisp rosé on a warm summer day, plucked from a cooler and shared on a picnic blanket with a lover wearing just a sundress. Or hot running water and a safety razor to shave one's face smooth, the better to enjoy the contents of that sundress. Forget cyberspace; the sublime journeys of exploration reside in the folds of loose gingham cotton.

I take a break from my research to compose a quick email to Annie informing her about the trip. I include my new mobile number with a Lithuanian country code in case she wants to reach me. Ezra, the café proprietor (Israeli, I'm guessing), assures me I'll be able to receive unlimited calls, place up to £10 in international calls, and send and receive 500 text messages. It's like my phone has undergone surgery for a new heart but the donor ticker only has a certain number of beats left. I don't want to seem cowardly so I'd prefer to call Annie to tell her about Sky, but I'm pretty sure she's still out of cell range in Yosemite. And I can be clearer with email than voicemail. Okay… click 'Send Message'… and then back to the browser.

What I have discovered about Rupert Salmons, all available with a Google search, is that his firm of solicitors mostly does trust and estate work but they also handle real estate transactions. More to the point, he was hired by The Queen's Club to negotiate their membership's buyout of the club facilities from the LTA – short for the Lawn Tennis Association and otherwise known in these parts as British Tennis. Some follow-up research divulged that the LTA had purchased Queen's in 1953 and used it as its headquarters until they built a national training center in Roehampton several years ago. This, presumably, was to produce more homegrown talent to exorcise the ghost of Fred Perry, in case Andy Murray couldn't do the job. All I knew about Queen's before was that it's a private tennis club in London that hosts an annual grass tournament in June that many pros enter as a tune-up for Wimbledon. Digging deeper, I have learned that the members didn't take kindly to the LTA holding their beloved club hostage to the inflated valuations of West Kensington property in the real estate bubble that was 2007. How is any of this relevant to my situation? I'm not sure, exactly, but my brain is going into overdrive to figure out something. Because in addition to the real estate angle, I have some personal history with the LTA. And if Rupert Salmons and I share British Tennis as a common adversary, that's more than I had to go on when I walked in here.

Looking at the Google street map, I realize it must be only fifteen or twenty minutes on foot to Queen's. So I log off my terminal, grab my tennis bag and head outside.

A construction crew is installing what appears to be bicycle docking bays on the opposite side of Penywern Road, so I take a closer look as I walk quickly westward. I've seen pictures of these municipal rental bikes in European cities like Paris and their simple, sturdy design seems a perfect marriage of form and function. Why can't we get something like this in San Francisco? Sure, pedaling a heavy cruiser up Nob Hill might be impractical, but a lot of the city isn't all that steep. To me it boils down to competing philosophies of urban planning. Do you let development occur organically or do you exert governmental influence? People resist change – that whole NIMBY thing – so sometimes, as bad as this sounds, only a disaster (natural or manmade) can clear a swath through a city and provide the clean slate to rethink how streets should be laid out and public amenities like parks included. Every storm has a silver lining, right? But absent a Loma Prieta earthquake or Great Fire of London, it takes a Baron Haussmann to impose the kind of grandiose public works scheme that results in the marvel of modern Paris. Yes, I understand the risk of imposing urban planning from on high. But can't we abide an occasional Robert Moses in order to avoid the urban jungles of Los Angeles or Houston? Try as Angelinos might to make their downtown user-friendly, who wants to live and work on a concrete atoll surrounded by automobile-choked freeways and devoid of green space? The genius that is Central Park need not be explained to a New Yorker.

I continue right onto Old Brompton Road from Eardley Crescent, trading beige brick and white columned Victorian row houses for post-war red brick flats opposite a large, walled-in cemetery. God, how I'd like to get back in the real estate game! And not just do a minor building here or there, but make something important – be a player. J. Paul Getty said a man can focus on his family or his career, but he can't do both. Was that my problem, not being ruthless enough about work? I'm guessing Annie would say it's a man's world, and women have the tougher row to hoe. Not that she complained. In her Midwestern manner, she preferred practicing gender realpolitik to fighting the Battle of the Sexes. And even though she's now with Jeffrey Schreiber, aka the Man with no (Evident) Flaws, I know that I'd have had no chance with her from the outset if I'd been one of those schemers or overreachers who puts macho ego before values. Yes, it's easy to dismiss the likes of a Silvio Berlusconi, a self-serving poseur whose only real status is as a buffoon. But what to make of the Frank Lloyd Wrights and Pablo Picassos of the world? Do we mark down their achievements because they treated their women badly? Or do we fault their wives for marrying the Black Prince and expecting Prince Charming?

Passing a newish entrance to a railway station I notice a plain-lettered plaque, which reads:

West Brompton Station
opened by
Glenda Jackson MP
Minister for Transport in London
1st June 1999

I realize, in my jet-lagged haze, this must be Glenda Jackson the actress, the one who starred in those serious British films of the sixties and then those comedies opposite Walter Matthau in the seventies. That's right, didn't she chuck it all for a second career in politics? I can't be sure of much in my present state but this seems to ring a bell. And if so, how about that? The world of drama certainly isn't a man's world, at least not since Shakespeare's day, but I'm guessing women are still a sizable minority in Parliament. Well then, Glenda – hat's off to you! Presiding over railway ribbon-snipping ceremonies may not seem as glamorous as Hollywood but people need to be transported away in more ways than one.

I know I need to bear right to get to Queen's but getting past the station is taking an eternity. So why the hell am I doing this? I've never even been to Queen's before, yet sight unseen it looms in the atmospheric void of my existence like some large planetary body exerting a huge gravitational pull. There's no rational purpose for me to make this trek – I have absolutely no idea what to do when I get there – but the fact that Queen's has a connection, however tenuous, to the solicitor I seek seems reason enough. And there's this: the faint tendril of hope that somehow I can prove Annie wrong.

Annie found London and the English charmingly quaint – and therefore alien – so she never really understood my ambivalence towards the place. And certainly not my lingering sense of injustice about the whole British Schoolboys Tournament fiasco. Not that Annie didn't have her impractical or romantic sides. She did. But they were about letting Mahler's *Second* wash over you and planning a perfect fall picnic hike, not dreaming about righting a past wrong. What would Annie have said to me when I first told her the story, if I'd given her truth serum? Probably: 'Trevor, get over it.' Maybe that's being unkind. But in fairness, how can one – even a loved one – truly empathize about a foreign experience?

Finally I'm able to turn onto Thaxton Road, another stretch of bleak, post-war red brick flats. Not exactly Prince Charles's 'carbuncles' but depressing just the same. This block must have been firebombed by the Luftwaffe. Or maybe a V-1 or a V-2? Man's inhumanity to man, once the shackles of civility come off. Ralph and Jack and Piggy and the conch. No, one mustn't succumb to pessimism. For look at this city now! Revival is in the air as part of a new Europe, with open borders and free trade. Can't we consign nationalism and other dark impulses to the ash heap of history?

I'm on Star Road now and a clearing of the skyline in the distance must mean – Queen's? My stomach tightens and my legs quiver a bit, a familiar feeling when I walk onto a court before a match, but I can't expect one today. That would be hoping for too much. Anything I can use – even a passing reference – to help convince Salmons to meet with me would be enough. Construct the point, with a drop here and a lob there. Don't always go for a winner.

A sign now says it: Queen's Club deliveries straight on, entrance to the right, so I follow Gledstanes Road past what are clearly grass courts beyond that fence. Okay, I need to figure a way to make him see this isn't a zero sum situation. Sure, there's a finite bequest to distribute, but unless his aim is truly mercenary – just racking up fees by dragging things out – there must be a way to make our interests allied. How did the article I read the other day go, about that economics genius? What was his name? Oh yes – John Nash, the 'Brilliant Mind' in the book, played by Russell Crowe in the movie.

It said he wrote his Ph.D. on non-cooperative game theory and got a Nobel for figuring out something called the Nash equilibrium, the point where two or more players who know each other's strategies reach a mutually satisfactory outcome. That is, before the good professor went stark raving bonkers and started hearing voices. Think, Trevor – this could help! Something about the prisoner's dilemma and the Kakutani fixed-point theorem, whatever the hell that is, and making your best decision given the situation presented. Wait a sec, didn't it assume equal status and no outside rule structure, like a legal system? Shit, how can I hope to win when he's got the upper hand? Appeal to his better angels? Throw myself on the mercy of the court? No, there's got to be a better way, a more clever way. If your opponent feeds on power, mix it up. Throw in some slice, use the angles.

The club entrance has one of those brass plaques next to the door that says it all: 'Private Establishment – Members Only.' I enter with my Wilson bag front and center and momentarily consider striding straight through the lobby until I see there's no avoiding checking in with the concierge. But I'm damned if I'm going to play defense so I go with the only thing I have, a name that springs from the deepest recesses of my memory like Athena from Zeus: Ronny Barnes. And I do what any jazz player does when a riff is unexpectedly tossed his way. I improvise.

"Is Mr. Barnes here yet?"

"Mr. Barnes, sir?" The concierge looked impassive.

"Yes," I say. "Ronald Barnes. I'm supposed to meet him. I'm his guest."

The concierge checks his ledger and I wonder what I should do next. Walk back to the Viceroy? Beg to see the manager to get a tour of the grounds? What hope in hell is there that Ronny Barnes is a member here? And, even if he were, that he's in the club this afternoon? Or that he would even remember me? For all I know he's dead or living in Moscow or Montreal.

"Sir, Mr. Barnes *is* on the premises. But he made no provisions for a guest today. Were you supposed to meet him here?"

Are you fucking kidding? Shanked ball, floating gently over the net, right at me. Calmly now… go with it, go with it…

"I'm sure he said so but you know Ronny – Mr. Barnes. He probably forgot. Could you just let him know Trevor Davis is here? From San Francisco?"

"Well, the club doesn't actually permit delivery of messages to members."

Shit, what is this, game over? Damn the Brits and their god-damned rules! I try not to look too crestfallen and consider my next move. But the concierge's expression softens without my saying a word.

"But I believe I know where he can be reached." The concierge reaches for a telephone. "If you wouldn't mind waiting over there, sir, I'll just see."

Mind? Are you serious? I raise my hand and nod as noncha-lantly as possible, then take a seat on a leather bench. Does this mean I've got a chance here? I mean, who really expects, when you throw a Hail Mary pass, that it will be caught? Well, I sup-pose on some level you always do, otherwise why bother? You buy the lottery ticket knowing the odds are stacked against you but believing you have as good a chance as anyone to hit the jackpot. And maybe better, if you can summon a little divine interven-tion. Zeus indeed! Or at least some measure of inspiration. And thinking of Ronnie – well, Trevor lad, *that* was inspired. Except... oh Jesus, no. What if there's more than one? It's a pretty common name and the population of London is, how many millions? Oh Lord, let this be Ronnie Barnes. *My* Ronnie.

9

One set and five games into my match, several things are readily apparent. One, while I spent the Oxford Wilderness Period playing on grass, it is now a totally unfamiliar surface to me. Two, Jeremy Sutcliffe is a lefty banger who cheats, a guy half my age who hits with the same reckless and unprincipled abandon as he makes line calls. And three, having that drink at the bar with Ronnie was a bad idea.

That all said, I took the first set 6-4 and it's 2-3 in the second with both of us on serve. Just need to compose myself during this changeover and hold for 3-all. One break of his serve should do it, I believe. I'm not serving great, especially my first serve, but my second serve has been solid enough that I don't think he'll break me.

Okay, just push Ronnie out of your head right now, and Frankie and Rupert Salmons, and *focus*. I don't want to lose to this asshole. Look at him, sitting there, ignoring me. Let's teach him a lesson. Christ, can you believe it though? I'm really here, playing at Queen's. And all because I dredged up a name from the past, just a minor acquaintance, really. I'm just lucky Ronnie remembered *me*. But the look on his face said it, when he burst into the club lobby and greeted me with a bemused smile and a hearty handshake.

"Trevor! How the devil are you? It must be, what, twenty years? Unbelievable."

"Closer to twenty-five I think. Good to see you, Ronnie. You look great."

I was lying, of course, as Ronnie had gained at least fifty pounds and the coloration of his nose indicated a serious drinking habit.

"You still playing squash?" I asked.

"Ha! Gave it up for Lent, old man. I'll have a knock up on the Real Tennis court once in a blue moon, but that's about it. Christ, has it really been twenty-five years? What are you doing here, anyway?"

I glanced at the concierge, hoping my cover wasn't totally blown, but he seemed preoccupied. The fact that Ronnie knew me must have satisfied him.

"I just arrived in London, here on a little family business with my daughter, and I felt like some exercise after the flight. I guess I figured old Ronnie Barnes must belong here and took a gamble you'd remember me."

"What? Are you joking? Absolutely! Who could forget that charming city of yours, with those little trolley cars."

"Right, the cable cars. Listen Ronnie, do you have a minute to talk? Can I buy you a drink or something?"

"Afraid your money's no good here, old chap. As it happens, I was just at the bar when they rang me you were down here. Let's catch up there. Bloody hell – twenty-five years!" And with that, Ronnie led the way. Like I said, sometimes you just get lucky.

Once at the bar, Ronnie ordered a fresh vodka tonic and I ordered a beer. I didn't really want one as I still had hopes of finding a tennis game, but it seemed the polite thing to do. And then Ronnie and I got down to catching up.

It seems almost an absurd concept because Ronnie and I barely know each other. We spent a three-day weekend together, or more accurately, I let him crash at my apartment after a mutual friend mentioned this charming, eccentric Englishman was coming to San Francisco with a group of squash players and needed a place to stay. George Zabassian, the mutual friend, knew Ronnie from a visit to New York and remembered that I belonged to the sports club that was sponsoring the squash event – this was before I joined my present tennis club – and that I had some connection to England. Anyway, that's how Ronnie landed on my doorstep. And he proved to be an ideal guest. He picked up the majority of the meal and bar tabs and was never at a loss for a funny quip or story. He did play squash, but it seemed clear after watching a match that he was touring with his London club's team for the travel experience rather than the competition. I don't think he won a single game the whole tournament and, even though I'd hardly played any squash, I'm pretty sure I could have taken him. Ronnie had other talents as a raconteur and a connector. And since I like to think I'm gifted enough socially, we hit it off quite well. But there's been no reason to stay in touch over the years, although this didn't seem to bother Ronnie in the least as we sat at the bar and brought each other up to date.

I gave Ronnie the abbreviated version of my last twenty-five years, omitting more recent details. I didn't really want to attract any expressions of sympathy, as I believe Ronnie traffics better in bonhomie. But I did mention the inheritance and the coincidence of the executor being the club's solicitor in the LTA transaction. Did Ronnie by any chance have any dealings with Rupert Salmons? As I'd hoped, Ronnie knew the fellow and believed he'd done a bang-up job on behalf of the club. I made a mental note to revisit Salmons and let Ronnie carry on. He'd eventually been promoted to Managing Director of Barnes Enclosures Ltd., the plastic pouch and container manufacturer his father had started, although after the old man's death Ronnie sold the company to a Hong Kong trading company owned by his in-laws. Yes, Ronnie had become married since I met him, which only seems surprising because he'd struck me as singularly committed to having a good time and avoiding responsibility. And married to a Chinese woman no less. He joked about his slant-eyed children in the inappropriate way a wealthy establishment Englishman characterizes anyone else: as amusingly gauche in their otherness. It was clearly a match of convenience, a family merger, and it freed Ronnie up to do what he did best: sit at the bar of The Queen's Club, drinking vodka and telling innocuous stories. Which is why Ronnie caught me so off guard when he asked if I'd heard about Frankie.

"You've seen Frankie?" I asked. "How? Why?" I'm not sure if I was more upset or surprised.

Francesca Kenwyn-Lloyd, or Frankie as I knew her, was my girlfriend at the time Ronnie visited San Francisco. She was English like Ronnie but otherwise they had little in common. Ronnie, in truth, was bourgeois and uninspiring, with the best accent his father could purchase and no particular ambition in life other than having fun. Frankie was exotic, idealistic and landed gentry, with her father's family – the Kenwyns – going back centuries as Cornish nobility and with an Italian mother who gave her both her name and her dark, sensuous looks. But more importantly, Frankie was – apart from Annie – the great love of my life. Everyone assumed we would marry, me included, and when we parted we never saw or spoke to each other again.

"Sorry, old boy – I thought you'd stayed in touch. We ran into each other after she returned to London, nothing much, just the occasional chat at some party or what not. Figured she was still stuck on you, as she got a lot of interest from chaps, but eventually she married that military fellow. You knew, didn't you?"

"Um, no."

"Dreadful tragedy, mind you I was never one of those critics of the war, calling Blair 'Bush's Poodle' and all that rot. Just one of those things, I'm afraid."

"Wait a second, Ronnie. What tragedy?"

"Frankie's husband. Thomas Smith, major in the Grenadier Guards. Imagine that – Francesca Smith. Ha! Anyway, he was killed in Iraq, Basra I believe. Last I heard she was back in Cornwall with her three children."

I was too stunned to speak. Not just about the death of Frankie's husband, but all of it, the sheer totality of it: husband, children, Cornwall, Frankie herself. How can you possibly process so many significant life events for someone you used to imagine spending your life with?

Ronnie must have noticed my shock, but I recovered quickly enough to make two requests of him: an introduction to Rupert Salmons and another for a tennis player at the club. He must have felt guilty for blindsiding me for he agreed, promising to make inquiries about the former while he rang the club pro to arrange the latter. And once I conveyed my ability level to the pro, the game materialized on the spot. One of the advantages of being a good player is you're always in demand.

"You ready?"

I realize Jeremy Sutcliffe is standing and is ready to continue.

"Yeah," I say, and quickly get up. I still feel somewhat light of head and heavy of foot, a combination of the beer, the jet lag and the news about Frankie, but I'm hoping this will all clear after another game or two. Let's focus on the positive: I'm winning and Ronnie agreed to put me in touch with Rupert Salmons. I know there are no guarantees, but it would be difficult for the solicitor to avoid me now.

A glance at my watch as I collect the balls reveals it's a quarter to seven. Sky's probably returned to our guesthouse by now. But I'm not worried about her. She'll be happy to hear my good news.

Just a quick mop of the brow with this nice fluffy white towel from the men's locker room before heading to the baseline. So nice it was too, with the wood paneling and marble, much fancier than my club's locker room back home. Maybe I should pinch a couple of towels and stow them in my bag, given the sorry looking specimens in our bathroom at the Viceroy. But I won't. Mustn't mess with the positive karma that seems to be flowing back in my direction.

Okay, time to rock and roll. And yet – are you kidding me, he's stooping to retie his shoelaces? After he asked if *I* was ready? Classic. Trying to psyche me out, I suppose. Well, he must know he's overmatched. What did he say his rating was, 2.1? I think that's roughly on par with my 5.0 USTA rating. Maybe.

"Take your time," I yell. "I'll just have another sip." And I walk back to my chair. Truth is, I could use some more water.

Why there isn't uniformity in tennis ratings I have no idea, with each country possessing its own system, each equally unintelligible to the other. There has been an attempt to impose an international system, a so-called ITN, with 1 being a professional and 10 being a beginner, but this has had as much success as Esperanto. Still, most of the scales use some linear sequence of numbers or letters, except the French who characteristically tried to impose logic with a handicap rating (e.g. 1/6 or 30/2 denoting set or game score differential) that is way more confusing than helpful. But whether you call Jeremy Sutcliffe a 2.1, an N4 or a Category 3, he's been able to hang with me. And that's got to stop.

I really used to love playing on grass and I'm sure, given enough time to re-familiarize myself, I would again. But I don't have that luxury of time. Jeremy's booming, flat groundstrokes have been skidding wickedly, whereas my heavy topspin – much more useful on hard courts – has been sitting up for him. The guy is all about blasting away for winners rather than constructing points; his game has as much finesse as the lead guitar in a heavy metal band. This has produced a litany of unforced errors on his part but also enough points to be annoying. Throw in his lefty slice serve and it's been a challenging match, but no way should it be this close. And it wouldn't, except the guy cheats.

I got my first taste at thirty-all in the first game, when, after a cross-court rally, I drilled a backhand winner down the line, a good three inches in.

"Out," Jeremy said, his finger pointing sideways to emphasize the call.

I was shocked – he was standing close enough to see it was in – but it's always possible he was unsighted.

"Are you sure?" I said. This is technically all one is allowed to say, but it often elicits the caller's uncertainty.

"Yes, sorry Trevor. I saw it out."

There are different kinds of cheaters in tennis, as in life, so I don't use the term loosely. There's the subtle kind, like a rampant foot-faulter who may not even realize he's doing it. His cheating isn't serious – it won't rob you of a point – but it's annoying since it gives his serve a small, unfair advantage. Then there's the more direct but still inadvertent kind, like the line caller who genuinely believes a close ball was out or maybe is the victim of wishful thinking. And then there's the blatant cheater, the guy who sees a ball in and calls it out anyway. On purpose. Because he can.

I've had discussions with friends about how to deal with a cheater and there's no consensus. In a tournament, if it gets really bad you can ask for a referee to observe and help keep your opponent honest. But in most situations this isn't possible. One school of thought is to immediately retaliate against a blatant cheater with a bad call of one's own, the idea being that this will send the right message and encourage better behavior. I've never subscribed to this theory. To me, that's sinking to the cheater's level. I don't want to play a match where bad calls become routine on both sides or where victory is tainted by my own need to cheat. No, when I encounter a cheater I go out of my way to make more generous line calls, in the hope *this* will encourage better behavior. It may seem counterintuitive, but this has worked for me before. But as much as I've tried to take the high road with Jeremy Sutcliffe, it has failed. Since that first game, several of his calls have been truly egregious.

Some players I know don't get bent out of shape by bad line calls, as if they're to be expected. After all, the thinking goes, who doesn't take an occasional water bottle from the honor bar or an extra pen home from the office? Psychologists say what upsets us the most in others is what we see in ourselves – what we fear becoming. And I suppose that's right. For instance, fat people have always bothered me tremendously, not because they're obnoxious or despicable but because on some subconscious level I worry *I* could lose self-control and end up like that. So maybe I loathe Jeremy's cheating because I see the temptation to do it myself. That may be true, and I'm certainly willing to look inward if necessary, but I have a more basic problem right now. His cheating has been costing me points. And I don't like to lose.

"Any day now, Trevor," Jeremy calls out. He's standing impatiently, ready to receive.

I nod and take a final sip of water and return to the baseline. Walking back, I allow myself a moment to take in the surroundings, which I have to acknowledge are truly magnificent. Despite Jeremy's ethical shortcomings, I feel grateful that I can play on such a court. The grass may be worn from the recent pro event but it's grass nonetheless. Surrounded by the brick façade and gable roofs of the clubhouse, I'd rather be here right now than anywhere else in London.

"Two-three," I announce before I serve. Jeremy is standing closer to the center line so I slice the serve wide in the deuce court, a ball he can't reach but calls out. I'm pretty sure it clipped the line but I'll give him the benefit of the doubt on this one, so I pause a moment, then serve again. He's drifted to his right, expecting another serve wide to his backhand, so this one I spin down the tee to his forehand. He has to stab with his racquet to reach my serve and he returns it without much depth. I take the ball on the rise near the service line with a backhand slice approach and rush the net. All Jeremy can muster is a weak lob that drifts over the net to my forehand side, a ball that I can easily hit for an overhead winner. As I turn sideways in the classic surfboard stance and raise my left hand to mark the descending ball, I stumble momentarily and roll my right ankle completely over. I recover in time to hit the overhead winner – he doesn't have a chance to get a racquet on it – but I immediately hunch over in pain, favoring the right ankle.

"Out," Jeremy says, reinforcing his call with his index finger raised.

"*What*?!" It's a reflex response on my part, since I can't believe my ears. My ball had to be four feet in.

"Yes, sorry, just long."

"Jeremy, there's no way. My ball was good. Fifteen-love."

I realize I've had enough – there's only so much cheating one can take – especially as the nerve endings in my ankle are firing and flooding me with adrenalin. So I collect the third ball and walk gingerly to the baseline. I can see out of the corner of my eye Jeremy is flustered. Maybe he sees I'm hurt, and instinctually you don't want to provoke a wounded animal. Or maybe he's not used to someone taking this confrontational approach. Whatever. I must keep my resolve and not give him the satisfaction. But as I ready myself to serve he approaches the net.

"Sorry Trevor, I see you stumbled when your ball flew long. You all right?"

"Sure. Just rolled my ankle but I'm fine. My ball was still good. Fifteen-love."

"See here, I don't know how they do it in the States, but it's my call. And I saw it out."

I approach the net slowly, testing my ankle and, upon arrival, stand as tall as I can to gain the full benefit of my perhaps one inch height advantage. I try to hide my wince as I put weight on the right foot, turning it into an insincere smile.

"Jeremy, I think I've been pretty tolerant. But that smash was clearly in. So why don't we say it's fifteen-love and move on. This is just a friendly match. Let's keep it that way."

"Friendly or not, what kind of match is it if you make your own calls from your side of the net? I called it out and I bloody well meant it. Love-fifteen."

I take a deep breath, sigh and then look directly at Jeremy Sutcliffe. He can't be beyond his twenties – twenty-seven is my best guess – and I realize I was playing national intercollegiate playoffs matches when he was still in diapers. Why do I bother, I momentarily ask myself, before realizing with the sad lament of my inner critic that *this* question, for me, is always rhetorical.

"Jeremy, you don't have to keep reminding me it's your call. I know that. Yes, it's your call. But you're missing the key ingredient here. You sound like some tin pot dictator insisting on the legitimacy of his election, as if he presided over a real democracy. 'I got ninety-nine point nine percent of the popular vote!' But if the system is rigged, who cares? Look, Jeremy, maybe you're having an off day. I don't know, I'm willing to make allowances. Shit, I've been having an off year. But here's the thing. I've got really good eyesight. Twenty-fifteen, every time I get it checked. It's kind of a curse, actually. So when I see a ball an inch or more in, I know it. All right. We've got ourselves a little situation here. What to do about it? Here's what I suggest. Forget about the score and look around for a sec. I mean, really look around. This place is amazing! Like I said, I've been having kind of a rough time lately, but standing here on this tennis court, a club like this, what could be better? It's summer, nice and warm, a couple of decent players out here having a competitive match on grass? Shit, we'd really have to go a ways to fuck that up. So let's not, okay? So here's my idea. Whenever you make a call – I'll do it too, to be fair – imagine someone you really respect is watching. Your mum, an old coach, I don't care, maybe it's the Queen of England herself. Or – could be – some girl you want to impress, so she'll see what a fabulous bloke you are. Taking care of business with that old geezer, straight up. Just imagine that, and then make the call. Okay?"

Jeremy has been listening to me, I'll give him that, but his expression has evolved along the way from curiosity to annoyance to, finally, disbelief verging on disgust.

"You are so full of shit," he says. "How can you even stand yourself?"

"Yeah, I admit that's sometimes a problem."

This actually cracks him up. A throwaway line like that, if you can believe it. Maybe his laugh is sarcastic, but still.

"Tell me something, Trevor."

"Anything, Jeremy."

"Has that wanker speech of yours ever worked?"

"Don't know," I say. "Never tried it before."

"Really? What do you usually try?"

I affect my most nonchalant expression.

"Usually, if the problem continues, I beat the living crap out of the guy."

He pauses, uncertain for a split-second, and then he regains his composure.

"You and who else?"

It's my turn to laugh. "Matthew," I say.

Now he genuinely looks confused. "Huh?"

"Chapter seven, verse twelve. They still teach that stuff in school here, don't they?" I point at my chest with my free index finger. "You thought I was American? I know, the accent is confusing. Nah, I'm English too. On my mom's side. Hey, you want to play some tennis or what? We keep standing here yammering, my ankle is going to be useless."

I turn to head back to the baseline before he can say another word. I move as carefully as I can, trying not to burden the ankle, and when I finally stand at the center mark I look back at Jeremy. He is halfway back towards his own baseline but also in the center, between the deuce and the ad courts, still with a confused air about him.

"What was the score again?" I say.

He doesn't actually shrug, at least I don't think he does, but something about his body language suggests it.

"Why don't you start over at love," he says.

Ah. Inside, I allow myself the tiniest of celebrations, making sure not to show it. However meaningless this match, this is genuine cause for self-congratulation. Isn't it? We go through life thinking we can educate grown men and women, trying to make them behave better. But that's almost always a fool's errand. Walking to net a moment ago, I figured I'm no more getting this guy to be a good sport than I was able to convince Gary Malloy to pay me what my bike was worth. And now? Well, the jury's still out on Jeremy – he hasn't had to make another close call yet – but maybe, just maybe, we've got ourselves a match here. And if so, no excuses. Certainly not about my right ankle, the one that's feels iffy right now. Hey, it's time to serve, bucko, so let's focus on the point at hand.

Standing to the right of the hash now, I toss the ball into the air with my left hand, bring the racquet back and gather and push off my feet – a regular first serve – but my right ankle gives way and the ball crashes into the net. Jesus. I mean, *Jesus*! I've got a serious problem here. That felt terrible. Do I forfeit now? What, after all *that*? And give him the satisfaction? No way. Christ. Maybe the ankle just needs to work itself out. I've rolled ankles before and recovered just fine. Okay, let me try again, not leaping this time. So I spin an easy second serve dead in the middle of the box. A surprised Jeremy eyes the sitter and crushes a forehand winner down the line. I mean, he hit it so hard he almost came out of his sneakers.

Oh boy. And – déjà fucking vu – it's love-fifteen. *Now* what?

10

The taxi's meter is already over five pounds, after what seems barely a minute of travel, but much as I detest squandering my limited money on a cab ride, I have no choice. I couldn't walk to a tube station, much less the guesthouse. Which makes it all the more remarkable that I finished the tennis match. Looking at my swollen ankle now, I realize my mind was in as much denial as my body. Once I stopped moving about the court, however, and returned to the Queen's Club locker room, the lower calf muscles stiffened around the damaged tendons and ligaments and it became fully apparent how bad the sprain was.

The cabbie looks straight out of Cockney Central Casting with his tweed cap and National Health glasses. Who says London cab-drivers are all Pakistanis and East Africans? He brakes in response to slowing traffic and I slide forward on the slippery rear bench seat. As we squeal to a stop, I manage to extend my left leg just in time to protect my right from striking the jump seat. The idling diesel clatters away and the meter tacks on another twenty pence.

In the category of Pyrrhic victories, my win over Jeremy Sutcliffe must surely rank high. Dale McKittridge, my coach at Cal, once told me that in his estimation losing feels twice as bad as winning feels good. Well, in this instance I'd have to disagree with him. Winning feels worse.

Jeremy played it smart the rest of the second set after I'd rolled the ankle, moving me around the court and picking up easy points when I couldn't reach his shots. After breaking my serve he held to even the match at one set apiece. I suggested a tiebreaker, hoping I could gut it out for a few more points, but he was having none of it.

"We didn't specify a tiebreaker at the outset."

"You want to play another set?" I said.

"That's right."

"Couldn't we agree now?"

"Sorry, those are the rules."

I didn't so much mind him throwing the rules back at me, after he'd been so blatantly cheating earlier, but sweet Jesus – why are the English always saying they're sorry? Especially when they aren't.

"If you want to retire, I'd understand. That ankle looks like it's bothering you."

By that stage, I figured it couldn't get any worse. And in fact my ankle had begun to feel a bit better the previous game. In for a penny, in for a pound, as they say in these parts. And so I gritted my teeth and soldiered on. I was damned if I was going to give him the satisfaction.

Once my mobility improved, I was able to take advantage of my more accurate shot making. He became visibly frustrated that I was returning better and he started to go for the same big baseline winners as he had in the first set. Fortunately, he sprayed just enough of them out to give me the crucial break I needed. To Jeremy's credit, we had no more issues with bad line calls. And he was even somewhat gracious in defeat, meeting me at net with an outstretched arm, a firm handshake and a terse "well played." Ordinarily it should have been as satisfying a win as they come. Yet it isn't. All I wanted earlier was a little exercise to clear out the cobwebs from the flight, but now I have the sour taste of a poorly played, contentious match. And I'm unable to walk.

My phone buzzes and I fish it out. It's a text from Ronnie. *Rupert can meet you 11am on Thur, his office. Good to see you again! Sorry bout the ankle, maybe it's time to hang it up old boy!*

Thank God this cheapo SIM card works and my phone is no longer a glorified paperweight. But shit, Thursday? That leaves all of tomorrow to sit around and wait.

I text back. *Thanks but any chance to see him tomorrow?*

The response is immediate, which is sort of remarkable given how many vodka tonics Ronnie must have had today. *He said he remembers your case, willing to meet but Thur soonest.*

So that's the best I can do. Well, not too bad considering. I suppose I should try to look on the bright side – it will give me a day to rest the ankle.

I let the scenery of West Kensington coming through the cab's windows wash over me, the large brick and whitewashed Victorian and Georgian and Edwardian facades as familiar as they are strange. This place evokes such distinct moments from my past: our family's arrival at the outset of the Oxford Wilderness Period, the trip Frankie and I took to meet her family in Cornwall, and my honeymoon with Annie in Italy (commencing in London at her insistence). But it also arouses a kind of confusion, or maybe a question. Are you friend or foe? Comfort or irritant? I suddenly remember those oft-repeated words of advice, about holding your friends close and your enemies closer. Well, what does that inform me about London? That I belong here? I certainly had the opportunity, when Frankie was returning from California. God, I always figured she'd marry eventually. But a career military man? Who got himself killed in Iraq? Leaving her to raise three kids? There's only so much the jet-lagged, pain-addled mind can process.

"Right you are, guv'nor," the cabbie says as he pulls up in front of the Viceroy. Nabbing one of the last real Cockney cabbies in London makes me feel proud for some reason, like I've won some travel bonus prize. God, how pathetic. That's what I view as success? Damn – just stop it, Trevor. Berating yourself never works, on or off the court. Keep it positive. One point at a time. We've got the meeting with Salmons now. Focus on the money. Aunt Philippa's bequest. That's what counts.

I grab my tennis bag and ease myself slowly towards the tar-smooth pavement, noticing with alarm how much more my right ankle has swelled during the brief cab ride. As soon as my right foot touches the Cromwell Road, waves of searing heat shoot up my leg, crisscrossing into my belly and lower back, up through my chest and shoulders and ricochet around my brain pan, literally compelling my body to shift all my weight onto the left leg. I breathe in spasms and swallow hard, all the time holding onto the cab door for support. Christ. That's really bad.

"Steady on there, guv'nor."

"No worries," I manage to exhale. "It's just a minor sprain."

The cabbie peels his cap off to smooth his stringy gray hair, smiles and indicates the meter. "That'll be eight pounds fifty pence." He resettles the cap on his head, despite the eighty-degree weather.

I fumble for my wallet, careful to keep my balance on my left leg, and hand the cabbie a tenner. He starts to make change but I wave him off. "Keep it."

"Cheers, guv'nor," he says. Like some latter-day Dickensian character he touches the tip of his cap, punches the meter to 'available' and pulls back into traffic, the diesel purring like a contented cat.

I heft the tennis bag onto my shoulders and hop up the steps to the guesthouse using the iron railings for support. Inside, the curry smell seems less pronounced. Or maybe my senses are just dulled by the pain. I spot Mrs. Chatterjee at the reception desk, talking on a mobile phone. As I approach, still hopping on my left leg, her face takes on an almost comically panicked expression and she abruptly finishes her call.

"Mr. Davis! Goodness gracious, what has happened to you, Mr. Davis?"

"It's alright. I just sprained my ankle."

"Are you in … considerable pain?"

I consider the question and force myself not to laugh. Considerable pain? Of what kind? Emotional? Spiritual? Or physical? As if it would matter.

"A little bit, yes. Might I trouble you for a large bag of ice?"

"A bag of ice? Yes, certainly, of course, Mr. Davis. It would be my pleasure. Just a moment, please."

"Um, did my daughter return by any chance?"

"Your daughter? Oh yes, a few minutes ago. I believe she is in the television lounge. Shall I bring you the ice there?"

"That would be wonderful, thank you."

Mrs. Chatterjee bustles away, her bangles tinkling as she goes. I eye the narrow staircase with dread, summon a deep breath, and hop towards it.

Once upstairs, I see Skylar slouched on the worn sofa, watching TV. The set is tuned to highlights of the day's horse racing – the announcer mentions 'Doncaster' – and I am momentarily annoyed. Couldn't she exhibit *some* enthusiasm for Wimbledon? Neither of the girls has ever shown the slightest interest in tennis, even though Sky showed genuine talent when she deigned to take some lessons in 3rd grade. I consider walking towards her, if only for pride's sake, so I gingerly try out the right leg again but the explosive reaction of my nerve endings makes me stop immediately. I toss my bag against the wall and hop towards her across the threadbare carpet with as much dignity as I can muster.

"What the fuck happened to you?" she says, looking up with contempt and not a jot of concern. "I thought you were going to meet the solicitor?"

"Check that box, the meeting's all lined up. So I figured I'd get in a quick hit and found a good game at Queen's. Real grass, just like at Wimbledon. Beat the guy too, even after I rolled my ankle. Mrs. Chatterjee is bringing me some ice. That should reduce the swelling."

Sky looks at my ankle more closely. "I'm not so sure. It looks fucking huge. You sure it's just a sprain? If you were a horse we'd order an x-ray."

"I appreciate your concern but I'm not a horse."

"I'm just saying."

I hop to the left side of the sofa and wait for her to move over.

"These old sets really had great color," I say enthusiastically. Sky scowls, then grudgingly shifts a bit. I plop down next to her and notice a dark purple smudge on her left ankle. Looking more closely, I see it is the outline of a horse's head, complete with bridle and bit.

"What the hell is that?"

She sees my right index finger pointing accusingly at her ankle and she giggles.

"Don't worry, it's just henna. I got bored so I found this shop on King's Road. Some gypsy woman with all sorts of vegetable dyes and shit."

As she talks I notice her shifting to cover her ankle.

"How much did you pay her?"

"What?" she asks with a nervous, upward rising tone. This I have learned in the past year is her 'tell.' An almost foolproof sign that she is lying. So I grab her wrist with my left hand and hold her foot still with my right. Her limbs start to tense and I realize too late that I've underestimated her strength from all the riding so that, by my holding on tight, we both roll onto the floor. My right ankle takes the brunt of the fall and I scream in agony. This must be enough to scare Sky so she stops resisting and just lays on the floor, looking at me with a shocked expression. Her foot is right next to me so I quickly study the ankle before she can react. There are pinpricks of blood oozing from what clearly are lines of midnight blue ink.

"That's not henna, Sky. That's a tattoo. You went and got a fucking tattoo? Without asking me? What am I going to tell your mother? She's going to crucify me!"

"What more can she do? She already divorced you. And took the house. It can't get any worse than that."

"This isn't funny, Sky. God dammit, you're only fourteen. I figured you were out getting tea and crumpets or something. And you do this?"

"Well, what about you? You were supposed to meet the solicitor about the inheritance and instead you go play tennis – I mean, big fucking surprise there, right? – and you come back with your ankle all fucked up. So I guess, what, we're even, right? Although, frankly, mine looks a whole lot better than yours."

"If you want to look like a … tramp." I can't think of anything else, I'm so mad, but for some reason this sets her off.

"Shut up!" She kicks her leg up and starts punching me, so I retaliate by grabbing at her, more in self-defense than anything. Sky is way stronger than I remember and things are getting out of hand, with the end table toppling over and a glass bowl of wrapped sweets going flying, when I hear another voice cry out.

"Please, will you both please, stop this!"

Startled, Sky and I do stop, and we turn to see Mrs. Chatterjee standing behind us. She is holding a small object that, upon closer examination, I realize might pass for a bag of ice. But only if the patient is the size of a small rodent. The plastic sleeve is something that could be used to purchase a few ounces of loose tea, maybe Darjeeling, and the ice inside would, in a pinch, fill a small glass tumbler, perhaps for a Pimm's Cup. I also realize that Mrs. Chatterjee has likely been standing there for some time.

"Here is your ice, Mr. Davis," she says, quickly handing it to me. With that, she hustles away in a cascade of gold bangles and a perfume cloud of lotus and patchouli.

The pouch of ice barely registers as cold on my right palm. Sky regards it and cracks up. "Good luck with that," she says.

11

I sit up in bed and readjust the proper ice bag Sky brought back to the room with the Indian takeout, after much coaxing on my part. It may be coals to Newcastle but I didn't feel like asking Mrs. Chatterjee if she had any extra dinner for purchase after she witnessed me and Sky having it out in the television lounge. And we were both hungry. I look across and see Sky is fast asleep. According to my watch it's 8.45 p.m. The light through the window is finally starting to seem more like evening than daytime and I'm reminded how much farther north London is compared to San Francisco.

I can't say the ankle feels better – certainly not worth testing with weight – but at least it's numbed up enough to fool me into thinking so. I'm beyond tired, and I consider turning in myself, but I figure if I force myself to stay awake until ten, I'll have a better chance of sleeping through the night.

I roll off the bed and perform my now-practiced hop to the door, grabbing the room key and shutting off the light as I go. Fortunately, we're on the 2nd floor so it's only one set of stairs down to the television lounge.

The lounge is occupied by a large, pale man – I'd guess German if I had to – and a blond, blue-eyed boy of around eight. They are watching something on ITV or another independent channel, given the advertisement playing. These ads, I recall, can run for several minutes, as the commercial interruptions are less frequent on British television.

"Hi. Do you mind if I check the Wimbledon coverage while you're waiting for your program?" I say it as politely as possible but the man frowns.

"We're watching a movie."

By his accent, I'm now guessing Dutch, although it could be Swiss for all I know. It's a fun game to play, if one is in the mood. Which I'm not.

"I understand. I just thought it would be okay to check the tennis score while these ads run."

"It's too late for tennis – look." He motions to the window where the light is much diminished.

"They sometimes play past nine. I just thought if I flipped over and back, real fast."

The man shakes his head, as the boy continues to stare at a Shreddies breakfast cereal ad.

"Our program will be over soon. You can watch the TV then."

I nod. In a perfect world, I'd go back to my room or downstairs to wait it out. I really don't want to hang out here in the spare arm-chair with these people. But in a perfect world we'd be in a hotel with a TV in our room. Actually, in a perfect world we wouldn't even be in London, at least not under these circumstances. But who expects perfection? Certainly not me. Although I wouldn't mind something a little closer to it than the seedy, overcrowded television lounge of the Viceroy Guesthouse.

After a seeming eternity the stream of ads finally ends and the program resumes. It takes a moment, then I realize it's Renée Zellweger in *Bridget Jones's Diary*. Not a bad movie, really, but as I watch her in a skimpy negligée cavort around her character's bed-room dropping f-bombs, I notice the kid's bewildered expression.

"Do you think this is appropriate?"

The man looks at me, unsure what I mean, and I indicate his boy. He looks at his kid then gives me a world-weary expression.

"My wife … she requires some time alone."

"I hear you, brother."

"Please?" he says, confused.

"Marriage. I feel your pain."

"Thank you." He stares at the screen, then looks back at me. "Who was playing in Wimbledon today?"

"A lot of folks. Where are you from?"

"Belgium."

"I think one of your guys was going this afternoon – Malisse."

"Xavier Malisse? He is from West Flanders. This is our region. Bruges."

"Right, Bruges – famous."

The man watches the movie a moment, then asks: "You have been to Belgium?"

"Brussels. Great beer. And the *moules, frites* – incredible. But not Bruges, no. I think my dad was in the Ardennes during the war."

"The Second World War?"

"Yeah. Not the first. I'm not that old."

He chuckles. "You are American?"

"Depends on who you ask." I smile with an apologetic shrug. "Yes."

He pauses, considering.

"Would you still like to see the tennis?"

I look at his kid, then back at him. "You sure?"

He nods sincerely. I lean towards the set, managing to just reach it by pivoting on my left foot, and punch the channel over to BBC Two.

The coverage is of a woman's match on Centre Court, a Slovakian, Daniela Hantuchova, against an American, Vania King. The scoreboard shows King won the first set in a tiebreaker and she is up 6-5 in the second set, but Hantuchova is serving at 40-15 to force another tiebreaker. Both women, I recall, are strong doubles players with aggressive net games ideally suited to the grass. Hantuchova ends up winning the point on a deft forehand volley and the English announcer observes that with the waning light there will only be time to finish the match if King can secure the set. Coverage switches over to the No. 2 Court, where coincidentally Xavier Malisse is playing the wily Spanish veteran Juan Carlos Ferrero, a clay court specialist who has managed to adapt his game to hard courts and grass. The match is now in the fifth set, but Malisse is up 5-1 and serving for the win.

The man from Bruges says something to his son in Flemish incorporating Malisse's name in an excited tone. The boy nods politely, not sharing his father's enthusiasm but appreciating it just the same. I was concerned the kid would put up a fuss at not being able to finish the movie but he doesn't seem the least troubled.

"It's looking good for him," I say.

Xavier Malisse, his hair in a ponytail, serves at 40-love. He cracks a serve that Ferrero returns into the net and the match belongs to the Belgian.

"*Ja, fantastiche!*" the father says. "He won!"

The kid says something to his father in Flemish with the word *kamer*, which I assume means room. The dad nods yes and they both get up to go.

"Thank you very much," the father says to me. He has a sincerity to his expression that I find touching.

"You're welcome."

As the Belgians depart the television coverage returns to the women's match on Centre Court, with Hantuchova up 3-2 in the tiebreaker. She takes the next point after King misses a relatively easy ball and the BBC commentator notes that visibility is no doubt becoming a problem for the players. The two women change ends and, if to emphasize the point, the coverage flips to a men's singles match on Court 18 that is being suspended at two sets all for lack of light. John Isner, an outsized American with a boyish grin, has just won a fourth set tiebreaker against a Frenchman I've never heard of, Nicolas Mahut. The umpire hops down from his chair as the two players stuff their racquets in their bags after nearly three hours of tennis. Looking at the score, I see Mahut did well to win the second set 6-3. At 6 foot 10 inches, Isner possesses a fearsome serve that is even harder to return on grass. I imagine the Frenchman is relieved he will have good daylight tomorrow for a chance at a first round upset.

I hear the familiar rustling and tinkling of Mrs. Chatterjee as she enters the lounge.

"Excuse me, Mr. Davis. Might I have a word with you, please?"

"Sure." I use my left leg to bridge the distance to the television to shut it off. I plop myself back on the sofa and shrug my shoulders apologetically. "Please forgive me for remaining seated. This ankle."

"That is fine," she says. But from her tight-lipped expression I can tell things are anything but fine.

"Is there a problem?" I say.

"Mr. Davis, I am afraid I must ask you to find another hotel."

Huh? Come again?

"Mrs. Chatterjee, my daughter is asleep in our room. I don't understand."

"You may stay tonight but please, not for tomorrow. This is a respectable establishment and we do not allow any hanky-panky."

"Hanky-panky? What are you talking about?"

"Please, Mr. Davis. I am sorry for any inconvenience. Check-out time is ten o'clock in the morning."

And with that Mrs. Chatterjee turns and quickly disappears down the stairs. I had no idea someone in a sari with all that jewelry could move that fast.

If I didn't have a severely sprained ankle I might go after her, but as my foggy brain tries to make sense of what just transpired, I reassure myself there are hundreds of budget places to stay in London. At worst this is a minor inconvenience, but still. I mean, Christ almighty. I shake my head and laugh. There's really nothing else to do.

"Hanky-panky?" I say out loud, for no reason but to hear the words again for my own amusement. "Are you fucking kidding me?"

I glance at my watch: ten past nine. Since my conversation with Ronnie I've been debating making a call. And I figured anything before nine-thirty is still okay. I've been waffling though, chickening out really, but now that I've been taken for some version of Humbert Humbert by the New Delhi branch of the Moral Majority, I seem to have found the resolve I need. I pull out my phone and dial 118.

After a series of automated voice recordings and requests for confirmation that I'll be charged for the call, I manage to get a human operator with a singsong female voice.

"Directory enquiries, what city please?"

"Um, I'd like to look up a number near Falmouth, Cornwall."

"What name, please?"

"Can you try Francesca Kenwyn? Or Smith."

"Which name is it?"

"Um, can you try both?"

There's a pause with some keyboard stroke sounds, then: "I have a listing for a Francesca Kenwyn-Lloyd in Penryn."

Bingo – right on the nose! Jesus, now what?

"Shall I ring the number?"

"What? No, wait… um… okay, yes."

"Connecting, thank you." The operator's voice trills off the line and is replaced by the distinctive double ringback tone of an English telephone. *Brrring-brrring… brrring-brrring.*

Of the telling cultural differences between Britain and America, this one seems the most succinct. The American phone's ring is uniform, patient, open – even friendly. *Riiiiing… riiiiing… riiiiing.* The British ring is clipped, insistent – almost formal. *Brrring-brrring… brrring-brrring… brrring-brrring.*

After about a dozen cycles of this, when I'm sure there will be no answer, there is.

"Hello?" It's a voice partly a man's and partly a boy's. Mature in depth but not self-assurance.

"Hello. I'm calling for Francesca. Is she there by any chance?"

"Just a second."

Holy Jesus. The phone receiver goes down on something hard, perhaps stone, with a loud *claacck* that reverberates in my left eardrum, and then I hear footsteps diminishing. Then, faintly, the gruff sound of "Mom" being called, and an answer in a woman's voice, with frustration, "Who is it?" The thumping footsteps resume, get closer, then:

"She wants to know who's calling."

"You can tell her an old friend."

This time he shouts it out – "An old friend!" – and I hear some muffled conversation then a new set of footsteps. Oh Christ. This is really it, isn't it?

"Hello? Who's calling please?"

"Frankie?"

Silence on the other end of the line.

"Trevor? Is that you?"

"Yes. Hi. How are you?"

"What? I'm fine. My God, how on earth did you get this number?"

"It wasn't that hard. You're listed."

"Am I? Oh dear. Right, well, we'll have to fix that."

I laugh.

"It's good to hear your voice," I say.

"Is it? I can't imagine why. Jesus. Trevor. Is everything alright?"

"I guess. I mean, that's a relative question, isn't it?"

It's her turn to laugh. "Yes, I suppose it is."

Wednesday

(Love-30)

12

There are at least a dozen trains each day from London to Penzance, but only one called the Cornish Riviera. As far as I know it has run continuously for well over a century – always departing Paddington Station just after ten in the morning – with that reassuring constancy that England still represents. Sky and I sit opposite each other in 2nd class window seats as a Great Western platform conductor blows his whistle and another slams the carriage door shut with a solid *thwunk*. The view out the window shows we are moving – you couldn't tell if you shut your eyes, it's that smooth a departure – and I check my watch. 10.08 a.m. Just two minutes late by the printed schedule in my right hand. A scandal by Swiss railroad standards but I'm more forgiving.

The one time I rode this train before was with Frankie in the summer of 1989. We were in the heyday of our relationship and she was showing me where she grew up and, not incidentally, introducing me to her family. It was a warm day as well, but without air conditioning in the railway carriage, so by the afternoon as the train rumbled through Devon, passengers were lowering windows to create some flow. Not that Frankie and I minded. We were in love, passionately so, and on vacation. It was all we could do to keep from mauling each other on the long train journey and the heat and the smell of wild honeysuckle only heightened the emotion. We felt as dreamy and primal as a couple in a Terrence Malick film. There was a lot of hand holding and nuzzling and gazing into each other's eyes. Anyone nearby watching us carry on like that might have been amused or annoyed, but it wouldn't have mattered. If there's a binary version of solipsism, with two souls imagining they're the center of the universe, we were believers.

This train car has air conditioning, however, chilling it to the temperature of a subterranean wine cave. I'm glad I wore jeans and not shorts, but Sky shivers in her cotton blouse, short skirt and sandals. My right foot is propped up on the seat next to Sky and when I try to readjust it the result is only to annoy her and send a fresh spasm of pain through my ankle. We were fortunate to find a traveler's wheelchair where our taxi dropped us off, although I found myself suffering a significant loss of dignity to use it. Sky had no such qualms, taking definite pleasure in my helplessness (the very definition, in fact, of that absurdly overused German word), but she soon tired of pushing me about the platform.

"Why couldn't I just ride in London?" she says.

"Wait until you see this place. They have real horses, not a stable full of rental nags."

"I'm not stupid, Dad. This isn't about horses. This is about you seeing your old girlfriend."

"That was a long time ago."

"But she *was* your girlfriend."

"Hey, you said I should move on. So I'm moving on."

I'm joking of course and Sky knows it but she still furrows her brow. She digs in her satchel for a sweater, which she pulls on, then she resumes reading the YA novel she had on the plane. She's been fuming about not having her smartphone since I collected her from riding camp but I'm secretly pleased she's rediscovered how to read a real book.

After she woke up this morning, I broke it to Sky that we'd need to find new lodging. While this wasn't exactly heartbreaking news, given her low opinion of the Viceroy Guesthouse, she still required some persuading to pack for a five-hour train trip. The prospect of riding a thoroughbred on a real English country estate had been the incentive, but I suspect Sky was actually more curious about my old flame than she let on. Sky was vaguely familiar with the name Francesca, having heard Annie joke about her years ago in the way secure married couples sometimes do in front of their kids. But I imagine she is somewhat shocked that I have reached out to her on this trip.

Well, I suppose that makes three of us.

Last night, as Frankie and I each got over the strangeness of hearing our once-familiar voices, I briefly explained why I was in London and how Ronnie had told me she was back in Cornwall. And of course I expressed how sorry I was to hear about her loss, but she quickly brushed aside any discussion of her late husband. We talked a bit about our kids and then I screwed up the courage to make my request: might Sky and I visit by train the next day? We had to change lodging, I explained, and I didn't need to be back in London until late Thursday morning. If she wasn't inconvenienced, I thought we could visit in the afternoon and then take the night train back to London. Riding in a sleeper carriage might be fun for Sky, I said. I didn't also mention that this would save us the cost of a hotel room.

Frankie was understandably taken aback by my proposal. Her initial response was to claim she had an afternoon appointment in Falmouth, something she wasn't sure she could reschedule, but I believe I detected a reciprocal curiosity on her part about Sky. Sky's interest in horses ultimately gave Frankie enough pretext to extend an invitation, once I assured her I was serious and then only after admonishing me, tongue-in-cheek, for being one of those "presumptuous Americans who invite themselves to people's houses while on holiday."

Frankie was always passionate about animals. When I first met her she was doing an internship at the Marine Mammal Center in Sausalito while she contemplated pursuing a veterinary degree at Davis. I don't know if she ever followed through on that ambition in England – we parted ways after she'd deferred admission a few times – but I suppose I'll find out this afternoon.

Jesus. Frankie. My Frankie. Well, she's hardly that anymore, with a dead Army officer husband and three kids. But still. Am I really going to see her again? In a matter of *hours*?

Sky faces the direction of our travel – her preference – and now that we're beyond Paddington's shunting yards and accelerating, it's an unfamiliar sensation to be traveling backwards so rapidly. The seats next to us are empty but a woman and a boy of about eleven occupy the aisle seats. They have the same olive skin and dark hair, and speak to each other in Spanish, not the

Mexican variety I'm used to hearing but full-on Castilian with those oddly comical sibilant lisps. By the woman's attentiveness – she's already doling out Cadbury treats – I assume she's the boy's mother. But you never know; Mrs. Chatterjee might conclude a more nefarious relationship exists. The woman meets my gaze and we exchange smiles.

"*Buenas dias,*" I say.

"*Buenas dias,*" she says. "*Hablas español?*"

"*No, solomente inglés. Bueno, un poco de francés. Pero nada de español.*"

The woman looks at me with a puzzled expression, then nods her head slowly, as if to simulate understanding, and returns her attention to the boy.

"What are you doing?" Sky whispers at me.

"Being polite."

"No, you're being weird. And since when do you speak Spanish?"

"I don't."

"Exactly."

"Well, you can't do construction in California without picking up a little."

"Dad, should I be worried? Maybe when you sprained your ankle you landed on your head."

I smile at Sky to reassure her – of what, exactly, I'm not sure – and I reach for my paperback edition of *The Sun Also Rises*. Sky sighs dramatically and turns her attention back to her book.

On the Virgin flight I started re-reading the novel but I was too distracted by the events of the day to let myself get sucked into it. Now, as I try again to reacquaint myself with Jake Barnes and Robert Cohn, it seems both an eternity since I read the book last – was it in college? – and something closer to a week. It's a distressingly common occurrence for me lately, this collapsing of personal space and time. The specifics of the Hemingway story have slipped from my memory: how many cafés and in which arrondissement the characters visit, and what kind of drinks they order. But the atmosphere and prose are extremely familiar, as well as the characters themselves. I could be back in Sproul Plaza on the Berkeley campus, soaking up the sun and reading, transported to Pamplona, while I wait for Valerie Pelletier, who was my girl-friend my sophomore year.

Why did I not end up with Valerie, or Rachel Adler who I dated after graduating, but Frankie, until I didn't? And then why not Susan Jenkins or Molly Dwyer, each wonderful in her own way, but Annie? My father and I used to talk about women sometimes, especially when I was between them, and he believed timing was everything. That is, after you factor in all the obvious stuff, like looks and brains and humor and values and chemistry. I suppose I could have committed to any of a handful of women other than Annie, who I married at thirty-three, but there was always something holding me back. Maybe it was timing – it's difficult to tie yourself down in your twenties when you aren't sure who you are, much less the other person – but in Frankie's case I had no doubts. And, so it seemed, neither did she. We wanted to spend the rest of our lives together and we talked in those terms. Kids, what the house would look like, the whole nine yards. Not some adolescent fantasy, but maturely, thoughtfully. Or so it seemed.

Which is a way of saying that I still do not understand why Frankie and I parted ways. Not that I didn't get over it. I did, as reasonably well-adjusted people do, after a period of heartache and mourning. The distractions and support and engagement of work and friends and family and, eventually, a new lover provided sufficient balm, and with time I moved on. When Annie entered my life I was myself again, or at least an older, wiser and more humble version. She'd had her own experiences as well and so we each brought to the other a sense of what we wanted and what we didn't. There was a wonderful chemistry, different to be sure but magical in its own way, and all those other givens. And, thankfully, the timing was right.

I look at Sky, engrossed in her book, and a surge of love and gratitude for her and for Abby swells yet again in my heart. They have been my saving grace through the dark days of divorce and not for the first time I wonder how I could have made it without them. Even Sky with her anger and angst – even all that, I'd like to think – is tolerable for what she adds to my life. My mother used to joke about me and Meg, when we were adolescents in Oxford and acting stroppy, that she wouldn't give anyone tuppence for another child and she wouldn't take a million guineas for either one of us. Fair enough, mom, I'd like to tell her now. Fair enough.

After Sky wheeled me up to the big departures board in Paddington, and we located our platform number, I continued to stare at the LED display in dismay. Who decided this was an improvement over the old display, with those split-flaps that updated with a loud *clack-clack-clack-clack-clack*? Feeling nostalgic, I noticed the statue of Paddington Bear and implored Sky to push me to it. She resisted and rolled her eyes of course, but I reminded her how I'd read the books to her and Abby when they were little, just as my mother had to Meg and me, and sentimentality finally overcame sophistication.

"Aw, how cute," Sky said with sarcasm, her way of forgiving herself for giving in to me. But it's true – the bear *was* cute. Forget for a moment the implicit middlebrow chauvinism of a domesticated bear from 'Darkest Peru' shipping out to a better life in England, or even the bourgeois preoccupations of the Brown family, with their nanny and their kids off at boarding school, despite a stay-at-home mom. The fact that the bear wanted so badly to be English, from his daily cocoa at elevenses with Mr. Gruber, to his ever-present jar of marmalade, was downright precious. And it begged the obvious question: what right-thinking soul – animal or human – *wouldn't* want to be English? Listening to my mother reading us Paddington's adventures, all tucked up in bed, I certainly did. I no longer had her accent – that got erased within weeks of starting kindergarten – and we lived in Los Angeles, a city incorporated after the birth of Queen Victoria's eldest son, for goodness sakes – but I still felt sort of English or at least a pretense to it. How ironic then – or is it fitting? – that when I was dragged there at the start of our Oxford Wilderness Period the yearning had passed. Completely. By fifteen I was fully American, inspired by Watergate to revere the Constitution, loyal to the Dodgers and the Lakers (and my father's Bruins), and openly scornful of British sports like cricket, where you wore white trousers and interrupted play to have tea. It might have been fine as a child to read Paddington Bear, but now I was lining up on Wilshire Boulevard with my buddies to watch *Star Wars*. Sure, the mincing metallic robot had an English accent, but that was for comic relief. The real hero was Han Solo, an American cowboy if ever there was. With role models like that, who wanted to be English?

But Oxford was my new reality and there was nothing to do about it but cope. And tennis became my coping mechanism. The more I played, the better I got. The game doesn't care whether you're practicing to escape or out of genuine passion for the sport. And the fact is, I *did* care about tennis. But as with a woman who responds to your touch, it's sometimes hard to separate your feelings about the object of your affection from the pride her reaction induces in you. And in Oxford, as the only tennis-playing American in my school, people behaved differently towards me because of it. I may have been the outsider, *that fucking Yank* or a *bloody wanker* to my more xenophobic classmates like Stomper, but on the court I was doing the school colors – white and navy blue – proud. School tournaments evolved into club tournaments and before long I was playing county events and winning. On the county level my status as an American was irrelevant. I was an Oxfordshire tennis player, with a typically British name and, in case anyone wondered, an English mother, playing the modern game invented by a Welshman and perfected on the lawns of Wimbledon. Maybe I hadn't fully surrendered my American identity, and Lord knows I was still lonely, but I'd found the ideal way to fit in. And isn't that what high school is all about?

At the end of my fifth form year my coach at the St. Clements Tennis Club, Richard Foxworthy, put me up for the British Schoolboys Championships. Organized under the auspices of the LTA, high school boys competed locally in singles and doubles, with the winners from each county – there are about forty of them – playing for the overall title on the grounds of Wimbledon immediately following the professional tournament. I'd been a dues-paying LTA member since my fourth form so there was nothing more to do; Richard simply entered me along with a couple of other boys he coached.

The level of competition in Oxfordshire was considered strong, given the population of the county and the number of grass courts in and around the University's grounds. I'd played most of the other boys already, always a benefit, and I was further aided by a growth spurt that saw me shoot up several inches since January, to nearly six feet. For a serve and volleyer, height is very useful. Yet even with those advantages, it never hurts to have some luck. My strongest opponent, Hal Abramson, picked up a stomach bug the evening before our semifinal match and was not at his best. But I also believe I wanted it more than anyone else, and in the end that might have made the crucial difference. For on June 23, 1978, I defeated Roy Curtis 6-4, 3-6, 7-5, to become the boys' singles champion for Oxfordshire.

Richard, my coach, couldn't have been more pleased – that's as elated as a middle-class Englishman permits himself to get – and my parents were understandably proud of me, knowing how much effort I'd put into improving my tennis. I was certainly happy, but what I was secretly thrilled about was the prospect of playing at Wimbledon. I'd never been there before, not even for a quick visit since we'd moved to England, and I'd grown up watching the championships on television back in Los Angeles. Because of the time difference the finals were always broadcast on NBC as *Breakfast at Wimbledon*, which might have made sense for the East Coast at 9 a.m., but made for a very early meal at 6 a.m. Nevertheless, I always made sure to set my clock radio to wake me up in time to watch the match, whether it was Jimmy Connors against Arthur Ashe, Billie Jean King against Evonne Goolagong or Stan Smith against Ilie Nastase. The American commentators made clear this was the most important major, that the English spectators were the most knowledgeable, and that the event was the most refined. No *Breakfast at Wimbledon* broadcast was complete without showing the strawberries and cream dispensed by the bowlful on the grounds. Imagine that – at Chavez Ravine you ate Dodger Dogs but at Wimbledon it was strawberries and cream. After all, a private club hosted the event, but not just any club – The All England Lawn Tennis and Croquet Club. With a name like that, what else could be served? Still, you couldn't begrudge the Brits their tradition, you could only admire it. Especially the way they carried it off, with so much poise and class. The class part was driven home after each finals, when actual royalty descended from their royal box, usually in the form of the Duke or Duchess of Kent, to deliver the trophy to the champion. And of course the champion would bow (or curtsy) when receiving that trophy. The unspoken message seemed to be: you might be the best player in the world, tennis royalty if you will, but you'll never be equal to one of us. Besides, it was surely a small price to pay, a modest dent to one's self-esteem, some minor dissage, as Sky and her contemporaries might say, in order to be crowned champion. Indeed, no one ever refused to genuflect. And in addition to the prize money, a million pounds to each of the winners this year, the club confers honorary membership. So you can be a complete outsider – even a crass American like John McEnroe or Andre Agassi – and belong to the All England Club. Just by winning the tournament. Incredible! It's not exactly a declaration of equality, but given the circumstances it's not too shabby either.

After winning the Oxfordshire boys' title, I spent the next week training at St. Clements with Richard Foxworthy and watching the pros progress through their Wimbledon rounds on television. Unlike with *Breakfast at Wimbledon*, the BBC covered the tennis from Day 1, but with very little actual commentary. In keeping with the decorum of the event, a terrific point might be met with polite applause from the crowd and a simple observation from John Barrett in the BBC broadcast booth, something like: "Borg's backhand looks as sharp as we've seen it." And in '78 it was indeed sharp, along with the rest of Bjorn Borg's game. A two-time defending champion, he was the favorite to win a third. The only player in his league seemed to be Jimmy Connors. On the ladies' side everyone was still giddy from Virginia Wade's victory the year before. It was too much to expect a repeat English champion, especially with Chris Evert and Martina Navratilova in the draw, but British fans could hope.

In the middle of the second week, as I packed for London, Richard Foxworthy rang our house on Observatory Street and asked if he could come by for a visit. That was unusual – he'd never been to our house before – but I figured he just wanted to make sure I was prepared. He'd be coming to Wimbledon for the

Schoolboys Tournament, even though I was making the actual train trip the next day with my parents. I can't recall if Meg was coming too, as my tennis bored her.

As soon as Richard entered the house I knew something was wrong. He was normally a cheerful, easy-going fellow. A solid tennis player, nothing flashy, but the ideal coach for someone like me who'd needed to perfect the grass court game and learn how to keep my emotions under control. Nothing ruffled Richard's feathers. At that moment, however, he looked both angry and lost, like someone had kidnapped his only child and left a garbled ransom note.

My parents invited him into the living room and as he sat, my mother offered to make tea. But Richard declined – his news just couldn't wait. My God, even a Luftwaffe air raid wouldn't prevent an Englishman from having tea. After a couple of stammers and stutters, Richard managed to get it out: the LTA had learned I was American and was threatening to deny me entry into the tournament.

"On what basis?" my father demanded to know. I was too dumbfounded to process what was happening so he did the talking for me.

It seemed, Richard said, on the basis that the tournament was for British schoolboys.

"British by residence or citizenship?" my father continued. At that moment, I'm not sure which was more unsettling to me: the prospect of not competing at Wimbledon or my father's newfound, take-charge manner. All I had seen since our arrival in Oxford was lassitude on his part. It was as if, having lacked any purpose in his life for months on end, my father finally had something meaningful to sink his teeth into.

Richard confessed his own unfamiliarity with the rules and told us that, as far as he was aware, the issue had never come up before. And he also wondered if he could still have that cup of tea, which I took to be a positive development.

Before Richard left our house, three things were clarified. One, that he was firmly in my camp and would do whatever he could to convince the LTA that I should be allowed to participate. Two, that the rules made absolutely no mention of citizenship and instead specified guidelines for a tennis tournament "to be contested by schoolboys from the various British counties." And three, as far as I was concerned, if necessary I was prepared to renounce my American citizenship and pledge eternal loyalty to Queen Elizabeth II herself.

The irony – and injustice – wasn't lost on me that the previous year I'd actually participated in the Queen's Silver Jubilee, when celebrations across Britain involved nearly every town and village. Twenty-five years on the throne was a laudable achievement by any monarch, especially one as beloved as Elizabeth, and the Britain of 1977 certainly needed a reason to throw a party. During the Queen's visit to Oxford there were parades and a ribbon cutting for a new hospital wing and, on the suggestion of the University sports director, a demonstration of lawn tennis on the grounds of Magdalen College. I didn't get to shake the Queen's hand but a group of us did present her with a bouquet of flowers. And Prince Philip winked at me, I'll swear to it.

But apparently that wasn't enough. Because the next day, when I should have been boarding the train at Oxford Station for the trip to Paddington, Richard was back at our house looking more morose than before. The LTA's Board of Governors had convened on the matter, he told us, and had issued their ruling. Even though the rules made no mention of citizenship, the 'spirit' of the tournament required it. Otherwise, I inferred, some uppity foreigner bent on usurping English glory might contrive to gain residency, enroll at a British school and enter the contest. The rules, of course, would henceforth be amended to clarify the point. But no exception would be made in my case.

Richard tried to console me by sharing that a debate was now raging on the Oxfordshire county level as to whether to withdraw its entry altogether. He was firmly in the camp protesting the LTA decision and was hoping to carry the day with his Oxford colleagues, but that hardly mattered to me. Whether Roy Curtis, the runner-up, represented Oxfordshire in my stead or not, I wouldn't be playing. LTA National had ruled on that point and wasn't going to budge.

To this day, I have no idea who ratted me out or why. I do know for a fact that plenty of boys who played in prior schoolboys tournaments were only British residents like me. But the rumor was, once the LTA learned about me, its chairman, Lawrence J. T. Willoughby, OBE, decided to clamp down hard. Call it coincidence, but Willoughby was the last Englishman to seriously contest for the men's singles title at Wimbledon after Fred Perry. And the opponent who beat him? Jack Kramer, arguably the greatest tennis player ever to come out of Los Angeles.

The train engine suddenly stops pulling, creating a sensation of floating, and the conductor announces the next stop will be Reading. Sky looks up from her book and frowns.

"Are we close?"

"Closer," I say.

I stretch my leg and accidentally tap Sky's hip with my foot.

"Ow!" we both say in unison. She pushes my foot away, which hurts even more.

"Stop! That really hurts!"

"Well keep your goddamned foot to yourself!" she says.

I notice the Spanish mother looking at us, either with concern or curiosity, but when I meet her gaze she immediately turns away. It reminds me of a trip I once took to Japan, when people would openly stare at me in the subway or on the street, but if I looked back they averted their eyes. When I mentioned it to my Japanese host, an investor in one of our building projects, he told me that a crowded island civilization needs a fairly rigid social structure to function, including a deep respect for privacy. But, he explained, people were also curious about me since I looked so foreign. I remember thinking about this in relation to the insular island nation I knew best – Great Britain. What was it that bothered the English so much about my Americanness? I certainly looked like most of them and, while I talked differently, it wasn't like they couldn't understand me. In California people were constantly telling my mother what a wonderful accent she had – literally asking her to "say something" since it sounded so cool – but all I got in Oxford was either ridicule or, at best, tolerance for how I spoke.

You could say my exclusion from the British Schoolboys Championships was the beginning of the end of our Oxford Wilderness Period. It seemed to light a fire under my father to get his career back on track, and I guess my parents figured the risk to their assets from the start-up loan guarantee had finally passed. While I initially took the LTA snub hard, believing I'd been wronged, my life actually improved as a result. My family rallied round me, including my sister – a minor miracle in itself – and my school and tennis communities were more than sympathetic. Once our family made the decision to return to the States, England somehow became more palatable to me. I won't say I was sorry to leave, but as the departure date loomed I found myself feeling something close to wistful about my time in Oxford. By that point the pain of the LTA decision had dulled and I was looking forward to collegiate tennis. The Schoolboys Championships, in retrospect, seemed small potatoes compared to the NCAA. I actually felt more sorry for Richard Foxworthy. He'd transitioned from competitive playing to coaching years ago so now his victories were purely vicarious. What if I'd been his most promising prospect? What if, had I gone to Wimbledon as planned, I might have won it all? Instead I would forever be that unresolved question mark, the 'what might have been?' in his coaching career.

"So why did you stop seeing this woman?" Sky's question is a bolt from the blue and I look at her with a dazed expression.

"What?"

"You heard me. Why?"

"Well… it's complicated."

"Not good enough. You stuck me on this stupid train, so the least you can do is answer my question."

"Listen, Sky, I'm not going to submit to your interrogation like some accused criminal."

Sky softens her face and give me a mannered smile.

"Okay. I'm just curious, father dear, why you didn't end up with her. Would you be so kind as to enlighten me?"

"I didn't end up with your mother either."

Sky makes a jarring sound like a game show buzzer. "Sorry, you're not getting off that easy." She tries a faux-sweet, beseeching tone. "Come on, I'd really like to know. I mean, you're my dad and I should find out more about you."

"So you'll tell me about your love life?"

She rolls her eyes.

"As if."

"As if you have one or as if you'll share?"

"Nice try," she says, "but you are so blatantly changing the subject. And all that tells me is this shit is big."

I stare at her a moment, deciding how to respond. I really don't want to talk about it, and certainly not with my more precocious teenage daughter, for any number of reasons. But I suppose she does deserve some kind of answer.

"Okay, the truth is most likely I would have married Frankie. But she moved back to England."

"Why?"

"Because that's where she was from and she missed her family and she wanted to get on with her career and she wasn't sure she wanted to live in America forever. But chiefly because her student visa ran out."

"So why didn't you go back with her?"

"Jesus, Sky! I don't know, because I had a job in San Francisco and I was building my career and maybe I wasn't ready to make that kind of decision so fast."

"But if you really loved her all that stuff shouldn't have mattered, right?"

"Hey, if I hadn't stayed and met your mom, you wouldn't even be here! You seem disappointed by the outcome."

Sky gives me an impatient look, as if to say, why are you trying so hard to avoid the subject?

"This is hard for me to talk about," I say.

"I get that."

I look out the window. We are slowing more and the Reading Station platform is just coming into view. I sigh, then I look back at Sky and speak to her as the young adult she is so rapidly becoming.

"Sometimes in life we make decisions we regret. The problem is, we're either not sure how to fix it or it's too late."

The train's brakes are applied in earnest and we come to a stop with a double-barreled *thump-thump*. Except for the faint sound of a carriage door opening several cars away, there is an eerie quiet stillness. No one in our car gets up and no one enters. I look at Sky and she looks right back at me. I believe I see my pain reflected in her eyes. With perhaps some panic of her own.

"Can I do anything?" she asks, in a tone close to a whisper.

I smile. "More than you realize."

13

I n June of 1979, before we returned to California, our family took a rail holiday in Europe. In those pre-Channel Tunnel days it wasn't fashionable in Britain to consider itself part of Europe, even though it was a member of the EEC. So you said you were traveling on the Continent. Anyway, we hadn't done that since we'd arrived in Oxford – money was tight and my folks figured there was plenty to see in England – but now that my father had secured a teaching job back at UCLA he was in a more celebratory mood. And my mother wanted to visit France. It wasn't a fancy trip – we travelled on 2nd class Eurail passes and stayed in the sort of budget hotels that made the Viceroy Guesthouse look posh – but it was a welcome breath of fresh air.

My mother, I realize now, had become something of the forgotten soldier during our Oxford Wilderness Years. Like the caregiver for a chronically ill patient, she did most of the behind-the-scenes work that kept our family going but received no credit for it. And with absolutely no whinging on her part, as the Aussies say. In the debate between nature and nurture, if we use the example of my mother's British stiff upper lip, nurture wins hands down. You had to remind yourself that she'd been born French.

Which isn't to say she wasn't complex. If we're okay making generalizations, and I guess I've already crossed that line, then there was plenty of the Gallic spirit in my mother as well. She could be excitable, argumentative, vain and needlessly intellectual – the sort of qualities one associates with a Parisian boulevardier, not a levelheaded Londoner. But her fortitude and capacity for hard work would have put Winston Churchill to shame. She'd talked her way into Shepperton Studios at eighteen and worked her way up to script supervisor, then quit and emigrated from

England four years later when she tired of post-war rationing and British servility. Eventually arriving in Hollywood with £500 and a large suitcase, she waltzed onto the lot of Columbia Pictures without an introduction – the accent probably helped, with *The Bridge on the River Kwai* about to go into production – and started over on the bottom rung.

I had been sharing with Sky some reflections about my mother and that long-ago rail holiday to France about the time the conductor called the next stop, Exeter St Davids. The rustling of gourmet sandwich wrappers by the Spaniards must have finally gotten to Sky, for she complained she was hungry. We'd each had croissants and coffee from a café in Paddington before boarding but I'd neglected to buy food for the train. By my calculation, after checking out of the Viceroy and buying our rail tickets (round-trip) and breakfast, my CashPort had a balance of $880 remaining, not counting the fifteen pounds in cash in my wallet. I could have sent Sky to the buffet car, but much as privatized Great Western might be an improvement over its nationalized predecessor, I have terrible memories of the soggy sandwiches and other inedible offerings that British Rail used to inflict on the unsuspecting or the desperate. This train has a dining car, however, catering mainly – but not exclusively – to first class passengers, providing hot meals cooked in an onboard kitchen. It would be a splurge for sure – and therefore difficult to justify – but I felt Sky had been a trooper and deserved a reward. So she and I walked slowly to the dining car, with me using aisle seat headrests as hand support to keep my weight off my right foot. I managed to make the four carriage journey with a fairly respectable scorecard: one painful foot planting (to counteract a sudden sideways lurch), two scowls from aisle passengers whose heads I inadvertently brushed against, and three backwards frustrated looks from Sky for the inconvenience of it all.

Once in the dining car, I caught my breath and we sat down at a linen-covered table for two. With a flourish a fresh-faced waiter of about twenty-five named Gerald presented us with napkins and menus. A glass vase with fresh flowers sat on the table and an older couple at the table next to us smiled warmly. Very nice,

I thought. Then Sky and I scanned the menu. She immediately raised her right eyebrow.

"You sure we can afford this?" she said.

Each of the entrées cost more than twenty pounds, so even if we skipped appetizers we were looking at close to a hundred dollars with VAT and gratuity. My first impulse was to immediately excuse ourselves. I believe Sky would have understood. This was an expense that I wouldn't have thought twice about in the past. But things were different now. My mind performed the mental calculation unbidden: if we ate here this meal would use up roughly ten percent of my total net worth. Just as quick as the thought appeared, I banished it. Like Al Gore's inconvenient truth, dwelling on that sort of thing was pointless. Absolutely no good could come of it. Better to find reasons to justify our staying here. For instance, we weren't going to have to pay for a hotel room tonight and by tomorrow I'd have my meeting with Rupert Salmons. And the deeper truth was, whatever I spent my meager remaining funds on, they weren't going to last very long anyway. Why not enjoy a decent lunch, and economize on dinner later? The alternative would be truly depressing: running the gauntlet of aisle passengers back to our seats and then making do with a bag of crisps, our tummies growling more and more with each passing mile.

Finally I sighed. "It's all swings and roundabouts," I said.

"What does that mean?"

"Something my mother used to say. It's sort of like, what you lose here, you win somewhere else."

"So we can stay? I'm really hungry."

I was pretty famished as well, the result of three long sets of tennis yesterday.

"Sure. Let's order."

"Awesome!"

And order we did. Sky started with the Highland Scottish salmon smoked over Somerset oak, with capers, cornichons, Dorset cream cheese and rye bread. For her main course she ordered roast West Country free-range chicken with tarragon sauce. Thankfully, main courses came with potatoes and seasonal vegetables. I offered to order her a Coke but, bless her heart, she opted for the complimentary mineral water instead. I considered skipping the appetizer but didn't want to leave Sky eating hers alone, so I selected the Bristol scallops, grilled in the shell with garlic and white wine, then for my main course opted for roasted breast of Devon duck, with orange and sage sauce. Gerald suggested a half bottle of Sancerre with such earnestness that I could hardly refuse. And in truth it seemed a relative bargain at sixteen pounds.

Sitting back, I marveled at the attention to detail in the décor and menu descriptions. This was so far removed from the Britain of the 1970s that it might as well be a different country. Perhaps the great cultural achievement of the Channel Tunnel was exposing the average Englishman to decent food (and wine) by providing an easy way to get to France. In so doing, centuries of ignorance and fear about those 'garlic-eating Frogs' got swept aside. And once he acquired a taste for something better than tough, mealy lamb and bland, overcooked vegetables, that Englishman now demanded more at home. Back in London it seemed there was a gussied-up gastropub on every corner, each proudly displaying its daily menu of seasonal, locally sourced ingredients. When I was a kid the only thing safe to eat in a pub was a ploughman's lunch, typically a hunk of cheese, some chutney and a thick slice of Hovis bread. You ventured beyond that at your peril: the fish was of dubious origin and likely frozen, and was served battered and fried in the same tired cooking oil as the soggy chips. But now everyone was getting into the foodie scene, it seemed, even the Great Western Railway. Like the lyrics in that old World War One song go, "how ya gonna keep 'em down on the farm, after they've seen Pa-ree?"

And indeed our lunch did not disappoint. Sky's smoked salmon was delicious – she let me have a bite – with just a hint of dill, and my shellfish was tender and flavorful. Our portions were appropriate, not too generous, leaving us sufficient appetite for the main courses. Sky was served a whole leg of roast chicken, perfectly golden and juicy, with garlic and rosemary-seasoned new potatoes and barely crunchy broccolini. My duck breast was surprisingly moist and the orange sauce both bright and restrained, not cloying. With the nicely chilled Sancerre, I found myself enjoying the meal more than any in recent memory.

"This reminds me of a dinner I had with my family in Lyon, before we returned to the States," I said. "I think I ordered duck as well. *Canard à l'orange.*"

"Did you have wine?" Sky asked.

"Absolutely. I was almost eighteen. Even Aunt Meg had some."

"Can I try some of yours?"

I looked around the dining car. There weren't any teenagers, but hopefully no undercover cops either.

"Sure," I said, pushing my wine glass towards her.

She sniffed the contents and swirled the glass, as she'd seen me do countless times, then took a sip. She made a little pucker with her mouth after she swallowed.

"It's okay," she said. "I've had beer before, you know."

"And now you have a tattoo on your ankle."

"Meaning what?"

"Meaning you're making your own choices. You're not our little girl anymore. But just because your mom and I can't control what you and Abby do, it's not like that makes your lives easier. Sartre said man is condemned to be free."

Sky looked like she's about to make a sarcastic response but she became thoughtful instead.

"Do you think you and mom will ever get back together?"

"I honestly have no idea. Why? Is that what you'd like?"

"Isn't that what every child of divorce wants?"

"She seems pretty happy with this new guy."

Sky wrinkles her brow. "He's okay I suppose. I just want each of you to be happy."

I paused and looked her in the eyes, taking in perhaps a new-found maturity. If this was a by-product of the divorce, then maybe that's some form of silver lining.

"So do I, sweetheart. So do I."

Later, as we contemplated the dessert menu, I told Sky how my mother had been so excited to visit France again on that trip. She was like a giddy adolescent, reveling in each café pastry and every *Bonjour, Madame* from a shopkeeper. Her French came back at first slowly, and then in a torrent, as if the underground stream of what she'd studied in school in England was suddenly flooded with the snowmelt of her early childhood fluency, and had burst to the surface. She took great pleasure in politely correcting our pronunciation and never tired of interpreting all manner of conversations, whether with a bored museum attendant at the Louvre or a philosophizing bouquiniste along the Seine. To the oft-posed question, *Êtes-vous Anglaise?*, she would reply with a shrug and a mischievous smile: *C'est compliqué.*

Sky finally decided on the curiously named Chocolate Nemesis with Cornish clotted cream while I virtuously declined the West Country cheese plate (Caerphilly, Double Gloucester and Stilton) in favor of a cup of coffee. By this point I was starting to have a prickly premonition that the bill might significantly exceed my estimate, but Sky was enjoying her dessert so thoroughly, each spoonful of gooey chocolate and thick yellow cream resulting in an explosion of pure joy starting at her mouth and spreading across her face, that I chided myself for worrying about what was now a fait accompli.

We were leaving Plymouth and approaching the River Tamar, the border between Devon and Cornwall, when I caught Gerald's eye and requested the bill, adding half-humorously to "be kind." And we'd crossed over the massive iron railway bridge designed by the great Isambard Kingdom Brunel and were almost past Saltash when Gerald sheepishly returned, the bill discreetly hidden from view inside a thick leatherette folder embossed with the Great Western logo. Sky looked at me with apprehension while I peeked inside.

"Bad?"

I affected nonchalance. "Ain't no thang."

That elicited the desired eye roll, this time tempered with a generous smirk, but much as I tried to disguise my shock, the damage was staggering. Our meal, wine and coffee included, cost £92. With 17.5% VAT and a 12.5% service charge, that brought the total to £119.60. I ran the conversion into dollars in my head and mentally recoiled. I was looking at about $180. Pulling out the

CashPort in a sort of daze, I realized I'd underestimated the cost of lunch by a factor of *two*. Instead of using up ten percent of my entire net worth, it was closer to twenty.

Jesus, I thought. Twenty fucking percent. I tried to calm myself so as not to ruin for Sky the whole benefit of the extravagance. But still – holy mother of God. My daughter and I had just consumed, in one sitting, one-fifth of everything I own in this world. A fifth! No, I reminded myself again, that's not entirely true. You have to figure Aunt Philippa's inheritance goes on my balance sheet as well. It may not be a cash entry yet, but it's definitely an asset. And like I told Meg on Monday, you have to spend money to get it. Hell, we had to eat anyway and this will be money in the bank, so to speak, in generating goodwill with Sky. So no worries. It's all going to work out fine.

Gerald thanked us solemnly and Sky and I pushed back our chairs and rose to return to our seats. I felt a bit wobbly and protective of my ankle, but I didn't want Gerald to think I'd drunk too much, so I summoned as much coordination as possible to navigate the dining car without the waiter's assistance, although I was grateful for the arm Sky offered. Once through to the next carriage, I took a deep breath and carried on, as slowly and carefully as possible. The journey back to our carriage therefor took on a kind of funereal quality, and it did occur to me with gallows humor that a condemned man is traditionally granted a last meal. Stop it, that's mawkish thinking, I chastised myself. Self-indulgent and counter-productive. Look at these people sitting here, reading their newspapers and drinking their beer. They're probably on holiday. Or if not, they have worries of their own. Do they care what I had before, and how much I've lost? Of course not! Negativity will only produce negative results. I've paid for a fine meal because I'm positive about getting a good outcome. That's what people want to associate with – positivity. Remember what Coach McKittridge used to say: a winning mentality leads to winning. Visualize the ball going in. Just one point at a time. That's all it takes.

So. I'm back in my seat, have been for a while now. I try to relax my shoulders some more and allow the shock of the lunch expense to fully dissipate from my body. Sky almost immediately fell asleep when we returned and she's still dozing, in her looks-dead-as-a-possum mode. The Spanish mother and son are gone – perhaps they departed at Plymouth – so the view through the windows on both sides of the carriage is now unobstructed. As I focus on the scenery, I notice Cornwall is perceptibly different from the West Country counties we've already passed through. It's less developed, almost wild. The train is running slower which seems to reinforce a trip back in time. The towns are smaller and simpler and have names like Menheniot and Lostwithial, names you'd likely find in the Domesday Book by the look of them. We seem very far from the wealth and modernity and frenetic pace of London. Indeed, we seem no longer in England. This place is foreign.

I suddenly remember a long-forgotten geography lesson from Oxford. The master – what my school called its teachers – was a Cornishman. A small, older gentleman with a neatly trimmed, white beard, his name escapes me now but of his origin I am sure. Because he told us exactly where he was from, and I see it on the train schedule as the stop after ours: Redruth. He pronounced it Re-*druth*, not Red-ruth as it might seem. The lesson was on the original Celtic nations, which numbered six, Cornwall included. Our teacher – damn, I can't recall his name for the life of me – said with some pride (maybe tinged with sadness?) that there were still some native speakers of old Cornish alive. Now, I wonder, all these decades later, do any remain? Or has the language finally become extinct? And if so, what was the *real* lesson, apart from some obscure fact that is now a minor historical footnote or might even evolve into a slim chapter for linguistics scholars to pore over? That social Darwinism is alive and well, meaning certain cultures aren't? Or that *everything* is impermanent: languages, peoples, species, continents, until the sun itself balloons up into a red giant that envelops the whole planet in its thermonuclear cloud? So hey, nonny, nonny! Make hay while the sun shines and gather ye rosebuds while ye may, for tomorrow we'll be dying. Summer's lease hath all too short a date, 'til that lamp of heaven burns too hot and leaves us crying.

I am feeling sleepy, so very tired, and Sky looks so restful, so – maybe just the briefest of naps. But mustn't miss our stop. So maybe not – there'll be time enough to sleep after I'm... after I'm... gone.

14

Truro is very warm, verging on hot – and humid. The foliage overgrowing the train station embankment is so lush and green that anyone familiar with a temperate climate who suddenly materialized here would immediately recognize the season: Summer! For me, habituated to the cool, dry Mediterranean version of coastal California, it provokes a kind of existential confusion. Should I relax into it or be on guard? Embrace the womblike temperature and beguiling fragrances or mistrust their charms? So I chose a steady state of awareness, on heightened alert.

I won't say I'm revived by my after-lunch nap but my fogginess seems more serene. And I did notice my ankle ache less as I half-hopped, half-limped across the platform. Maybe a side effect of the robust meal and long period I elevated it. Sky, however, stepped off the Cornish Riviera groggy from her sleep and is now grumpy as all get-out. She scowls and squirms in a much less comfortable seat on the empty, single carriage train parked on a track adjoining the main platform.

I reach towards a metal holder for a printed schedule of the Maritime Line, linking Truro with Falmouth. We won't be going to the final destination though. On the phone last night, Frankie said to get off at Penryn and she'd meet us there.

"You didn't say we had to take another train," Sky says.

"I did. Maybe you forgot. It's okay – it's just a ten minute trip."

"We've been *sitting* here for ten minutes!"

"I have a feeling things run a little slower in Cornwall."

"No shit," she says.

I instinctively look behind me to see if anyone else has boarded the train but no one has. It seems odd to even refer to it as a train. It's more like a streetcar, only beefier. I look at my watch again, wondering if we've got this wrong. As if on cue, a weathered man of at least sixty wearing a navy blue uniform and a thick gray mustache steps out of a shed on the platform, makes his way towards the train and enters our cabin.

"Good-day. Tickets if you please," he says in a heavy West Country accent. He looks and sounds like something out of a Masterpiece Theatre production of a Thomas Hardy novel. I hand over our tickets and he examines and punches them.

"You'll be wanting Penryn, then. That'll be stop after Perranarworthal." If I hadn't just seen the train schedule I'd have absolutely no idea what the last word he uttered was meant to be. It came out more like *Purrrunerrrrrwerrrrthlll*, as if he'd just taken a big, meaty bite of a Cornish pasty and hadn't swallowed yet. Sky looks at me with her eyebrows raised high but thankfully the railroad man doesn't notice so he can't take offense. He walks to the front of the coach, sits, and presses a button that starts the motor, as if this were a bus. And then there's a *clunk* as he engages the transmission and a *hiss* from the brake lines and we're on our way.

We gather momentum deliberately, with the tightly wound compression that characterizes a diesel engine, and then the driver changes gears with a lurching *ka-chunk* and the rising crescendo of the motor's whine and rheumy exhaust note resumes. It suddenly reminds me of a train we took in that summer of 1979 in the Dordogne. Swap out the exterior color of the train – I recall the French carriage was a pale teal, while this one is a royal blue – and the other pieces fit, from the solo engineer to the moist, warm weather to the cranky American teenage girl. Normally my parents let us work out our stuff on our own, especially in later teenage, but for some reason my mother got on Meg for her grumpiness that day, and then turned on me when I inevitably piled on my sister. Like some minor flame that sows the seeds of a wildfire, this relatively modest altercation soon engulfed my parents themselves and they were having at it: an exceedingly rare marital spat, at least from what we were ever privy to. I realize now there must have been something else at play, something pent up and ready to ignite. And like the tinder-dry sagebrush that Californians fear every October, when the Santa Ana winds blow, any spark will do. In my experience my father never raised his voice, but here he was yelling and gesticulating like a Roman taxi driver. And my mother, who could certainly do those things on occasion, was cursing in – French! We'd heard her sound off in the past, in a sort of PG-13 Anglo-Saxon – a *bloody hell* here and a *sodding bastard* there – but only for short bursts when she was provoked enough. Yet here she was letting loose in her native tongue, I mean her *real* native tongue, at length and in full voice. I can't recall what she said, mostly because I didn't understand half of what she was saying, but it seems to me now that the nearly three years of our Oxford Wilderness Period that she'd kept bottled up was pouring forth in pure histrionic Norman. Lord knows she had reason to vent, with all the frustrations she'd endured, and she was doing so in the form of an operatic geyser. My father must have been as surprised as Meg and I, because he stopped his arguing and fell completely silent. And so the three of us, mouths agape, sat and watched this bravura performance on the part of my mother. At least she *looked* like my mother. But honestly, you'd have thought she was possessed by demons or aliens or *something*. She wasn't speaking in tongues though, rather *a* tongue. Her mother tongue, with words and phrases probably learned on her mother's knee and stored in the recesses of her brain all those years.

After the aria ran its course she wasn't met with applause but tears – her own – and voluminous apologies. We all joined in immediately, my father most fervently and impressively, and there was a wonderful family catharsis that resulted, if memory serves, with ice cream and a *citron pressé* for Meg and a *panaché* for me at the first café we could find in Périgueux. My parents ordered pastis, not because they liked the licorice taste, but out of admiration for the cloudiness the cold water produced when poured in. Like the aftermath of a summer thunderstorm, all the tension and drama seemed washed away, leaving a moist warmth to the ground and a gentle, ionized freshness in the air.

We pass Perranwell station without stopping. I look at the schedule, confused, since I thought the name was different, longer – the word the conductor had slurred.

"Did we miss it?" I ask Sky, then immediately realize she doesn't know where we're going.

"What?"

"Wait, no I think we're okay." I look at the schedule again and see it's listed as Perranwell *for* Perranarworthal.

"Christ, that's confusing," I say.

"You okay, Dad?"

"Yeah."

But I'm not. I feel fluttery and worry that I must look worse. I could ask Sky but that would be too obvious. Plus, wouldn't she tell me if my nose was smudged or my hair was sticking up in back? No, probably not.

"I look fine to you?"

"You mean other than your gimpy leg and you're usual dorkiness?"

"Yeah. Other than that."

"Jesus, you're nervous to see her again, aren't you? Oh, this is good."

"Gee thanks. I knew I could count on you."

The train is coasting now, past a sloping viaduct, and I check my watch. Just five minutes or so to Penryn.

Sky places a hand on my wrist. "You look fine, Dad."

I smile at her and nod my thanks.

Frankie and I didn't take this train when we travelled here together; her father met us in Truro. I remember him as tall and impressive, both in his confident bearing and his aristocratic good looks. He was decidedly masculine and took pleasure in outdoor pursuits like sailing and hunting, but he had a thoughtful, almost erudite quality as well. Over the next few days, as I interacted with him more, I came to see that there was an underlying confusion to him, with what seemed a foot in both the present day and the distant past. He'd ask politely about doings in London or the States but he didn't seem to really want to know. I realized what Frankie had once said was true: that his Kenwyn family lineage was actually a burden, tying him to the region for his income, and even though he'd ventured to London and Paris in his youth and married an Italian woman with no connection to Cornwall, they'd returned to his family's estate at Trewithy, overlooking the Carrick Roads, when it came time to start a family of his own. Frankie later confided that she was convinced Trewithy had sucked the life out of her parents and their marriage. She vowed never to live in Cornwall again, even though she was happy to show it to me and help me understand the locale that had shaped who she was. So when Ronnie said she was back here, my shock was mixed with sorrow. She'd once meant so much to me, almost the world really, and even though time and loss and life have tempered those feelings, the intensity of what I've felt in the wake of Annie's departure makes me feel especially empathetic. Whether I feel her plight more because of our shared history or just on a human level, as one would react to anyone's suffering, I don't know. But does it really matter? The important thing, it seems to me, is the concern. The compassion for someone else's feelings.

"Sky, can I ask you a question?"

"You just did." And old joke between us, but I'm too distracted by my real question to acknowledge it.

"At lunch you asked about me and mom ever getting back together. How much did our splitting up affect you? I mean, on a scale of one to ten, one being a minor annoyance and ten being it completely rocked your world, which was it?"

"Dad, parents who divorce when their kids are teens are always overestimating the harm based on their own suffering. But adolescents already have a relatively well-developed sense of self and are actually not that interested in their parent's inner world."

"Where do you get this stuff?"

"I read."

"Seriously," I say. "Give me a number."

"Why do you care? It's already a done deal. I mean, it's not like you can get a do-over."

"I care. Please, give me a number."

"Including the fact that it cost me Moondancer?"

I sigh. "Yes. Including Moondancer."

"An eleven. Off the fucking charts. Why do you think I've been acting out so much? I mean, hello? So you'd better start saving up for my therapy trust fund. Oh, wait – sorry, I forgot you were broke."

"How come I never know when you're serious? Sky, really – I want to know."

"You want the truth?"

"Yes."

"You want the truth? You can't handle the truth!" She does her version of Jack Nicholson in *A Few Good Men*.

I shake my head, defeated. She pats my arm reassuringly.

"Seriously, Dad. Don't worry. I'm good."

I look at her. "Really?"

"Really. But it's Abby you should worry about. This whole divorce has fucked her up big time." She smiles a close-lipped, wicked smile. I feel like Charlie Brown, failing to kick the football after Lucy has yanked it away yet again. Why do I fall for it?

I check my watch again. Five past three. We should be at Penryn by now according to the schedule, but I'm pretty sure we left a couple of minutes late. Up ahead, out the train window, the vista starts to slope downwards until some water is visible. Falmouth Bay? After another switchback I see what looks like a broadening of the area on either side of the track. This must be it. Penryn Station. I have a quick scan of the platform as the train starts to slow. I can't see anyone yet but there's that covered space over to the right. She must be in there. Christ. Francesca Kenwyn-Lloyd. Frankie. After all these years. My Frankie.

15

S ky and I stand on the Penryn Station platform next to our bags. The train has rolled on towards Falmouth and there's no Frankie in sight. Or anyone else for that matter. The station, which has no building or interior space, just a series of benches (the central portion of which are covered), is completely deserted.

"So?" Sky says.

"She must be running late. Let's sit over there."

Sky starts rolling her suitcase towards the nearest bench and I lift my tennis bag when I notice a figure in the distance, near the parking lot. It's a young man, I think, must be, by his appearance. He has long, brown hair, cut surfer-style, with shaggy bangs and he seems to notice us. I start to walk towards him but my right ankle doesn't like that so I stop.

"Where are you going?" Sky asks it in a frustrated tone. Then she sees the guy as well. He starts to walk in our direction, hesitant at first, then with increasing purpose. I stand and watch him approach and Sky does the same.

"Are you, um, Mr. Davis?" The young man is about fifteen or sixteen I figure, really more of a boy but tall for his age. He speaks with an English accent of indeterminate origin – could be local, I suppose, with the right education, or more likely from one of the Home Counties. The striking feature about him, apart from his general good looks, is his eyes: a piercing Mediterranean blue.

"Yes, I am. Trevor Davis. This is my daughter, Skylar. And you are?"

"Michael. Michael Smith. My mother said to say sorry, she's running late."

"No problem. I think she said she might have some meeting in Falmouth. Is that it?"

"Must be," he says. "There's a café close by. She said she'd meet us there."

"Great," I say. "Did you drive?" I motion towards the cars parked diagonally in the lot but Michael frowns.

"Sorry, no. I mean, I *can* drive, but not, you know, legally. We can walk."

I realize Sky hasn't said a word. I look at her and she's staring at young Michael Smith with a kind of wonderment.

"Well..." I say to Michael, and this seems to snap Sky out of her reverie.

"My dad can't walk so good, I mean so *well*, because he sprained his ankle. Back in London, playing tennis yesterday when he should have been attending to business, but whatever."

"Oh," Michael says. He looks either confused or bemused by this torrent of information. Or possibly both.

"Yes, thank you, Sky, for the blow-by-blow. I'm okay if it's not too far, Michael. What are we talking about, distance-wise?"

"Well, I'm not really sure. Not far."

"Less than a quarter mile?" He nods.

"Hmm," I say. I scan the train platform and I pick out a luggage trolley, but not the sort of passenger cart you find at airports, rather a flat bed trolley that porters use to load large amounts of baggage. Still...

"Do you think it would be okay if we borrow that for a few minutes?" I indicate the trolley across the platform.

"Jesus, Dad," Sky says.

Michael smiles an attractive, reassuring smile. The sort that says he's dealt with far worse predicaments than the legalities of appropriating railroad equipment.

"Why not?" he says, and he's already moving towards it.

Sky immediately falls into step next to him and I do my best to follow, hoping a question might slow him down a bit, so I ask why the rail station is so deserted. Michael explains that most people are home or at a pub watching England take on Slovenia in the World Cup. To the obvious follow-up question – why isn't he also watching it? – Michael proclaims a complete lack of interest in football. Sky beams at this response and fastens me with an expression that seems to say, 'See, an intelligent male who doesn't go in for ball sports!' She asks about his interests, in that giddy sort of conversational stream typical of teenage girls, and by the time we have our luggage loaded on the trolley, Sky and Michael have compared their favorite popular songs and singers, names that are largely meaningless to me, Katy this and Nicki that and Kelly the other. Meanwhile I stare at the heavy steel trolley and reconsider.

"I don't know," I say. "Do you think you both can really push me?"

Sky looks at Michael, who assesses the trolley then meets her gaze. "I'm game if you are," he says.

"I like his can-do spirit!" she says, as if she and I were the only ones conversing.

"I do too," I say. So I gingerly pull myself onto the trolley and, with our luggage serving as a chaise longue, face my legs forward and grip the sides. Sky and Michael take up positions at the trolley's rear and start pushing on the attached bar. The trolley's steel wheels turn surprisingly easily on the concrete railway platform and we all exchange self-satisfied smiles at our ingenuity.

The going gets a little more challenging once we reach the edge of the platform and descend a ramp to the street, both in containing the trolley's acceleration on the ramp and then overcoming friction from the softer and more uneven asphalt of the road. I don't say anything, so as not to discourage Sky or Michael, but I can see them each working hard to maintain the trolley's headway. So we soldier on, with me as powerless as I was in the wheelchair at Paddington, except now with Michael serving to temper any mischievous inclinations on Sky's part.

By the time we reach the far end of the station parking lot the kids look in need of a rest, so I suggest they take one, but Michael wonders if getting the trolley moving again from a standstill might be difficult. I notice the grade start to slope downwards ever so slightly, enough to aid their effort, so I say sure, keep going. I even try on enjoying the ride, like an ill-fitting Halloween mask, willing myself to ignore the indignity of sitting prostrate like this and musing that were it not for the World Cup match making the immediate station area seem as desolate as a Kansas corn field in winter, we probably couldn't pull this off. The incline is now such that the kids exert no effort at all, and merely need to guide the trolley, or even retard its progress slightly, and they are grinning now, especially when they allow the speed to pick up enough to require a jogging pace. I suppose I should be concerned that we might be going a tad *too* fast, but Michael seems adept at grabbing hold of the trolley's bar and slowing it down when required. That is, until the road takes a sharp bend to the left and the downslope increases dramatically out of literally nowhere.

In one of those out-of-body time-compressed moments that seems to permit only observation, not action, the trolley immediately accelerates and it's all Sky and Michael can do to hold on to it, much less steer. I am looking straight ahead and Michael shouts, "That's the café!" and indicates towards our left, as if my knowing where we are supposed to meet Frankie will help me even slightly as I tighten my grip on the now-careening trolley. Sky by this point has dropped away and it's only Michael holding on, or more precisely being dragged along by a luggage trolley that is now completely out of control, as he alternates between flailing his legs to keep up with it and, occasionally, planting his feet in a futile attempt to slow it down. The face of my Sixth Form physics master, Mr. Renshaw, pops into my consciousness. He's explaining Newton's laws of motion and how an object's energy converts from potential to kinetic when acted on by the Earth's gravity. 'Davis!' he barks out. 'What's the formula?' But I'm too preoccupied to remember, not that I could anyway. Instead my eyes dart to the café, maybe because there's nothing else they can safely fasten onto, certainly not the cars parked at the bottom of the street that are now directly in the trolley's path. The café is painted blue and white and has the ever-so-cute name, *Turn a Tin Ear*. I'd forgotten the British penchant for silly puns, especially for small businesses, even though this one does give a legitimate nod to Cornwall's mining history. I'm not sure what surprises me more, that my brain has chosen to work out the wordplay rather than calculate how quickly I'm gaining velocity and, by extension, the odds of my surviving jumping from the trolley versus crashing into one of the parked cars. Or that, God forbid, we haven't yet encountered a moving car driven by some elderly man who, like

Michael, ignores soccer and has embarked on what he presumed would be a simple afternoon drive to the grocers. So instead I do nothing, just grip tighter as Michael finally drops his hold on the trolley's handle with a grim expression of resignation that conveys some sense of abject apology but really contains more, maybe even the tragic loss of his father, if I'm not presuming too much.

"Dad!" It's Sky, screaming after me, but I can't worry about her now either. I can only concentrate on holding on and hoping, maybe, just maybe, the trolley can thread the needle between a parked white Vauxhall sedan and what looks like a large palm tree of some sort and find the upslope of a narrow driveway. It's hard to know but I guess I must be doing about thirty miles an hour, which is a terrifying pace when you think about it, on a heavy steel luggage trolley in the middle of a public thoroughfare, certainly scarier than on a nimble, rubber-tired Moto Guzzi doing eighty with fully functioning ABS brakes. In the moment right before the trolley suddenly veers to the right and mounts the partial curb of an intersecting street, putting me directly behind a large Range Rover *descending* in approximately the same direction – finally, a moving vehicle! – I have a fleeting thought: *I should have updated my will!* Followed right on its heels by yet another: *No matter, since I have nothing left!*

And then I brace myself for the impact.

Instead of the Range Rover braking, however, as most drivers would typically react to a manned Great Western Railroad luggage trolley suddenly materializing in their rear view mirror, the SUV's driver accelerates and veers away, which alters what would have been a serious collision into a glancing blow. Only then does the driver brake and, in doing so, he departs from my view, leaving me and the trolley on a billiard shot trajectory skidding towards what appears to be a gravel and dirt meridian. Then – *crunch!* – the wheels dig in and I'm decelerating. Fast. So much so that I feel in perilous danger of ejecting from the trolley like a human cannonball in some circus act. I shift my grip to push myself backwards and instinctively wedge my left foot against the front edge of the trolley to counter my forward momentum. Which works to keep me attached. But attached to what? I've never ridden one of those mechanical bulls but this must be similar, the way the trolley is bucking and jerking around. And then it dawns on me: this gravel meridian is functioning like those runaway truck ramps you see on Interstate 80 when you descend from Donner Pass towards Sacramento. I am actually slowing! And the trolley is miraculously staying upright, despite a pronounced list to starboard. As the last remnants of velocity dissipate I can finally acknowledge to myself that I won't die, at least not just yet. So I exhale and take in a breath of fresh air to prove the point to myself.

"My God! Trevor! Are you alright?"

I look up to see Frankie, large as life and twice as natural.

"Well, I suppose that's a relative question," I say.

Frankie's expression changes from horrified concern to... what, exactly? Incredulous bemusement? Anger? It's too much to process, in any case, so I look away and take in my immediate surroundings.

The nearest object to the trolley is the parked but still idling Range Rover. It must belong to Frankie, I realize, for the driver's door – on the right side of the vehicle, of course – is ajar and she is standing next to me.

"Mom!"

It's Michael's voice, so I realize he's addressing Frankie as he comes running up. I see Sky trailing him by about twenty paces. "Are you okay?" he asks me, panting and out of breath.

"Michael!" Frankie says. "What in the world...?"

"It was my idea," I say and she fastens me with such a sharp glance that I almost retract my confession, but as I've always told the girls, it's not what you do wrong, it's what you do about it afterwards. It's just... this isn't anything like I imagined how things would go with Frankie. Our Grand Reunion. Lord, what a fiasco. I'm pretty sure I – or rather the trolley I was riding on – collided with the left side of her Range Rover, and even though it could have been much, much worse, the damage must still be substantial. Frankie doesn't appear injured but maybe it's just the shock of seeing me like this. Maybe she actually *is* hurt and just doesn't realize she suffered whiplash or a cut on her scalp.

"Are you okay?" I ask.

"Me? Yes, I'm fine."

"What about your car?"

"Well, we'll just have to see about that. But what possessed you... I mean, why were you *riding* on this thing in the first place?"

"I rolled my ankle yesterday. I've been trying to keep it elevated so... it seemed like a good idea at the time."

"Really. To ride on a luggage trolley. On a public thoroughfare."

"Yes."

Then she notices my tennis bag. Raising her left eyebrow she indicates the bag with an accusing right index finger.

"Sprained it playing tennis?"

I nod. Guilty as charged.

Skylar finally arrives on the scene, and as strange as it seems, the priority shifts to introducing Sky and Frankie, now that it's clear no one – me included – was injured. I take Frankie in for the first time, properly, but still in a sort of altered state of consciousness. She looks much the same as I remember – I'm sure I would have recognized her – but of course she's older too, most visibly by her formerly chestnut hair now substantially gray. Most women back home would have corrected this, so it's surprising at first, but I then notice how natural it looks. Frankie's face remains much the same, her cheekbones still wide and well defined and her complexion midway between Italian olive and English porcelain. And, oh my God – she still has those dimples. Well, dimple-like pockets really, but they're just as they were, visible in each cheek as she talks.

"So I'd ask if your trip down from London was alright, but under the present circumstances...."

I'm off the trolley now, my feet on the ground, and I'm leaning against it next to her to keep the weight off of my still tender right ankle and I realize she's making a joke at my expense and that the kids are smiling. Sky and Frankie have already shaken hands, so it seems a little late for me to – what? Hug Frankie? Kiss her on the cheek? Christ, shake her hand? So... nothing.

"It was great. I treated Sky to lunch in the dining car and it was excellent. I mean, *really* good."

"Wonderful. So you've both eaten. No need for the café then? I thought we might head back home so we can get Skylar sorted out with a horse. Would you still fancy a ride, dear? Your father mentioned you might like that. If you aren't too unsettled. And if anyone wants tea I can put a kettle on."

"Yeah, absolutely," Sky says. "I mean, to the riding."

Frankie looks at me. "Right, shall we do that?"

"Sounds good to me," I say.

"Now then – what are we going to do about this?"

Frankie indicates the luggage trolley.

"Skylar and I can push it back to the station," Michael says.

"You bloody well will not," Frankie says. "Look what happened the last time."

"It's loads lighter without the bags. Or him," Michael says.

"Him?" Sky says.

"Sorry," he says to me and I wave it off, neither offended by his reducing me to a pronoun or implying that I am, to any degree, overweight.

"He's probably right," I say to Frankie. "And we know there are no downhill parts to worry about."

Michael looks at Sky to assess her game worthiness and she flashes him a thumbs up: she's in. That's my girl, I think. Even though I'd be fine leaving the damned cart right where it is.

"Alright, you two. Have a go and we'll meet you at the station. But for goodness sake, don't crash into anyone." Frankie and I lift the luggage off and watch as Michael and Sky roll the trolley, which appears completely unscathed, back onto the road. Once we are satisfied they can manage the slope back up to the station, we walk over to Frankie's Range Rover and inspect the damage. Or rather Frankie walks and I do my combo shuffle-hop.

There's a visible dent on the Range Rover's left rear fender, and a scrape to the paint job about eight inches long. It's somewhere between a gash and a scratch, not all that bad, considering. It could have been a whole lot worse.

"I'm really sorry," I say.

"I suppose it wouldn't have happened if I hadn't been running late."

"No doubt. Apology accepted."

Frankie's beleaguered expression substitutes for an eye roll. "I had a meeting in Falmouth," she continues. "Something that might involve a bit of work. "

"Work. Is that, I mean, I don't even know what you do now."

"Yes, I'm sure there's rather a lot to catch up on." Suddenly she looks distracted. Or, is it upset?

"Frankie?"

"I'm not sure this was such a good idea," she says.

"It would mean a lot to Sky to have some time on a horse."

"Well, I suppose there'll be no riding for you."

I look at my gimpy ankle. "Ah, no. Not today." She regards my tennis bag and shakes her head. "Some things never change."

I look for some leavening sarcasm or humor in her expression but I'm not sure what I read. Disapproval? Indifference? Maybe she's right. Maybe this trip wasn't a good idea. So I focus on the brown Range Rover. It's an older model, the boxy one that looks too big for its chassis, like some toy car a kid might make by tying a cardboard box on top of a red wagon. I recall Frankie telling me why her family always drove brown cars: it was her father's tribute to their combined English and Italian heritage. You see, she explained, in international automotive racing England's color is green and Italy's is red. And when you mix red and green, you get brown. When I first learned of it – Frankie drove a brown Toyota hatchback when I met her in California – and saw it confirmed when her father collected us from Truro in a brown Jaguar sedan, I wasn't sure whether to label the gesture as quaint or sentimental or romantic. But I do remember thinking it was something my father would never have done, and that made me oddly envious.

"You're still driving a brown car."

"Yes."

"Some things never change," I say, with as disarming a smile as I can muster.

She looks at me sharply and I wonder if this is a momentary way station before anger. But she relents and cracks a smile and we both laugh.

"Okay, I guess we're even," she says.

"Wipe the slate clean?" Her smile suddenly vanishes and is replaced by a haunted expression. Even though it seems for some reason to have little to do with me, I realize I've pressed too soon and too hard. Idiot!

"Let's get the kids," Frankie says.

I nod towards the café. "Mind if I use the loo first?"

"It can't wait?"

"Um, no. As a matter of fact, it can't."

"You sure it isn't too late already?" Her grin has rematerialized, flashing those dimples. Christ, must she do that?

"Are you implying I shit in my pants? On the luggage trolley?"

"Excuse me, I wasn't implying that!" She cracks a guilty grin. "Just that you might have peed yourself."

We both start laughing again. The laughter feels like a balm, a long-forgotten remedy for life's everyday ills, and I remember how easy it always was for us to find things to laugh about. Little things. Anything really, no matter how silly or mundane. Frankie might be having a similar thought because her smile suddenly changes to a chastened expression.

"Go on then," she says. She turns and busies herself with loading the luggage in the Range Rover. I want to help, but I realize that's just male pride and it would only slow us down. She's more than capable without me. So I take her in and see, fully, how alluring Frankie still is. It's no one specific attribute – her height is average and her figure more lean than curvaceous – but the combination has always thrown me for loop. Something about the planes of her face and her smooth skin evoke for me the refined beauty and earthy pleasures of Italy. Her Englishness only heightens the potency of the mix, the same way, I suppose, that the gin in a Negroni makes the Campari not just exotic but intoxicating. My reaction feels unsettling, like stepping too close to the edge of a steep cliff, so I lean backwards and quickly turn around.

I make my way into the café and ask the receptionist if I can use the restroom, eliciting a cheery smile and a "Yes of course!" Once safely in the bathroom at the rear of the café I relieve my bladder, grateful that my sphincter muscle managed, somehow, to maintain its composure on the trolley. Must be all those tight matches over the years, I muse. Who says tennis isn't practical? Maybe that could be my nickname. Trevor "Nerves of Steel" Davis. So calm under pressure, he sinks to the bottom without even exhaling. Jeez, I do crack myself up. But seriously, what's the good of stressing out? On the way back out I'm unstressed enough to observe that the television in the café's bar area is tuned to coverage of Wimbledon. I have a closer look and notice that the players are from yesterday's suspended match, the American John Isner and the Frenchman Nicolas Mahut. I squint to see the score in the fifth set, which seems to be... seventeen games all. *Seventeen?* I do a double-take and the older man at the bar notices.

"End of the first period," he says.

"What?"

"England is leading, one-nil."

"Oh. No, I was looking at the score here."

He brightens. "Remarkable, isn't it?"

"I guess they're both serving well."

The man nods. "At this rate they could be out there all day." We share a momentary chuckle at the absurdity of the notion. All day? Inconceivable.

16

There's something about the way Frankie handles the large SUV that reminds me of Annie, a particular skill and confidence in her driving. She reaches the bend in the road where my luggage trolley excursion went from adventure to near-disaster and we spot Sky and Michael next to the station platform.

"Skylar is lovely."

"She has her moments. Michael is your eldest?"

"Yes. We'll see Samantha later. Tim, my youngest, is off with a friend and his family camping on Bodmin."

Frankie pulls to a stop and calls out her window: "Well done you two!" Sky beams. Michael shrugs, then opens the rear door and lets her in first. He follows after her and shuts it behind him – *thunk* – and we're on our way again.

As we drive back through Penryn, then navigate a series of roundabouts and eventually peel off in the direction of Mylor, I feel I'm in a dreamlike state. Not the jet lag-induced trance of yesterday – I've mostly recovered from that – but a different kind, one that seems both ethereal and distinct. So much is unfamiliar – the summer day's humid warmth, sitting as a passenger in the wrong front seat, the tidy, round-cornered road signs, and the stone and slate roof houses – and yet it's not so foreign as to be alarming. Quite the contrary. There's a comforting quality to it all, a realization that maybe the British finally figured things out, with their Continental-inspired cuisine and their efficient traffic circles and their new-found respect for service. My God, I think – have I become Paddington Bear, finally succumbing to the notion of British superiority? Or is it that England is no longer threatening to me, no longer something I feel excluded from or ridiculed by. Or maybe it's none of those things. Maybe it's that I'm back in the company of Frankie after all these years. And that this is both strange and welcoming in equal measure.

Frankie follows Bissom Road, until it becomes Rosehill as it winds down to the village of Mylor Bridge, and then Lemon Hill as it rises up the opposite side, in the peculiar way streets here change names. I sneak another glance at Sky, who's been marveling at the postcard-worthy scenery. When she isn't checking out Michael, that is. At my prompting Frankie has been explaining some local history: about the Falmouth packet ships that carried mail to far-flung continents for centuries; how packet captains often settled in remote corners of Falmouth's vast natural harbor, like Mylor Bridge; and why the Cornish gained a reputation for piracy and smuggling and wrecking owing to the dangerous coastline and their entrenched poverty.

"Did we have any pirates on Papa's side of the family?" Michael asks.

"The Kenwyns? Not that he would have admitted to. But you don't receive and maintain a baronetcy all those years without some kind of skullduggery." Frankie twists her head and shoots me a grin.

"No comment," I say. "We had to send your lot packing when you started taxing our tea."

"Ha!" she exclaims. "I was wondering when we'd get to that. So how are things faring in the colonies since we left you to your own devices?"

It's an old joke between us and I can tell Michael and Sky are enjoying the exchange, so for the life of me I have no idea why I choose to deviate from the script.

"Not so well. We could probably use a little help from the motherland."

Frankie looks at me appraisingly, then she purses her mouth and returns her focus to the road.

"I saw this thing on the Internet written by John Cleese," Sky says with excited enthusiasm. "You know, from Monty Python?"

"I know who John Cleese is," Michael says.

"Right, well this was supposed to be a letter from the Queen about how America had screwed things up and she was revoking our independence. It was hilarious."

"I used to love Monty Python," Frankie says. "They *were* hilarious and I'm glad they're still going strong."

We're past the church and houses of Mylor Bridge, on what is now Carclew Road, and are skirting tall hedgerows, the irregular stone walls covered in heather and brambles that make the fields look like a patchwork quilt from above. Frankie continues for maybe a half-mile – it's hard to judge without reference points – and finally turns right at a sign for Trewithy Estate.

"Michael, are you interested in riding as well?" Frankie asks.

"Not really," he says.

"No, I didn't think so. Right, well let me drop you and Trevor off and then Skylar and I can get sorted out at the stable."

We drive up the private lane to the estate and I search my memory for differences. The driveway appears the same, still wide with an arching canopy of huge oaks on either side. The trees are as majestic, and with the windows down the Range Rover's interior is filled with the scent of honeysuckle and fuchsia. When we reach the wide oval clearing at the top of the driveway, ringed with large magnolias and graceful rhododendrons, the house itself seems identical, a massive two-story stone mansion that, as I recall, was originally built in the fifteenth century and remodeled in the eighteenth. The only change appears to be a sign designating a car park and another with an arrow pointing to *Reception*.

Frankie doesn't stop; she keeps driving along the side of the car park and past some stone sheds and garden equipment.

I must look puzzled and Frankie notices.

"My brother conveyed the estate to a trust after Father died. It rents rooms in the main house to vacationers and conducts horticultural tours of the gardens."

She pulls the Range Rover up to what looks like a crofter's cottage and parks.

"Here we are. Can you and Michael manage for a little while?"

"No problem," I say.

Michael and I get out and Sky switches, at Frankie's urging, to the front seat, but not before she's interrupted by two dogs who come running up to greet her, their tails wagging madly. One is a Border collie, with the typical black and white coloring, and the other is a golden retriever, making up in friendliness what it lacks in frenetic energy.

"Oh, how sweet!" Sky says as she pets them both. "What are their names?"

"The sheep dog is Jake and the retriever is Gwyn," Michael says.

Sky fusses over them and I do as well, until Frankie asks Michael to call them so Sky can get back in the Range Rover. Sky seems visibly reluctant to leave the company of the dogs but then she has always been the most animal-loving in our family. She's probably missing our dog, Bruce, a rescue mutt who has lived with Annie and the girls since the separation.

"See you later then," Frankie says.

"Have a good ride," I say. Sky waves goodbye and I wave back. I'm not sure if it's a happy or a worried expression on her face – let's call it apprehensive – and I realize I have no idea if she's meant to ride alone or with Frankie or someone else. The thought occurs to me that I'm her father so I probably ought to have found out, but I trust Frankie enough to do what's best. Michael is already going through the front door of the cottage so I follow him. The dogs seem content to stay outside so I hesitate to be sure, then close the door.

The living area of the cottage is cozy enough, with modern appliances in the kitchen and a comfortable-looking sofa and armchairs, but I'm still recovering from the surprise that Frankie's family no longer occupies the main house. I know it's common for some of the larger estates to get sold or become upscale B&Bs when the death taxes and upkeep become too much for the heirs, but I didn't figure the Kenwyns belonged in that group for some reason. Maybe because the house isn't that grand or is in such a remote place like Cornwall.

"Do you need anything?" Michael asks.

"No, I'm fine." I say. "Actually, do you mind if I turn the TV on? It's probably over but I want to check on a tennis match."

"Sure," he says and he locates the remote control. He turns on the smallish flat screen television and the BBC One coverage of World Cup football come on. England still leads Slovenia 1-0 with time running out in the game. Michael flips the channel to BBC Two and I see that Isner and Mahut are still going strong.

"You're really not interested in the World Cup?"

"I don't follow sports," he says.

I hop towards the set to get a better view. Nicolas Mahut is serving, with the score in the fifth set 23-24. He is down in the game, love-thirty, but fires an ace to take the score to fifteen-thirty. The announcer says that John Isner, in the previous game, broke the Wimbledon record for most aces in a match, with sixty-two.

"Wow, this is incredible," I say. I explain to Michael that the match is in its second day and how improbable it is for a fifth set of tennis to last so long. That in the U.S. Open, in fact, this would never happen since the tiebreaker is employed in all five sets.

"If Isner wins two more points he's got the match," I say. I can't tell if Michael is at all interested. He telegraphs apathy but he is watching nonetheless. Is he just being polite, I wonder? I take a closer look at Nicolas Mahut, the lanky Frenchman, as his image fills the screen. He has the angular face and spiky hair of a rock guitarist, but he's all business – focused and serious as he prepares to serve. He manages to win the point, and then the next, but he can't close out the game as Isner takes it to deuce on a nice cross-court forehand from behind the baseline.

I sit down on the sofa and Michael hovers behind an armchair, still watching.

"Have you played any sports?" I ask.

"Not really. I tried rugby at school but didn't really see the point."

"It gets pretty physical in the scrum, that's for sure." Mahut wins the point at deuce and moves over to serve from the ad court. The chair umpire intones 'Advantage Mahut,' and I recognize him as Mohamed Lahyani, considered one of the best officials on the professional tour. Already an elegant looking man with straight dark hair, parted on the side, and an olive complexion, he seems even more so with the French blue shirt and navy tie that Wimbledon umpires wear.

"You know about rugby?" Michael seems surprised.

"Well, we do play it in the States, but I'll grant you it's not as popular as football or even soccer." Mahut dumps a first serve into the net and tries again.

"But I went to high school in Oxford so I played a few times. Too rough for me." I motion towards the television. "I'm a tennis guy."

Mahut's second serve goes long and the crowd groans. The BBC announcer with more of an English accent – the other one sounds American although they both, oddly, seem somewhat Mid-Atlantic in their delivery – says that this makes fourteen double faults for the Frenchman.

I motion to the set. "You don't play at all? Even for fun?"

Michael shakes his head. "No. I tried it once but I was hopeless."

Mahut lines up to serve again in the deuce court.

"My younger brother plays a little."

"Yeah?" I say. "I could never interest either of my girls in tennis. For Sky it was always about horses."

Mahut serves a strong first serve and follows it to the net, where he puts away Isner's return for a volley winner.

Lahyani calls 'Advantage Mahut' again.

"I'm sorry about your father," I say.

Mahut lines up in the ad court to serve.

"Did you know him?" Michael asks.

"No."

Mahut misses the first serve long. He walks back to the base-line from midcourt.

"I didn't really know him either," Michael says. "I was twelve at the time and he was away quite a lot even before he went to Iraq."

Mahut spins the second serve in, allowing Isner to hit a strong backhand passing shot that Mahut can only just get his racquet on, and the ball flares out.

'Deuce,' Lahyani says.

The BBC announcer who sounds more American says, 'Looks like we'll have to do it again,' and the other announcer chuckles. 'That seems to be the theme of this match,' he replies.

Mahut serves and it's a winner, Isner's return going into the net.

'Advantage Mahut,' Lahyani says.

"So there's no limit to how many deuces they could play?" Michael says.

"No limit," I say.

Mahut's first serve goes into the net.

"He loses this point and they do it again. But each deuce he's thinking, lose two points and I lose the match."

Mahut serves again and Isner returns the ball. A rare baseline rally ensues, with both players stretching and making shots on the run. Finally, after it seems neither one can play any better or gain the upper hand, Mahut gets a short ball to attack and he does so with a slice approach to the corner, generating a weak lob on Isner's part that Mahut smashes for a winner. The crowd erupts in applause and the commentators echo it with comments of 'Well done' and 'Superlative.'

'Game, Mahut,' Lahyani calls out. 'Isner to serve; score is twenty-four games all.'

"And now his reward is to receive serve from a guy who's six foot ten and fires missiles that are practically unreturnable," I say.

Michael moves from behind the armchair and sits down.

17

Watching a singles tennis match, especially the one Michael and I have been watching the past couple of hours, is like being a voyeur. It isn't true voyeurism, of course, as the players know they are being observed, most importantly by each other. But because Nicolas Mahut and John Isner are playing on an outer court with fewer spectators and are so focused on their task, there are likely stretches of time when they aren't conscious of the onlookers. And certainly not the ones following the action in front of a television set like us. But from what I have seen so far, there has been no hint of weakness, of betraying negative emotions. They have each been going about their business with courage, point after point, doing what they have trained so hard to do.

I have tried to convey to Michael a little of what it's like to play such a match, at the risk of becoming a bore. He has seemed interested, and the nature of the tennis has permitted a conversational back and forth between us to develop, since not much back and forth has been taking place on the court. You could almost call the games routine holds, with a raft of service aces and winners interrupted by a rare point scored by the returner, except there's not much routine about a fifth set at Wimbledon with the score surpassing twenty-five games each.

Michael has shared that his favorite school subjects are math and music, and that he's made a stab at forming a band with some friends. The band, he said, if he had to pin it down, is alternative rock and has its roots in blues and jazz. I observed that even though I don't have any experience as a jazz musician, I imagine the effort required is similar to tennis: the concentration on the notes others are playing and the focus on one's own note-playing in response. How you can't get too far ahead of yourself – that *staying in the point* is like staying in the song – but you also need to be aware of the bigger picture. For Mahut, this might mean that John Isner doesn't move as well, so an occasional drop shot – especially as the big man seems to be tiring – might be a good tactic.

I've always thought competitive junior tennis was excellent preparation for business, since it teaches you to (literally) think on your feet and solve problems by yourself in a stressful, adversarial setting. But ever since it became clear to me at Cal that my tennis skills weren't sufficient for a professional career, I've wondered whether I could have sustained the single-minded focus necessary for success on the tour. It's said that certain pros burned out because they were interested in a broader world than hitting a tennis ball. I don't know if that applies to Bjorn Borg, the great Swedish champion who walked away at the height of his ability. But if curiosity killed the cat, it might also be lethal for a career in professional tennis.

Isn't this one of the great challenges in life, though? So much about achievement seems to be bound up in steadfast dedication and obsessive repetition. We tell our children to follow their passion – I've certainly said as much to Sky and Abby – but doesn't overfamiliarity breed contempt in work as much as relationships? I suppose the goal is to choose a career with enough variety and challenge to keep things interesting.

At some point during our first hour in front of the television Michael asked me what I do for a living. This is ordinarily a question I dislike, even back when it was possible for me to answer with an honest sense of accomplishment, because it has always seemed such an unimaginative way to get to know someone, but in this case I was thrilled. It seemed a victory that Michael was curious enough to ask. So I told him what I did. Or rather, used to do. How I started working summer construction jobs in college to earn extra money and keep fit for tennis. How my liberal arts education – a history major and English literature minor – left me with few options after graduation, but that I'd discovered I had a head for business after doing some office work for a builder during my junior year. How that, combined with a budding interest in architectural design and urban planning, led me to join the company full-time. How I still swung the occasional hammer, but mostly I was managing projects and learning the intricacies of competitive bidding and construction financing. And how it led to me eventually striking off on my own.

If the tennis match in this stretch of games could have been set to music, it would have been a movie soundtrack. And not the thrilling crescendo of strings or crashing percussion of conflict, but the soothing, restrained woodwinds of routine. It practically begged for dialogue on our part, so I obliged by telling Michael about my mother as well, how she'd grown up in Shepperton, just a stone's throw from Michael's previous residence in Farnborough. And how she'd developed an interest in the business of film-making by combining her talent for organization with her passion for visual storytelling.

Eventually, during a changeover – a forced lull in the action – I asked Michael about his late father's choice of the military as a career, aware that I was treading on sensitive ground – both for him and for Frankie. Sometimes, when I've had conversations with friends of my girls, I've been leery of poking too deeply into family matters. Even simple questions, innocuous and polite on the surface, can elicit responses from guileless youths that their parents might consider intrusive. I know, because I've seen it happen in reverse. One mom in particular had a knack for digging family information out of Abby with the skill of a smooth-talking country lawyer. Michael's response didn't surprise me: his father's family had a history of military service, in particular the Grenadier Guards. Michael's grandfather was an officer in this the most senior infantry regiment in the British Army, as was his great-grandfather, who – and Michael seemed to exhibit something close to real pride relating this – distinguished himself by leading the orderly evacuation of the British Expeditionary Force from the beaches of Dunkirk in 1940.

What I naturally wanted to know was what attracted Frankie to a man like Michael's father, who'd followed such a well-trod family path into the Army. Despite being the daughter of a baronet (that anomaly of British nobility beneath a true peer but above a knight), Frankie had never professed a fondness for the monarchy, which in Britain is so closely affiliated with the military. And she had always expressed abhorrence for guns and violence of any kind, even institutionalized and sanitized in the manner of NATO armed forces. But of course I couldn't ask Michael. Not that he would even know. Sometimes love transcends all differences. Maybe Thomas Smith was a sensitive, brainy stud. And we all know how women react to guys in uniform.

It's all well and good to joke about how his parents came together, but this kid has a lost quality to him, and it doesn't take a degree in psychology to realize his father's untimely death has to figure in there somewhere. Seeing him sitting across from me, watching a sport on TV that he didn't care about with some strange foreigner who used to date his mom, I felt an overwhelming sadness. And it made me want to apologize for the war that took his father from him.

Now I know I'm not personally responsible. I may be American but Lord knows I didn't vote for the man who blundered into that conflict. And if Tony Blair had wanted Britain to be a true ally to the United States he would have declined to go along with Bush's folly. Like the saying goes, friends don't let friends drive drunk. Sure, if you really wanted to play the 'what if' game and go back far enough, it's the British themselves who created the whole damned mess, drawing the boundaries of modern Iraq with their mandate in the wake of World War One and the division of the Ottoman Empire. It's no accident the Grenadiers were in Basra, for goodness sake. I learned enough history in high school to know about British occupation of the city before and after the Great War. Yet all of that seems beside the point. I might be way off base – and it certainly wouldn't be the first time – but what seems the crux of the matter is what we as Americans let ourselves become in the aftermath of 9/11. When nineteen mostly Saudi true believers so rattled the world's remaining superpower with their naïve ingenuity that our response was to wring our collective hands and permit our elected officials to shred the Bill of Rights and invade a sovereign nation absent direct provocation or credible threat. When common sense and historical perspective and respected allies were shouting at us: Stop, please stop, for pity's sake – stop! But it's easier to look the other way when you've got an all-volunteer military and the hawks are wrapping themselves in the flag and labeling (libeling?) dissenters as unpatriotic and the commander-in-chief is telling everyone to go shopping to support the economy and that the mission is "accomplished." So I fumed and I spewed like my fellow Bay Area liberals but I re-shelved my vow to leave the country if that all-hat-and-no-cattle Texan got re-elected president. *That* would be too inconvenient with two daughters in school and a thriving business to run. To assuage my guilt and to convince myself I was effecting real change I wrote bigger checks to the opposition candidate in 2004, an actual war hero, just like the blunderer's father, who fought a real aggressor in the Pacific during WW2 and another in the Persian Gulf as Commander in Chief – the very same despot his son would attack, not coincidentally – but had the wisdom not to pursue to Baghdad when the aggression was dealt with. Meanwhile, as I wrote my self-satisfying checks from the comfort of my home office, another man of honor and duty, this young man's father, one Major Thomas Smith, was deployed overseas. To meet his fate from an improvised explosive device or a sniper's bullet – I don't have the heart to ask Michael *how* it happened – thereby transforming, back at home, a wife into a widow and leaving three children fatherless. And for what? Could anyone honestly say Michael's father gave his life for some worthy cause? To foist democracy on traditional antagonists at the barrel of a gun? To protect capitalism from the fluctuating price of a barrel of oil? Not me. It seems to me, in my not so humble opinion, precisely the opposite is true: that he died in vain. We all must die; this is a certainty. But please, dear Lord, let it not be in vain.

In the 66th game of the fifth set, with Nicolas Mahut (again) serving to stave off defeat, Mahut routinely won the first point but then lost the next three in a row, the last on a blistering backhand winner by Isner down the line to give himself not one but *two* match points. The crowd stirred, sensing the end was nigh, and Isner waved his right hand up and down to exhort the crowd to make more noise, not to rattle his opponent, I'm sure, but to provide a surge of energy for him to feed on. Michael and I perched on the edge of our seats, straining to follow the image of the ball on the television. Mahut, betraying not a whiff of nerves, calmly readied to serve and… hit his first serve long. Match point still, 15-40, but now on a second serve.

"Well, this looks like it," I said to Michael.

"I'm not so sure," he replied, and damned if the kid wasn't right. Mahut managed to get his second serve in – talk about *sang-froid* not to double-fault when it's 32-33 in the 5th set! – and win the point on a steely forehand volley. And then the next on a service winner. Now at deuce, the Frenchman collected himself and won two more points in a row to hold serve and even the match once more. Supporters in the stands were on their feet, clapping and cheering madly. 'Nico, Nico, Nico!' they chanted, so Michael and I had no choice but to follow suit. I raised my arm in front of him and he grinned and high-fived me. But we weren't rooting for Mahut alone. We were rooting for both guys, for the match to continue, as implausible as that might seem.

"This is crazy," I said to Michael. "It has to end at *some* point."

"Apparently not," he said.

Isner and Mahut each won their next service games without losing a point, but in the 69th game it was Isner's turn to falter. After winning the first three points he lost the next three to go to deuce. But the exceedingly tall American, who has the curious habit of bouncing the ball between his stilt-like legs with his left hand before serving – perhaps a holdover from his basketball days? – calmly pocketed the hold with a first serve winner and then an ace.

Mahut again easily held serve the next game but Isner is now back in trouble on his service game. After being up 40-15, it's deuce. The crowd is chanting and Mohamed Lahyani beseeches them to be quiet. Suddenly, I hear the dogs outside barking and the sound of the Range Rover pulling up. I check my watch: 6.15 p.m.

A car door slams and the barking diminishes. Meanwhile, Isner serves long.

"Crickey," Michael says.

"Fun, isn't it?"

"You call this fun? It's bloody nerve-wracking!"

The front door swings open and Isner fires an ace. A second serve ace!

"Double crickey!"

A girl who looks about twelve with sandy blonde hair and wearing what can only be described as a summer frock bursts into the room and sizes up Michael and the television and me.

"Are you Skylar's father?" she asks.

"Sam, shut up!" Michael hisses.

"Yes, I am," I say. "You must be Samantha. Or do you prefer Sam?"

"Either is fine," she says, "but you can call me Sam."

The girl curtsies – I kid you not – and I heave myself up to give her a formal bow.

"Trevor," I say. "But you can call me Mr. Davis."

She hesitates, not sure at first if I'm serious, then she laughs, immensely pleased. The sound level coming from the television drops suddenly so she looks towards it. "You're watching tennis?" she says. "What fun!"

"*Will* you be quiet?" Michael implores.

Out of the corner of my eye I see John Isner serve a winner and mercifully the game is over, making it 36-35 in the final set with the players walking to midcourt so they can sit and guzzle more water before they must change sides.

Sky and Frankie enter, both in riding gear, and Frankie looks at Michael with bemusement and then at me.

"Don't tell me you've turned him into a sports fanatic," she says.

Michael considers responding but merely shakes his head in annoyance.

"It really is an incredible match," I say. I fill her and the girls in on the situation but I can tell from their reaction either they don't understand the significance of what is now, officially, the longest match in not just Wimbledon but grand slam history, or they don't care. At least Frankie is willing to patronize us, by saying how "gripping" it all sounds. She offers to make tea, roping Sam into the effort, and I gratefully accept, while Michael grunts assent.

Sky hovers near Michael, clearly still taken with him, so I ask how the ride went and she gushes about her mount, a mare named

Demelza, and Frankie's horse Pasco and how beautiful the countryside is where they rode, which even afforded them a view of the River Fal. Fortunately Nicolas Mahut has another routine hold at love so Michael doesn't risk bursting Sky's balloon by shushing her as well.

The dogs, Gwyn and Jake, are inside now and they shuttle between the newcomers and their more familiar companions, accepting a pat on the head or a stroke of their backside with a wagging tail as steady and constant as a windshield wiper, and then plopping on the floor with a *thud*, only to hop up a moment later and move to someone else and repeat the process. There are encouraging domestic noises emanating from the kitchen: the strong, full-throated whistle of a heavy kettle at full boil, the rattle of china on a metal tray, and the rustle of what sounds like parchment paper, all amid Frankie's confident voice and the silly giggles of girls (Sky has joined Sam and Frankie there now). John Isner holds serve, easily this time, and Mahut does as well, and the summer afternoon takes on a dreamy quality, the light in London as beamed through the television set the same golden hue as the light streaming through the cottage's windows, as we approach what a cinematographer friend of my mother's once called the magic hour. I know it is an illusion but my real world worries seem somehow pushed away and shored up, at least temporarily. My lack of money doesn't matter here, nor my lack of a job, nor my lack of a house, nor my lack of a wife. There's not one but two dogs at my feet – they certainly don't care about such things – and there's this sweet young man sitting close by, with the soul of a surfer to match his haircut, who genuinely wants to connect with me. Rupert Salmons and his blasted inheritance laws seem very far away and Jeffrey what's his name more distant still. What do I call him, the Man with no (Evident) Flaws? Well, this place seems pretty flawless, with its horses and its dogs and its boats and its tradition. And these tennis players, these gentlemen warriors, how can they be any more perfect? They're sitting now at their changeover, at 38-37 in their 5th set, having played four full sets yesterday, and they're still energized, still up for more. What more can you ask of a man? Or of a moment in time? Abby told me

Jeffrey doesn't even play tennis. Of course he doesn't. She thought he did yoga. *Practiced* yoga, she said. Or maybe jogged. So, how could he understand? Even Michael here gets it. That all the other stuff is … what's the word? Ephemeral? That's it, ephemeral! But this, this moment in time – *this* is real. This has meaning. This has weight. This has importance. This has *significance*.

Frankie, Sky and Sam re-enter, each bearing a tray. There is tea of course, the pot covered in a blue quilted tea cozy, with a small pitcher of milk and a jar with demerara sugar. There are cups and saucers and small plates, in a jumble of nonmatching china patterns that, I recall, is Kenwyn family tradition. And there are two larger plates, one piled with thin ham, brown mustard and watercress sandwiches and the other filled with small round pastries that Frankie calls congress tarts.

"In honor of your esteemed colonial government," she says with a cheeky smile.

"Hopefully more sweet than unsavory," I say. There is much good-natured groaning, and Frankie pours the tea as Nicolas Mahut secures another routine hold and we all tuck into the food. The tarts have a delicious raspberry almond filling but are robust, almost crunchy, unlike the more delicate frangipane tarts you'd find in a French patisserie. Sky and I offer Frankie profuse compliments for them that she modestly rebuffs until her bluff is called by Sam, who laughingly outs her mother for having purchased them at a bakery in Mylor Bridge. Michael joins in the repast but remains focused on the tennis, watching John Isner serve his way to another routine hold of his own. Sky seems a bundle of confusion: the distraction of Michael, who pays her no notice; Samantha's girlishness, speaking to her inner child; Gwyn and Jake, who have settled on the rug next to Frankie, clearly the alpha dog; and my banter with Frankie, sparking a curiosity about her father's past. So Sky dives into the tea, replenishing her fuel tank from the ride, and lets her attention drift from one locus to the next, until a large black and white tabby cat materializes on her lap. The cat, we are told, is named Merlin, after the Arthurian sorcerer who inhabited Tintagel Castle on the north coast.

Watching Sky munch on a sandwich as she scratches Merlin's neck, I realize it's been awhile since she and I had our railway lunch. My tea is just the way I like it: dark and strong, with just a small splash of milk and less than a teaspoon of sugar to take the edge off. I ask Frankie about her meeting, what the work might entail, and she brings me up to speed on her career. That she shelved vet school for good when she returned to England and worked with several non-profits in London doing wildlife relief. Until family obligations got in the way and she tended to the children after she and Tom moved to Hampshire when his regiment was posted to Aldershot Garrison. And since moving back to Cornwall, how she's been doing some contract work with the Cornwall Seal Sanctuary in Gweek and teaching an occasional course in marine biology at the community college in Newquay. Earlier today, she had an interview with a new eco-tourism company planning to run marine wildlife safaris out of Falmouth. They were interested in having an expert on board but she wasn't sure she wanted to spend her time spotting basking sharks and leatherback turtles so vacationing Russians and Germans could snap photographs while drinking cold beer. Still, the family's military survivor's pension only went so far.

Frankie seems uncomfortable with where the conversation has drifted so she asks about my work. I give her the thumbnail version of events, trying not to sugarcoat it or sound dispirited. It's an odd interaction, to the say the least. Her natural inclination is to be understanding, but my not following her back to England – in order to continue my real estate career – hangs over us like the ghost of Banquo at the banquet. Plus there's something else, of what I'm not sure. It's not exactly guilt on her part – that would make no sense. Maybe something causing her discomfort. Or is it embarrassment? I'm grasping for meaning but a dark thought surfaces: maybe she wishes I'd been successful so at least our breakup wasn't in vain. Damn! What's all this vanity in my thinking, I wonder? I try to channel some better spirits of humanity, a little selflessness leavened with responsibility. Notice the psyche's need for self-blame then let it go, finding a middle way to compassion and connection. Be in the moment and accept it. This woman once meant so much to me, and I to her, but I'm a different person now and so is she.

"Here we go," Michael calls out, a dramatic edge in his voice. It's thirty-nine games all and Nicolas Mahut has taken John Isner to deuce on a lovely cross-court backhand return. Frankie looks amused again and the girls feign interest. Or is it more sincere now? I reengage in the match, noticing the American looks somewhat wearier and the Frenchman still sharp. Maybe, if he can just get a break here, he'll have a chance. But Isner fires an ace and then a first serve winner and he weathers the squall.

Frankie asks about our travel plans and I dig out the train schedule to confirm: the Night Riviera departs Truro at 10.17 p.m., after the connecting train leaves Penryn at 9.43 p.m. I check my watch reflexively and am surprised and disheartened to see it's nearly 7 p.m. It feels like we just got here and I say so. I knew our visit wouldn't afford a lot of time to catch up but I also didn't expect we'd spend it watching a first round Wimbledon match between two little-known players. As much as I might wish the match to end now, to give me and Frankie a few moments alone to talk, Mahut holds easily again and it seems he and his opponent each have the will to play on. And having apparently hooked Michael on this epic struggle, I can hardly suggest turning it off or ducking out myself. That would seem… treasonous somehow. So I take a deep breath and relax again into the moment. This strange confluence of events that we call life has conspired to put me in the Cornish countryside with Sky and three members of an English family, not quite strangers and becoming something beyond acquaintances as the match continues.

I notice a buzzing sound, which ends then returns a few seconds later. It dawns on me it's my cell phone, which has been inactive for the most part since its SIM card transplant surgery. I dig it out of my travel wallet and try to identify the caller but that doesn't seem to be possible post-op: the display shows a confusing hodgepodge of digits, parentheses and hyphens.

"Hello?" I say.

"Trevor, is that you?" The connection isn't great but I recognize the voice.

"Annie?"

"Is Sky okay? Why are you in Lithuania?"

"What? No. Just a second."

I excuse myself to Frankie and the others and step outside the cottage, to the obvious consternation of Michael. I'm stiff from sitting on the sofa and the ankle seems tighter, but I manage to hop a few paces away from the front door so that I should be well out of earshot.

"Trevor? Are you there? What's going on?"

"We're fine, everything's fine. Don't worry. We're in England. I left you a voicemail. Didn't you get it?"

"Yes, I know, that's why I'm calling. To Lithuania."

"No, the *cell* number is Lithuania. It's the chip, anyway, never mind – you got ahold of me. Sorry for any confusion."

"Well that doesn't explain why you brought Sky with you. Jesus, Trevor, what were you thinking? The very day we agree on custody? To up and take her out of the country? Are you crazy?"

"Probably. Believe me, it wasn't my plan either. Look, she got kicked out of her camp and she absolutely refused to stay with anyone there. What was I going to do? You were gone and I had to decide."

"Trevor – I'm still in Yosemite so I can't really deal with this now, I mean I just got Internet access for the first time since Monday. But – this is really serious. Did you close out my bank account with Sky? I got an email notice from B of A."

Christ. Okay, here we go. "Annie, things got complicated. The whole reason I'm here is to get some funds to get started again, this inheritance. I didn't have enough to pay for Sky's airline ticket. She insisted. It's her money, she said."

"Trevor." I can hear her trying to calm her voice down, which at any moment threatens to get hysterical. "Let me make this very clear. You are going to put her on the next flight back to San Francisco, today."

"Annie, there's an eight hour time difference. It's almost nighttime."

"I'm sure they have night flights."

"Look, we're not in London right now so that's going to be hard. But I can look into it tomorrow."

"Wait, what do you mean you're not in London? Where are you?"

I am silent, weighing my response.

"Trevor, I *said*, where are you?"

"In the country. We're taking the train back to London in a couple of hours."

"*Exactly* where are you?"

"Southern Cornwall."

There's a silence on her end.

"Isn't that where your old girlfriend lived? Francesca?"

"And now she's back here with her two daughters and son. She took Sky horseback riding earlier."

"Okay, I see. She's divorced, I presume." There's no jealousy in her tone, more a note of triumph, like she's fully unraveled my deception.

"Widowed actually. He was a British Army officer, blown to bits in Iraq."

"Jesus, Trevor. That wasn't necessary."

"No, it wasn't. Waste of a good man, from what I can tell."

"You know that's not what I meant."

"Annie, I have to tell you something. So brace yourself. Sky got herself tattooed. It's not very big, just a small outline of a horse's head on the inside of her ankle. I think she was pissed at me that the hotel where we were staying in London wasn't the Ritz so she found a tattoo parlor and must have pretended to be old enough."

Another silence. Then: "Okay. Thanks for telling me."

"You're not angry?"

"At you? Not about that. It doesn't sound like it's your fault. I suppose she could have done that in San Francisco just the same."

"Okay. Well, thanks for that, then." As I say this I realize I actually feel disappointed she didn't chew me out, thereby revealing her unreasonableness. But no such luck.

"I still want her on the first flight home tomorrow. Are we clear?"

"Does it ever get tiring always being right?"

"As opposed to what? Being the good cop? The free spirit? The jerk with a heart of gold? Yeah, it got real tiring. Tomorrow, Trevor.

189

Send me the flight information as soon as you have it. And you can replenish Sky's account when you get your money."

The *click* ending the call is actually audible in the transatlantic connection, a split-second before we're fully disconnected. I stare at the phone, then look around, a conscious attempt to reorient myself. The cottage is still there, sturdy as stone, and the thick leafy copse beyond. The brown Range Rover is still there too, practical and whimsical at once. That's a hard trick to pull off, I realize. It's usually one or the other. There was a time with me and Annie and the girls when we seemed to manage something like that. Suddenly that Tolstoy line about families pops into my head. Maybe it's this setting. I suppose it could be a stand-in for the Russian countryside, even though I've never been to Russia. All I've seen of it is in photographs and Hollywood depictions, such as *Doctor Zhivago*, and in my mind's eye reading a few of the great works of Dostoyevsky and Chekhov and Pushkin. What is it about those damned romantic, melancholy Russians?

'Happy families are all alike; every unhappy family is unhappy in its own way.'

Well, Count Leo, when you're right, you're right. It even used to be a point of pride for me, when things were good with Annie, the happiness pervading everything like the intoxicating, fragrant warmth of a spring day. That we were one of *those* families. The happy ones. And when things weren't? Good, that is? Well, it must have begun as a gradual slide past indifference and into frustration, until we found ourselves in a unique labyrinth of misery, a contorted puzzle of dark alleys and dead ends, with no way back to the starting place. We may be divorced now, but there's no real freedom in that, not when you're co-parents. That's another truism. So add this to your inventory of clichés, Mister Tolstoy: divorced families are and they aren't. Families, that is. What was that vapid bumper sticker I saw when I was driving to get Sky the other day? *Reality Sucks*. Well, yes – sometimes it does. Maybe even often. This might lack the elegance of Tolstoy but it sums things up pretty well.

I do my limping walk back towards the cottage but I stop before reaching for the doorknob. I lean against the Range Rover instead, stuff the phone in the front pocket of my jeans and cup my face in my hands. I so want to be grateful in this moment, to feel some measure of calm. I know my time-honored tricks to get there. Remembering the truly unfortunate, the hungry and war-torn in Africa. No, it would be cynical to call it a trick. Maybe it's a method but there's nothing wrong with that. Maybe I have only First World problems but they're my problems, dammit, and they require First World methods to solve them. And if you really want to talk about cynicism, then this whole First World-Third World (whatever happened to the Second World?) dichotomy can be Exhibit A, a form of holier-than-thou political correctness that might go so far as to label two white guys spending hours hitting a tennis ball for money on the finely manicured lawns of a private club as precious or decadent or worse. *Laissez-faire*, I say. If they aren't bothering you, don't bother them. And if you love someone, set them free. It's just, with Annie... that's hard to do. Was she even the tiniest bit jealous? No matter. Must keep trying. One goddamned point at a time. I take a deep breath and reach again for the door. And I open it wide.

Once inside, it's as if I'd never left. Everyone is in the same place – people, dogs, cat. And on the television screen: tennis players, ball boys, chair umpire, linesmen and spectators. The real persons in the room all swivel their heads towards me and then back to the screen. I can tell from Michael's nervous expression that something is up in the match.

"Isner is serving," Michael says. "Fifteen-thirty."

"Fifteen-*thirty*?" I repeat.

"One of the commentators on the telly said if Nicolas Mahut can win another point, he'll have two chances to break John Isner," says Samantha. She pronounces Mahut's given name 'Ni-co-lah' and his surname 'Ma-who' with a charming Anglo-French accent.

"Break his *service* he meant," Michael says softly.

Isner gets his first serve in, but Mahut returns it well to the deuce court. Isner, looking even more tired, lumbers over to his right to retrieve it but hits his forehand wide. 'Fifteen-Forty,' intones Mohamed Lahyani. The crowd is on its feet now, clapping and cheering and urging both men on, it seems.

"What's the set score now?" I ask.

"Fifty games all," Michael says. "And get this. The electronic scoreboard on the court has packed it in. It's frozen at forty-seven games each."

"Incredible," I say. I make my way back to my spot on the sofa and sit down. Isner fires a first serve that Mahut barely gets a racquet on and the spectators let out a collective gasp, followed by a mixture of scattered applause and murmurs. 'Thirty-Forty,' Lahyani says.

Sky shoots me a glance and I return it.

"Your mom says hi," I say. Sky nods, then immediately returns her attention to the screen. Well, I think, this is a first. Sky interested in tennis – televised tennis, no less. Frankie leans over and gently touches my shoulder.

"You okay?" she whispers. Her face is full of concern. I readjust my mouth in some semblance of a reassuring smile and nod stoically. Inside my throat a lump forms and I swallow hard to keep from losing it altogether. Our eyes hold each other for a moment, then perhaps a moment too long, until I form the words "I'm sorry" in scarcely a whisper. Frankie searches my face for more meaning, as if the answer lies there, then we both manage to break our gaze at once and return our attention to the television.

Isner lines up to serve in the ad court, bouncing the ball an extra few times.

"He looks knackered," Sam says.

"Well you'd be knackered if you were out there all day, wouldn't you?" Michael says. Isner serves and again Mahut returns it, but not that deep. Isner drives a two-handed backhand deep to Mahut's backhand side, then charges the net. Mahut brings the racquet back on his one-handed backhand yet instead of attempting a passing shot he hits a lob. But it's not high enough; the American easily camps out under the arcing parabola of the ball's path and puts away an overhead winner. 'Deuce,' the chair umpire says. The crowd is instantly on its feet again, yelling and clapping. 'Remarkable,' says the British commentator. 'How about that, Greg?' The American-sounding commentator says: 'Just amazing. For Isner to still have that kind of energy on the smash? Fantastic.'

I realize he must be Greg Rusedski, a former Canadian player who switched allegiance mid-career and then played for Britain, reaching the finals of the U.S. Open over a decade ago but never winning a major. With his big serve and volley game he'd been a threat to be the first British player to expunge the ghost of Fred Perry and win Wimbledon, but unlike Tim Henman I don't believe he ever made it past the quarterfinals. It must have been tough competing against the likes of Becker and Sampras in those days. So now he's doing television commentary for the BBC? Well, why not? He had his run at the brass ring and certainly knows more than most what it's like down there on the grass, slugging it out. Although, with the light fading for the second straight day, these two players still playing the same fifth set as they have for the last six hours, really no one could know what they're going through. It would take a voyeur of the soul to understand what's keeping each man upright and battling.

John Isner readies himself at the baseline to serve, then misses long. But his second serve seems a rocket of almost equal speed and forces a return error. Advantage in. He seems to summon some extra energy, from where God knows, and lines up more quickly to serve. Then he delivers another winner – Mahut can barely touch the ball, and it flies wide. 'Game Isner," Mohamed Lahyani calls out. 'Isner leads fifty-one, fifty.' The players trudge yet again to midcourt to sit. And the crowd gives them yet another standing ovation.

I feel I'm bearing witness to something truly special, bordering on the surreal, and if I'm not mistaken the others with me here do too. The television commentators have wisely gone silent, letting the moment speak for itself. Each athlete sits alone in his chair, just a few feet from the other but without outward acknowledgement, as it should be. It isn't dark yet but it could fairly be called dusk. Official sunset may be an hour away but we're well past the magic hour, the light now seeming scarce and fading fast, as a quick glance outside the cottage windows reminds me (the television cameras are not reliable, with their adjustable lens apertures). Spectators can be seen donning sweaters and coats to ward off the newly cooler air; even Mohamed Lahyani has put back on his chair umpire's navy jacket with white trim. But not Isner and Mahut, of course. They are still sweating from their exertions and, for the fiftieth time this set, Lahyani calls time and they each summon the energy to stand up, pick up their racquet and walk back on the court. As he has all day, Isner wears his white baseball cap backwards, like some goofy, giraffe-sized third grader. Mahut's only adornments, apart from the practical white sweatbands he, like Isner, wears on his wrists, are a string choker necklace, perhaps made of leather, holding a single disk of shiny metal, and a ring on his left pinky finger. With his electrified hair and hollow cheeks he really could be the front man in a punk rock band. But whatever he does for kicks, one thing is clear. He is a superb, gutsy competitor, just like his opponent.

Some might argue that the quality of play is not actually that high, that what we are witnessing is two guys serving extremely well and not much else. That this kind of situation is exactly why Jimmy Van Alen invented the tiebreaker: to prevent a succession of uninteresting service holds. But that would be missing the essence of what is happening. Not only have these players proved the value of playing out the fifth set because of the margin by which they've exceeded previous match records, they've created something else: a unique event, a dual work of art, a surely-never-to-be-repeated microcosm in the larger universe that is the Wimbledon tournament. What they've fashioned, by sheer willpower and luck, is a transformative experience. For themselves and anyone watching. John Isner and Nicolas Mahut are transforming the very nature of what it means to play a tennis match.

But to them they're doing nothing so grandiose. To them, they're doing the same thing they've been doing from the start of the match yesterday. They're playing one point. And then another.

So that's what they keep doing, in the continually waning light. There are no threats to break, just more aces and service winners. Each man holds. Every two games, they sit and drink more water, eat another banana and stare straight ahead. And then they get up and do it again. And we in this stone cottage in Cornwall watch, transfixed. As no doubt others do in other parts of England and – I can only guess – elsewhere in the world.

Finally, when it seems something surely has to give, it does – there is a break. But not a break of service. At fifty-eight games apiece, right after Mahut has won his service game and Isner is about to serve, the chair umpire calls for a break of play so the players may visit the locker room. A wave of laughter goes through the crowd. A bathroom break! I check my watch – 8.45 p.m.

"How long will this last?" Sam asks. "Will they continue playing?"

"It's not clear," Michael says.

"They'll sometimes let matches go until nine-fifteen or nine-thirty," I say.

"Well, I tell you what, then," Frankie says. "If they're having a bathroom break, we should as well."

And that's what we do. Taking turns, we each get up and use the bathroom. And like a spellbound gawker returning to the scene of an accident, each time someone finishes up he or she rushes back to the others of us still gathered in front of the television and asks: "Have they started again?"

By some miracle of timing, when the last person returns – which happens to be me – the players have returned as well and play quickly resumes. And John Isner starts the game off with an ace. A few points later, he does the same to win the game. 'Isner leads fifty-nine, fifty-eight,' the chair umpire announces.

During the changeover, Mahut looks somehow different. I wouldn't describe it as worried, but there's an apprehensiveness about him. Maybe, like everyone else, he's wondering when the officials will call the match for lack of light. Or maybe he's having genuine difficulty seeing the ball. Any player would, and I seem to recall he was the one struggling the most in the darkness of the fourth set tiebreaker yesterday.

Sure enough, even though Mahut starts his service game with an ace, he double-faults the next point with a ball into the net. And while he manages to win the next two points, he loses the two after that, the second on a framed shot where he clearly lost sight of the ball. The score goes to deuce. The crowd seemed somewhat subdued after the bathroom timeout but they are fully engaged again, on their feet and clapping and cheering. There's a sense this could be it, one way or another. The end of the match or the end of play. I feel anxious too, but there's something more. A rising sense of, what? Indignation? I hate the thought of Mahut losing because the light is too poor to properly see the ball. After all we've witnessed that would seem an injustice.

"God, I'm nervous," Frankie says.

"Me too," Sky says.

"Imagine how Nico feels," Michael says.

"Come on!" Sam says.

"Who are you rooting for?" I ask.

"Both of them," she replies, in a matter-of-fact tone, as if any other possibility would be completely nonsensical.

"That doesn't make any sense," Michael says.

"Well then who are you supporting?" Sam asks.

But Michael remains silent on that topic.

Mahut readies himself and serves into the net. Sighs all around. He serves again and the cry of a line judge rings out, clear and loud. Double fault.

"Oh my God," Sky says. There's rising panic among the spectators. After such an epic match, to end like this? 'Advantage Isner," Lahyani says, but what he really means is, match point. Just one more point for John Isner and we're finally done.

Nicolas Mahut stands in the ad court, toes the baseline and readies again to serve. What must he be thinking, I wonder? No matter – for he serves another ace, right down the tee.

What was panic before is now bedlam. The crowd is beyond joy. For Isner, clear disappointment. And for Mahut? No visible emotion at all. Just readying himself for one more point. It is still deuce, after all.

Finally, with a nudge from Lahyani, the crowd quiets enough for him to serve again. A miss long. Big sighs. He spins in the second serve – he's bound and determined not to double-fault again – and it sits up, a big juicy meatball to John Isner's forehand. Isner winds up and – shanks the ball long. Isner doubles over in agonized disbelief, grabs his shirt in his left hand and stuffs it into his mouth. Mahut looks at him, perhaps distracted, but he can't permit himself the loss of focus and he gets back to work. Ad in. I steal a glance at

Sky and Sam and Michael and Frankie. They all have the same mesmerized expression. I permit myself a momentary mental time-out to wonder what I've wrought by asking Michael to turn the match on, like Frankenstein might have wondered upon regarding his scientific handiwork, then I let myself get pulled back into the tennis again.

Mahut gets his next first serve in, strong to Isner's backhand, and the return sails wide. Game Mahut, 59-59.

Nicolas Mahut, instead of preparing to return serve, walks to the chair umpire. We can't hear what he is saying, but he is gesturing and it isn't hard to guess. He is complaining about the lack of light and wants to stop. Soon John Isner joins him at the net, in front of the chair umpire, and enters the conversation. He apparently wants to continue. But it isn't really an argument, more of a calm discussion, using Lahyani as intermediary. In due course a tournament referee carrying a walkie-talkie is summoned. We all watch the proceedings without saying a word. There is more talk, while the clock keeps ticking and the light keeps fading. Each player is now leaning on the net. They are tired.

Like some weird kabuki drama unfolding, the four men – two players and two officials – look to each other seeking an answer. They seem to know what it is, but no one wants to state it. Then finally, with the universal signal of two hands slicing away from each other on the horizontal plane – cut! – the referee decides. Play suspended. Done. Over. At least for today. The match has lasted ten hours already. Ten hours! Far longer than any match before it. And still it won't end.

18

It's hard to say exactly who is responsible for Sky and me not being on the train from Penryn to Truro. We are at the Pandora Inn on Restronguet Creek instead, at a long, communal table on the patio outside, along with Frankie, Michael and Sam. The Pandora sits all by itself at the foot of a steep hill on an inlet to the Carrick Roads, a whitewashed two-story building with a thatched roof. It looks like it's been here forever, although the menu says it dates to the 13th century. The kids are drinking sparkling lemonade while Frankie and I sip from pint glasses of a cask ale called Tribute. A double order of steamed mussels is on its way while we mull over the main courses. The prices, thankfully, are reasonable, but the thought of my nearly depleted Cash Passport threatens to sink my newly buoyed spirits, especially as I feel duty-bound to treat Frankie and her brood.

After Michael turned off the television set back at Trewithy Cottage, it took a few moments for everyone to emotionally collect themselves. Watching the tennis match had been that draining, especially with the lack of a resolution. At Frankie's prompting, the kids took the dogs outside to give them a bit of exercise and, ostensibly, afford us an opportunity to chat. But after checking my watch I realized we had at best a few minutes before we had to leave for Penryn, so we only managed a frustrating exchange of enhanced small talk before joining the kids. There seemed an intuitive understanding between us that delving into any real conversation would be an exercise in futility. Or worse. There was simply too much ground to cover and too little time. On the way out the door, Frankie handed me a wooden cane, which she said her father had used the year before he died. My initial response, apart from being touched, was to decline the offer: it seemed too precious an object for her to part with. But she insisted and seemed to leave open the possibility of a future meeting, saying I could "always return it when my ankle healed."

Outside, the kids had formed a large triangle and were calling Gwyn and Jake between them. It was fun watching them – the dogs were being run ragged, so were as happy as dogs can be – and I hated to end the party. But we had a train to catch. I used the cane to help me approach Sky but she cleverly avoided me by continually stretching the triangle. Finally, I had no choice but to be firm.

"Sky, come on sweetheart. We need to go."

"I don't want to go yet."

"Can't she stay a little longer?" This, from Sam.

What followed was a rondel of sorts, with me and Frankie half-heartedly trying to engineer the departure and the kids resisting. No one really wanted us to go, except I knew we must. I just couldn't miss my meeting with Rupert Salmons. It was Michael who volunteered the information that there was an early morning train that we might possibly take. I actually had seen it on the schedule earlier.

"Really?" I said. I looked at Frankie for some hint of opinion on the subject, one way or the other. Of course the kids followed suit so there were four sets of eyes set upon her, apart from the dogs who just trotted around in circles, panting, wondering why all the fun had stopped.

"But would that work with your meeting?" she said. That was all the opening I needed. Pulling out the train schedule, I confirmed that the Golden Hind train arrived London Paddington at 10.02 a.m., giving me plenty of time to make my 11 a.m. appointment in the City. But the train departed Truro at 5.38 a.m., before there was any connecting service from Penryn. Surely that was too inconvenient for Frankie, Michael and Samantha. Now instead of four sets of eyes, Frankie was greeted with a chorus of demurrals from her kids and entreaties from Sky. No, it was no bother at all! Couldn't we stay? It was the summer holidays after all! They didn't mind leaving so early. It could be a slumber party and everyone could sleep properly after our departure. The drive to Truro was scarcely any farther than going to Penryn!

In response to all this, Frankie simply smiled and give me a look that said, nicely done. She'd been snookered and she knew it. But not, I submit, completely unwillingly. After that, the only remaining piece of business was what to do about dinner, and it was decided unanimously by the locals that we should all pile in the Range Rover and drive to the Pandora. After Frankie and Sky changed out of their riding clothes, that is. Sky seemed thrilled by the turn of events so I figured no good could come from telling her that her mother wanted her on a flight home tomorrow. That bit of news could wait for the train ride back to London.

The Pandora is busy, with the outdoor tables mostly full, and everyone seems to be in a festive mood. Between the England victory in the World Cup and the warm summer weather, there's no doubt plenty to be cheerful about. And perhaps others here were watching the tennis match as well. The Pandora has a pontoon pier to allow customers to arrive by boat, in addition to the small car park, and I noticed a Falmouth water taxi departing as we arrived. The temperature, if I had to guess, is in the high sixties – still comfortable enough to eat outside even though the sun has disappeared. The air contains a lively mixture of odors: food aromas from the kitchen, garlic and onions and grilled beef, mostly; a mild brininess from the creek; and night-blooming jasmine from somewhere near the footpath below the pub.

The kids seem to have bridged the gaps in age and gender and nationality and have found common ground. From what I overhear in brief snippets, the conversational threads include celebrities (music and film), what certain friends are doing (even though this must be largely meaningless to the others), technology (social media sites, cool products), cable television shows (Sky likes *Mad Men*? Since when?), and differences between California and Cornwall. In any event, it does free up space for me to finally talk with Frankie. Not in true privacy of course, but at least at some length.

We ease into the topic of our former spouses by sharing some sympathetic observations on marriage. How hard it is to get in synch with another person when you're with them either too much or not enough (this was more a problem for Frankie with Tom's frequent work absences) or one of you is neater or messier than the other (Frankie and I were both the messier ones, we agree). The wonderful, maddening conundrum of kids, who both bring you closer to your spouse and push you apart, with inevitable differences in parenting style and fewer opportunities for intimacy. And how sex and money are often the unspoken topics with other couples, as no one feels comfortable divulging how much they want or get or can do without. Frankie and I have a small, ironic chuckle after the awkward pause that greets our broaching this last topic.

"Okay," I say. "I admit, I had to draw the line with Annie at once a day. I was just getting too exhausted with the demands she was placing on me for more."

"Yes, I can see that would be a problem," Frankie says. "But Tom and I reckoned twice a day was about right."

Our laugh now is both heartfelt and rueful. For different reasons, of course. But rueful just the same.

"He must have been quite a guy," I say, delivering the line straight with no hint of sarcasm. This catches Frankie off guard and I can see her visibly struggling to keep her composure.

"Christ," she finally says. "After all this time."

"Sorry," I say.

"No, it's … it's been fine, really. Being down here has helped enormously. There are none of the usual reminders. I mean, I miss Tom, of course, but I worry about the kids, Michael especially. I thought Paul would be good for him, having an uncle nearby to be a male influence, but he's been pretty useless, really. Not that he's any better with his own children."

"You must think couples who divorce are mad, given what you've gone through. Or worse."

"Why? It's not like Tom and I didn't have our problems. I can't imagine most couples don't entertain the idea at some point. For us though, I think we were just too busy muddling through. And it sounds like, with you and Annie, the loss of your business was a huge strain."

"No doubt. And I certainly give myself the lion's share of blame. But I can't help thinking a stronger couple would have survived. I mean, I know one couple who dealt with the wife having an affair. They said it made them stronger in the long run."

"Not me. I always told Tom I'd kill him if I caught him cheating."

I get a devilish urge and Frankie looks at me with trepidation, realizing she's left herself open for some kind of zinger of a response. She of all people knows I'm a firm believer in the sanctity – even necessity – of black humor. If we can't laugh at our misfortune, then what else is there to keep us sane? But I realize I can't do that to her, not about this.

"He'd have been a fool to leave you. Believe me, I know."

This clearly catches Frankie off guard. "Trevor, please, let's not go there." She nervously looks at the kids but they're oblivious to our conversation. So I lean in closer and lower my voice.

"Fine. This is all I want to say. I'm sorry I didn't come after you. I was scared and I thought I needed to stay put but I was wrong. I don't regret meeting Annie and having Sky and Abby but I do regret not following you."

"You do realize how contradictory that is, don't you?"

"So what? Fitzgerald said the test of a first-rate intelligence is the ability to hold two opposing ideas in the mind at the same time."

She laughs. "You're saying you have a first-rate intelligence? Now that clearly is grounds for the loony bin."

"Okay. Maybe you're right."

Our waitress arrives with the appetizer: two large bowls of dark mussels in an enticingly steamy broth that smells of garlic, wine and fennel, in addition to the briny mussels themselves. Together with a half-baguette of warm, crusty sourdough bread and a ramekin of fresh butter, this seems a meal unto itself. But the kids dig in as if tea never happened, or was at least several hours ago, which of course it was.

The five of us speculate about the outcome of the tennis match tomorrow, with the consensus being that John Isner and Nicolas Mahut will keep playing until the match is again called for darkness. The minority opinion is that Mahut will prevail, because Isner appeared to be more tired and therefore his service is bound to falter first. The kids seem relieved when Frankie and I allow them to drift off into their separate adolescent conversation and we resume our own, over fresh pints of ale.

It seems that a clearing of the air has occurred between us, if not fully then at least sufficient for us to fall into both familiar and new patterns of discussion. Topics like politics (world and national), animal rights (conservation and husbandry) and the state of the novel (still thriving) vs. popular music (possibly tapped out) can be lightly touched on or drilled into more deeply, even seriously, as the mood strikes us, in an easy flow that reminds me why I was so attracted to Frankie in the first place, apart from her more obvious attributes. It's as if we've rediscovered an old two-person skiff in a boatshed, weather-beaten from prior use and dusty from non-use, and lowered it into the water to find, lo and behold, the seats still fit, it's still seaworthy and we still know how to row it. More confident now, our oars back in rhythm, we can raise our heads up and look around and say: 'Remarkable! Well, where shall we row it now?' But it's a question I don't wish to even entertain. For I fear we are rowing in a narrow, closed canal.

Our dinners arrive: beer-battered fish of the day (plaice) for me and Frankie, and burgers (Cornish beef) for the kids, with shoestring fried potatoes and side salads all around. Even before tasting, I can tell this is vastly superior pub food than we got in my childhood. The beer we've been drinking is a true session bitter, moderate in hops and alcohol, so before we're too far into our fish and chips Frankie and I order another pint each. I feel a pleasant mild buzz, nothing much but just enough to heighten the sense of conviviality and soften the more painful edges of reality. It's as close to a state of serenity as I've experienced in quite a while. I am still aware that tomorrow will be a day of reckoning, but it's now a compartmentalized thought, not an overwhelming one.

Frankie and I share some dreams and frustrations about our respective fields of work, in effect bringing each other up to date on well-known aspects of ourselves. One of the things that drew me to Frankie was her passion for the marine animal kingdom: protecting endangered species; safeguarding and treating particular animals that have or might be harmed in the oceans or on shore; and raising environmental awareness. I'd like to think she held a reciprocal appreciation for my interest in urban design and renewal, even though she personally prefers living outside of cities. But it occurs to me now, watching her react to me talking about my frustrations with the current skyline of San Francisco and the design review process, that had our interests actually over-lapped more we might have found a way to stay together. So I run this up the flagpole for her consideration. And instantly regret it, based on the frown it produces.

"I've never thought that mattered," she says. "What does Annie do?"

"Now, she runs the admissions office for the private school the girls attend. Before, she worked at USF administering an interdis-ciplinary program for undergraduates."

"So her passion is education."

"I suppose that's right. Although I always thought of her more as an academic who never committed herself to research or teaching. Maybe her passion lies in learning."

"Well that sounds fairly urban. Or is certainly consistent with it."

"What about Tom?"

"His being in the Army?"

I nod, yes. Frankie looks away, maybe to gather her thoughts, and then turns back.

"The thing I discovered about the military is that all different sorts go in for it. Politically, emotionally, you name it. I suppose that was the biggest surprise. I mean, obviously, they were all suf-ficiently patriotic – Tom wasn't any different there – but in some regards he was the least likely person you'd expect to be a career soldier. Although he swore his joining had nothing to do with it being a family tradition."

"Did you believe him?"

"I had to. The man never uttered a falsehood in his life, as far as I can tell."

"That's remarkable," I say.

"Tell me about it. Believe you me, it was no fun trying to live up to that kind of example day in and day out. But he seemed to tolerate my failings without a fuss. Apparently he only set a lofty standard for himself."

"And he had no problem with using military force?"

"Quite the contrary. He had tremendous problems with it. You've no idea how reticent the officer corps is to commit troops into combat. Especially the ones who'd had firsthand experience. Even though Tom didn't, I think he was smart enough and sensitive enough to understand. I mean, not just the risks – you only have to read the names on the war memorial plaques in any school or village to see that – but the complexities. The folly of best intentions."

"So… how did he react when he was…" My voice peters out, as I worry that I'm treading on inappropriate ground.

"When he was sent to Iraq?" She looks directly at me and squares her mouth. I nod.

"He was thrilled."

"But you said…"

"I know," she says, "and it probably makes no sense. Ever since there'd been discussion about invading Iraq he thought it was a huge mistake. And he hated the idea of leaving the kids and me. I'm sure it must have occurred to him that he might not return. The only sense I can make of it is that he figured he'd do a better job of looking after his troops, so better he go than someone else. And…"

She turns her head towards the creek, dark now expect for the lights on the dock. After perhaps several seconds she turns back.

"I think Tom was curious. To see how all their work, all their training would be reflected. I didn't ask him this, of course. I didn't want to put him on the spot and I was upset enough about his having to go. He would have wanted to tell me the truth – that damned honest streak of his – and it would have made him seem small-minded or bloodthirsty or something. After he was killed I was angry at him for that, for not resisting or arguing with his superiors about what a stupid mission it was, but now I realize he could never have done that. It was his chosen profession and he knew the protocol as well as I. Anyway, my anger was just one of the stages of grief. But I only made real peace with it when I remembered something he'd said to me once. About how fairness isn't seen in the moment but in the big picture. I'd been beating myself up about how I'd scolded Michael. He must have been six or seven, still very much an innocent boy, really. I'd caught him hurting a lizard and I was really harsh, saying how cruel he was, how no child of mine could behave that way towards animals. Later, after I'd apologized, Michael was still upset, so naturally I was very upset with myself, the way we parents are sometimes, and Tom tried to cheer me up. He said what matters wasn't how I behaved as a mother in that instance but how I approached the whole enterprise of mothering."

She pauses and fixes me with that direct look from a moment ago.

"I don't think Tom died in a good or just war but I know he viewed his job itself as vital to civilization, a necessary evil if you will, and that he approached it with goodness and justice. And when I realized that, it gave me enough comfort to deal with losing him."

Looking at Frankie now, I'm filled with a cascade of emotions. Gratitude for her honesty and openness in sharing such an intimacy with me. Warmth and longing for her, or maybe it's a left-over desire for Annie or just a certain type of woman in general, the uniquely sexy combination of sweetness and strength that has always been my undoing. Relief that she doesn't blame America – and by extension me – for Tom's death. And guilt for having questioned whether he'd died in vain.

"This may sound silly but I was worried you'd hold a grudge against anyone American – even me – for what happened to Tom."

She gives me an odd, almost confused look and I realize I've probably said too much. Out of some misguided need to equal Tom in the honesty department and unburden myself.

Frankie lifts her beer glass to her lips and then sets it back down without taking a sip. "After we talked on the phone last night, I realized that on some level I *was* angry at you. But I don't think it was about the war, even though I do admit that I hated America, or a certain aspect of America, after Tom was killed. What I felt was… a bit of the emotional memory of our breakup. How painful it was, not having you come back with me, want to be with me."

"I *did* want to be with you," I say.

"Please don't argue, Trevor. I don't want to rehash what we went through all those years ago. It really doesn't matter anymore. It really doesn't. We made the choices we did and our lives moved on. After I got over my heartache and I met Tom, I was happy, genuinely happy. No regrets. I don't say that in a mean way, it's just how it was. But after you called, hearing your voice again, some of those old feelings came up for me. And if I'm being totally honest, I was disappointed in myself for saying yes to your visit."

"Are you still sorry you said yes?"

Frankie smiles and reaches for her pint glass again. "I haven't been for a ride in ages. And I got to meet Sky."

"Ouch. Forget I asked."

Frankie turns serious.

"Trevor, I know you've had some real loss so hopefully you can understand. Everything I've been through – Tom, my father, now my mother – what all that has taught me is, look for the small nuggets of everyday joy and avoid the drama. I just don't need any more sadness in my life, okay?"

"I'll drink to that." I lift my glass and clink Frankie's, then swallow what's left of the beer.

The kids have finished their burgers by now and have migrated to the pontoon dock. I ask Frankie if she thinks they'll want dessert but she says no, let's not stay – there's some sweet at the cottage if anyone wants it. A chill passes through me – I almost want to say 'someone walked over my grave' because the old Britishisms seem to be bubbling out of me lately (even though I always hated that one) – and I wonder if it's just the cooling night air or the last few minutes of conversation with Frankie. Well, even if that's how we need to leave things, I'm glad I reached out to her and invited ourselves down here. She might think I've stirred things up but I feel like we've cleared some unfinished business. She's a grown woman, after all, and she could have said no, don't come down. And the fact is, we've had some really enjoyable moments today. I feel like I've shown Sky a little more about who I am than she knew before, which can't be a bad thing. It also felt nice connecting with Michael earlier, watching the tennis match. Little moments, to be sure, but maybe it's something he'll remember. Even the smallest connection can make a day – a shared kind word and a smile with a grocery checker – and this was certainly more than that. Like Frankie says, mining the small nuggets of everyday joy.

Frankie excuses herself to visit the ladies room and I wait for our waitress to finish delivering drinks at another table so I can get the bill. She finally looks over and I give her the universal 'scribble signature' sign, and she nods, smiles and departs, giving me perhaps my first moment alone today. To honor and savor it, I slowly take in and then exhale a huge breath of air.

If the bill comes in about what the train lunch cost, that should leave me roughly $500 on the CashPort. More than enough for meals and transport in London tomorrow for Sky and me. And once she's safely on her flight home, I only have myself to take care of. But I reacquaint myself with a certain nagging thought that is starting to feel like a toe rubbing inside a shoe. The thought is: Should I prevail upon Rupert Salmons to release my (and Meg's) rightful inheritance, he isn't likely to issue a bank check on the spot. I try to dispel this concern with the confident belief that, if the settlement were a done deal, Meg would advance me some petty cash to last until the check clears. And if I'm not successful with Salmons? Well, that doesn't bear thinking about. What's the point of imagining losing a match while you're in the midst of playing it?

The waitress reappears to take another table's order and then disappears again, without leaving the bill. This momentarily frustrates me until I realize I'm not used to the more relaxed restaurant customs in Europe. At home, the bill would have materialized before I asked for it, in order for the restaurant to turn the table. I want to take care of this before Frankie returns, to spare her the perfunctory need to offer to share the tab, but no matter. It will be dealt with just the same.

Frankie reappears and sits down with a warm smile, those dimples as visible in the lantern light and just as beguiling. I catch a hint of her fragrance, not as strong as perfume (which was never her style), but subtle and feminine-earthy, like expensive milled soap mixed with what remains of a healthy athlete's dried perspiration several hours later. My attraction to her was apparent to me at the Penryn coffee shop and often since, but this is the first time it's felt primal, as a deep lustful yearning.

"All right?" she asks.

"Great. Just waiting for the bill."

"Oh. That's already taken care of. I hope you don't mind."

"What do you mean?" I'm genuinely confused.

"My treat. Now please don't make a fuss. You're on my turf and we invited you out."

"Frankie, what are you talking about? I invited *us* down here. And we've overstayed our departure time to boot. This is on me. I insist."

"Oh dear. Well, the thing is, I've already paid. So let's not worry about it, all right? It really has been my pleasure, Michael and Sam's as well. All these years, my goodness. I know you've got delicate financial matters to attend to tomorrow. Let me do this for you."

As she says this, I realize I haven't gone into minute detail about the extent of my impoverishment, just that I came to London needing to address my mother's waylaid inheritance. But the way Frankie just phrased it, that word 'delicate,' the 'let me do this for you,' makes me wonder. How much does she know? And from whom?

"Did Sky say something? I *can* pay for dinner."

She averts her eyes and I detect a note of guilt in her expression.

"She did, didn't she? Jesus."

"Look, I didn't want to embarrass you in any way. Please don't say anything to Sky, it's not her fault. You know how kids are. She must have wanted to share something with me, maybe as a way to get to know me. The point is, I know you, Trevor. You aren't some macho guy who thinks the man has to pay for everything. And it's not like we're on some date anyway. Okay, you're a bit strapped for cash right now. No problem. You'll get it sorted out, probably start another real estate firm that's even bigger than your last one, and this will all be long forgotten."

"Will it?" I hold her eye but she looks away in discomfort.

"That didn't come out right. I meant... well, you damn well know what I meant."

"I'm not sure I do. But I'm not going to fight you for the bill. I certainly don't want to be accused of being some macho Neanderthal. So I'll just say 'thank you.'" My male pride definitely feels bruised but I don't want to make a scene.

She looks at me with genuine gratitude. "You're welcome." Then she's suddenly her old, feisty self, possibly more for effect. "Hey, I said macho, not Neanderthal."

"Whatever," I say with a semi-forced smile. She looks pleased and relieved. We seem to have a tacit understanding that nothing should be allowed to spoil this day, not a petty disagreement over who pays for dinner, nor a misunderstanding on the appropriate bounds of discussion about the war that killed Frankie's husband.

"Right, then," she says. "Shall we round up the others?"

I grab her father's cane, tipping it in her direction in acknowledgment of her kindness in providing it to me, and I push myself up from the table.

"Let's," I say.

It takes a small search to find Michael, Sky and Sam, who are now near the public footpath beyond the dock. There are some older teens along the path – I detect a whiff of a joint – but as far as I can tell our children aren't up to anything other than wanting to be near where the 'action' is, whatever that means. Sky seems to be enjoying herself, maybe because she can be the older, more interesting female in Michael's eyes. And indeed, he appears less annoyed with her than before, while Sam continues to be in her thrall. They give me and Frankie a bit of good-natured grief about leaving so soon but then they hatch some plan in whispered voices to continue the merriment back at the cottage. And then we are walking back to the Range Rover.

Frankie and I utter not a word on the drive to Trewithy. It's all silly banter from the kids in the back seat, Samantha leading the fray. In the front, Frankie concentrates on the narrow road as illuminated by the surprisingly less-than-powerful headlights. I sit in the passenger seat as before, holding the cane in my left hand and the armrest with my right, and I allow the moment to wash over me without conscious thought. Except the realization, midway through the trip, that life is funny. A couple of days ago I had absolutely no earthly notion that I'd find myself here, in the remote Cornish countryside, being driven home from a pub dinner by a long-lost love. A cruel joke from above? How things just happen? Or part of some cosmic plan? I have no answers, so I let the questions slip away like flotsam on an ebb tide and surrender to what is.

Once back at the cottage we're greeted by Jake and Gwyn as if they haven't seen us in weeks. It's hard to be philosophical when confronted with not one, but two tail-wagging dogs. Nothing's more simple and grounding. They seem to have an endless reservoir of unalloyed loyalty and love, which is the whole point of having a dog, isn't it? Apart from the ones who perform actual jobs. I finish a mental note – started earlier, before we left for dinner – to get another dog when my living circumstances permit. But since that probably won't be soon I make sure to get my fill of these two lovely creatures, fussing over them to the tune of "what a good boy!" and "hello there, girl!" I sense Frankie might be indulging me for she delays opening the cottage's front door.

Inside, Sam heads straight for the television and turns it on – apparently this was the grand plan she orchestrated back at Restronguet – then flips the channel from a news program to one showing a movie. It takes but a second for me to recognize the film: Juliette Binoche, playing a French-Canadian nurse, tends to Ralph Fiennes as the eponymous (and impressively charred and shriveled) *English Patient*. Frankie starts to protest the TV going on at this late hour – it's past eleven-thirty – but Michael reminds her what we all agreed, about not bothering to go to bed given our early train departure. She looks at me for affirmation and I shrug.

"It's fine," I say. "Sky can sleep on the train." So the kids settle in while Frankie and I move to the kitchen.

"What about you?" she says. "You need to be at your best for your meeting with that solicitor." She fills the kettle from the faucet and puts it back on the stove.

"I'll grab a couple of hours on the train as well. A little spruce up in the washroom at Paddington and I'll be right as rain."

She laughs. "Right as rain, is it? When did you become so English?"

"Hey, if you can't beat 'em, join 'em."

"You're forgetting you did beat 'em," she says.

"Did we? I'm not so sure."

She looks at me with a puzzled expression. "I have no idea what you mean and it's far too late and I've had far too much beer to try to figure it out. Would you like some coffee or tea?"

I shake my head. "Let's save that for later, when I really need it."

She seems a bit adrift, looking at the kids in the living room, then to the stove and back at me.

"You sure you don't want to rest? You could doss out in the boys' room for a bit."

"Are you going to watch the movie?" I ask.

She wrinkles her nose. "I've seen it before. You know me, I'm no good with romantic weepies. They reduce me to a warm puddle of snot."

"That would be bad."

"It would!" She laughs and I'm not sure if it's at her or me.

"Let me use the loo" – I grin to let her know I'm laying on the Brit-speak intentionally thick – "and we'll come up with a plan for my remaining hours of captivity."

"Captivity?!" she says, her eyes glinting with gold-flecked daggers. "You can jolly well walk to Truro in that case."

I start towards the bathroom. "Do people still say jolly? Well, isn't that smashing!"

She grabs the tea cozy from the tray on the counter and swats my butt, playfully but hard enough to make a solid *thwack*.

"Oww! Hitting cripples now? Very nice, that is!"

"Get on with you," she laughs, and I make my way to the bathroom. As I shut the door the urge to urinate is suddenly intense, even painful, making my teeth and jaw ache, and when I start to relieve myself it takes what seems at least half a minute to feel close to comfortable again, then another half-minute to finish.

"Fucking horse," I say to myself in the mirror, for no other reason than to try to amuse myself. But I don't feel very amused. I find a tube of toothpaste in the medicine cabinet, squirt a generous dollop on my right index finger and go at my teeth and mouth to try to freshen my breath. I don't feel much of a buzz from the beer anymore, but I realize I'm dehydrated so I run the cold-water tap to both rinse the toothpaste and drink from it. Finally, I splash some water on my face and dry off with the hand towel. I won't say I look or feel good but it's an improvement over a few minutes ago.

Back in the hallway, I stand still a moment, listening to the television. It sounds like the Sahara desert sandstorm scene when Kristin Scott Thomas and Ralph Fiennes get trapped inside their vehicle. I can hear Fiennes, as Count Almásy, describing the different winds: the *Ghibli*, the *Harmattan*, the *Simoun*, and I'm torn – I want to watch along with the kids but I'd also like to have a quick peek in the cottage's bedrooms, which I haven't seen yet. There are just three bedrooms, it seems: one for Michael and his younger brother, Frankie said, one for Samantha and one for Frankie. The cottage isn't large; the footprint is actually smaller than our house in San Francisco, which had all three bedrooms upstairs, but the stone walls, flagstone floors and thick wood beams lend it a substantial, generous feel. A fine blue and beige Persian runner covers the length of the bedroom hallway – Isfahan, I believe, judging by the repeating floral pattern – and for the first time today I feel less the intruding outsider and more a genuine houseguest.

I inch towards the doorway I assume belongs to the master bedroom, even though the hallway's ceiling lamp doesn't throw much light inside.

"The boys' room is that one," Frankie says, pointing to the doorway across the hall. She materialized behind me so suddenly that she startles me. And judging by her reaction – a quick, muffled laugh – I think she enjoys having done so.

"The cottage is wonderful," I say, remaining deadpan. "It would be great as is, I'm sure, but you've made it feel really cozy."

"Thanks. I wanted it to be a sanctuary for the kids. It wasn't easy, uprooting them from Hampshire, their schools and all their friends. At least they'd already spent holidays here."

"On the train Sky told me that parents underestimate their children's ability to cope with change. But she hasn't forgiven me for selling her horse."

"She will, just give her time. Oh, I meant to tell you – she's a remarkably skilled rider. But I'm sure you know that."

I nod and drift into Frankie's room, or as close as one can be said to drift with a gimpy ankle and a cane, and Frankie follows, flipping on the light switch. I blink from the brightness and look around. The room is perhaps twelve feet square and is furnished simply with a full size bed, a single nightstand, a bureau and an armoire, all antiques of different yet harmonious dark-stained woods. The walls are white plaster with three unframed oil paintings, modern landscapes just this side of abstract by presumably the same artist. I point to the nearest one and Frankie says: "My cousin, Emily. All of them." I nod and say, "Nice." The nightstand has on it a recent photograph of Frankie with all three of her children overlooking the sea and several books, mostly unfamiliar novels and a biography of Gertrude Bell. The bureau has about a dozen framed photos on it, including a larger one in the middle of a sandy haired man in an officer's uniform, not dress blues but the more casual open-collared khakis. I step towards the bureau to have a closer look. He was good-looking, no doubt about it, but the dominant sense I get of him is of amused detachment, like he knows the photograph won't reflect who he really is.

"Yes, that's Tom," Frankie says, placing slow and equal emphasis on each word as if she were addressing a child or someone unfamiliar with the English language.

I look at her and she's observing me carefully, like a cat ready to pounce or flee at the slightest provocation. Or remain perched where it is, guarded and watchful, if there isn't a provocation requiring a reaction. Yet.

"I am so very, very sorry," I say.

She evidently wasn't expecting this, for I see her lower lip start to quiver and she looks away, then she starts to crumple into a sort of half-bend from the waist, before she catches herself and stands back up, erect, but facing completely away from me. I'm at a loss for what to do, whether to comfort her or leave her be, so I reflexively move towards the doorway. She must hear me moving, for she turns and looks at me again, wiping a tear from her eye as she does.

"I'm okay, really I am. It's just… emotions."

"Sorry, I didn't mean to… upset you."

"You don't need to apologize. It's what you felt."

"That's true," I say.

Frankie sighs and sits on her bed, midway between the head-board and footboard, her toes just touching the floor.

"Trevor, there's something I need to say to you."

"Okay." I draw the word out, cautiously, and remain standing near the doorway. She turns her head gently and looks at the bed space to the right of her and then back at me. Her hands remain resting on her lap – she didn't pat the top of the duvet cover where she looked – but her direction seems clear enough: sit next to me. So I do.

"Earlier you said you were scared about following me back to England. That you regretted it, even though you didn't regret eventually meeting Annie and having your girls."

I nod.

"Well, I was scared too. Scared to follow through with vet school. That I wouldn't be good enough, couldn't handle the heavier science courses or would be too squeamish to operate on cadavers. Just silly fears I created in my mind so I kept defer-ring enrollment until the visa ran out. And I was scared I'd end up like your mother, an Englishwoman married to an American, disconnected from her family back home and living in a country I wasn't sure I wanted to embrace. And… this is really hard for me to admit. At some point in the aftermath of our breakup, after a lot of soul searching, I realized that on some level I'd sort of wanted to give you a test, to see if you loved me so much that you'd follow me back to England to be with me. And when you failed the test, this stupidly false test I'd imposed, well, then I told myself it must not have been meant to be, that our love must not have been big enough."

I sit, stunned. Once that initial shock wears off, a feeling of gratitude and warmth replaces it, a sensibility verging on contentment or even happiness, that Frankie cared enough to share this with me.

"Wow," I finally say.

"I'm really sorry," she says.

The gratitude hasn't worn off, but the shock waves are still reverberating inside of me.

"Wow."

Her face turns to an expression somewhere between annoyance and guilt.

"Could you please say something other than 'wow'?"

"Okay," I say. "I'm really glad you told me. I'm sure it wasn't easy."

"It wasn't, no."

"And I... I'm not sure what I'm supposed to do now."

"You don't have to *do* anything. I just needed to tell you."

"Okay. So, let me get this straight. I've unburdened myself to you, and you've unburdened yourself to me, and now we're supposed to just go on our merry way. I'll take Sky back to London in a few hours and get my nest egg released so I can start over back home, and you'll do your marine animal work and continue raising your kids and then probably meet some great guy, I don't know, a gentleman farmer or something..."

"A gentleman farmer?!" The way she says it, I might have suggested a serial murderer.

"Whatever," I say. "And we'll go about our separate lives, glad that at least we were able to tell the other what was really going on when we broke up."

"Who says I haven't already met some great guy?"

I look at her, newly shocked again. "Oh, shit. Have you?"

She smiles, pleased with my reaction. "No, I haven't. I mean, not someone I didn't already know."

I look at her and I feel my insides melting, like scoops of vanilla ice cream in a bowl just thawing to room temperature and suddenly placed in a 550 degree oven.

"Not fair," I say. "What am I supposed to do with that?"

"What's all this 'supposed to' talk? What about what you want?"

"What I want?" I say it out loud, even though it's more for myself to consider.

"Uh-huh."

Only one answer occurs to me. So I lean over, pull Frankie towards me and kiss her.

Thursday

(Love-40)

19

I wake to a dull throbbing in my head and a mouth that rivals the Gobi for dryness, then the panicked awareness that it's light outside. So I jerk my head up, which makes the throbbing much worse. I reach across Frankie, still very much asleep, for my watch on the bedside table and carefully grasp it so as not to wake her. 4:58 a.m. That *seems* okay, until my sleep-deprived brain – did I get any more than an hour? – recalls that our train leaves at 5:38 a.m., and from Truro, not Penryn. That's what, fifteen minutes away? Twenty? Fuck! I need to get Sky up and going, if she's asleep, and Frankie as well, since she's our ride, then there's the obligatory group goodbyes that always slow things down.

I tumble out of bed, completely forgetting my bum ankle, but by sheer luck I land squarely on my left foot. I'm not spared the shock of my own nakedness, however, and last night's events wash over me like an oozing tide of embarrassment. My face flushes and I have a sudden sense memory of wetting my bed at a 5th birthday sleepover party at Johnny Fowler's house. Total misery and shame, with no means of escape. Well, no use getting mired in the past. So, need to focus. Money. Solicitor. Meeting at eleven o'clock. Christ, the time! A glance at my watch – it's now past five o'clock – triggers a prickly, fearful sensation that creeps from between my shoulder blades to the base of my skull. I simply cannot miss that train.

I thread my legs through my briefs and jeans, careful not to put any weight on my right ankle, then pull on the same teal drip-dry shirt I wore yesterday. I re-button it as I make my hobbling way around the bed and out the door, both wishing Frankie would wake up and also that Sky and I could somehow make our getaway without her knowing. Fitzgerald at work again? In the hallway I notice Sam's bedroom door is closed but Michael's is ajar. There's enough light seeping through the family room windows to see Michael asleep on the sofa with a quilt half-covering his bare, hairless chest. I'm about to reverse course and look for Sky in one of the kid's rooms when I notice an oval of matted, auburn hair peeking out from the quilt next to Michael's left hip.

"Sky?" I say it louder than I intend, with a tone that betrays more concern for the circumstances than the time.

Michael opens his eyes and he takes a full second to recognize me before he goes into a full panic. He reflexively grabs a handful of the quilt and pulls it up towards his neck, but that makes the other end of the quilt slide off the sofa, revealing Sky's legs. She squirms in discomfort and I see she must be completely naked under the quilt.

"What the fuck!" I blurt it out, and now Sky's eyes are wide open as well and she's staring back at me with a mixture of anger and horror.

"Shit!" she yells.

"Oh my god!" Michael chimes in. He's now re-draping the quilt decorously around Sky's torso, a gesture that my reptilian parental brain would somehow like to acknowledge as chivalrous if it weren't so hung up on the fact that my underage daughter has, by all appearances, been having some kind of carnal knowledge of Frankie's son, Michael. So I repeat, with more emphasis:

"What the fuck!!"

Sky's emotions are now fully unified: she's furious. She points her finger at me and then towards the hallway.

"Go! You, you, go!"

Frankie has somehow materialized by my side wearing a multi-colored robe decorated with all sorts of marine wildlife – cormorants and flounder and penguins and starfish – a robe so ludicrous that I would have no choice but to tease her about it in any other setting. But I have no notion of doing so now and I merely note the robe's preposterousness in passing, the same way I must have perceived the café's name yesterday while clutching onto the speeding luggage trolley. Mercifully, Frankie is oblivious to my thoughts and as she hastily assesses the situation, her expression morphs from confusion to comprehension to resolution.

"You two – get dressed, now!" She waves her hand for emphasis then grabs hold of my arm and gently, but firmly, pulls me back to her bedroom. She closes the door behind us and puts her hands in the air as if to forestall my protests.

"I'm sure it looks worse than it is."

"Really? It looks pretty clear to me. It *looks* like your son was fucking my daughter."

Frankie's eyes flare and I can see her almost visibly controlling herself from exploding.

"Come on, Trevor. They're kids. They were just cuddled up. Maybe they fooled around a little. It happens."

"It *happens*? You do realize Sky's underage, don't you?"

"As is Michael. He's never had a girlfriend in his life. Surely you must have seen how she was… paying attention to him."

"What are you saying, that she *seduced* him? Like some … some… Lolita?"

Frankie doesn't say anything and I steal a glance at my watch. 5:11 a.m.

"Christ, we don't have time for this! I've got a train to catch, like, now!"

"Okay. Give me a minute and I'll get Sky ready. Probably best if I deal with her, don't you think?"

I raise my hands up, palm side out, conceding.

"Look Frankie, about last night…"

"Please, you don't need to worry about it," she says, more hasty than reassuring. Because of course I *am* worried, terribly so. What man wouldn't be? I look for clues in her eyes. Does she mean it? Before I can probe she turns and leaves the room, shutting the door behind her.

I look around to collect my things only to realize I never unpacked. My tennis bag must still be in the Range Rover. I'm at a loss what to do instead so I remake the bed.

A moment later the door opens and Frankie bursts in.

"Okay, she's all set." Frankie looks at me quizzically. "What are you doing? Come on, we need to go! I can do that later."

I shrug, embarrassed in yet another way, this time that I have been caught treating her bed like an Etch A Sketch with some awful design that needs to be shaken clean. I can feel my face flushing bright crimson yet again.

"Oh Trevor. It's all right. Really."

"Easy for you to say."

She wrinkles her face, but the resulting outbreak of dimples only makes things worse.

"Come on. If we race I think we've got a chance to make your train."

I grab the cane and follow Frankie out of the cottage in a kind of blur, dimly aware that there's no one else about, not Michael, not the dogs, just Sky slouched in the rear seat of the Range Rover, studiously avoiding my gaze and looking miserable. Frankie dashes for the right front door, saving me from mistaking it for the passenger side again, so I get in the left side.

"Michael is staying behind to look after Sam in case she wakes." Frankie says this with a firm cast to her face, brooking no dissent. Sky says nothing, I nod meekly and we're on our way, fast. And I mean fast.

I had no idea Frankie could drive like this. And on narrow country lanes, in an old, lumbering Range Rover no less. Whether she's channeling her inner Mario Andretti – no, let's make that Sterling Moss – or she otherwise doesn't mind imperiling us and any unsuspecting sheep farmers tending their flock at this early hour, in order for me to make my meeting, I don't know. In any case I have no choice but to surrender to fate. And isn't not knowing a more natural state of being? Well, I guess not. Because after watching Frankie accelerate onto the A39 and treat it like her very own *Nürburgring*, I begin to have hope. Enough that I can't resist a quick peek at my watch, but quickly, so Frankie doesn't see. Damn. Almost 5:30 a.m. And I realize, with a suffocating distress that has become all too familiar, that if the Golden Hind departs Truro Station on time this morning, Sky and I won't be on it.

20

My watch reads 6:56 a.m. and I'm staring out the train window at the station sign: Bodmin Parkway. I don't see anything as grand as a parkway or even a dinky road. There's no one on the platform getting on and no one has gotten off, but I guess that's how it is when you've missed the express train and you're on the fucking local, the morning milk run, stopping at every damned podunk town in Cornwall. This is the fourth stop since Truro and that was only about half an hour ago. Fuck! At this rate it's really hard to believe the train will get to Paddington at 11:24 a.m. But that's what the schedule says. Anyway, who cares? It'll still be too damned late for my 11 o'clock meeting, even 'fashionably' late or with a grace period, neither of which means anything in the business world. Maybe after eight or nine I could try to call his secretary and reschedule, see if he can see me later, but my hunch is no, not the way things are going. And then I'll be well and truly fucked.

I feel like shit. No other way to say it. My head is pounding again – I need coffee or water or aspirin or *something* – and I'm a mess. A total fucking mess. I'm so mad at myself, not just for allowing us to miss our train, but also for losing my temper with Sky on the platform, that whole scene with Frankie, everything. I'm worried, not just about the meeting, but what might have happened to Sky. My God, what if she got… if he really… no – I believe her. I *have* to believe her, that that didn't happen, not all the way. And… yes, I'm embarrassed. For what didn't happen, with me and Frankie. Christ, embarrassed is when you fart out loud. I'm not embarrassed, I'm mortified. For what I couldn't, wasn't able, to do. Never, I mean that has *never* ever happened before. Every guy has it happen sometime, right? But not me, ever. And it happens then? One moment flying high, full of confidence, ready to charge and then the next, nothing – in free fall, tail between my legs, full retreat. Fuck. What's the matter with me? *Was* the matter with me? God, I could use some coffee. At least the train is moving again. For what that's worth.

Sky is wiped out, sleeping, which is a blessed relief, I suppose, given how we went at each other earlier, like two foul-tempered dogs. I'd give anything to be able to sleep right now, just close my eyes and shut it all down, which is pretty goddamned funny I suppose because I haven't got much left to give, money-wise. Sure, there's still *something* on the frigging CashPort, a few measly bucks, but how long is that going to last? I mean, really? Jesus, what a fucking mess. And the way my head's buzzing now, nineteen to the dozen, I couldn't sleep. Not for all the tea in China.

God it was nice, though. For a while, with Frankie, before things got carried away. Just kissing and making out in her room, like a couple of teenagers. I'd forgotten how nice that is. The simple wonder of it. Lips on lips, tongues exploring mouths, kisses that go on and on. Sweet, gentle caresses and the weight of another against your body. Why the hell couldn't we leave it at that? I could have kissed her all night, held her close to me, then gotten up by five, that was the plan, hustle Sky out the door, a quick ride to Truro and then on our way. Allow some mystery, some anticipation, for a next time. What's the old rule from vaudeville? Always leave them wanting more. Well, that's what happened, all right. But not the way it's supposed to.

And Sky. And Michael. Jesus! Are you serious? The kid basically ignored her all day. And there they are, under the blanket on the sofa. Sweet, innocent Samantha in her bedroom, asleep, while the others get it on in the living room. What did Sky say? They were just *hooking up*. That it was no big deal. So when did *that* become the norm? Practically strangers, for God's sake. And what the fuck does 'hooking up' mean anyway? Sky swears it's not sex, but after Frankie left us at the station and I lit into Sky, I realize I'm having this surreal discussion with my fourteen year-old daughter like she's Bill Clinton and I'm Kenneth Starr and we're parsing what the meaning of 'is' is. I mean, why don't you just fucking shoot me now! All I want to know, all I *need* to know, is did he or didn't he? Go in her. *Release* in her. I mean, I don't blame the boy, really. She was giving him the eagle eye since we got there and she does look mature for her age. And she's sexy, if a father is permitted to say that. He may be a nice kid but he's got hormones like any teenager. I reacted badly, I know I did, but what father wouldn't? But it's not even about that. I just need to be able to tell Annie. Or not. And how would that script go? "Oh, hi Annie. Here's Sky's flight information. And by the way, you know how I told you yesterday that she got a tattoo? Well now she got herself knocked up. Uh-huh. Yeah, the older son of my old girlfriend. What? 'What was *I* doing?' Oh, I was in the other room, trying to do the same to his old lady. And failing miserably." Yeah, that's a phone conversation I really don't want to have. Please, dear Lord, let the kid have gotten a simple hand job. A blow job, even. But nothing more.

The cruel irony is how wrong Annie got it about Siobhan. Sure, I wanted her – I don't deny that – but much as I fantasized, with everything working just fine in the goddamned shower, thank you very much, I never laid a hand on her. Never so much as a kiss. So yeah, if an emotional affair is as bad as the real thing, if I "lusted in my heart" like Jimmy Carter, then I'm guilty as charged. But then toss me in San Quentin and fire up the gas chamber, because I fantasized about killing Annie's boyfriend too. Which would make Jeffrey Schreiber's only (evident) flaw demonstrating a legal absurdity. Either that or exposing me as a coward.

Okay, I need to calm down. Take stock and figure out what to do. But first, Christ, I really need something. What's that over there, in the seat back pocket – a half-filled plastic water bottle? Must have been left behind by a passenger. What about the germs? Fuck it, I'm drinking it. All right, that's a little better. I could still use a couple of aspirins but… that's *better*.

So, let's take stock. Nobody died here, did they? Well, my parents did, but that was a year ago, and they *were* getting on and, well, there's nothing to be done about that now. Jeez, I can't believe Annie said that on Monday, in our courthouse *tête-à-tête*, when I asked her what she meant about my mood in recent years.

"Maybe I was distracted," I'd said. "But *melancholy*? Don't you think that's a little extreme?"

"Trevor, you were acting like you were mourning something, some great tragedy, as if your dad had been killed in the war. If that isn't melancholy, I don't know what is. And when you finally got some real loss in your life – please, don't get me wrong, it was a terrible shock and I loved your parents too – it's like you'd pre-empted your capacity to feel it."

How could she be serious? *Pre-empted*? She doesn't know what the hell she's talking about. Is that what happens when you grow up playing on the manicured streets of Evanston fucking Illinois? It's not like she's ever lost a parent or a close family member. Okay, maybe a grandparent, but at our age that doesn't really count. The point is, there's been a lot of distracting shit the last decade. Plenty to get upset about. But despite it all, I kept my focus, kept my priorities straight. Family, work, community. So I play a little tennis. So what? It's not like golf. Plenty of guys I know play golf, and they don't call their wives golf widows for nothing. And okay, I'd go for an occasional ride on the motorbike to clear my head. Is that a crime? But "pre-empted my capacity to feel"? What a crock! Believe me, I'm feeling plenty right now. Not in a good way, but still. Anyway, I mustn't get sidetracked. I was taking stock. Oh yeah – no one died. And, apart from this twisted ankle, everyone's healthy. I mean, last night doesn't count, it had to be something else – stress, unfamiliarity, whatever. And assuming Sky isn't, you know… in the *family* way… Jesus, mustn't even joke about it. It is *not* funny. No, we're putting her in the healthy category. So, then, what? This little money issue? Okay, I don't need to recapitulate the whole damned thing, I just need to sort out the meeting time. Hey, things come up, he's got to realize that. Alright then. Prioritize. Get Sky on a flight home, stretch what remains on the CashPort until I can convince Salmons the inheritance is valid, then Bob's your uncle. But what about… Frankie?

Oh boy. Deep breath, pal. She'll understand. She probably does already. About my going off about Michael, yes, *and* that other thing. Shit, I've been under a lot of pressure, she knows that. A total aberration. And when things are more settled and I get this cash flow problem fixed… what then? Sigh. Come on, let's be realistic. If we had geographic issues before, when it was just the two of us, what about now? She's got her three kids and I've got my two. I'm not going to convince Annie to let the girls live in England, now am I? Wait a second. Whoa – let's slow way down, buddy. What am I even talking about? But come on – why not? Talk about it, I mean. Otherwise, what's the point? I can no more deny the feelings I was having for Frankie than she can. Amazing, after all these years, that we still feel that way about each other. Yes, *feelings*. So, why don't you just pre-empt *that*, Annie.

Sky is still fast asleep, lying across from me. The rail car is otherwise empty – who else is fool enough to travel to London at this hour, and on the local? – so I scout around for something to read. There's no way I can sleep, so I might as well divert myself. And I don't have an appetite for the Hemingway right now, not remotely. So, let's have a look. Ow, fuck me! – that damned ankle. Where's the cane? Okay then.

My recon mission about the carriage turns up exactly one newspaper, a copy of *The Daily Telegraph*. I normally take a vacation from news when I travel, but these are not ordinary times. So I grab it, even though I know it leans heavily Tory and reads more like a tabloid than a broadsheet. At least it's today's edition.

Sure enough, the British monarchy is front and center, but has equal billing with tennis under the headline, 'Wimbledon's longest match: Isner v. Mahut continues as Queen visits SW19.' The article recounts the details of yesterday's match and sets the stage for Nicolas Mahut and John Isner – "unknown to the wider sporting world yesterday, household names this morning" – dragging their weary bodies back on to court this afternoon to resume the longest match in tennis history, as the Queen makes her first visit since 1977. I read on with a sort of morbid fascination. Not about yesterday's match, which of course I'm familiar with, but the fact that QE2 – the person, not the ocean liner – hasn't ventured onto the grounds of the All England Club since Virginia Wade won her singles crown in that Silver Jubilee year, the very summer I participated in the Oxford lawn tennis exhibition for the Queen and her husband. My God, I think: what kind of weird symmetry is that? Or maybe we've both just been around a long time. Today she's supposed to have lunch with some tennis notables and then watch Andy Murray play his second round match against Jarkko Nieminen of Finland. And how odd that the Queen is attending during the first week of play and not when Murray is contending for the finals or the championship itself. The article gushes the particulars of the club's preparations in its fawning royalist manner, right down to the menu for lunch: salmon millefeuille starter, a main course of orange and honey marinated chicken on fruity couscous with roasted vegetables, followed by strawberries and cream with a mint syrup. That dessert choice seems either intentionally traditional or ironic – or both. Perhaps the club official in charge of selecting the meal has a sense of humor. "Let's give Her Majesty what every commoner at Wimbledon eats." The article goes on to explain how the invited female tennis players are all in a dither about their curtsy technique, including Serena Williams, who is planning to "dress more conservatively than usual and has been practicing a less dramatic and more natural curtsy." Well, I marvel, for Serena this is a long way from the mean streets of Compton. So good for her, I say, and may she curtsy as dramatically and unnaturally as she likes. I mean, exactly what about a royal curtsy is *natural*? A lot of tennis players I know don't care for Serena's temperament and manner – there's not much about her game itself you can criticize – but having grown up in L.A., I know about South Central neighborhoods like Compton and Watts and Inglewood. For Serena and her older sister, Venus, to have become successful, independent women is truly remarkable, quite apart from each of them becoming multiple Grand Slam and Olympic champions. So I cut Serena some slack.

In startling (and surely unintended) juxtaposition, the adjoining article is about the "burger diplomacy" of President Obama, who yesterday invited the president of Russia, Dmitri Medvedev, to lunch at some greasy spoon named Ray's Hell Burger in Arlington, Virginia, to discuss issues like trade, nuclear disarmament, and, presumably, which is better on the side, French fries or onion rings. No fruity couscous for you, Comrade President! One of the things I shared with Frankie last night is that my proudest moment as an American was the night Barack Obama was elected president. I'm sure I'm not alone in this regard and I'd wager the sentiment crosses multiple political, economic and racial divides. Now, growing up as an African-American on Oahu is probably not as challenging as South Central Los Angeles, but for the son of an absentee Kenyan father with the shared middle name of Hussein to reach the White House is certainly more remarkable than conquering Centre Court, given the prior accomplishments of Arthur Ashe and Althea Gibson. And for her part, Frankie acknowledged that the election made her feel a kind of kindred sympathy towards America for the first time since her husband had been killed.

I scan the first few pages of the newspaper and I'm surprised how many headlines relate to the United States. "Fed Chair Ben Bernanke needs fresh monetary blitz as US recovery falters." And, "BP oil spill: Suicide of fisherman 'distraught at size of Gulf clean-up.'" And, "Barack Obama to replace Gen McChrystal with Gen Petraeus over Rolling Stone comments." Even the tabloid fodder has an American slant, to wit: "Al Gore behaved like 'crazed sex poodle' with Oregon masseuse." But thankfully, there's always the beleaguered royal family to bring us back to home, with: "Memory of Diana 'keeps us going every day' say Princes William and Harry." The actual stories are depressing to the extreme, a catalog of manmade environmental catastrophes, military adventures gone wrong, continuing global economic ruination and marital perfidy, so I don't linger on the details and flip instead to the feature pages, in hopes of finding something uplifting. The headlines there are worse, however, if only because of their personal significance. "Off-road motorcycling for all the family" is both a sad reminder of my Griso's recent forced sale and Annie's frequent complaint (despite her own passion for bicycling). "Strict and loving relationship key to stopping teenagers going off the rails" has, I suppose, some potential for inspiration, but the article contains such a litany of dysfunctional behavior that it merely reminds me of my early morning fight with Sky on the Truro Station platform. And "When, and how, to tell the kids you're moving on after a divorce" doesn't even bear reading, nor does "Holiday spending: how to beat the budget blues." I know the old chestnut, how after a break-up every song on the radio reminds you of your own life, but this is ridiculous. Do the editors of *The Daily Telegraph* have it in for me? Is there nothing in these pages that will provide, if not actual comfort, some distraction? Even "Magnets can improve Alzheimer's symptoms, study finds" only serves to hark back to Frankie telling me yesterday about her travails with her elderly mother in Italy. But when I'm about to toss the paper aside, I find something seemingly innocuous – "Large Hadron Collider: scientists create sound of 'God particle'" – that plants in my mind the tiniest seed of hope.

The article explains how physicists at CERN in Geneva plan to 'listen' to their data in order to more easily identify the crucial 'Higgs boson' particle, also referred to – but not by those same physicists, I'm fairly certain – as the 'God particle.' As I read on, the details of the overall experiment become vaguely familiar, how dozens of countries have spent decades and billions of euros building a 27 kilometer circular tunnel under the Swiss-French border for the sole purpose of smashing proton beams together and observing the subatomic particles that result. There is no military application, I recall, nor any likely economic benefit. This is pure research, with the goal to better understand the fundamental building blocks of matter and how the universe was formed. The 'Higgs boson,' the story explains, is the missing piece to the so-called 'Standard Theory' of quantum physics, as predicted by a British physicist named Peter Higgs in 1964. And now it seems, with the additional (no doubt crucial!) collaboration of classical musicians in London, the search may be nearing its successful conclusion.

When I entered Cal as a freshman we were given a campus tour that passed, without visiting, an odd, igloo-domed structure known as 'Building 51.' I later learned it housed the Bevatron, a pioneering particle accelerator that produced many new periodic elements and Nobel Prizes for the Berkeley professors who discovered them. Because the Bevatron was part of the Lawrence Berkeley National Laboratory, with direct ties to the nuclear weapons lab in nearby Livermore, it was more than a little controversial among the student body and faculty. I didn't have any problem with it, however, since I figured you have to let scientists understand the physical world before you accuse them of conspiring to wipe it out.

Remarkably, after reading about this seemingly contrived collaboration between musicians and physicists, I feel marginally better. I hope the good folks at CERN find their missing boson, and if it helps to call it a 'God particle' or turn the data into a concerto, however gimmicky, to continue to get funding or for people to pay attention, that's fine too. The important thing is that a higher purpose is being fulfilled. Maybe the highest. I don't mean this to sound like some high-minded cliché, but I believe what separates us as a human race, at our best, is our quest to go beyond our individual, often mundane lives, and find a deeper meaning in our existence. And quite frankly, sitting on this empty train with my sleeping daughter who loathes me as we travel away from the one woman who seems (still?) to reciprocate my desire, I desperately need some meaning. To know – or at least have belief – that it isn't all some cruel hoax of a world, like that backyard anthill from my childhood, occupying the methodical efforts of dozens of worker ants until the six-year-old me, in my own thoughtless yet naïvely superior way, stomped on the anthill and rained Armageddon down on those innocent ants. Those dumb idiots, I thought then: they haven't a clue what's happening. But even then the light was dawning on me that I just might, in my own way, be a larger, more intelligent (but certainly less humane) version of an ant, trudging off to school and back and otherwise fulfilling my minuscule societal role. And yet – if we could understand what it means to be human, and how the molecules and neurons in our brain make us sentient and possess unique personalities, *that* would be fundamental progress, wouldn't it? And even, with our large telescopes and our huge accelerators and colliders, if we could map the furthest reaches of the universe and the tiniest subatomic particles and how they all relate, wouldn't that mean something special?

About the same age when I was thoughtlessly wreaking apocalyptic destruction on that undeserving ant colony, I was also drinking Tang, the ersatz orange drink used by NASA in the sixties. It didn't take all that much for General Foods and its Madison Avenue ad agency to motivate a California kid like me to rehydrate from powder and consume an awful-tasting version of a beverage that was readily available, cheap and fresh, in our local Ralph's supermarket. If Gus Grissom and the other Gemini astronauts squeezed Tang from a plastic pouch while in orbit, like some latter-day Royal Navy sailors taking their daily grog ration, well the least I could do was give up orange juice too. This will last only a month or so, I reassured my mother, who strongly disapproved of paying more for an inferior substitute. But what started as a lark became a solemn act of solidarity when Grissom and his fellow Apollo 1 crewmembers, Ed White and Roger Chaffee, perished in that horrific Cape Canaveral launchpad fire. Not a drop of real orange juice would pass my lips, I vowed, until we successfully landed on the moon. And I kept my promise for well over two years, long after my dislike of Tang turned to out-and-out loathing, until Neil Armstrong and Buzz Aldrin not only reunited in lunar orbit with their command module pilot, Michael Collins, but they all splashed down in the Pacific and were safely aboard the USS Hornet. Has there been a similar sacrifice in Sky and Abby's lifetime, symbolic or otherwise? If there is, it eludes me. Yes, they and their classmates did give up peanut butter in their kindergarten lunches in support of kids with (alleged) life-threatening nut allergies. And Annie and I regularly took the girls to food banks during the holidays to serve hot meals to the needy. All worthwhile causes, to be sure, but nothing with extraterrestrial significance. And, if I'm being truly candid as a parent, nothing that came from their own instigation. But maybe they've never been given a big enough cause to believe in, like the war bonds – and the war itself – of my parents' youth. I mean, just think about it! President Kennedy laid down the challenge and we followed through: before the decade is out, land a man on the moon and return him safely to Earth. Ten years later, done and done. JFK didn't live to see it, but still – that's some legacy.

I know it became – and maybe still is – fashionable in certain circles to criticize NASA's not-insignificant budget as a waste of taxpayers' money, especially after the euphoria over Apollo 11's success waned. Liberals questioned why we were planning missions to an uninhabitable planet like Mars when we could target inner-city poverty instead, while conservatives argued we could simply lower taxes. The joke was that all we got out of the space program was Velcro, some moon rocks and *The Right Stuff*. Well, if true, that's not a terrible trade-off – both the book and the movie were terrific – but of course that's not the point. We as a species are explorers. It's in our DNA. Yes, often the exploration leads to conquest and economic exploitation. That seems to be in our DNA too. I doubt the Spanish crown funded Christopher Columbus for scientific reasons but I also imagine he cared as much, if not more, about the big ideas than turning a colonial profit. I'd prefer to think so, anyway.

And with this train of thought my mind naturally dredges up Nungesser and Coli. I'd call them a childhood interest, but maybe an obsession would be more accurate. I don't need or want to go there now, do I? Let's stick to the train I'm on, this damned local. What, are you kidding me? We're stopping again? And at, what, St Germans? This is Cornwall! Who named a train station St Germans?

Alright, I need to calm down. Maybe it would help, to remind myself of the aviators' story. Like watching a videotape of a match that went awry. What was it Coach used to say? A focused mind is a productive mind. And there must be some reason it's haunted me all these years. If I could only figure out why.

When I was in 4th grade, my teacher at Warner Avenue Elementary, Mr. Allen, assigned our class a paper to write on a number of possible topics, including 'Pioneers of Aviation.' In those days, doing a research paper meant going to the school library and copying entries longhand from the World Book Encyclopedia supplied by the librarian, Miss Perske, then 'writing' the paper by changing just enough to avoid being accused of plagiarism. This was 1970, a year after Neil Armstrong's historic 'small step and giant leap' that I'd followed so closely, so choosing an aviation pioneer to write about seemed to me the obvious course of action. I'd paid my Tang-drinking dues; I'd built my Revell scale model of the Saturn V rocket; I'd re-enacted the lunar landing countless times with my best friend, Phil Webb, lurching around like we were in one-sixth Earth gravity and unable to control our momentum.

But once I opened the encyclopedia there were so many possibilities, so many worthy candidates, making the initial choice seemed more daunting than researching and writing the paper itself. Should I pick the Wright Brothers? Glenn Curtiss? Charles Lindbergh? Amelia Earhart? Or maybe someone more modern, like Chuck Yeager, or his female counterpart, Jackie Cochran? How about John Glenn? Or even the *man* himself, Neil Armstrong? But after spending an entire library period perusing the various encyclopedia entries, I chose Nungesser and Coli. Who? Exactly.

Charles Nungesser and François Coli were French aviators and heroes of World War One. Their entry in the World Book Encyclopedia was not for their wartime achievements, however, but their ill-fated attempt to cross the Atlantic and win the same Orteig Prize that Lindbergh sought in his *Spirit of St. Louis*. In other words, they were pioneers for what they *failed* to do, not for what they achieved.

On May 8, 1927, twelve days before the Lone Eagle (that cool nickname alone made the choice even harder) left Roosevelt Field on Long Island, bound for Paris, Nungesser and Coli took off from Le Bourget Field in their open cockpit single-engine biplane named *L'Oiseau Blanc*. Escorted to the English Channel by French military aircraft, *L'Oiseau Blanc* was sighted over England and again over Ireland and presumed safely on its way to North America. But despite multiple reports of its passing over Newfoundland, Nungesser and Coli were never heard from again. The fate of *L'Oiseau Blanc* remains a mystery to this day. I know, because every so often I'll check – just a quick Google search to see if anything new has surfaced. There have been plenty of false alarms, everything from backwoods crackpots claiming to have seen the flyers alive to official government investigations testing the metallurgy of salvaged engine parts. But as to solid evidence? So far, nothing. A part of me keeps hoping that one day some Maine hunter will discover the wreckage of *L'Oiseau Blanc*, solving the mystery and allowing Nungesser and Coli a posthumous claim on the first trans-Atlantic flight.

Mr. Allen, God bless him, gave me an A- for the paper (my penmanship was poor and I made some spelling errors). But he was an open-minded teacher and maybe he had a soft spot for noncon-formity. Still, his indulgence notwithstanding, I do realize it was an odd choice on my part. Sitting on this train now, forty years later, I try to take myself back to that moment in the library so I can figure out *why* I picked Nungesser and Coli as my 'Pioneers of Aviation.' Because, strange as it seems, I don't remember that part.

My strongest initial impression is of Miss Perske, the librarian. She couldn't have been much older than twenty and she dressed in an intriguing combination of Summer of Love hippie and sophisticated Playboy playmate. Her long, straight hair and her fragrance – was it sandalwood? – were as intoxicating as her cen-terfold-worthy figure, so she must have made it doubly hard for me to focus on my task at hand. What else? I remember sitting in one of those Eames-inspired colored plastic chairs with the square rear cutouts, the same chairs we used in our classroom and pushed violently backwards when we had duck-and-cover drills, hud-dling on our knees under our desks with our arms 'protecting' our heads in simulation of a nuclear attack. But did we take those drills seriously? That I can't remember either. Still, they must have made an impression.

What then? Why the seemingly pessimistic choice of the two dead French airmen? And why has their plight stayed with me ever since? Maybe Annie is right and I do have a melancholic streak. Oh, for goodness sakes, Trevor! That's just self-indulgent nonsense. Anyway, I *do* remember being taken by the reaction of the French to the loss, as recounted in the surprisingly lengthy encyclopedia article. Is it possible it was written by some nostalgic Frenchman who somehow prevailed on the American editor for leniency? And if not, then why the included photograph of a mon-ument erected in Nungesser and Coli's honor on the coastline near the village of Étretat where *L'Oiseau Blanc* departed France? I still remember its soaring, triumphant quality with a concrete spire of unmistakably Art Deco design – it could easily coexist with the Golden Gate Bridge – abutting the figures of the two heroic airmen, in flying suits and helmets, chests thrust forward. These poetic elements formed the fuselage of an otherwise flattened outline of the airplane itself, the two-dimensional propeller spinner pointing out to sea in the direction of England and, ultimately, America. What also struck me was that the German army had destroyed the vertical components of the monument – the spire and the busts – after occupying France. What so offended the soldiers, I wondered? The fact that the pilots had fought against Germany in the previous war? Or that they'd tried – and failed? – in their historic trans-Atlantic flight? I don't recall any light being shed on that issue. But maybe *that* was too touchy a topic for World Book's editors, who'd devoted columns of glowing copy for Werner von Braun, the brains behind our colossal Saturn V, even though he'd been the top Nazi rocket scientist at Peenemunde lobbing V-2s at Britain during the war. In any case the French eventually rebuilt the spire, but in a mid-century design, a leaning point reminiscent of the Seattle Space Needle, and well forward of the airplane's outline, which remained. The figures of Nungesser and Coli, however, were not replaced.

Come on man, think. Why those pioneers? Why the doubles team? I always prefer singles to doubles. Sitting here on this sad and lonely train, I have to believe, if I can get this right, think it through, I'll be onto something. Some answer. So, no – maybe it wasn't the monument. For as poignant and dramatic as the saga of the monument must have seemed to my nine-year-old sensibility – did the German troops use dynamite or jackhammers? – I have to believe that what most impressed me about the story was how the French people treated Lindbergh after he landed at Le Bourget. Remember, this was the very airfield Nungesser and Coli had departed from amid a throng of well-wishers, and then this impossibly dashing, earnest American materializes in the sky and lands before they had finished grieving. But the historical record is unequivocal: Lindbergh was embraced enthusiastically, if not ecstatically, as if he were one of their own. A 'hero's welcome' might seem perhaps too trite a phrase to use, were it not exactly what he received – and precisely what he became – in France and at home as well, at least until his own flirtation with Nazi Germany. Admittedly it's a challenge for me to recall but perhaps, as I sat at that library table, I tried to imagine our having lost touch with the crew of Apollo 11 halfway to the moon – Armstrong and

Collins and Aldrin perishing, never to be seen again – and another nation's astronauts returning from a successful moon landing less than two weeks later and splashing down in the Atlantic near Cape Canaveral for Americans to welcome back to Earth. What strength of character that would require. Or, to use a French word, what *largesse*.

Yes, I do believe that must have been the tipping point for me. In sports it had been drummed into me from an early age that, win or lose, you were supposed to behave graciously. Shake your opponent's hand at the net and look him in the eye and congratulate him. "Nice match," you'd say, even though the bitter taste of defeat was still fresh. I'd started my lessons with Win Brenneker two years earlier and was by then playing a lot of tennis matches. So I'm sure the reaction of the French to Charles Lindbergh would have made an impact on me. They fêted him and showered him with praise, genuinely and with passion. And in their hearts they were also feeling, what of Nungesser and Coli? The men who reached for greatness. And fell short. Maybe one day I'll visit that monument in Étretat and pay my respects. A modest goal perhaps, when compared to theirs. But still.

21

Sky opens her eyes and blinks from the daylight. She stretches her arms and scrunches her features in an exaggerated pantomime of waking up, except it's legit. Her eyes finally focus on me and her expression sours.

"Where are we?" she says.

"The last station was Pewsey."

"Where?" She looks confused, still sleepy.

"I'd guess Wiltshire if my life depended on it but honestly, I've never heard of it. By the time we get to London I figure we'll have stopped at every village in the West Country."

"It's not my fault."

I'm about to ask whose fault it is, if not hers, but I realize this will just ring in Round Two of our Truro donnybrook. So I refrain.

"I'm thirsty," she says finally, seemingly disappointed that I'm not re-engaging.

"What do you want?"

"Coffee I guess."

I fish in my pocket and re-discover the fifteen pounds I've been carrying around. I hold it up in front of her.

"This is all the cash I have until we can get to an ATM. I'll have coffee too. And whatever looks edible."

She looks annoyed. "*I* have to get it?"

"Could you? My ankle is still sore."

Sky grudgingly takes the money and gets up. I point towards the front of the train.

"I think the buffet car is that way." She scrunches her mouth in acknowledgement and I add: "Hey Sky?"

She looks at me, her eyes uncooperative, sulking.

"Can we start over?"

"Go screw yourself," she says and then she's gone. I look after her, letting the sadness wash over me then slowly dissipate until I can shrug my shoulders.

"I guess I'll take that as a 'no.'" I say it for my own benefit, even though I feel no lift, no lightening of spirit. Why bother, I think? Why indeed.

Before Sky woke up I was thinking about Annie, replaying the tapes of the past, those ever-present tapes. Things said and done (and not done), what it was like before Abby and Sky were born. And after. You replay those tapes in your mind, hoping for answers, but you end up wondering if it's better to do like Rose Mary Woods did for Richard Nixon and erase them, or at least the crucial nineteen minutes. But no such luck: the gaps are wishful, not real. If, with each replaying, I blame Annie less and less for giving me the heave-ho, when can I blame myself less as well? It's little consolation but maybe there's this: if we believe Whitman, we are indeed large and contain multitudes. Then what of a married couple, the union of *two* sets of multitudes? If I contradict myself alone, the possible conflicts *together* are staggering. And then, just to make things interesting, introduce children: individual souls with inchoate multitudes of their own. Is it any wonder why Tolstoy weighed in the way he did about unhappy families?

I had a symbolic logic class at Cal my freshman year that satisfied a mathematics requirement. I figured it would be more interesting (and easier) than calculus, but I should have known better, because it was in the philosophy department. All men may be mortal, and Socrates may be a man, but the following is also true:

A.	All philosophy professors wish they were like Socrates.
B.	No philosophy professor is as wise and humble as Socrates.

∴	Taking a philosophy class involves getting your brains twisted inside out and watching the professor take pleasure in humiliating you.

Needless to say, I never took another philosophy class again. But I suppose enough formal logic stuck to me to know a fallacy when

I see it. So what do I think when I contemplate the possibility of marital bliss? I won't say I'm a disbeliever on the subject, but let's say I'm strongly agnostic. I reach for a pen and a piece of paper from my bag to try to amuse myself – anything but the reality of this God-forsaken train – by putting that long-ago symbolic logic to use, but before I can begin I realize I don't remember the symbolic operators and how they all relate. I am momentarily distraught at what *has* vanished from my memory – 'Rose Mary, that's the wrong goddam nineteen minutes, Rose Mary!' – but I never understood it all that well anyway so I jot down what I have in mind, the premises that seem relevant.

A.   Very well then, I contradict myself (the "Whitman Theorem").

B.   I am large, I contain multitudes (the "Whitman Corollary").

C.   All happy families are alike (the "Tolstoy Theorem").

D.   Each unhappy family is unhappy in its own way (the "Tolstoy Corollary").

E.   Nothing is funnier than unhappiness (the "Beckett Theorem").

F.   Laugh and the world laughs with you; weep and you weep alone (the "Wilcox corollary").

G.   Hell is other people (the "Sartre Theorem").

H.   I miss you like hell (the "Millay Corollary").

∴   Women, can't live with them, can't live without them (the "Erasmus Proof").

I realize I'm beyond punchy when I look up to see Sky returning with two containers of coffee and a paper bag. Like Pavlov's dog, I feel my mouth water and my stomach growl and my head swoon. I thank her, genuinely grateful, but receive no acknowledgement in return. Ah yes, the silent treatment. Skylar's particular specialty. Well, maybe we'll both feel better with some breakfast in us. The milky coffee is somewhere between hot and lukewarm and not the freshest brew but I don't care. There are three sugar-dusted doughnuts in the bag – they look like the kind with jelly in the middle – and I momentarily puzzle at the odd number.

"Two for me and one for you," she says. It would be easy to be exasperated by her, even angry, but her insolence is so base and childish that I opt for reverse psychology. This hasn't worked on Sky since she was five – it lasted considerably longer with Abby – but she seems to be regressing.

"Seems fair to me," I say.

"Why?" She seems offended by my non-offense.

"Because you went and got it."

"Jesus! You're too stupid to realize you're being fucked over."

I chew on the doughnut and slurp some coffee.

"Too tired and too hungry. Really, Sky – thanks for getting it."

She rolls her eyes heavenward and gives up, starting on a doughnut herself.

The dual singsong tone of the train's public address system sounds and the conductor announces the next stop as Reading, with a coach connection to Heathrow. I check my watch: 10.45 a.m. Since nine o'clock I've been dialing the office number for Rupert Salmons every fifteen minutes or so, but the phone just rings, with no answer, not even by a voicemail system. This is odd and troubling because I'm supposed to meet with Salmons in fifteen minutes and we won't arrive at Paddington for another forty. Maybe something happened on his end as well. Does this give me a plausible excuse because I've been trying to reach him? Or... is it possible my Lithuanian SIM card isn't working properly? The *driiing-driiing* has sounded like a proper call going through, and I double-checked the number on his office letterhead in my manila file folder, so what gives? I'd hoped, if I could postpone the meeting, to sort out Sky's flight first and the conductor's announcement forces my hand.

"Your mom and I talked yesterday."

Sky glances at me briefly then returns her attention inward.

"She wants you to fly home today. First thing."

"Fine with me."

I'd expected an outright refusal, or at least an argument. But not acquiescence. It should please me; it certainly simplifies my life. But I feel nothing but sadness.

"Okay. I was going to have us get off at Reading and take the bus to Heathrow. But I haven't been able to reach the solicitor so I'm thinking we should go to Paddington first, in case he can still see me earlier."

"Whatever. You figure it out."

All this compliance. If it were wholehearted it would be fine. Even ambivalence I could deal with. But not complete disinterest.

"Maybe I should have insisted you stay with Aunt Lin. I'm sorry if things didn't work out the way you expected."

This strikes a chord.

"The way I *expected*? Like, we'd come over here, you'd get your money and I'd get Moondancer back? Or like you wouldn't totally humiliate me in front of Michael and his mother?"

"You really care about him, don't you?"

"No, Dad. I'm just some slutty whore who gives it up for any guy who comes along."

"Jesus, Sky. Try to pretend I'm your father. This isn't easy for me."

"Good. That makes two of us."

"Look, I'm sorry if I humiliated you. That wasn't my intent. We just needed to catch a train and… you caught me off guard."

"But you're supposed to be the grown-up! To have some maturity!"

"Ah, now you're confusing me with your mother. I'm the screw-up."

"Please, don't play the pity card. It doesn't suit you," she says.

I realize a number of nearby passengers can hear us, so I lean close to Sky and ask her in a whisper to please lower her voice.

"What's the matter, feeling *embarrassed*?" She makes no effort to lower her voice. If anything, she's even louder. I notice the middle-aged woman in the aisle seat look at us sharply but I avoid any eye contact and instead focus on Sky as directly and sympathetically as I can.

"Sky, I'm not playing any games here. Cards on the table – I'm worried. I needed to make this meeting and now I'm going to be late."

With that, she shrugs her shoulders and makes a 'who cares' expression with her face. Like I said, why do I bother? So I resign myself to enduring the solitude of my private worry for the remainder of the rail journey. And in the peculiar way that activity – even inactivity – stretches out to fill the void of time, our train rolls along, one agonizing mile after another, and not a single word passes between me and Sky. I sink into my seat and, as difficult at it is, I refrain from trying Salmons's number yet again on my phone. I refrain from engaging with Sky. I refrain from calculating what's left on the CashPort, as if more money will somehow materialize by doing so. If Albert Einstein really said that insanity is the repetition of past actions expecting a different result, who am I to argue with genius? But does this mean that Sisyphus was insane or just hopeful? We all have our personal crosses to bear, but the Greek Gods were exceptionally cruel in meting out punishment, whether it was Prometheus with his regenerating liver or that damned boulder that keeps slipping free. On the court, if the game plan isn't working you're supposed to try something different. But not hitting the ball? That doesn't seem a very winning strategy.

I look around and realize our train has come to rest. And not at yet another station en route, but Paddington itself. Paddington! A porter pushes a trolley outside the carriage and Sky is collecting her bag from above so I stand up to do the same. Pain immediately emanates from my right ankle, so I balance on my left foot to grab the cane and my tennis bag, then gingerly follow Sky to the platform. We make our way towards the main concourse and I feel the onset of both elation, that we've finally arrived in London, and dread, for what sort of reception my tardiness will bring. So I focus instead on taking measured steps, planting my cane carefully, to keep my weight off of the right leg as much as possible. Once inside the station proper, I see a row of three pay phones, all unoccupied. They aren't the classic red pillbox variety – do those even still exist? – but modern, low-slung ones with LCD screens. Still, they accept coins, so this is all that matters. I ask Sky, who is sulking again, for the change from the fifteen pounds I gave her earlier. She hands over one pound and seventy pence in coins.

"This is it?"

She shrugs her shoulders. I feel exasperation begin to rise inside me – could two coffees and three doughnuts really cost that much? – then I cut it off. I'll get some more money off the CashPort, but first I need to make this call. I dial the office number for Salmons and a crisp, female voice answers on the first ring.

"Solicitors. How may I direct your call?"

"Rupert Salmons, please."

"I'll connect you with his secretary."

"Thanks."

Sky gives me a sarcastically encouraging smile and a thumbs up but inside I'm kicking myself. Why didn't I realize my phone wasn't working properly? I glance at my watch and see it's now 11.42 a.m. Christ!

"Hello, this is Mr. Salmons's office."

"Hi. This is Trevor Davis."

"Mr. Davis. We were expecting you at eleven."

"Yes, I know. I'm terribly sorry. My train was delayed and for some reason my cell – my mobile – wasn't working properly. Is Mr. Salmons there? I'd like to apologize to him."

"Just a minute, Mr. Davis, let me check."

This can only mean that Salmons is there, but the question is, will he take my call?

"Mr. Davis? I'm afraid Mr. Salmons can't talk right now. Shall I take a message?"

I can barely hear her over the noise of a departing diesel loco-motive and a public address announcement, on top of the ordinary background hubbub.

"I totally understand if he's not interested in talking to me. I'd be upset too. But here's the thing. Sorry, what's your name?"

"My name? Sally. Sally Talmadge. I'm Mr. Salmons's secretary."

"Okay, nice to meet you Sally. Sally, I'm sorry to burden you, but I've had kind of a rough twenty-four hours. Well, a bit longer than that, actually, but I just arrived at Paddington Station with my daughter, Skylar, and while I need to get her to Heathrow at some point today so she can fly home to California, I'd be happy to come by your office anytime, even right now. It's very important that I get just a few minutes of Mr. Salmons's time and I feel terrible about making him wait. I'd say it's inexcusable but the thing is, I actually have an excuse. So do you think we can work something out?"

"Mr. Davis…

"Please, call me Trevor."

"Mister… Trevor, I have Mr. Salmons's schedule in front of me and he's going to be completely unavailable the rest of the day. He's instructed me not to…"

"Sally, can I ask, do you have any children?"

"Um, yes. A boy."

"A boy, great. I was blessed with two girls. I'm not complaining, we don't get to choose, do we?"

"No, we certainly don't."

"How old is your son, Sally? If I may ask?"

"He's eight. Look I don't see what this has to…"

"Sally, please indulge me. Well, your boy isn't a teenager yet, but I'm sure you've had moments that try your patience, when his will and your will diverge. I only say that to give you a little context. If I'd been able to make my meeting with your boss earlier, if my daughter and I hadn't had a divergence of wills, you can be sure I would have. And here's the further issue. At this moment I'm here in London with very little left in the way of cash. I mean, next to nothing. It's a long story that I won't bore you with, but my meeting with Mr. Salmons would have a direct impact, hopefully in the positive, on that situation. So it's imperative that I see him sooner rather than later, if you see what I'm saying."

"Mr. Davis, I…

"Sally, it's Trevor, please."

"All right, Trevor. I'm not sure he'd appreciate me telling you this, but he's leaving the office in a few minutes for a lunch meeting and then he'll be out the rest of the afternoon. "

"Can I ask where he's having lunch?"

"Well, I don't suppose that matters. It's not a restaurant, it's at the All England Club."

I'm momentarily floored. "You mean Wimbledon?"

"Yes, that's right. So I'm afraid there's no way he could see you today. And he won't be in the office tomorrow, as he's starting a family holiday."

"I see. Can I ask who he's meeting for lunch?"

"I'm not at liberty to say. I really shouldn't have said this much."

"I understand. And I'm most grateful."

"I hope things work out with you and your daughter."

"Thanks, Sally. I'm sure they will. They always do, don't they?"

"I suppose so."

I hang up. Sky is looking at me quizzically.

"Well? How'd it go?"

"Not great. But I have a plan. We need to get some money first."

I look in my travel wallet for the CashPort.

"What's the plan? Are we going to Heathrow now?"

"Not yet. We're going to Wimbledon first."

Sky rolls her eyes. "Jesus, tennis again? Dad, you need to focus on getting us…"

"He's there. Salmons. At Wimbledon. Or he will be in a few minutes."

"No way!"

"I know, right? Damn, where did I put that?"

I've been looking for the CashPort to no avail. In the travel wallet, in the exterior pockets of my tennis bag, nowhere. Which are the only places it could be.

"Sky, answer me seriously. Do you have it?"

"Have what?"

"You know damned well what – the Cash Passport! Jesus, you do have it, don't you? Look, honey, no fucking around. I know you're pissed about earlier, but just give it to me and we'll get everything sorted out, okay?"

"Dad, I'm telling you, I don't have it."

I grab her by the shoulders, not hard but enough to get her attention, and I look her straight in the eye. She doesn't flinch and she looks at me right back.

"Tell me straight," I say. "Do you have it?"

"No," she says. "I swear. I don't."

I release her shoulders and look around, then back to the tennis bag.

"Alright, think, Davis. Where the hell could it be?"

"How much is on it?"

"Not that much, but enough. We just need some walking-around money. For tube fare, to start with."

"Are you sure you looked everywhere?" she says.

I give her another appraising look. Is she messing with me? But at this point I have to believe her. What does she have to gain anyway? She doesn't even have the PIN for it.

"Alright then. My bag first, then yours. Let's go through them from top to bottom."

And we do. Methodically at first, then more frantically. Until all the contents are strewn on the asphalt in front of us. As the possibility starts to settle in that I might not have the card, I feel a new variety of fear physically manifest itself. It starts on the nape of my neck, like a tingling, wet coldness, then moves down my back, up through my crotch and settles in my lower belly. I see Sky looking at me with genuine concern now and I hope that I don't vomit right here in front of her. There may only be a few hundred bucks left on the CashPort, but that's all I have, apart from the £1.20 in coins in my pocket. I know everything is relative; in the land of the blind, the one-eyed man is king. So it might not be much even to a person of modest means, but please, dear Lord, let me find this card. I need this money. "Again," I say. And we go through all our belongings one more time.

At some point, after scouring every nook and cranny of our bags and combing repeatedly through all of our pockets and every last garment and toiletry – enough, I suppose, to near the point of insanity – I look up and shake my head. We haven't found the CashPort and I don't expect we will. I can only guess I lost it somewhere between dinner in Cornwall and our arrival back in London. So it could be anywhere. Swept into a dustbin at Truro Station, hidden under a cushion at Frankie's cottage, obscured by the gravel of the Pandora Inn car park, you name it. Regardless, at this point I've got to consider it well and truly gone.

I quickly run through the options. Try to contact First Regency Bank in San Francisco, rolling the dice that they'll allow me to access the remaining balance and retrieve it. But even if that were possible it wouldn't happen today, so I'd lose any hope of meeting with Salmons before he's gone on vacation. Plus, Jolene at the bank said the card had a chip that could be recharged with cash. So it's probably impossible to verify the amount remaining on the card without the card itself. And even if it *were* possible to track the withdrawals, and I figured out the right person to call, my cell phone isn't working and Sky and I don't have enough pocket change remaining to risk a toll call.

I can't risk calling anyone else back home for the same reason. It's almost noon here so that's 4 a.m. on the West Coast. Even if I managed to arouse Meg or Dore or Diana from their slumber and convinced them to wire me some funds, I doubt it would come through in time to be of any use today. And there's the same problem with telephoning: will 120 pence stretch for the length of an overseas call? Unlikely.

So… what to do? Think Trevor! I look at our possessions, trying to locate something sufficiently valuable that we could sell on the spot for some quick cash. Even ten pounds would be useful. My tennis racquets? But who would want them? I scan the station quickly, as if there's some experienced tennis player walking through who'd want a couple of dinged-up Wilson frames, the old Pro Staff 90 model, strung with gut on the mains and poly on the crosses, grip size 4 5/8 (I have large hands). Doubtful. Would a pawnshop be interested, if I could find one close to the station? In used tennis racquets? Realistically I can't imagine getting even a pound. On eBay or Craigslist they'd be worth something to a knowledgeable player. But there's no time for that.

I check my watch again – 12.03 p.m.

"If he's having lunch, we can still get there before he's finished," Sky says. She's become remarkably helpful since this latest crisis, completely shelving her earlier sullenness. Well, thank goodness for small favors, I suppose. As if I don't have better things to think about, my stupid brain invests a moment on contemplating a hypothetical bargain with the devil: getting the CashPort back in return for Sky's positive mood change. I push the thought aside and I try to focus on a real solution. I'm annoyed with myself on a number of fronts: my carelessness at losing the card; my having got us into this whole financial predicament in the first place; and my seeming willingness to sell off my daughter's newfound emotional stability for another day's spending money. And now I'm annoyed at my annoyance, which is completely counter-productive. It's like beating yourself up for muffing an easy overhead in the previous point when you're now serving love-forty at two games to five. Total rookie mistake. You've got to forget the points you've already lost, especially the egregious ones. Focus on winning the next one.

"Don't you think?" Sky says.

"What?"

"That we have enough time."

I look at the earnestness in her expression – is it just concern or actual devotion? – and my heart skips a beat, or rather it beats two or three little thumps in place of a normal one. I hold my breath and wait for it to settle into a regular rhythm again. Jeez, that's all I need: a myocardial infarction at Paddington Station. Although an ambulance would solve the transportation issue. 'Never mind the ticker, gents. Would you mind dropping us at the All England Club?'

"Yeah," I say. "Plenty of time for sure."

I undo the leather strap of my watch and examine its back, with the engraved inscription to my father. The cursive letters seem so old-fashioned, like the watch itself. I look up and see Sky regarding me with a horrified expression.

"No way. Dad, no way! It was Grandpa's!"

"It's just a watch, sweetheart. And it's not like he wore it that long. Less than a month."

"That's not the point! They gave it to him for what he did in the war. You told me yourself, it was the most important battle in Word War Two. Maybe ever. Right?"

"Maybe. There's certainly a good argument."

"So you can't sell it. End of story. We'll figure out something else."

"I might not have to sell it. They have these people called pawn-brokers. They…"

"I know what a pawnbroker is," she interrupts.

"You do? How?"

Sky looks uncomfortable.

"Never mind, I just do. Jesus, Dad, I wasn't born yesterday. I know things! The point is, it's too big a risk. They wouldn't give you a fraction what it's worth and you might not get it back. You'd end up regretting it forever."

"I doubt it. It's just a watch, a material possession. A piece of metal and glass with a bunch of gears and springs inside. People are what matter. Me, you, Abby. Your mom." Yes, Annie too. But did Sky have to use that word, regret?

"And Grandpa. It's not the watch, it's what's written on the watch!"

She grabs the Longines from my hand and reads the inscription.

"'To William G. Davis, U.S. Army, from the grateful citizens of France. June 6, 2009.'"

I meet her eyes and smile, hoping she will soften her imploring expression but she's having none of it.

"How many other watches say that?"

"None," I say.

"Exactly."

"Okay, so what's *your* plan then?" I ask. "We have exactly one pound and twenty pence. How are we going to get from here to Wimbledon and inside the tennis grounds so I can talk to Rupert Salmons?"

"Okay. Let me work on that. But first things first, we've got to get you cleaned up. No way you're meeting him looking like this."

I look at my clothes. I'm wearing a rumpled pair of Levis and the short-sleeve drip-dry shirt I've had on since yesterday morning, but I realize it's much worse than that. I feel my jaw—there's more than a day's growth of stubble. If my eyes appear as red and puffy as they feel, I must be a frightful vision, and I don't imagine I smell too good.

"I was planning on grabbing a shave and a shower but now we don't have the money."

Sky goes into extreme 'can do' mode, straightening her posture, scanning the platform quickly, then looking at me with an expression so serious and adult that I don't know whether to feel reassured or concerned.

"Okay," she says. "You wait here. I'm going to do a quick scouting mission. All right? Don't move. And for God's sake, don't do anything with this." She hands the Longines back to me.

"Okay," I say. "I won't."

"Put it back on."

I nod solemnly. "I will."

"Not 'I will.' Put it on now!"

I do as she commands. "Happy?" I ask.

She puts her hands on her hips but doesn't bother to roll her eyes. "Overjoyed. Thrilled to the fucking marrow. Now wait here!"

Before I can say another word she's gone, dashing across the huge terminal in the direction of the statue of Paddington Bear. With nothing to do other than wait, I reach towards my tennis bag to pull out my phone. Maybe the damn thing has managed to reset itself and will make a call now. But as soon as I touch it, another thought dawns on me: I might be able to get a wireless Internet connection. Excited, I press the button to wake it and wait impatiently for the software to respond so it can search for any WiFi signals in the vicinity.

The little circular 'I'm working on it' symbol spins away for what seems thirty seconds, then a minute.

"Come on, come on," I say out loud, as if I can somehow implore it into functioning more quickly. But nothing. This Lithuanian SIM card must have really screwed it up. I know logically that shouldn't be the case – the phone function must operate on a different circuit entirely – but what other explanation can there be? Finally, after perhaps another minute of electronic futility, the circle stops spinning and the screen starts to populate with the names of WiFi routers discovered. All have the padlock icon denoting password-encryption, except one: WH Smith.

"Yes!" I quickly click on it and, in a mere second or two, the three semi-circular bars of a positive WiFi connection appear on the top of the screen.

"Right here!" I say. I often talk to myself on the tennis court, a kind of positive reinforcement that isn't meant to disrespect my opponent (I keep my voice low) but to inspire myself. Roger Federer has his "Come on!" after a winning shot and Justine Henin, the great Belgian player with a one-handed backhand so beautiful it should be bronzed, has her "*Allez!*" For me, it's always been: "Right here!" A kind of shorthand to tell myself that, whatever's come before and however poorly I've played or however dire the circumstances, it's time to put all that aside and make it happen. Right here and right now.

I reflexively click on the Mail button, then immediately regret it as the segmented circle starts spinning again. I probably should have opened a browser first, to make sure the signal was working or to log in. I consider doing that now but that would likely over-load the hapless device beyond any hope of recovery. I'm consid-ering my next step, watching that interminable spinning circle whirl away – maybe a forced restart – when Sky suddenly reap-pears and sits down next to me, half out of breath.

"Okay," she says. "Here's the deal. Near platform twelve you can get a hot shower for five pounds. So if we can scrape together a few more pounds, you should do it. And get this! I found one of these little 20p pieces on the ground right in front of it. Can you believe that? They're barely bigger than a penny and that's worth, what, a quarter?"

"A bit more." I was tempted to say, 'A bit more than two bits,' but this is no time for stupid puns. Besides, she might know about pawnshops but no way she knows what two bits means.

"Okay, then. Awesome. I'll have another look for loose change but meantime the men's washroom is only 30p so I think you should go there right now. You can shave and change your clothes, so who needs a shower anyway? With the 20p I found, that'll only cost us ten pence!"

"What then?"

"What do you mean, what then? Then we're in business! You're all cleaned up, feeling like a new man, we get on the underground for Wimbledon and you knock his socks off."

"You're forgetting we don't have enough for tube fare."

"Are you sure?"

"Not even close."

"Okay. You let me figure that out. But come on – we're wasting precious time! You need to go get cleaned up."

I realize she's right of course. So I take the 20p piece from Sky, find a 10p coin in my pocket, return the phone to the outer pocket of my tennis bag and put the bag on my shoulders. Then I put an arm around Sky and kiss her on her forehead. She recoils from me, disgusted.

"Eww! Did I mention you stink?"

I smile. "I'm planning on fixing that."

"Good! The sooner the better! So go!" She motions me away with a flicking motion of her fingers, palms downward. Like Cleopatra might have done to send her troops off to battle.

I take a step, feel the sharp pain in my right ankle, and remember the cane leaning against the bench. I retrieve it and start walking. The sign for the men's room is just visible beyond the Great Western ticket office, and as I head in that direction one thought becomes paramount in my mind: will there be hot water? This isn't a given in public restrooms and I don't want to try shaving with cold water. The results could be disastrous. But how could they charge 30p if they don't provide hot water? Well, the voice of negativism in my head continues, because if you're desperate to take a piss or a dump, you'll pay, and who cares if you wash your hands with cold water after?

Rather than get ahead of myself I realize I need to stay in the moment, so I make a conscious effort to take in the sights and sounds and smells of the platform as I walk. It's not rush hour and there are many fewer passengers milling around than when Sky and I departed on the Cornish Riviera yesterday morning, but there is still plenty of activity, enough to generate, with the enhanced acoustics of the arched roof, a constant background hum. It's already quite warm – it will be hotter than yesterday according to the forecast I read in the *Telegraph* – and the dominant smell in my nose, apart from the occasional whiff of coffee or food, is that of coal. Not diesel exhaust, which is an odor I'm familiar with, but coal. Or more precisely, burnt coke. It's as though the heat bearing down from the sun has released a trace hydrocarbon deposit from the very bones of the station, as if a century of coal soot emitted from the thousands of steam locomotives running back and forth on the tracks under the station roof and the countless fireplaces in the vicinity of the station, from early Victorian times onward, through the Edwardian era and whatever one calls the George-Edward-George do-si-do period that followed, had somehow become so trapped in the pores of the brick and steel and glass and stone, so compressed into the gaps of the building's very molecules themselves, that despite more than a half-century of regular cleaning and nature's wind and rain, enough continual scrubbing and dowsing and blowing, presumably, to remove every last trace of coal dust, that on a hot summer day like this enough still remains to seep into the immediate atmosphere and reach my nostrils.

As I descend the stairs to the men's room, the faint soot smell still evident, I wonder if I could be imagining it, and in the very next moment I decide no, definitely not, and in that same moment I also remember the time I visited the USS Arizona Memorial in Pearl Harbor and witnessed the eerie oil sheen on the water, a remnant of the million plus gallons of bunker fuel that went down with the stricken battleship. That visit was almost a decade ago, when the girls were maybe five, and the ship had been submerged for over fifty years. As far as I know, the Arizona continues to seep fuel oil to this day. So couldn't this be the same, with the soot?

I ask the washroom attendant about hot water and he confirms with no trace of insult or amusement its availability. So I hand over my thirty pence and find a clean enough-looking sink to use and dig out the toiletry kit from my bag. I look at myself in the mirror for the first time today, then instantly wish I hadn't. A discouraging sight. Well, it's not going to improve by staring at it so I remove the shaving cream and razor from the kit, turn the hot water tap and get busy.

As I scrape away at my whiskers my thoughts drift back to my visit to the Arizona Memorial and the incongruity of that tranquil, tropical setting being visited with aerial attack, and the particular devastation suffered by that ship and her crew: a direct hit to the forward ammunition magazine. My mind was both repelled and fascinated thinking about such an explosion, and the horrors that would have resulted, the way one learns of some heinous terrorist beheading posted on YouTube and is tempted to view it, even though, after the fact, you'll wish you hadn't. So I focused instead on the majesty of the floating memorial itself, an austere, white Noah's ark preserving not animals but the names of the sunken ship's dead, hundreds of eighteen year-old boys much like my father who, for whatever twist of fate, didn't wade ashore in cold Atlantic breakers but whose lungs filled with the warm Pacific while trapped below decks. And if, in that moment, there was an awareness in them that life was to be no more, there must have been no sense of cause, just or otherwise, or community or family. Or anything. Just loneliness of the worst sort, devoid of meaning or hope. Staring into the dark and empty abyss.

I shake these morbid thoughts from my head and force myself back into the present, where I'm at the sink in the men's washroom under Platform 1 of Paddington Station. And I permit myself to admire my handiwork. I am now clean-shaven and, thanks to the small hotel freebie I'd kept from my last trip, my hair is freshly shampooed. True, I can't shower or bathe, but I throw caution to the wind and risk the ire of the washroom attendant by taking off my shirt and washing under my arms with hot, soapy water. That done, I gather my stuff into my tennis bag and enter a toilet stall, where there is barely enough room to strip down to my socks, give the rest of my body an improvised sponge bath with a cotton undershirt, then towel off, apply deodorant, and re-dress in a clean pair of underwear, khakis pants and a blue button-down shirt.

Back upstairs, I locate Sky on the platform near the entrance to a Ladbrokes. She gives me an exaggerated once-over, nodding and smiling for emphasis.

"Not bad, not bad all," she finally says.

"I'm glad you approve."

"More important, I'm sure the solicitor will too."

"From your lips to God's ears."

Feeling suddenly upbeat – as if! – I'm tempted to walk into the bookmakers shop and see if they're offering any odds on the

Isner-Mahut match when it resumes, either who's picked to win or whether it will even finish. It would be a momentary diversion, perhaps a reassurance to Sky (and myself) that we're not overly consumed with our plight, but before I can suggest it, Sky gets an urgent, serious look on her face.

"Hey, do we have Oyster cards?"

I'm momentarily confused – oysters? – then remember this is what London Transport calls their discount program.

"No. Since we weren't going to be in London that long I didn't bother."

"Damn. If we had Oyster cards your fare would be one pound eighty and mine would be just a pound."

"And the cash price?"

She frowns. "Four pounds each."

"Shit," I say.

"Tell me about it."

She and I stare at each other a moment and my right hand goes towards my left wrist.

"No," she says. "Out of the question."

"What else can we sell?"

"Dad, I scoped out the ticket barriers. I could hop over easily. If you pushed off your good leg, I think you could too."

"And then what? Run for it?"

"I doubt anyone would follow us. It must happen all the time. What would they care?"

I can't deny the thought occurred to me earlier, but I dismissed it. Not so much on practical grounds, for I believe my daughter is right and we'd probably get away with it. But on moral ones. I don't mean to sound high and mighty (as if I could, given my recent track record) and I really don't have any qualms about denying London Transport our fares, which surely amount to an insignificant gnat's worth of their elephantine annual budget, but – sigh – it's the damned principle of the thing. If I cheat riding the Tube I might as well cheat playing tennis against Jeremy fucking Sutcliffe. I've let Sky down so much. So is that the example I want to set for my daughter, even *in extremis*?

"I'd care."

"Jesus, Dad, come on! We just need to get there."

"Wait a second, let me think."

I've been so focused on what physical items we might have to sell, to generate some quick cash, like my watch or my tennis racquets. But what if we had something else to offer? And then it comes to me. Yes! Something Sky and Abby used to listen to and imitate when there were younger. Crazy, perhaps, and we don't have much time. But still – who knows?

"Wait here," I say to Sky, and I leave my tennis bag with her and walk, cane-aided, into Ladbrokes.

"You're going to gamble? With one pound?" I can hear her voice even as the smoked glass door closes, but I'm on a mission so I don't turn to respond. I approach the counter and ask a middle-aged, thickset man wearing half-moon reading glasses if I can have a piece of cardboard and borrow a marking pen.

"You want what?"

I repeat my request, emphasizing in the politest terms its urgency, and I can see him waver between telling me to bugger off and helping out. Thankfully there are no customers so he's got nothing better to do than entertain my odd request.

"What do you want it for?"

He looks suspicious, like I've asked for a knife or a spare Molotov cocktail. I sigh and I'm about to tell him when he shakes his head, as if realizing the irrelevance of his own question, and he goes in search.

I say a muffled 'Right here!' to myself and wait as patiently as I can for him to return, which he does in short order carrying a piece of white card stock, maybe twenty inches square, and a blue Sharpie.

"Will this do?" he asks.

"That will do magnificently." He hands them over and I move a few feet away to a countertop and start writing. When I'm done, I recap the Sharpie and return it to the man.

"Ta," he says.

"You're a lifesaver," I say.

I smile and show him the sign, which he quickly scans. He nods as if it's nothing out of the ordinary and he turns his attention to some paperwork, so I rejoin Sky outside.

She sees me carrying the card stock as I approach and I can tell she's curious but I hold it edgeways so she can't read it. I can feel an impish grin begin to get the better of me so I surrender to it.

"What?" she says.

I flip the sign around so Sky can read it. I've written in block letters as neatly as I can:

WE LOST OUR MONEY AND NEED
TWO TUBE FARES TO GET HOME.

IF YOU LIKE OUR PERFORMANCE,
PLEASE BE GENEROUS!

She looks from the sign to me, her puzzlement beginning to morph into worry.

"Performance?" she says.

"I was thinking we'd do 'Who's On First?'

22

It's funny how being on a moving train can give you a sense of purpose, like you're getting somewhere. And since Sky and I are on a Wimbledon District Line train – yes, that was the actual destination showing on the front of the train as it pulled into Paddington – I suppose I should feel some forward momentum, other than in the strictly Newtonian sense. It's just there's that nagging question that seems so constant lately: now what? So we'll get off at Wimbledon and leave the underground station and then ask ourselves, now what? Walk to the grounds and watch all the fortunates pull out their tickets and go inside? Sky and I scored a remarkable fourteen pounds back at Paddington in barely fifteen minutes of busking, but after paying for our tube fares and adding in the pound we already had, that only leaves us with seven. No way some scalper is going to sell me even an unreserved grounds ticket for seven pounds, not on a day the Queen is visiting, Andy Murray is playing, and John Isner and Nicolas Mahut are set to resume their already historic match.

I realize with a heavy heart that I'm not going to solve this problem now. So I suppose I should simply be grateful for small miracles, like Sky was willing to do the old Abbott and Costello skit with me in the first place. Lord knows she didn't want to, and it seemed like, try as I might to convince her, she wasn't going to, but after cajoling her about a dozen times with different versions of: "Who's your first baseman?" she finally responded with a meek "Yes."

I don't remember when 'Who's on First?' entered our family's consciousness. Maybe Annie and I were talking about baseball – her father is a big Cubs fan (poor wretch) – or maybe we'd got on the subject of comedians. But for some reason we ended up searching for, then playing, a recording of Lou Costello and Bud Abbott performing their signature skit and the girls were hooked. They couldn't stop laughing at the zany absurdity of it. After that they asked us to replay it regularly. So much so that the girls began reciting the lines and eventually would entertain guests by doing the entire thing from memory. Abby, true to type, played Costello's earnest questioner, the befuddled guy asking about the names of the players, while Sky played Abbott's impassive in-the-know character with the absurd answers, a guy as confounding as he is fascinating because he must realize the nature of the other man's confusion but he never lets on.

Once Sky began to respond, as I peppered her with the infield roster queries her sister used to ask, she fell completely into the rhythm of the cockamamie routine, like an old tennis player rediscovering her swing. Soon we were both at net, batting volleys back and forth at a furious pace, neither of us wanting to let the ball bounce or miss. And like a great player when they get into the zone, Sky seemed to transport herself from where we really were: on an asphalt station platform in a foreign country begging for money. I wasn't sure at first if anyone would either understand what we were doing – it's about baseball, after all – or appreciate the effort enough to chip in some spare change, but when a small crowd formed to watch, maybe ten or so, I thought we might have a chance. And then the coins started dropping into the tennis cap I'd left on the ground near the card stock sign and had primed with our last pound. And not little coins, but one pound and fifty pence pieces.

"Well, what's the left fielder's name?"

"No, What's on second."

"And the left fielder?"

"Why."

"Because!"

"Oh, he's centerfield."

Plop, another coin.

The beauty of the routine is you can pretty much keep going forever, riffing off the crazy names of the pitcher and catcher, Tomorrow and Today, once you've mined the basemen sufficiently, and I was so enjoying taking this nostalgic joy ride with Sky I almost didn't want to stop, but at some point I figured we had more than enough for the Tube and we should be on our way. So I set up the final joke by going on a sarcastic rant about how I suppose Who picks up the ball and throws it to What, who tosses it to I Don't Know, then back to Tomorrow for a triple play. Continuing, I said: "And I guess another guy gets up and hits a long fly ball to Because. Why? I Don't Know! He's on third and I don't give a damn!"

"What'd you say?" Sky asked.

"I said, 'I don't give a damn!'"

"Oh, that's our shortstop." Delivered completely deadpan on her part.

We actually got some applause and a big grin from an old woman. She couldn't have had a clue what a shortstop was, but she seemed delighted by our skit anyway, even though she didn't leave any coins. Oh well. Sometimes the best rewards aren't monetary.

I look over at Sky, who's sitting and staring ahead without focus. I'd say she's pensive but I have no idea if she's thinking about anything at all.

"You okay?" I say.

No reaction. She's been in that weird adolescent period the past year where you'd swear she's heard you but there's absolutely no response. I could have said, 'Moondancer just poked his head in the train' and it would have received the same (non) reaction.

"Sky." I say it loudly.

"What?"

"You okay?"

She shrugs and looks anything but okay. Whatever boost she might have received from our performing the Abbott and Costello has vanished.

"That was fun back there, doing the skit with you."

"Yeah."

Something about the cast of her eyes and set of her jaw gives me a notion what she's brooding about.

"For what it's worth, I liked Michael too."

She looks at me sharply. "*Liked*? You sound like he's dead."

"Like. Sorry. Like."

Sky suddenly drops her emotional shield and looks at me with a vulnerability I haven't seen in a long time, at least directed towards me.

"Dad?" She says it in a scared, little girl whisper.

"What sweetie?"

"Will I ever see Michael again?"

I look at her and feel the thin membrane of my heart, what's left of it, rip right down the middle. Her pain seems so familiar that I'm dangerously confused whether I'm feeling genuine empathy for my eldest daughter or some mirror image of my own suffering.

We're sitting side-by-side, only an armrest between us, so I lean over and envelope her in my arms. She dissolves into my embrace and it feels good. I rest my head over hers then I kiss her gently where her forehead meets her hair.

"I hope so. "

What feels like a series of switches in the track jerks the train sideways and back several times and I hold onto Sky through the violent motion until a particularly heavy jostle, coupled with the carriage's sudden deceleration for the next station, tosses us both from our seats and her from my arms. We each regain our balance and sit back down but the moment, once interrupted, has passed. I pat her on her thigh but she nods without looking at me so I look out the window instead and wait until I can see the name of the station appear. Earl's Court. It seems an eternity since we were here last but then I realize with an electric jolt that it was only yesterday morning, after we'd unceremoniously checked out of the Viceroy Guesthouse and I had to walk to the Earl's Court tube station without the benefit of a cane. Christ, what a twenty-four hours she's had. I should be used to the pain that summer lightning can produce, even though I'm not, but for her? Sky puts up such a tough front but I now realize how much she's suffering. I wish I could give her a better answer about Michael but, with how things are between me and Annie, or rather aren't, and how I left things with Frankie, I feel more uncertainty about my life than I can ever remember feeling. And I'm no unsullied teen; I've got almost fifty years of wear and tear, certainly enough to know better. But maybe the complacency of middle age has left me soft and vulnerable. And now, with what's been thrown my way, it's like I have no future whatsoever, or at least no expectation of all the things that reasonably prosperous middle aged people take for granted: a place called home to return to, preferably also occupied by a loved one; a next meal to fill one's belly (I already feel hungry but I force myself to ignore it); and a job, both to provide a sense of purpose and to pay for the home and the meal. Instead, I have that question: now what?

I realize that some wealthy types, at least in my neck of the woods, go to great lengths to try to attain an analogous state of disconnectedness, in the belief – however misguided – that doing so will provide enlightenment. I know plenty of them; they fill the zendos and ashrams of Tassajara and Green Gulch and Spirit Rock and similar places further afield in California and Oregon looking for something close to what I seem to have achieved on a south-bound District Line train passing through Earl's Court. Maybe what they haven't realized is that true spiritual awakening, of having a real oneness with the moment, will elude them as long as they insist on keeping their cars and houses and jobs and spouses. Or perhaps, just to play devil's advocate, they really *are* better off with all those things but they just haven't learned how to appreciate them. What did the Dalai Lama say, in one of those talks that those wannabe Buddhist friends of mine are always quoting?

'It is better to want what you have and not have what you want.'

Not bad, really, coming from a guy whose country was swallowed whole by China and whose job forbids him having a sexual partner. And yet this guy, in his maroon and saffron robe, and his Michael Caine glasses, insists on chortling through life like it's all a cosmic joke. Which, come to think of it, may be the point.

Anyway, the only problem with wanting what you have, from my standpoint, is the damn goalposts keep shifting. I don't seem to have a fighting chance to want what I have, because five minutes later I don't have it. So after the downsizing of the past year plus, accelerating the past couple days like some going-out-of-business sale on steroids, what do I still have that I'm supposed to want?

Apparently, judging by my and Sky's recent vaudeville performance, I should be glad we have a marketable skill that can generate pocket change in a relatively short period of time. But how sustainable is that? I've already considered reprising 'Who's on First?' in front of the All England Club, keeping at it like an endless infielder's game of 'around the horn' until we raise enough cash to get me inside. But something tells me Sky's indulgence has been pushed to the limit and the ghosts of Bud Abbott and Lou Costello can cease spinning in their graves. And without Sky, I'm screwed. Nobody wants to hear me recite just one part. So then what? Unless my barely-Karaoke-ready baritone miraculously acquires operatic quality, there's nothing I can perform solo. Developing urban real estate and hitting a tennis ball. That's about the extent of my talents. And apparently neither one sufficient to matter.

Jesus, what's this – self-pity? Again? Well, there's certainly no market for that. And – have I forgotten so quickly? That it's not talent that matters all that much, it's setting a goal and plugging away. You know, the old Woody Allen line, how eighty percent of life is showing up. So… just keep your powder dry, Trevor lad. We'll find a way into the bloody All England Club. Slice backhand approach down the line, ball skidding near the baseline. One point at a time.

I look around the train carriage. Other than Skylar and me, there are eight souls. An elderly couple dressed as if it were thirty degrees cooler and six younger solo passengers, variously occupying themselves with books, newspapers and smartphones. An ordinary tube train trip, in the middle of a warm June weekday. That's the strange thing about mortality, isn't it? The on-ness of life, just going and going, then stop. It's like: here, here, here, here, here, here, here, here, here, here, here, here, here, here, here … here, here, not. For a life that reaches middle age those consecutive 'here's stretch on for pages before the 'not' arrives. And there's no warning – unless you have some incurable disease – that your ordinary state of being is about to shift into sudden nothingness. If I were a fatalist I suppose I might conclude that I've been getting some sort of warning. Not in a medical way – my badly sprained ankle, as painful as it still is, can't be mistaken for anything terminal – but perhaps in tragic, dramatic terms. 'The signs were all before him; the trajectory was clear. And so his inevitable downfall was nigh.'

Okay, Christ – how is substituting melodrama for self-pity an improvement? Do I really believe my recent past defines me? That a run of bad luck – admittedly, a *really* bad run – can't be reversed at some point? Take that guy over there, the snappy dresser with the silk shirt and linen trousers. What's to say *he* isn't the tragic figure here and he's heading home to discover his wife in bed with his best friend, which all ends with kitchen knives and massive bloodshed? I'm done with being the poster child for that Chinese proverb – the one about living in interesting times. No Sirree Bob, I'm due for a spell of really boring times. Okay, not *too* boring; I'd like Frankie to be part of the picture to spice things up. But other than that, plenty boring enough.

I look at Sky again. No change in emotion, at least by outward demeanor. I touch her gently on the arm.

"Sky, you remember a couple of years ago, when you and I got that bad cold?"

"Huh?" She realizes I've spoken but too late for the sounds to be intelligible.

"We got really sick, it took like two weeks for the cough to go away, but Mom and Abby never got it."

"What about it?"

She looks like she understands what I'm talking about, but I'm not entirely sure.

"I could tell we had exactly the same virus because whatever symptoms you got, I got them a day later. Normally I'd be concerned with massive sinus congestion that lasts for days but since you were suffering the same thing, I didn't worry."

"Uh-huh. So what's your point?"

"I guess I don't have a point."

She looks more confused than exasperated, although there's some of that as well.

"Okay," she says. "So, you just like remembering being sick."

"I guess I was just making conversation."

She looks at me briefly, then stares off into the middle distance. When she turns back she has a determined expression.

"That I'll never find something else to be good at."

"What?"

"You asked me to tell you my biggest fear. When I was riding yesterday I remembered how it feels to be really good at something."

"You'll be good at a lot of things, Sweetheart. You're still young."

"You don't understand," she says.

I have to force myself not to laugh. Don't I? Once, a long time ago, I was pretty good at grass court tennis. Enough to play for Oxfordshire at Wimbledon.

"I might have some ..."

"No," she interrupts. "I don't want to talk about it."

"But you just..."

"No! I told it to you. End of discussion."

Her eyes burn into mine with a naked ferocity.

"Okay?"

"Okay." I'm actually not okay but she isn't giving me much choice. And right now I'll select peace over conflict whenever possible. I try a modest smile and she looks away.

"So," I say. "What's the plan when you get home?"

"You cannot be serious," she says.

"What do you mean?"

"You want to talk about my summer schedule? Here?"

"Well, maybe you can make it easier and give me your approved topic list for discussion."

"Okay, fine," she says. "How about how you're going to get into Wimbledon and meet the lawyer so you can get the fucking money and I can go home. *That's* the approved topic."

"I'm working on it."

"Great. When you have a plan, let me know."

I look at her, glad that she's got some oomph back in her but always surprised to see how take charge she can be as well.

"Jeez, when did you get so grown up and practical?"

"Someone has to be," she says.

Hmm. No argument there.

I look around and notice enough people have entered our carriage the last few stops to make it feel occupied, if not crowded. The train starts to decelerate for the next station and I check the map overhead to see if we're close to the end of the line, Wimbledon. Slowing to a stop I see the station is Southfields, then all of a sudden most everyone on board stands up and exits the car. It occurs to me just as the doors are about to close that they all look like the kind of people who might attend a tennis match.

We're moving again and in a panicky confusion I check the map. It shows two stops after Southfields: Wimbledon Park and Wimbledon. Is it possible that the All England Club is located near Southfields?

"Shit, I think we just missed our stop."

"Don't worry," Sky says. "We can always go back a stop." I realize she's right, but I check my watch – 1.20 p.m. – and also realize that the time window to catch Rupert Salmons before the conclusion of his lunch meeting is rapidly closing. A train going in the opposite direction might not show up for ten or fifteen minutes.

I lean over to a man of about sixty who looks by dress and aspect to be a native Londoner.

"Excuse me, do you know the best stop for the All England Club? We're on foot."

"That would have been Southfields. But Wimbledon Park or Wimbledon are nearly as good."

"How much further are we talking about?"

"Oh, I believe ten minutes at most.

"Thanks."

I motion to Sky – time to get off.

I try to look through the window but all I see is my reflection back, the guy who keeps screwing up. How much more leeway do I have? Cats have nine lives but surely I've exceeded that number. The luggage trolley fiasco alone ought to have cashed in my chips. Sailors and aviators talk about nature sometimes permitting one human error, but that two are usually fatal. I've been given so many chances, so many do-overs on the really big stuff. Maybe I'm so tapped out on mulligans that even something trifling, like not bothering to scope out the correct tube station, does me in. And if so, who's to say it doesn't serve me right?

23

Sky and I walk down Home Park Road, with solidly upper-middle-class houses on our left and a leafy tree-lined expanse of parkland on our right. The road gently curves counter-clockwise in an infuriating manner, infuriating because, as I know now from the map outside the tube station, this will take us very much further from the crow-flies direction of the All England Club before we can dog-leg back towards it. I check my watch again – 1.27 p.m. – and curse myself again for not exiting at Southfields.

Sky grabs my arm and points to a sign indicating a footpath to Wimbledon Park.

"Would that get us there faster?"

I hesitate while I bring up the image of the map in my head – I've always been good with maps – and mentally trace ourselves heading north past the big lake to the public park.

"No, better to keep going. We'd just end up backtracking even more."

"Are you sure?"

"No, I'm bloody well not sure, but trust me."

She scowls and opens her mouth and I brace myself for some sarcastic jab about my dubious trustworthiness.

"If you're going to swear, swear like a fucking American."

We're walking quickly now, each of us pushing the pace a little bit more, but I'm at the limit of what I can manage using Frankie's cane. As it is, each time my left foot leaves the ground completely and the cane can't absorb my shifting body weight soon enough, a yelp of pain shoots up my leg from my right ankle. I try a few paces with a kind of herky-jerky hopping motion, but I can't get the correct cadence to sustain it and it only saves up the nasty stuff and deposits it all on one awkward stride, ratcheting the ankle pain to another level entirely and introducing an annoying sloshing of my tennis bag like a piston that alternates banging against my left hamstring and the base of my skull. Trying to bamboozle my ankle like this is how I imagine it would be inside a free-falling elevator, and trying to time a vertical jump just before the elevator hits the ground, cheating death like in those Wile E. Coyote and Road Runner cartoons. Only you can't outfox gravity. Like the lady said in the old margarine commercial: 'It's not nice to fool Mother Nature.'

Sky is going faster now, remarkably controlling her roller suitcase so it keeps in line, and a video clip pops into my head of a gangly male athlete in a floppy cap speed walking around the Munich stadium track. That was the first time I recall watching an Olympics on television and a rush of sounds and images from the summer of 1972 suddenly flood my brain. Mark Spitz with his iconic mustache and Speedo, either dripping water from the pool or dripping gold medals from his neck. Helmeted kayakers paddling furiously against an artificial, concrete-enclosed torrent to reach a dangling pylon and then releasing themselves to navigate to the next gate, only to madly dig again against the flow like some waterborne Sisyphus. And the dark, haunting coverage of terrorists in ski masks in the Israeli section of the Olympic Village. No thrill of victory there, just agony of defeat.

"Wait up!" I call to Sky. While I've been lost in my reverie she's opened a gap of ten feet between us and is pulling further away by each stride. She looks back at me and shakes her head.

"We need to go faster," she says over her shoulder.

"Shit," I mutter. The pain from my ankle is now reaching Brobdingnagian proportions and I can feel a headache forming. Plus it's damnably hot and my clean shirt is damp all across my back beneath the Wilson bag and below my now-weeping armpits. What was the point of cleaning myself up at Paddington if I'm going to get disheveled again?

I try to push my cane-assisted speed walking up a tiny notch in pace, seeking some incremental sweet spot where the pain is almost tolerable, but my ankle is having none of it. My head is throbbing fully now, starting at my temples and expanding all around my crown. Rivulets of sweat are trickling down my upper arms into the crook of my elbows and onto my wrists and hands.

"Sky!" I yell, but her stride doesn't waiver and she merely gives me the briefest of backwards glances with – is it possible? – a droll little smile. A moment later she glances back again but seemingly just so I can hear her clearly when she yells.

"Come on! Give full effort!"

Give full effort. That's something I used to say to the girls, in the days when I had a credible claim to being a constructive influence in their lives. If one of them brought home a sub-par report card, for instance, I wouldn't get upset, I'd just ask if they'd given full effort. It's all anyone can ask of us, I'd say. In sports or in school. Or in life.

"Why you rotten little..." My voice rises in volume, each word geometrically louder, then I stop myself. She can't hear me. Something suddenly distracts me, a different image in my periphery, so I provisionally set aside my anger and focus on a gap in the foliage to the right. Is that ... a golf course? Yes, it must be, with the telltale fringe of rough transitioning to fairway grass and a flagstick marking the pin in the distance. The park has given way to a golf course that likely rings the lower portion of Wimbledon Park Lake. Extrapolating from the distance we've already covered and the station map, and assuming it's no executive course but the regulation 18-hole variety, it should then border the All England Club itself. If we could find a way through the fence and across the ditch, we could probably lop a good ten minutes off our remaining journey. That offsets my missing Southfields station, swapping a debit for a credit on the ledger sheet.

"Sky, wait!" I yell as loud as I can, for she's at least fifty yards ahead of me, but either she ignores me or doesn't hear. And, it occurs to me with resignation, this fence-ditch combination probably runs the length of the golf course. Why wouldn't it? You'd want to keep out all sorts of undesirables from a club like this: drunken yobbos, football hooligans, assorted lower class riff-raff and of course the occasional down-on-his-heels gimpy American looking for a shortcut to the tennis grounds. And yet... what is that gate up ahead?

As I get closer I see it's a private car park and the sign, when I'm near enough to read it, confirms it belongs to the Wimbledon Park Golf Club. The gate is one of those rolling electric jobs, probably remote controlled. There are thirty or so spaces in the car park, but no one is in sight. Beyond there's just a grass fairway, some sand bunkers and the lake. Open terrain, in military terms.

"Sky, dammit – stop!" I come to a halt, releasing my bag and bending over at the waist to try to catch my breath, but the extra blood that pumps into my head takes my already throbbing headache to an altogether excruciating level, so I quickly unbend back to vertical again and clench and unclench my jaw in hopes of lessening the grip of the headache.

"Sky!" I scream it as loudly as I dare without risking exploding my skull open, which seems actually possible, as if it were an overheated coconut placed in front of rock concert speaker blasting at 15,000 watts. But she just keeps on trucking. And with the curve of the road she's just about to pass from sight. Fuck!

The car park gate starts to rumble sideways and I realize that a blue and white Mini has slowly pulled towards it on the other side in order to exit. So I grab my bag and step to the side and try to act nonchalant, as if I pass this road all the time and have no reason to show interest in the golf course or its private car park. Once the gate is fully open the Mini's driver, a woman with ash blonde hair in her late twenties or early thirties, pulls into the road next to me, gives me a quick glance, then reaches to her remote to close the gate. She hesitates a moment, then hits the accelerator. The gate, meanwhile, trundles ever so slowly closed. So slowly, in fact, that I know I can slip past it. It's one of those split-second decisions: leave Sky to take the (presumed) shortcut or try to struggle on after her. Like some mental coin flip, I don't think, I just act. And I'm inside.

I take a few steps towards the fairway and only then do I see the clubhouse to my right. We must have passed it on the road, unseen, only because it was completely protected by trees. Now what? As easy as it would be to walk onto the course, it would be even easier for someone in the clubhouse to spot me. Christ.

Well, who cares? I mean, what are they going to do? Throw me out? That's fine with me; I'm not here to sneak a quick nine holes.

After the harsh asphalt of Home Park Road the fairway grass feels springy and soft. But I know I've made the right call when I look between two large elms and see the unmistakable outline of Centre Court. It's so close, I can't help stopping to gawk at it. The freshly mown fairway turf is redolent of the fescue grass courts we lovingly rolled at St. Clements in Oxford, and the Wimbledon grounds look so inviting, in their forest green splendor, it's tempting to rest here a minute and just take it in. But I know I shouldn't, so I keep walking. A nascent worry is already troubling me, about how I will meet up with Sky. But no matter: I must press on.

As soon as I am across the open stretch of fairway and among the trees that separate the adjoining fairway I feel less exposed. I still need to skirt the lake that blocks my direct path but I'm almost to its edge now. Given the savings in time I know this shortcut will produce, I allow myself to walk, cane-assisted, at a more humane pace, not exactly languidly but nothing close to Sky's race walking speed. I can now see clearly the edge of the lake, which seems to peter out into a sort of marshy bog, and I mull how close I can dare to cross that area without getting muddy when I hear a distinctive *crack*, and then half-hear, half-feel a golf ball *whizz* over me like an artillery shell, close enough for me to instinctively duck. Once I regain my wits I look around and notice a tall, stocky man holding what appears to be a seven-iron. He shakes it at me violently and yells, "Stupid tosser!" Maybe thirty yards beyond this man's bag of clubs-on-wheels are three other men, all shorter and less stout, who appear to be staring and laughing. Without waiting any longer, I start off again. I'm guessing they'll be more interested in finishing their game than hunting me down, and by the looming shape of Centre Court I can't be more than a few minutes from the edge of the course.

"Oy, you there!" The voice, coming from the opposite direction of the golfers, catches me completely off-guard, and I whirl around to see the blur of an electric golf cart moving at full speed towards me. Before I can react further, the cart brakes to a stop and the silhouette of a driver is revealed to be a man of my approximate age, with similar height and hair, wearing grey overalls. Really, despite the different accent and clothes, we could be related. Must be a groundskeeper, I think. Something seems odd about the steering column of the cart, though – it seems to reach almost to the man's shoulder blades – and it's only after looking closer that I see his arms are actually short, mal-formed flippers. The instant I realize it I move my gaze upwards to the man's face. But not quickly enough, for I can see he's noticed my reaction. Which honestly hasn't been one of revulsion or anything negative, just surprise. But still – the recognition in his eyes bums me out both on a purely human level, as I've no wish to cause this man any further distress, and because I'm already a trespasser and I know how protective groundskeepers can be of their golf courses, if that is indeed his job. A one-word conjecture forms in my head: thalidomide.

"What in blazes are you doing?" he says.

"I'm really sorry. I know I shouldn't be here."

"No, you bloody well shouldn't."

I open my mouth to respond and then shut it. What can I say that will make any sense?

"Well?"

"I would tell you the whole story if I had time, I promise, I really would, but I need to get there," I say, pointing to Centre Court. "Right away."

He looks at me more closely, taking in my tennis bag, and then he smirks.

"What, I suppose you're late for your match? Who's your opponent, that Spaniard, Rafael Nadal, is it? Come on, you must be as old as I am."

"Look, as much as I'd love to banter with you, I believe we have a common objective here. You want me off your golf course, sir, and I do too."

"Maybe so but don't call me sir. To the best of my knowledge, there have been no knighthoods in my family."

"Yet. Yet! As an Englishman, one mustn't give up hope, must one?"

The groundskeeper gives me a fresh appraisal and allows a quick half-smile before returning to serious form.

"Bloody Americans. You like to take the mick out of us, don't you?"

"Not me. Hey, do you mind if I get in?" I ask.

"What?"

"Can I get in? If you can just run me to the edge of the course over there, I promise I'll be on my way and won't trouble you any more."

I can see him about to protest. He'd have every right to bring me over to the clubhouse, call the police and charge me with trespassing. But something pricks his balloon just as he's about to puff himself up and he skooches over slightly.

"All right, get in, before someone bloody well hits us both."

I toss my bag in the back, where the golf clubs normally go, and slide in beside him. His legs and feet are normal size and shape, or as well as I can tell since he has shoes and trousers on.

"I'm Trevor. Trevor Davis." I reach out my right hand close enough for his right arm to grasp it. He hesitates momentarily and then does, shaking my middle three fingers – all he can manage to encircle – with a surprisingly strong grip.

"Stephen. Stephen Farisher."

"Pleased to meet you Stephen," I say. He slips the cart brake off with his left foot and presses the accelerator with his right and the cart jumps forward. He swings the steering wheel around with considerable dexterity and, thankfully, aims it in the direction of Centre Court, or at least the gap in a hedge that seems to connect to an access road leading towards it.

"Warm weather we're having, isn't it?" I offer this without any obvious sarcasm, but Stephen Farisher shakes his head as if dealing with an impudent child.

"Get on with you," he says, but he smiles just the same.

"You're probably more used to golfers than tennis players."

"All the same to me," he says.

I look down and notice several brightly colored plastic bracelets on the console of the cart next to the steering column. I point to them and ask what they are.

"Passout bracelets."

I reach towards a bright green bracelet. "May I?"

He shrugs and I pick it up to examine it. It looks like a hospital bracelet but instead of patient identification it says *Wimbledon 2010 The Championships* and, above that, *Wednesday, June 23*.

"Ticketholders who leave the grounds need to have those on in order to get back in."

"Why do you have them here?" I ask.

"I reckon some of the patrons of the All England Club are too lazy to find a rubbish bin. I collect at least a half-dozen every day, this side of the wall along Church Road."

"Today is Thursday, right?"

"You don't know what day it is?"

"It's been a little... chaotic lately."

"Yes, it's Thursday," Stephen says.

"Do you have any bracelets for today?"

Stephen furrows his brow, then with his right arm reaches into a chest pocket in his coveralls. He removes two yellow-colored bands and offers them to me. I take them and see they are dated today's date.

"They're no good to you without tickets."

"I understand. You don't mind if I keep these then?"

"Saves me the bother."

"Thanks."

We are now well beyond the lake and fast approaching the access road. But instead of stopping at the edge of the course, Stephen pulls into the driveway and heads towards what I assume is Church Road. The All England Club is so close now I can hear the crowds cheering on various courts and see the heads of spectators inside the club grounds.

"So your doubles partner misplaced your player passes, did he?"

"Something like that. Honestly, it would take me ten minutes to explain and even then I don't think it would make any more sense to you than it does to me."

Stephen brakes the cart to a stop at another electric gate. He presses a remote on his console and the gate begins to swing open.

"Go on then. We don't want anyone wandering uninvited onto the golf course, do we?"

"No," I say. "That would be a problem." I grab my tennis bag, and heft my cane, testing my ankle with a wince.

"Good luck playing with that," Stephen says, nodding towards my cane.

"I suppose one learns to make do."

Stephen holds my gaze for a moment. Do I detect some sort of gratitude on his part for my nonchalance about his condition? Or would that be assuming too much? Regardless, I'm pleased we're ending this encounter better than how it began.

He clicks the painted sheet metal gate shut and as I step towards Church Road it closes until I no longer see him or his golf cart.

I turn and look up and down the road, which is filled with more pedestrian traffic than cars. Christ, how am I going to find Sky? I identify what looks like a ticket entrance towards the left and start walking towards it. Oddly, instead of feeling worse, my ankle actually feels better. And the headache I had earlier seems to have dissipated. But my shirt clings to me, damp with sweat, and my shoes are covered with grassy stains. Well, what's more appropriate for Wimbledon? Reaching the gate, I marvel for a moment at how impressive the tennis grounds look, at least from the outside. The club reeks not so much of tradition, but of wealth. All the signage and fixtures and buildings look modern and substantial and clean and, well, expensive. I see a sizable production cart in a parking lot inside the grounds filled with a coil of large diameter cable and it occurs to me: television rights. And mostly American television rights, at that. All those *Breakfast at Wimbledon* broadcasts from the Sixties onwards, through the Seventies and Eighties and Nineties and into the new century, but especially the Seventies when tennis had its modern resurgence and viewers were eager to buy the new metal racquets and wear stylish tennis apparel and advertisers wanted to capitalize on it. Sure, this place already had its tennis tradition and would have done fine without things going crazy, but still – this sort of wealth is something else. The kind of wealth that allows a private club, without blinking, to build the huge, retractable roof I see up there, just to enclose the show court for the few times when rain interferes with the TV schedule. That's hundreds of thousands of Californians like me watching hours of advertiser-sponsored tennis coverage up there. Christ, they ought to escort me into the place on a red carpet. What did Reagan say in that New Hampshire gym, "I paid for this microphone"? Well, I paid for that roof!

"Dad!" I turn and see Sky. She seems pleased and relieved to see me, and more than a little surprised. "Are you okay?" she asks.

"More or less, no thanks to you. Why the hell didn't you wait for me?"

"I thought you were behind me."

"Bullshit, Sky. You could see I couldn't keep up."

"I was trying to *motivate* you."

"Really. And how come you're so goddamned motivated all of a sudden?"

"Why do you think?"

Right. That damned horse. Never mind dear old Dad and *his* worries. Let's focus on some stupid four-legged creature whose only purpose is prancing around a ring and jumping over fake fences. Why couldn't she have taken up something normal? Like soccer for instance. Or field hockey.

"Sorry," she says. "I should have stayed with you." She looks like she means it.

"Never mind," I say. "I managed to take a detour. Through the golf course."

"Cool." She suddenly brightens. "Hey, guess what? This couple? They, like, *gave* me their tickets."

She holds up a couple of grounds passes for today.

"They said they only wanted to see the Queen and they weren't that interested in the tennis. But then this guy told me the tickets are no good without some kind of bracelet."

"A passout bracelet," I say.

"Yeah, I guess. But anyone who has one of those would be going back in. So I guess we're, you know, pretty much back at square one."

"Not necessarily," I say, reaching into my pocket. "Our luck might be changing."

24

The maddening thing about being inside the Wimbledon grounds, apart from not being able to find Rupert Salmons, is realizing I should have come here before. Because I really would have enjoyed it. My excuses always seemed plausible, even to myself. Some business deal to attend to. A prior family obligation. Or just waiting for the right opportunity. But who was I kidding? All these years I've denied myself a pilgrimage to my sport's Mecca over a teenage slight, out of some misguided sense of personal justice. So they didn't let me compete in the Schoolboys Tournament? Because they interpreted the rules against me, after the fact? Fine – then they won't get my money. Never mind that British Lawn Tennis doesn't control Wimbledon; they're just parties with a common purpose. But even if they were one and the same, at some point you have to let bygones be bygones. And now that Sky and I have gained entry on the sly, through the re-admittance gate with discarded credentials, I see in vivid Technicolor what I've been missing. This place is a tennis-lover's nirvana.

As I've dashed around the Centre Court Complex, or as close to dashing as one can with a cane and a bum ankle, in the apparently mistaken belief that Salmons would have scheduled his lunch in one of the Centre Court restaurants, I've made a mental promise to myself to reserve some time later this afternoon to just wander the grounds and soak up the atmosphere. Maybe watch an outer court match. All the same, a kind of nagging reality check informs me that, *even* if I'm able to track down Salmons, and *even* if our meeting goes well, I won't actually be able to enjoy my visit to the All England Club. Not as I might have in years past, when, instead, I seemed intent on cutting off my nose in spite of my face, Wimbledon-wise. Let's get real, my conscience tells me: I'm an interloper here, like I was in Oxford. And this visit is strictly business. Which I suppose is a bargain I'd grudgingly accept, if I could just find the bastard and conclude our transaction.

To give myself more freedom to find Salmons and because she was getting stroppy again, I parted ways with Sky after our entrance and told her to meet me, come rain or shine, at three-thirty sharp at the statue of Fred Perry near Centre Court, the best landmark I could think of. It's now 2.15 p.m. and, standing on a small concourse between Court 16 and the No. 1 Court stadium, this is what I know:

- I wish I'd asked Sky to remain with me. Her resourcefulness and spirited company outweigh her bitchiness. Sort of.

- Queen Elizabeth II, after her lunch with the tennis world glitterati, moved to the royal box at Centre Court, where she is currently watching Andy Murray play Jarkko Nieminen of Finland. The Scot is leading 6-3, 5-4 (40-15, with Murray serving for the set), and my sense is everyone here is both pleased and relieved he's putting on a good performance for the Queen. Other than Jarkko and his team, of course.

- The Queen is wearing a pale blue dress with white trim and a matching wide-brim hat. I haven't confirmed it myself, but several people who witnessed her arrival or have seen her image on the large TV screen in Aorangi Terrace, behind the No. 1 Court stadium, have volunteered this information. As if it's important to keep track of such things. I even overheard one Wimbledon staffer say with unabashed delight that the Queen looked "smashing." I guess this royalty stuff still matters over here.

- The method that wealthy folks use to bypass the highly restricted membership of the All England Club is buying a 'debenture' to gain access to Centre Court or Court No. 1. The exclusive lounges and restaurants on the grounds seem to be reserved for members or debenture holders.

As best I can tell, a debenture is meant to provide the club with money for capital improvements even though it most likely isn't a true bond, in the securities sense, just a fancy way of describing a season ticket package (or in this case, a five-year package). Judging by the way debenture holders dress and the amenities and price lists of their facilities, my guess is a debenture costs a boatload of money. The recession doesn't seem to have affected these people at all.

- Because I don't have member or debenture credentials, just a lowly grounds pass, I've not been able to get inside the spots where Rupert Salmons is most likely to be lunching. At the toney Wingfield Restaurant in the Centre Court building I did my best to convince the receptionist to let me take a quick peek, but to no avail. After checking her reservation records she assured me that no Rupert Salmons was there. At least she (finally) acknowledged that if the reservation was in his lunch companion's name, Mr. Salmons might well be there after all. However, no amount of claiming dire circumstances on my part would convince her to allow me in to have a look. No credentials, no admittance. Folks with boatloads of recession-proof money don't like seeing riffraff wandering in their midst. Sadly, I speak from experience here. Not the recession-proof part, though.

- Rupert Salmons could be on his way to Majorca for all I know.

I'm standing at the Debenture Holders entrance to Court No. 1 in the faint hope that he's not on his way to Majorca but is inside, maybe in The Renshaw (this building's version of the Wingfield Restaurant). The receptionist here, who seems marginally more accommodating than her counterpart in the Wingfield, has promised to check for me. I've been told to stand outside and wait. So I'm doing just that, following the matches on a scoreboard. If I squint I can just make out some live action on Court 17, which is a men's singles match between an Italian, Fognini, and an American, Russell.

"Mr. Davis?" I turn and see it's the receptionist.

"Yes?"

"I managed to locate your party."

I can scarcely believe it. I want to kiss this woman. Maybe I will.

"Bless you. Thank you."

"You're welcome," she says. "He asked me to show you to his table."

"Please, lead on!" And I follow her inside.

Christ. Okay! I found the guy. I actually found the guy! Time to get my head in the game. Aunt Philippa's will. A simple bequest to my mother. What more can there be?

Once we're past the reception area, and into the restaurant proper, I allow myself a moment to look around and take in the Renshaw's dining room. I have to admit, the design and décor are extremely well done, understated yet refined. Natural wood, nickel and putty green leather are the dominant materials and tones, bridging modern, almost Scandinavian chairs and tables (covered in cream damask linen) and hanging pendant lighting consisting of concentric circles. The overall feeling is one of clean lines, elegance and taste. The thought occurs to me that if I'd returned to England with Frankie all those years ago and established my business here, *this* is the kind of project I might have done. As quickly as this notion occurs I banish it for being the regret-laden, counterproductive intrusion it is.

The room is maybe three-quarters full of patrons and I try to guess at which table Rupert Salmons is sitting, until the receptionist indicates a four-seat table with two men sitting opposite each other: a balding man of medium height and sporting a reddish-gray goatee, and a taller, clean-shaven man with a full head of brown hair. The bearded man seems about my age and the taller man maybe a decade younger. The receptionist departs and I hesitate, not sure which man is, in fact, Rupert Salmons.

"Mr. Davis, is it? I'm Rupert Salmons," the bearded man says. He stands and offers his hand, which I shake.

"Yes, Trevor Davis," I say.

The other man introduces himself as John Pankhurste and we all sit down, me next to Pankhurste. From the coffee cups, empty dessert plates, and Champagne flutes in front of them, and the upturned bottle in an ice bucket, it appears they've had quite the lunch. A waiter passes by carrying two entrées and my stomach gurgles, reminding me I've had nothing to eat since the doughnut on the train this morning. It gurgles again, more insistently this time, and I wonder, could it be audible even in this busy dining room? God I'm famished. What I wouldn't give for a lousy bread roll.

"Sorry for intruding on your lunch like this," I say.

"We're mostly finished," Salmons says. "You get top marks for ingenuity. My secretary said she only told you I'd be lunching at Wimbledon."

"It wasn't easy."

"Might have been simpler just to meet at my office earlier," he says. He and Pankhurste exchange smiles, nothing mean-spirited, but in my present state I'm not disposed to even good-natured ribbing.

"Yeah, well – sometimes life has a way of tripping you up."

"Indeed," Salmons says.

Pankhurste indicates my cane, which I've leaned against my chair.

"You weren't using that, were you, when you dispatched our boy Sutcliffe at Queen's?"

I look at Pankhurste, confused.

"If so," he continues, "British tennis is in a sorrier state than I thought."

My confusion deepens, then I realize Ronnie must have related my match details to Salmons, who has probably just shared it with this fellow Pankhurste. Is Pankhurste an LTA official? On the board of Queen's? God, I really need to eat or drink something. I can barely form an intelligible thought. Except this: I wish I'd pocketed some of the Twinings English Breakfast when Sky and I checked our bags at Left Luggage before entering the grounds.

"Do you think I could get some tea?" I ask Salmons. "It's been quite a day."

"Of course, I should have asked." He signals to a waiter who immediately arrives to take my tea order. The waiter asks if I'd like anything else. I give Salmons a quick glance and he seems to indicate that I'm welcome to, but for some reason I decide against it, so I tell the waiter just the tea and he nods and departs.

"Sorry," I say to Pankhurste. "Where were we?"

"You were about to explain how you humiliated one of our better young players while hobbled with a bad ankle," Pankhurste says.

"Careful, John," Salmons says. "It seems Mr. Davis here is one of us."

"Please, call me Trevor," I say.

"What?" Pankhurste says.

"British national, through his mother," Salmons says.

"You don't say," Pankhurste says. "Bloody hell. We could have used you. In your prime, I mean."

Ordinarily I'd welcome this kind of badinage. And I know that this John Pankhurste, whoever he is, has no knowledge of my history with the LTA and the British Schoolboys Championships. Maybe it's because I'm at such a disadvantage here. Or maybe it's because I'm hungry and thirsty and the waiter hasn't brought my tea yet. But it's all I can do to not tell Pankhurste to take the empty Champagne bottle and shove it up his fucking arse.

"Trevor," Salmons says. "If I may." He looks at me with a genuinely kind expression. "I'm very sorry for your loss."

I look at him, completely bewildered.

"Your mother, I mean," he adds.

"Thank you," I say.

I realize he's probably refreshed his memory by re-reading my file, including Aunt Philippa's will, in anticipation of our meeting this morning. Get a grip on yourself, Trevor lad. He's just doing his job. Remember – he thinks Ronnie and I are friends. That bit of luck earned me the meeting. Keep your eyes on the ball. The bequest.

The waiter arrives with a tray carrying a teapot with two bags of Taylor's English Breakfast. He sets it down in front of me with a small pitcher of milk, a bowl of demerara sugar, and an empty cup and saucer. I thank the waiter, pour myself a cup, add more sugar and milk than normal, and give it a quick stir with a teaspoon. The first long sip tastes wonderful, truly glorious, like I imagine a cup of spring water would to a Bedouin after marching days in the Sahara without a drop. I have a quick pang of worry about Skylar – is she as bad off as I am? – but I remember how resourceful she is. There are drinking fountains on the grounds, I realize, and she doesn't eat much when she isn't riding. What do they tell you on an airplane, in case of emergency? When the oxygen masks drop, take care of yourself first, then your child. I pour myself another cup of tea, add the milk and sugar, and take a smaller gulp.

"Steady on there," Pankhurste says with concern. "You alright?"

I feel immeasurably better actually.

"Just fine," I say. "Bit of a transportation issue earlier. Nothing that a cup of tea can't fix."

Pankhurste smiles. "You were right," he says to Salmons. "He is one of ours."

Salmons looks at me, evidently relieved I'm not going to collapse, and smiles at Pankhurste. "One of yours you mean. If he were Scottish he would have asked for whiskey."

"Christ, you bloody Scots. Three hundred years of union and you still won't let it go. Speaking of which, let's see how your lad is doing." Pankhurste reaches for his phone and pulls up the Wimbledon app. "Excellent. Up 4-1 in the third. The Finn looks finished." He casts an impish grin in my direction. "Sorry, not very original I know, but can't resist. Anyway, I'd best be going, let you gents talk. Her Majesty will want to make a quick exit no doubt." He nudges me conspiratorially. "She absolutely *detests* tennis. If it doesn't involve horses or dogs, she couldn't be bothered. Had to move heaven and earth to get her back here."

Pankhurste stands up, so Salmons and I do as well. There are handshakes all around and Pankhurste thanks Salmons for lunch, then he departs. Salmons and I retake our seats.

"What does he do, exactly?" I say.

"John? Hmm, that's a good question. His title is executive something or other but he's a sort of professional liaison."

"Liaison between what?"

"The crown and other entities. Athletics, especially tennis, is John's special interest but there are dozens of royals and they are patrons to literally thousands of charities and organizations."

"Rule Britannia," I say.

"Indeed."

"By the way, Jeremy Sutcliffe isn't all that good."

Rupert looks amused. "You aren't suggesting Ronnie was embellishing his story, are you?"

"Perish the thought."

"Well, it was to your benefit. So, Trevor. Now that you've tracked me down, what can I do for you? I'm afraid I don't have much time. As I believe Sally mentioned, I'm off on holiday this afternoon."

"You're not staying to watch the tennis?"

"Sadly, no. This was a business lunch."

I take another slurp of tea and look directly at Salmons.

"Okay. Well, you probably have an idea. Can I call you Rupert?"

He gives me a look – please, of course.

"Rupert, I believe it's pretty clear my great-aunt Philippa intended her bequest to go to my mother."

"I agree," he says.

"You do?"

"Absolutely," he says.

"Great. Then how soon can you release the funds?"

Jesus, this was easier than I thought. Was it the Champagne or my persistence? Anyway, who cares – just so long as I can get this wrapped up.

"Not so fast," he says. "There's still the matter of documenting your mother's status."

"But you just said…"

"What I *said*," he interrupts, "is there is no doubt she was the *intended* beneficiary. But estate law requires more than that. I explained this to your solicitor already. Did he not communicate with you?"

"He said that he explained the circumstances of my mother's birth, how her adoption records had been destroyed in the war, but you were still refusing to release the funds on a technicality."

"A technicality? Is that what you said?"

He looks affronted and I am momentarily baffled. Have I insulted him somehow? Do Scottish estate lawyers take umbrage at straight talk?

"Trevor, let me see if I can put this in context for you. You're a tennis player. The game has rules, some of them quite technical."

"It's a pretty simple game, actually," I say. "I hit the ball. If it bounces in, my point. Bounces out, yours."

"And if I return it?"

"Same thing. In or out. Sooner or later someone misses."

"Okay," he says. "Now let's suppose I hit a short lob, an easy put-away. You rush forward, hit your smash, a dead winner, but your knee just barely grazes the net."

I know immediately where he's going and I don't like it. This is one of those rules that gives players and, in officiated games, umpires fits. It's surprising how many experienced players don't know the proper rule, so it's doubly annoying that Rupert appears well versed.

"If I've hit the winner, it doesn't matter. My point, whether I touch the net or not."

"No, you've hit what *should* be a winner, a tremendous over-head smash. The ball landed in, then bounced way up, outside the court. There's absolutely no physical way I could retrieve the ball. I'm walking away, conceding the point, but right before it bounces a second time, several courts away, you just lightly brush against the net. The hairs on your leg really, not even your skin."

I sit there in silence for a moment. There really isn't anything more for me to do except take the last sip of tea in my cup.

"Your point," I say.

Rupert doesn't say anything, he just nods, apparently in appreciation that I've acknowledged the principle he's demonstrating. He doesn't seem the least bit happy about it, as if he were a chair umpire having to make the same net violation call at match point in the finals of Wimbledon. Rules are rules. Even if we don't like the results they produce.

"So what happens? I suppose, what, the crown gets our inheritance? Maybe your buddy John can liaise with some royal society that wants to use our money."

"Trevor, you *do* have the opportunity to get the proper documentation from the French authorities. Didn't your solicitor explain this? Christ, I tried to walk him through it but he seemed adamant that I see things his way."

"I wouldn't know where to start. Even if my mother were still alive, she was too young when she left France to remember anything about it."

"You don't strike me as someone who gives up so easily. We just need something in the file. Any certificate will do, really. The French are awfully good about that. Bureaucrats to the core, but there's always some *notaire* to stamp a document for a fee."

"Rupert – I just don't have *time*. Or the money. I'm tapped out, completely. Maybe if you could find your way to make an advance…"

"You want me, the will's executor, to advance you funds, on a specific bequest? Ludicrous. How in the world did you get here, then?"

I give an involuntary laugh, something between a gasp and hiccough.

"It wasn't easy."

Salmons looks suddenly embarrassed.

"How unfortunate. Well, you must see, this isn't my concern. Look, what about your community?"

"What?" I say it without thinking, even as I have some inkling what he means.

"Your community, man!"

"It's sort of… fragmented."

I can barely hold his gaze, for the embarrassment he felt a moment ago now fully inhabits me, coursing through my blood vessels with the cold clamminess of a physician's vaccination. He's right, course. He's done his part and has given me the chance to do mine. But I've fallen short. Like Alejandro Falla against the mighty Federer. And I've got nowhere to hide.

289

All of a sudden Rupert Salmons pushes back his chair and stands up from the table.

"Stay if you like," he says in a soft voice. "I must be off."

I nod feebly but make no attempt to stand. Even if I wanted to, I do believe I'd be unable. The feeling I have is of a crushing weight, pushing down on my shoulders and pressing me into the chair and, in turn, into the floor. So, it occurs to me almost in an offhand way. Is this what defeat is like? I know ordinary defeat, at least the kind that occurs on a tennis court. Or in a business meeting. And even in a divorce court. But this feels different. This feels… absolute.

I manage to bend my neck back so I can look up at Rupert.

"Good luck, Trevor," he says. And he turns and walks out of the restaurant.

I watch him go. Slowly, almost imperceptibly, the sensation of weight pressing down on me abates. I realize I have been tensing myself against it, that I must have been trying to resist it, fighting to keep my shoulders and torso erect. But now that the force relents, I relax too. Until I slump back in my chair. I feel exhausted, utterly spent. My mind as well – hollow, tapped out and devoid of ideas. But it refuses to shut down entirely. Instead, it dredges up one last thought. An early childhood memory, of my father teaching me to play chess. We are in the den of our Hilgard Avenue house and I must be five or six. He has pulled out a simple wooden board with the classic Staunton pieces. Patiently, he explains how each piece moves: the rook, the bishop, the knight, the pawn, *et cetera*. I ask about the knight again and when I finally tell him I understand we play a game, just to get my feet wet. Inevitably, understandably, he soon has me in checkmate; I'm a rank beginner after all.

"What do I do now?" I ask him.

With an apologetic smile he reaches over and pushes my king onto its side. "You resign," he says.

25

C ourt 11 is one of those remote outer courts, bunched in a group with seven other courts so you could almost forget you were at Wimbledon and were instead at a run-of-the-mill tennis club. It could even be a municipal court, except for the quality of the players and the fact they're wearing white. Maybe I've gravitated here because this is closer to my own tennis experience. True, there are spectators watching the action. But not that many.

The match is almost over and, from the ten minutes or so I've watched, it won't go down in the record books as anything special, just a first round men's doubles match among the dozens to be contested this week. Two tall, strapping Australians, Carsten Ball and Chris Guccione, are leading 6-4, 6-2, 4-2 and the points are going quickly. A big serve – Guccione, a ginger-haired lefty, has a particularly monstrous one – followed by an immediate approach to net. If there's a volley exchange it doesn't last more than a shot or two, but most points end on a service winner or a first volley put-away. There's something about watching, though, that feels calming and good. I sit off to the side, away from the other spectators, and observe the action. The Aussies clearly know and like each other and they encourage each other between points with a fist bump or a "Come on, mate!" These guys can earn some solid money this fortnight, especially if they could win their way through to the next week, the kind to make their whole year, but the casual fan focusing on the marquee singles players will recognize neither of their names. Call them journeymen tennis pros if you like. They won't get rich playing ATP tournaments given the travel expenses so in that sense they're really more amateur than professional, if by amateur one means playing for the love of the sport, not the money. Even though I never made it to this level, this seems like my community. I always preferred singles to doubles, since there's no one to blame but yourself, but watching these two players urge each other on makes me feel, well – I don't want to say *happy* – but maybe … comforted.

I check my watch. 3.25 p.m. The Queen's departure from Wimbledon has caused all the energy in the grounds to shift from Centre Court to Court 18 where John Isner and Nicolas Mahut are due soon to resume their fifth set. As much as I'd like to watch some of that match, since my grounds pass would grant me access, Court 18 was already full when I departed the Court No. 1 building, before the players had even arrived to warm up. Besides, being on this side of the grounds and watching this lopsided doubles match has given me a chance to consider my next steps. Because, as much as we sometimes like to wallow in a little self-pity, I cannot allow myself the luxury of total defeat. Yes, I've suffered a setback. Perhaps a significant one. But enough to say the game is not worth the candle? No. And as our new President so eloquently stated upon taking office, problems are also opportunities. In my case, it's a chance to mend some fences.

First thing, once I can figure a way to make a phone call, is to reach out to my sister Meg. I realize now there are still hurt feelings on her part about what happened to her half of the inheritance – the one we actually got, from our parents.

For years she'd been hearing how well I was doing with my real estate business. As she and Manny struggled to make ends meet on his modest supermarket manager's salary, she would tell me that if there was ever an opportunity for them to get into one of my building funds they'd be grateful. But Fred and I had always established our LLC's minimum investment at $25,000 and that was just too rich for Manny and Meg. Until, with the death of our parents, they were suddenly flush with a tidy windfall.

Thank God I insisted they put some of it aside to pay down their mortgage and start a college fund for their kids. But I should have declined all of it. True, it ultimately was her choice to evaluate the risks, to invest or not, but I could have said no. While the writing wasn't fully on the wall for my company's destiny, I could already see marks and scratches. How does that quote go? From

Lenin, I think it is. Money tarnishes all human relationships. Well, in Meg's case, we were never all that close. But she is my sister.

I also need to come clean with Sky about Moondancer. I suspect she knows that, even once I'm back on my feet economically – and I mean fully, not just with the inheritance – there's no reason to believe his current owner would part with him. Maybe Sky was complicit in flying here, but I shouldn't have indulged her fantasy. I'd like to think there's some virtue, as a parent, in shielding her from the pain of sacrifice, but what price is dishonor? She might blame me forever for depriving her of a horse, but I'll risk that for a chance to earn her respect.

On my way out of The Renshaw I helped myself, with the waiter's blessing, to a couple of bread rolls with butter. So while I'm still hungry, it's a functional sort of hunger, not the all-consuming craving I felt before. Dealing with the immediate money issue is another matter. I still need to get Sky on a flight home tonight; thankfully I bought a return ticket for her at SFO. But as to my larger dilemma, Rupert Salmons has, oddly enough, given me hope. Even though he didn't provide me the answer I wanted, he gave me some hope. Which is all a man needs, really.

I pick up my cane to go meet Sky but I hesitate a moment and examine it. This is my material connection to Frankie, I realize, through her father. I glance at my wrist – I've got two minutes to get to the Fred Perry statue – and realize my watch is my material connection to my father. But do we really need material connections? Aren't the emotional ones enough? This body I inhabit I will have to relinquish at some point, too. The material is borrowed. Just like time itself. It's knowing when to let go that matters, I suppose.

Do I still need this cane? I'm not sure, so I test the ankle. Perhaps a bit better, it seems. Marginally less painful. There's something positive, something to build on. But this cane isn't mine to sell, it's merely on loan. From a woman who meant so much to me, long ago, and still does, I've been surprised to discover. Some fence mending there has begun. But perhaps there can be more to do. So then, what? The Longines, my father's watch, a gift from the grateful citizens of France.

I propel myself along the walkway that skirts the Centre Court building near Church Road. The Fred Perry statue is just now visible and I squint to see if Sky is waiting there. The bronze figure of Perry, not quite full scale, stands atop a marble pedestal and shows the old champion with his racquet back and high for an unhurried forehand. I recall that Perry wasn't well regarded by the British for most of his life; he was treated as an outcast, really. I suppose after so many years without a men's champion the club felt honor-bound to erect the statue. What might be a cynical gesture to one person is an effort to make amends to another. Here's to you Fred, regardless.

A little closer now and to my immense relief I see Skylar standing where Fred's imaginary tennis ball should be. She looks okay and I call out to her.

"Did you get it?" she says when I reach her. Somewhere between curiosity and concern.

"Hi sweetie. Are you all right? I was worried you'd be hungry."

"I was. But I explained my situation to a woman at one of the First Aid stations and she gave me two packets of biscuits and a token for strawberries and cream."

"That's my clever girl."

"What about you?" she asks.

"I got some rolls and butter. I'm okay, thanks."

"Oh. Good. But I meant about the solicitor. Did you get it?"

"Well, lawyers don't just hand over checks for fifty thousand bucks."

I hear a vaguely familiar voice addressing me from over my left shoulder.

"He was more American than English." I turn and see it is Bennett Dixon, and his wife, Naomi. I must look dazed and confused six ways to Sunday, so Bennett points to the statue.

"Perry, I mean."

I greet them and re-introduce Sky in case she doesn't remember them from the Heathrow baggage carousel but Sky ignores the Dixons and fixes me with an angry, determined stare.

"What do you mean, fifty thousand?" she says. "That's not enough to get Moondancer back. You said you have to split it with Aunt Meg."

"Honey, let's talk about this later, okay?"

"Bullshit, later. You tricked me, didn't you? This was never about Moondancer. You were lying to me all along!"

"That's not..."

"Stop!" she interrupts.

I reach for Sky to try to calm her down but she bats away my hand. I direct a quick, apologetic smile towards Bennett and Naomi and they avert their eyes politely.

"You're nothing but a pathetic liar!" Sky wails. "I hate you!"

"Sky, come on!" I move towards her but she backs away, tears streaming down her face. I want to argue with her, how she's got the arithmetic wrong, or even chastise her, for feeling entitled to a pedigree show jumper when we've all sacrificed, especially my mother, who got by at Sky's age on food and clothes rationing and no memory of her real parents, but the words needed seem useless and even cruel, as the tears keep gushing. So I move towards her again. This time she flings her hands down and bolts at a full sprint, heading in the direction of Centre Court. I look in desperation after her, then to the Dixons, who register my distress, so I give an embarrassed shrug and start to follow after Sky.

"Trevor, wait," Naomi says, her hand gently touching my shoulder. "Why don't you let me? I have a little experience with teenage girls."

I sigh and look at her fully. Her eyes radiate no agenda other than kindness and empathy.

"She doesn't mean it."

"Yes, she does. I've worn out my welcome with her."

"Sometimes they just need some space. Or a fresh shoulder to cry on."

"It's my mess. I've got to clean it up."

Naomi shoots Bennett a look of concern and he nods back in encouragement.

"No offense, Trevor, but you look like you could use a hand."

I exhale a little laugh, then pause before taking a breath. My emotions feel balanced on a precipice and I'm scared it'll be one of those juddering inhalations that sends me over the edge and into the abyss. Then my body decides it needs the oxygen enough to risk it.

"You really wouldn't mind?"

"Of course not, I'd be happy to. Truth is, I could use a little break from all the tennis. It's more Bennett's thing."

"She might be a little hungry," I say. I reach in my pocket and retrieve the seven pounds I have left from our 'Who's on First' performance at Paddington, but Naomi waves off my money.

"Should we meet you both here?" Naomi asks.

"We could use our Centre Court seats," Bennett says to me. "But I really want to get onto Court 18 for the Isner-Mahut marathon."

"Bennett – we tried already," Naomi says. "Half of London is there. It's hopeless."

"We should be able to watch on the big screen behind Court One," I say.

"Perfect!" Bennett says. "Can you meet us there, sweetheart?"

Naomi smiles at her husband, then touches me reassuringly on the arm.

"If you don't see her on the grounds, you might try the infirmary," I say. Naomi nods, then disappears into the crowd.

"That's really nice of her," I say.

"She wasn't kidding about wanting a break." He motions to the cane in my right hand. "What's up with that?"

I tell him about my match with Jeremy Sutcliffe at the Queen's Club as we make our way towards Court One.

"I hate players who cheat," Bennett says.

"Hate the sin, love the sinner."

Bennett fixes me with a skeptical expression but I betray not a trace of irony so he looks contemplative.

"Hmm, well, it's too bad about your ankle in any case. You thirsty? I wasn't expecting London to be so hot."

"Who does? Sure, I could drink something."

Bennett suggests Champagne but I demur, knowing that on a nearly empty stomach and in my present emotional state I'd likely pass out. Besides, Champagne feels celebratory and I don't. I would like something more substantial than water, though, so I propose getting a shandy.

"A *panaché*? Great idea, but I don't think they sell them."

"Tell you what, you get two beers and I'll get two lemonades and an extra cup."

Bennett looks thoughtful again.

"Why didn't I think of that?" he says.

"That's why I make the big bucks," I say. He laughs an innocent, hearty laugh and I think, if he only knew! Or maybe he does. I'm sure word got around the tennis club that my real estate business tanked. But Bennett has been too polite to mention anything, although my argument with Sky must have him wondering. He heads off towards the beer and wine concession while I seek out the stand selling the non-alcoholic drinks. The queue is maybe twenty deep so I take my place at the rear, when all of a sudden there's a loud commotion coming from the direction of Court 18. I check my watch. It's just shy of three-forty and I realize John Isner and Nicolas Mahut must have arrived to warm up. There's a large crowd standing in front of what I take to be the spectator's entrance to the court but the line isn't moving; the stands must indeed already be packed to the rafters. Court 18 isn't an outer court but it isn't exactly a show court either so there's no way everyone who wants to get in today will be able to. Luckily for us, the All England Club at some point in the past installed an enormous television screen on the side of the No. 1 Court, facing onto the large slope named Aorangi Terrace that everyone seems to call Henman Hill, after the recently retired English player. Tim Henman bravely contended for the championship during the late nineties and early part of the last decade but never managed to put the hoary ghost of Fred Perry to rest. Funny – Perry's tribute is a less-than-life sized statue but Henman's is an enormous amphitheater. Go figure. I gather Tim Henman has a rather posh accent, so you can do the math.

Once I get within sight of the café menu overhead I see lemonade costs £2.25. I reach in my pocket and retrieve the seven pounds. I do a quick calculation and scan the rest of the menu.

It hardly seems possible but bacon sandwiches cost only twen-ty-five pence more. And I'm ravenous. I feel a deep twinge of guilt about Sky – shouldn't I share this with her? – but I realize Naomi will take care of her. I'm about to pass out, I'm so hungry. At the front, the bacon smell goes from enticing to intoxicating. So I order two lemonades and one bacon sandwich and part with the last of my money.

I place the two cups of lemonade and the sandwich in a card-board carrying tray and step to the side of the concession booth. Standing there with my cane propped against my left hip so it won't fall, I tear back the paper wrapper and devour half of the bacon sandwich, which has been divinely slathered with mayon-naise and layered with ripe tomatoes. I honestly can't remember anything ever tasting so good. Of all people, the words of a favorite history professor I had at Cal, Neil Woodbine, come flooding back to me. Neil liked to illustrate his points during lectures with clever references to popular music. He would preface a remark by saying, "As the philosopher Morrison once said..." or "as the philosopher Dylan noted..." and then quote some of the singer's lyrics. In this case he would have said, "As the philosopher Jagger observed, 'You can't always get what you want. But if you try sometimes you just might find you get what you need.'" Amen, brother Jagger. I wrap up the rest of the bacon sandwich and start to go, then remember we need an extra cup.

I reunite with Bennett at the base of the hill and we find a spot about two-thirds of the way up for us to sit. We divvy up the beer and lemonade and make a toast to tennis. I apologize for not offering to get him something to eat but he dismisses it, saying he and Naomi had an ample lunch in the Centre Court café. The shandy tastes better than wonderful and I take a gen-erous second gulp to wash down the rest of the bacon sandwich, quenching a thirst that hadn't adequately been addressed by the tea I had earlier.

"So how are your children?" I ask Bennett.

"Laura just made partner at her firm in L.A.," he says. "But she's decided she really wants to be a federal judge."

"Kids these days," I say. "No ambition."

"Tell me about it."

"And your boy?" I ask.

"Prentice is managing the wine shop in San Francisco. That and making buying trips to our sellers in France and Italy."

"A chip off the old block."

Bennett nods. "Truly, my cup runneth over."

"What's your secret?" I ask.

"To what?"

"How about to a happy marriage?"

He laughs, more of a snort than a chuckle. "Hell if I know. I guess I got lucky with Naomi. She puts up with me, that's my best explanation."

I purse my lips and think about Annie for the first time in, what, several hours? That's progress, I suppose.

"I'm really sorry about you and Annie, Trevor."

"Thanks," I say. "Me too."

On the TV screen we see that Nicolas Mahut and John Isner have finished their warm up. The chair umpire, Mohamed Lahyani, quiets the crowd and John Isner toes the baseline to serve at fifty-nine games apiece. A murmur passes through the crowd, both on the hill and, at a slight delay, from Court 18, when Isner double-faults the first point. But any lingering questions about the big man's fitness to resume play seem answered when he wins the next three points, once with an ace. Mahut manages to take the game to deuce but Isner responds by winning the next two points to hold serve, including one more emphatic ace.

"Settle in, *compadre*," Bennett says. "We may be here for a while."

"After this they'll probably require tiebreakers in fifth sets."

"Do you know the previous longest match?"

He asks it casually, but with a sliver of a dare. So I rack my brain. Budge vs. von Cramm? Vines vs. Cochet? No, those are clearly wrong.

"Hint: it was before tiebreakers."

Duh – I figured as much. I'm glad nothing's riding on this, even a friendly wager, but it's still galling. Because I'm lousy with – I mean, you know, *good*, with tennis factoids. The more trivial the better. I'm pretty sure I *did* know, at some point, but

I'm not certain. Christ, Donald Rumsfeld and his goddamned unknown unknowns.

"I got nothing," I mutter.

"Pancho Gonzales against Charlie Pasarell. First round, 1969."

"Shit – that's right! Gonzales won, didn't he?"

"After surviving seven match points, over two days. He lost the first set something like 24-22, then Pasarell nearly bageled him as the light was fading. Here he was, forty-one, broke, washed up, a chain-smoker, unable to compete at Wimbledon all those pre-Open Era years when he had to kick around the so-called pro circuit, playing for beer money in cold high school gyms, and now he's back on Centre Court on the second day, body aching, down two sets to love, playing Charlito, his protégé, the pride of Puerto Rico, a guy in his absolute prime. I would have liked those odds."

Pancho grew up on the wrong side of the tracks, I recall, a Chicano with a perpetual chip on his shoulder, self-taught in tennis because he couldn't afford lessons, then often banned from junior tournaments in lily-white Los Angeles. He lost years to Navy service and afterwards played in the shadow of Jack Kramer, who then shrewdly signed him to a long-term contract on the fledgling pro circuit. Gonzales became a cautionary tale in the tennis world, detested by his fellow players even as they revered his graceful athleticism and competitive fire. He married and divorced a half-dozen women, fathered and alienated even more children, and died alone and destitute in Las Vegas. He was the archetypal lone wolf, rakishly handsome and either charming or vile, as the mood possessed him. Those who saw him play swore he had the greatest serve and volley game ever.

"You know what Jimmy Connors said about him."

I can instantly tell I've stumped Bennett. It feels nice to return the favor, like a nasty dribbler of a net cord winner.

"No, what?"

"'If I needed one person to play for my life, I'd pick Pancho Gonzales.'"

As we follow the match, it seems odd to be watching it with Bennett and not Michael, but comforting nonetheless. I wonder if, down in Cornwall, Michael is watching it now. Maybe even with his sister Samantha? I hope so. I wish my phone was working so I could call or text him and find out.

Mahut holds his service game easily and the match resumes a familiar rhythm. Bennett asks me about the progress of my family business in London, so I fill him in on my trip so far, omitting nothing. I give him the backstory of my company's collapse, my divorce, my great-aunt Philippa's inheritance, even our trip to Cornwall and visit with Frankie and her kids. The players, meanwhile, are winning on serve easily, the aces continuing to come in bunches from both sides and no games going to deuce. Just like with Michael, it affords a deep and genuine conversation with Bennett that provides enough background distraction to prevent the focus from becoming too sharp. Like having a conversation on a road trip, I suppose, with the set score ticking over like the miles on the odometer and the tennis play itself passing by like scenery outside the car windows. Once in a while something different to notice, but otherwise – much of a muchness.

At some point I ask Bennett about his real estate project, the one he wanted to pick my brain about, more to give myself a breather, both emotionally and vocally. He tells me that he's decided to open at least one retail store in France and we talk through the ins and outs of renovating an older building space, and the opportunity he has not just in Paris but elsewhere in France, and perhaps Italy as well.

"What's your preference, Italy or France?" I ask.

"You mean for what, business?"

"Anything. You've spent enough time in both places. Do you have a favorite?"

He laughs. "That's a loaded question, like asking me to pick my favorite child. The short answer is, I love them both. And I know each of their virtues. And shortcomings."

"Very diplomatic," I say. Isner wins another service game on an ace to take the score to sixty-seven games apiece and I for a brief second wonder if the consensus at dinner last night at the Pandora wasn't right and these two tennis players will again duel to a draw today. Christ, what a thought. Well if I have to endure that, I suppose I'm happy to be doing it with Bennett, despite the circumstances. He's got a good heart and he's decent company.

"What about you?" Bennett says. "Italy or France?"

"Or England," I add.

"Or England."

I smile. "Well, I have a theory," I say.

"I figured you would." He says it good-naturedly so I continue.

"My theory is that France has always found itself caught between two poles, England and Italy. They may have a hard time admitting it but the French admire the English their propriety and their discipline. Meanwhile, Italy speaks to the Frenchman's heart: the passion, the flair, the love of life. So for the French it's always that internal confusion, that delightful complexity. The silly and the serious. The industrious and the irresponsible."

"Okay, even if I buy that, it doesn't answer what your preference is."

"Well, we're Americans," I say. "We don't have to choose. We can just cherry-pick the parts we admire, like their wine, and leave the rest."

"Something tells me you're more emotionally invested than that," he says.

During the next player changeover Bennett asks me to resume my story so I tell him about my meeting with Rupert Salmons at The Renshaw earlier. How he might have given me a roadmap for extricating my inheritance, by way of France. And how, with the purchase of the two lemonades and bacon sandwich, I am now officially penniless.

"Christ," Bennett says. "You've been through the blender, haven't you?"

I exhale a short blast of air through my nostrils. "Yeah, I guess that about sums it up. But it could be worse."

Bennett looks thoughtful. "What's the worst thing that could happen to you?"

"Me or anyone?"

"Anyone. In life."

"The worst thing?"

"The absolute worst thing," he says.

"The death of your child," I say.

"God forbid." He shakes his head, as if banishing the thought. "And what's the best thing that could happen?"

I pause, thinking. Is this some kind of test?

"Other than winning Wimbledon?"

He smirks. "Uh-huh."

"Once upon a time I'd have said finding your soul mate."

Bennett nods, slowly and thoughtfully, then stops. "Finding?"

"Finding. And committing to."

"And now?"

"Maybe curing cancer. Or making the world safe for democracy."

"Way above my pay grade," Bennett says.

"So first guess, best guess?"

"Usually is."

On the TV screen Nicolas Mahut is serving again, the score now 68-69.

"Mahut is supposed to be even better at doubles," Bennett says.

"Mister Isner might disagree."

Bennett laughs. "No, seriously. Maybe it's like relationships. You know what they say. You have to be good for yourself before you're any good for someone else."

"You been listening to my ex-wife?"

Bennett laughs again but with a wary, cautious look.

At thirty-all, a normally benign score, Mahut comes in to net and executes a well-placed half volley but Isner places a blistering forehand pass right on the sideline and all of a sudden he has break point against his opponent. Which of course means match point.

The crowd on Court 18 rises and stirs like a buzzing beehive, only settling again on Lahyani's urging. And before we can fully process the magnitude of the moment, Mahut follows his first serve to net and floats enough of a volley to Isner's backhand that the big man is able to line up and rope a passing shot down the line and just beyond the outstretched racquet of Mahut. Realizing what has transpired, Isner crumples to the ground. Game, set and match, John Isner. And just like that, the longest singles match in history is over.

The entire hillside of spectators erupts in applause, echoing the sound of clapping and cheering from Court 18, but I am too stunned to do anything except stare at the television screen. Isner, being the good sport he is, quickly gets to his feet – or as quickly as a nearly seven foot tall man can who has played three consecutive days of strenuous tennis – and joins Mahut at the net for a warm embrace. I don't know about them but my emotions are in complete turmoil. I'm happy for Isner, who has triumphed despite the extra physical toll his XXXL body must have endured. But I am bereft for the Frenchman who has had to serve so many times in the fifth set down a game – sixty-nine times, to be exact – a colossal disadvantage that, in the end, proved insurmountable. I can only imagine the sense of loss he must feel to have given so much, point after point, game after game, and come up short by such a tiny margin. It doesn't seem fair and for perhaps the first time I realize how cruel the game of tennis, at its core, can be.

"God, what a match," Bennett finally says.

"I can't believe it," I say.

"I know."

We watch, spellbound, as several Wimbledon officials take to the court and, with the players and the chair umpire, Mohamed Layani, commence an impromptu ceremony. One official pulls out a microphone to address the crowd while another carries boxed gifts of some sort for the participants, but I can't take my eyes off of Mahut, who clearly wants nothing more than to return to his locker and probably to sob into one of those oversized green towels the club provides to the players. How he can endure it to stand there and off-handedly share his observations with an interviewer before the live crowd and TV audience, like he's chatting with Oprah, and then even be made to pose for the photographers with his vanquisher in front of the scoreboard, is utterly beyond me.

Finally, after several minutes of this no doubt well-intentioned folderol, the players are permitted to depart the court. From our vantage point we can see them, or what we must assume is the two of them, pass from the court's ivy-covered entrance through a throng of spectators lined with policemen and tournament officials, like Moses parting the Red Sea.

I shake my head in disbelief. "Incredible," I say.

"Truly. So, Trevor, what are you going to do now?"

"What?"

"I mean, about your situation."

What I want to do, right now, is go after Nicolas Mahut. To try to console him and congratulate him on his effort. And, if possible, pose a question. If I could, I'd say, *Excusez-moi, mon ami. Bon courage – je suis désolé – mais*, and then I'd ask him if he has any regrets. With profuse apologies for intruding, I'd say, if it isn't asking too much, could he enlighten me? Knowing what he gave on that grass court day after day, the fortitude it took to play each point on its own terms, even facing down multiple break chances, each one a match point. Only to be defeated by a routine backhand. If I could I'd ask him, was it really worth it? *Le feriez-vous à nouveau?* Would you do it again?

I realize Bennett is waiting for an answer about my predicament so I unstrap the Longines from my left wrist and hand it to him.

"I'm going to sell this for whatever I can get, put Sky on the first flight home to her mother, then catch a train to France."

He slowly nods his head, in seeming agreement with my plan.

"You know, the Chinese ideogram for crisis combines the symbols for danger and opportunity."

"I didn't know that," I say. Hell, I think, all those crazy right-wingers who accuse Barack Obama of being a closet Kenyan have it wrong. He's really from the Middle Kingdom.

Bennett admires my father's watch but fails to notice the back of the bezel so I tell him to read the inscription.

He does and looks up at me, startled. I suddenly recall that Bennett got some big award in France for his services to the wine industry. Maybe even a knighthood, if that's possible.

"What did your father do?"

I explain about my father's war record, how he was one of the youngest officers to go ashore in Normandy on June 6, 1944, and how his regiment fought off German Panzer attacks that December in the Ardennes and somehow managed to avoid capture during the worst military defeat the U.S. Army has ever suffered.

"Did I ever tell you about my brother?" Bennett asks.

"No."

"I was kind of an accidental surprise for my parents. My brother and sister were both a lot older. Carter was the star – he ran varsity track at Stanford, Dean's List, Editor of the *Daily*, in line for a Stegner – the whole package – but somehow he couldn't abide sitting out the Vietnam War in a cozy Palo Alto dorm so he volunteered before graduation. Ninety days later he shipped out of San Diego a 2nd Lieutenant, 1st Battalion, 9th Marines. A month later he was leading his infantry company across the Cam Lo River when an NVA sniper killed him."

"Jesus, Bennett. I'm sorry."

"You can't sell this watch, Trevor."

"That's what my daughter says. But it's just a watch."

"Tell you what. How about you consult for me for a few weeks on our French store. I could really use your help."

"Thanks but I don't need your charity."

"Bullshit. It isn't charity, you idiot. I'm talking about hiring you."

"What do I know about building out retail shops in France?"

"I'm sure more than most people. Plus, I trust you."

I look down the grassy terrace and see Naomi and Skylar scanning the hillside, looking for us. I grab the cane in my right hand, extend my arm upward and wave it back and forth until Sky sees me.

"Life isn't a singles match," Bennett says. "There's such a thing as community."

I consider this a moment. I know on some level I agree with him. But then why do I resist?

"Is that why you never beat me?"

"Go to hell!" Bennett says. His face assumes an aggrieved expression that fails to mask his underlying good humor and I can't help but smile. I look down and see Sky and Naomi making their way up towards us and I transfer the focus of my smile towards my eldest daughter, who looks so beautiful in the late afternoon light. A puff of breeze ruffles the flags behind us and brings with it the distinctive scent of star jasmine. I feel a surge of relief and gratitude that begins, ever so slightly, to wash away the disappointment I feel for Nicolas Mahut. And for so much more.

Bennett points to my right ankle. "I like my odds against you now."

"I bet you do," I say. "Just give me some time."